Valkyrie
Rising

Valkyrie Rising

Ingrid Paulson

HARPER TEEN
An Imprint of HarperCollinsPublishers

HarperTeen is an imprint of HarperCollins Publishers.

Valkyrie Rising
Copyright © 2012 by Ingrid Paulson

Library of Congress Cataloging-in-Publication Data
Paulson, Ingrid.
    Valkyrie rising / Ingrid Paulson. — 1st ed.
      p.   cm.
    Summary: While visiting Norway, sixteen-year-old Ellie must step out of the shadow
of her popular older brother, join forces with his infuriating best friend, and embrace her
Valkyrie heritage to rescue teen boys kidnapped to join the undead army of the ancient god
Odin.
     ISBN 978-0-06-202572-2 (trade bdg.)
    [1. Valkyries (Norse mythology)—Fiction. 2. Supernatural—Fiction. 3.
Kidnapping—Fiction. 4. Loki (Norse deity)—Fiction. 5. Odin (Norse deity)—
Fiction. 6. Norway—Fiction.] I. Title.
PZ7.P28433Val 2012   2011042307
[Fic]—dc23   CIP
                                                            AC

Typography by Carla Weise
12 13 14 15 16 LP/RRDH 10 9 8 7 6 5 4 3 2 1

First Edition

To my grandparents, who encouraged me to dream,
and to Alex, who helped those dreams come true

1

Half the school came to Graham's eighteenth birthday party. People were everywhere—crowded around the pool, crawling all over the patio, and crammed onto the sofa in the family room. Even though they were within plain sight of my mother, almost everyone had added a little something to their Coke—or replaced the contents of the can altogether.

That afternoon I was watching from a safe distance at the kitchen window, a whole story above the fray. I told myself I was up there to help keep the refreshments flowing, but truth be told, no one would note my absence. Even my friends were so focused on blending into Graham's crowd, they'd probably forgotten I existed. After all, I wasn't memorable in my own right. I was just Graham Overholt's little sister—no different from his many other accessories. Something halfway between a lacrosse stick and a football helmet.

I opened the sliding glass door and leaned on the deck railing outside the kitchen—one of the few places where I could watch my brother holding court without being seen. His height and shock of messy gold hair made him easy to spot. The group around him was laughing hard at something he'd said.

At moments like that, it blew my mind that we were related. But maybe he'd have felt the same way if he had looked up just then, to see me peering out at the party from behind Mom's potted geraniums like some senile old hermit. It was ironic that I got nervous at parties, given that I shared a gene pool with the most popular person on the planet. Then again, trying to live up to Graham's legacy was what usually triggered the diamond-crushing pressure behind my eyes.

It was pretty much impossible to say or do anything that wasn't somehow eclipsed by or attributed to Graham. By the time I'd hit high school, I had gotten tired of trying.

While I stood there playing Peeping Tom, Graham's best friend, Tucker Halloway, snuck up behind me and pinched my arm. Hard. Then he took a long step forward and leaned on the railing right at my side. I turned my head, just enough that I could smell his breath.

"What if my mom catches you?" I wrinkled my nose and glanced down at the silver flask dangling loosely in his grasp. "You're screwed. She'll absolutely call Colette."

"Can't." Tuck gave me a smug smile. "Colette has a migraine. She's at the spa."

I raised an eyebrow at that. "Again? What's this—her third time this week?"

"Fifth," Tuck said.

Colette, Tucker's mom, was from another planet. France, specifically. She was exotic, glamorous, and the only person I knew whose parties required cocktail attire. Or were catered, for that matter.

Tuck never had food in the fridge, but he always had designer clothes on his back—his appearance was the one thing about him that held Colette's interest. But that was no surprise. Tuck made pretty much every female pause and smooth down her hair.

I had to resist the urge to do it myself as I turned to look him straight in those impassive gray eyes. I never could tell what he was thinking, even after knowing him my entire life. "Still, though, my mom will totally tell Colette," I repeated lamely.

Tuck grinned. That famous wicked smile. "Is that really supposed to scare me?" He put his arm around my shoulders and leaned in. I staggered a step to keep my balance. "Where do you think we got this in the first place? Colette sent me over here with a bottle of thirty-year-old scotch for Graham with, I quote, her compliments."

I had to admit that was a bit shocking, even for Colette. "Her compliments on what, exactly? Your ability to talk your way out of anything? My mom won't let it slide this time. And don't pretend her opinion doesn't matter to you."

"True," he conceded, sliding the flask into his back pocket. "But your opinion matters to me even more." His tone was as silky smooth as his words, but I wasn't taken in for a second. Well, maybe for a second—the exact second he turned to meet my gaze, a mere six inches from my face. When I looked at him that closely, at those white teeth framed by that deceptively innocent smile, I knew why Tucker Halloway excelled at getting whatever he wanted—especially from girls.

And I couldn't fathom why he was wasting that particular talent on me when bullying and mockery had always been the accepted currency between the two of us.

"What do you want?" I asked, instantly wary. "Shouldn't you be enjoying the party?"

His smile curled up at one corner, proof positive he was up to no good.

But then he did something weird. He just shrugged and stood there, looking back down at the party without saying anything at all. After a minute like that, his silence was more unnerving than his usual fast talk. Anyone who looked up at us then could definitely get the wrong idea.

I glanced down toward the pool, half expecting to see an army of girls watching me, planning their revenge.

"Are you leaning on me because you're drunk?" I choked out, once the silence had stretched itself so far and thin it was fine dust coating my throat. Then I grasped for the only logical explanation. "If you're trying to make some girl down there jealous, you should cozy up to someone else. No one would ever see me as a threat."

"Why do you say that?" His grin reappeared, settling in and preparing to stay for a while. And marking the return to familiar footing. The muscles in my shoulder started to uncoil.

"Because of who I am." Freshman year, Graham had thrown a boy out of a party for ignoring my polite hints. And he had interpreted my one-time plea for help as an open-door invitation into my love life. Or lack thereof, thanks to his constant interference. I wasn't supposed to know that my touch carried a social stigma second only to leprosy, but word gets back to you eventually.

"I meant, why play games? I get by just fine on looks alone." His smile was blinding, driving his point home.

"Don't forget your charming personality," I said, and my stomach flipped when his grin widened at my words. Making Tucker laugh was the best kind of rush. "I hear modesty is quite the aphrodisiac," I added.

"Listen to you." He lifted those gray eyes to meet mine. "Graham would die if he heard sweet little Ellie use a word like that. And die all over again if he thought you knew what it meant."

"Lucky he's not here," I said.

"Lucky indeed," he said slowly. "For more than one reason."

His smile was so pretty, I almost sighed out loud. Fortunately, that was all it took to remind me of the manifold dangers of dropping my guard around Tuck. Because he was softening me up. It was a dance I knew all too well, even if he usually preferred a more direct assault with me.

"What do you want?" I repeated.

"Time with you," he said sweetly. "Your undivided attention."

"Cut the crap, Tuck."

"Isn't that the right answer?" he asked, all false innocence. Tipped with sarcasm. "Seems to me that's what most girls want to hear."

"For the record, insincere compliments work better when you don't point them out," I said. "And I'm not most girls."

"Duly noted," Tuck muttered before rallying and changing tactics. "I came to the right place, since you're such a wise woman, seeing through all my subterfuge. I know you'll be my savior."

Apparently his plan was to exasperate me into submission. "For the third and final time, what do you want, Tucker Halloway?"

"Last name too? Bad sign. But here goes." He leaned closer, knowing full well how destabilizing his proximity could be. Before I could help it, I was batting my eyelashes right back at him. A reflex as involuntary as the knee-jerk test at the doctor's office.

"Hypothetically speaking, if a person urgently needed the key to the cabinet in the china hutch, what would that person need to do to acquire it?"

"Mug my mother," I told him. "Hypothetically speaking, of course." I held up one hand when he started to object. "You have a flask. That should keep you busy for the afternoon. I'm not helping you steal more alcohol."

"Not everyone drinks scotch," he said with a wink. "And Graham put me in charge of fun. Plus, I've already taken care of the hard part. We only need to put this back before anyone notices." He held up a small glass bottle of gin that he pulled right out from the tangled green leaves of the geraniums. So that's why he was really here, loitering around with me. He'd come to retrieve the bottle and was fortunate enough to find me standing here, a potential minion to do his dirty work. "You'll be righting a wrong, so to speak," he added. "Very noble of you, by the way."

"Impressive," I said, and I meant it. "It's not easy to get around my mother's radar."

"Thank you, Ells," he said. "It's nice to be appreciated. Graham would have flipped. You, on the other hand, always understand."

"Graham doesn't know?" As far as I knew, Tuck never kept secrets from Graham. I'd assumed Graham had sent him to me for damage control.

"We don't want to ruin his birthday with unnecessary stress," Tuck said. "We owe it to him to handle this ourselves."

I wasn't sure how Tuck's problem had suddenly turned into a "we" situation. But no one was more persuasive than Tuck when he was in the zone like this. His smile. The sweet, beseeching look in his eyes. Like I really *was* the only girl on the planet who could give him what he needed. I couldn't believe I was falling for it.

Too many other girls had shown me where this particular road dead-ended.

"Fine. I'll make sure it's unlocked tonight," I heard myself say. "Just put it all back by morning, or we'll both be screwed." Then I wiggled free of his arm, ashamed when I immediately missed it. But it was pointless to let myself pretend he was there for any reason other than covering up his typically Tuckish crime.

I expected him to leave now that his mission was a fait accompli. But he stood there a second longer, elbows propped on the railing, like he too needed a moment to catch his breath before plunging back downstairs.

"What are you two doing up here?" Graham asked. We both jumped and turned in unison, a little too fast.

Somehow Graham had extracted himself from his entourage and made his way up the deck stairs without either of us noticing. He looked at me, then at Tuck, and his eyes narrowed in mock suspicion.

I squirmed, uncomfortable he'd found us like that—locked in private conversation when the whole world was downstairs. Especially since Tuck and I now shared a secret.

"I could smell you five feet away," Graham said, glancing at me, but then dismissing the thought as he zeroed in on Tuck. "Is that why you're hiding up here? Seriously—lay off the scotch." He made a grab for the flask, but Tuck was slippery as an eel. "If you're hung over during practice, I'm not covering for you again—I don't care if you throw up." But his smile told a different story.

"Oh, I would never do anything to compromise my athletic career," Tuck said, parroting the serious, grown-up voice Graham saved for teachers and college interviews. Graham made a valiant effort to stay annoyed, but it was too late. He grinned and ran one hand through his hair. Only Tuck could manage him like that.

"I'm being serious," Graham said, carefully avoiding the responsible voice. "I'm outta here at the end of the summer. And I'm telling you, senior year is harder—with college applications. You've gotta pull yourself together."

"There's gratitude for you," Tuck said, catching my eye. "Without people like me for contrast, no one would recognize how perfect you are."

Graham shifted impatiently on his feet, but Tuck kept right on talking, paving over his transgressions with a solid foot of bullshit. I tuned out until something caught my ear. "I already talked to Colette," Tuck was saying. "She got me a ticket to visit for two weeks."

That was hardly a surprise. "Visit Graham at Stanford?" I confirmed. Graham would be leaving for college at the end of the summer, but Tuck was a year younger than Graham and a year older than me. Which meant Tuck and I would be left behind together. Or, more accurately, Tuck would be left with the half of his friends who were also his age. It wasn't like Tucker Halloway would hang out in our house every night once Graham was gone.

"Nope." Tuck grinned first at me, then at Graham. "Norway." Tuck was aglow with the good news, whereas I felt a bit queasy.

"You're coming to Norway?" I asked in a very small voice.

He nodded.

That summer our mother was ushering a group of rowdy college students through a summer art history program in

Italy, as part of her ongoing battle for tenure at UCLA. And we were being shipped off to Grandmother Hilda's house in the country—eight full hours from Oslo.

"I thought I was getting away from you. At least for the summer." It came out louder than I'd planned, like someone had turned on a hidden microphone. "When did this happen?" As much as I wouldn't admit it, especially not to Tuck, it wasn't actually unwelcome news. The tiny town we'd be trapped in could get slow after a week, much less two months.

"A couple of weeks ago," Graham replied, shrugging.

"Fantastic." I frowned, even though the addition of Tuck would probably be a good thing—no one was more fun than Tuck when he wanted to be. Still, I was annoyed to be finding out like this. It was another example of Graham not telling me things. Like I wasn't a person who deserved common courtesy, but just one more planet that should slip obediently into orbit around him.

"Tell me what you really think," Tuck said drily. "Really, don't spare my feelings. You're far too sweet."

"Play nice," Graham said to us both. "Next year I won't be around to mediate."

But the momentary lull in the universal battle for Graham's attention was over.

A football whizzed through the air toward the side of Graham's head. Without taking his eyes off me, he caught it in one hand and threw a perfect spiral back in the general direction of his friends, somehow still hitting one of them squarely in the chest. "It'll be fun," Graham told me. "You two can use this summer to practice world peace. You know. Get along."

A deep voice called Graham's name, and a girl shrieked with laughter so loud it could be heard above the music.

Graham's attention snapped back to the party. My ten seconds were over. Duty called.

"C'mon. Tuck," Graham said. "Everyone's asking for you. And I'm not leaving you alone with Ellie and a flask of mystery liquid."

"Mystery liquid?" Tuck waved his flask in the air. "This is thirty-year-old scotch!"

"Shh," Graham and I hissed in unison.

"You realize the scotch is old enough to legally drink? I'm pretty sure that gives me some kind of immunity to local statutes." He nudged my shoulder. "C'mon, Ells, you've got to start somewhere, and I promise it doesn't get any better than this."

Graham's smile faded as Tuck slipped the flask between my fingers.

"She doesn't want to," Graham said. "You know she's too young."

It didn't matter that he was right about the first part. It only mattered that once again he was speaking for me. And being a huge hypocrite. Everyone knew that he and Tuck had been up to far worse when they were my age—Tuck was barely eleven months older than me. Plus, it wasn't like he was legally old enough to drink either.

But before I could object, Graham had already charged forward, disappearing down the stairs. His golden head was a periscope marking his progress as he submerged into the sea of people below.

Tuck slipped the flask into his back pocket and started to follow, but hesitated on the second step.

"You coming?" he asked.

I shook my head.

"Maybe that's for the best," he said. "If he was actually paying attention, Graham would realize how much he hates that dress."

"What's wrong with my dress?" I demanded, flushing pink at the thought that maybe I'd looked ridiculous all day, especially during the two hours I'd greeted pretty much everyone at the door.

"Nothing," he said, flashing me a grin that I felt ten feet below my toes. "Let's just say I won't be the only guy who finds himself stopping to chat longer than he'd expected."

I had no idea what to say to that.

Fortunately, Tucker never gave anyone the chance to sneak in the last word. He was in motion before the words had even left his lips, slipping down the stairs and into Graham's wake.

I retreated back through the sliding glass doors and into the cool shadows of the kitchen. From the windows overlooking the pool, I could watch Tuck weave his way through the party. Sure enough, a senior girl latched onto him like a tick. I was disappointed when he leaned in close and whispered something in her ear. Whatever he said made her laugh so hard that her face pinched up until she almost looked less pretty. Almost.

A full ten minutes elapsed, and I was still watching Tuck.

I swear he talked to every girl there. Which was no small feat.

Clearly, flirting with me, or whatever it had been, was about as noteworthy in his day as breathing and walking upright. Not that I expected anything otherwise. It really should have been a relief. Especially since we'd be in close quarters if he was coming with us to Norway. The last thing we needed was my ridiculous imagination tagging along and making me feel awkward around him.

After loitering in the kitchen long enough that the same person had walked through twice to use the bathroom, I decided to make an attempt to be social. Plus, I knew there was no way Graham was paying attention to the dwindling food situation. I grabbed a tray of sandwiches and made my way down the stairs and into the melee.

"Hold up." A guy I'd never seen before shifted in front of me. Assuming he was hungry, I extended the tray.

"Want to sit with us?" He motioned toward a group of unfamiliar faces clustered around a table.

"There's only one chair," I pointed out, because it was the first thing that popped into my head.

He nodded. Apparently he thought we'd be sharing it.

He had to be from a different school—someone Graham knew from one of the dozen or more after-school activities that had dazzled college admissions officers across the country. From the way that boy smiled at me, he had no idea who I was. Or what Graham would do to him if he tried to sleaze all over me. Not that it necessarily would have stopped someone who had so clearly drowned each and every one of his inhibitions.

"Tempting," I said. "But I'm busy."

"What's the hurry?"

I hesitated. There was no hurry. There was no reason I couldn't sit and talk to him and his friends. Graham would never know. Except when I turned and finally looked the boy squarely in the face, something in me sagged with disappointment. His eyes were glassy from a day of drinking in the sun, comparing unfavorably to the way Tuck was always sharp, even when you knew he shouldn't be.

"Want some help with that?" The boy reached for the tray, misreading my hesitation.

"No, thank you," I said, turning away. "I've got it."

"No, really, let me take it." He grabbed for the tray again.

Even though he was annoying and harmless, I started to get mad. At myself, for stopping to talk to him. At Graham, for making me second-guess and worry about every little thing I did. And at Tuck, for lighting my nerves on fire in the first place. I could feel my temper snapping, threatening to break free, when the boy's other hand materialized on my hip.

"Don't touch me." My voice was unnecessarily harsh, even to my own ears. I turned to face him, startled by the vehemence of my reaction, by the force of my own anger. But at my words, an odd shadow settled across his face. His eyes were distant and cloudy, like a fog had drifted across his pupils. They weren't just unfocused like they'd been earlier; instead, they were utterly empty. As I watched, his jaw fell slack and he bobbed on his feet, putting his full weight on my outstretched arm. The same arm that was supporting the tray.

For one terrible moment, I thought he would knock me and all the sandwiches right into the pool. But a steadying hand caught my elbow. The tray was lifted from my grasp. "Can't take you anywhere," Tuck said. "Although I guess you had an equally incompetent assistant. Looks like I'm not the only one who appreciated that scotch."

I shifted my eyes toward the boy, hoping Tuck would catch my plea for help. And of course he did.

Tuck looked at him, a smirk on his face. "Do me a favor and get a water from the cooler over there."

But the boy just stared at me blankly for a full count of five. There was something unnatural about his lingering, vacant stare; it sent a glacier of ice-cold fear sliding down my spine. Had my rebuff been so harsh that I'd made him catatonic? Or maybe he was slipping into some sort of alcohol-related coma? But just as my panic reached a fever pitch, he snapped back to life, blinking furiously as if waking from a deep sleep.

"Sure," he said. That boy might not have known who I was, but everyone knew Tucker Halloway. "Be right back," he added.

"You came down," Tuck said to me. "Are you staying, or are you catering?" He grabbed a sandwich off the tray. "Thanks, by the way. Famished."

"Neither," I said, stepping away and deciding right then to just leave Tuck to deal with the tray of sandwiches if he was gonna be snide.

"Don't let that jerk chase you away," Tuck said, following me through the crowd. "I'll get rid of him."

"Isn't that what you just did?" I stopped and turned to face him.

"I mean for good." The alcohol on his breath was surprisingly sweet, as was the look in his gray eyes. But I wasn't going to be tricked a second time.

"I don't want murder on my conscience, if that's what you mean."

"It's not," Tuck said. "Even I have my limits."

"Good to know. Tucker Halloway's limit is just shy of manslaughter," I said. "Maybe we tie him up and stash him in the pantry instead?"

Tuck laughed. Usually that would make me feel ten thousand feet tall. But even his smile wasn't enough to shake off what had happened. The memory of the boy's vacant face had triggered an ominous, jittery feeling in my limbs, and it was building by the second. I wanted more than anything to be alone, away from the party.

"How about we tell him who you are?" Tuck said. "Unless you want an afternoon to be someone else. Graham's too busy to play dad."

Ordinarily I might have considered his offer. Or at least paused to ponder what Tuck would exact from me in return. Tuck never sided against Graham.

But I was too confused and distracted to navigate whatever maze Tuck was coaxing me into. I shook my head, looking up to find Tuck watching me closely. Testing and quite possibly trapping me.

"Did you notice anything weird about that guy a minute

ago—about his eyes?" I asked.

"No, but I wasn't the one gazing into them," Tuck replied. It was my prompt to smile, to play along. And when I missed it, he surveyed me like a surgeon deciding where to cut. "You okay?" Concern creased his forehead. "You look weird right now. Did that guy do something to you?" The edge in his voice was a reminder that as reckless as he sometimes appeared to be, Tuck was every bit as intense as Graham. Protective vibe and all.

"Yes . . . I mean, no . . . I'm fine," I stammered, wanting to get away. For so many reasons. "I—I left the oven on. I have to go."

"Odd, given that none of the food I've seen requires heat." He arched one eyebrow but let me go without another word. Still, I knew he was following my every move as I wove through the party.

My feet felt far away as they carried me up the deck stairs and into the house. The boy's white pupils filled my mind. As did the way his face had fallen slack, empty, as he tipped right into me.

Once in the safety of my room, with two inches of solid oak protecting me from the world outside, what had just happened was easier to rationalize. It wasn't like I'd wanted to join the party in the first place, and while there, all I could do was worry about Graham and whether I'd embarrass him. Or if he'd humiliate me by acting like my parent. Last Friday night, he had dragged me to a party, only to kick me out a half hour before my curfew. In front of everyone.

Either way, it was starting to seem like a good thing that I was leaving for the summer. If I was hiding in my room during the party of the year, and quite possibly hallucinating, it was a sign I needed a break from all the chaos and pressure of Graham's world. Eight weeks in Skavøpoll, Norway, would give me just that. Graham's shadow couldn't possibly reach all the way across the Atlantic—at least not until he arrived and took over that town, too. But I would have a week to myself before he'd join me, while he stayed home to complete the circuit of graduation parties. And even when he did get there, there was only so much excitement he could stir up.

After all, there was no quieter place in the world than Norway. Nothing *ever* happened there.

2

The trip to Norway was thirteen hours in the air, with a layover in Newark. After a cramped eight hours sandwiched between the tallest person I'd ever seen and the fattest, I arrived in Oslo. There I switched to yet another plane for the short flight to Bergen, where my grandmother would pick me up at the airport. By the time the captain announced our approach and imminent landing, I was dying to get off the plane. Even the rinky-dink town of Skavøpoll would be a welcome sight after that epic bout of confinement.

My grandmother was waiting for me at the baggage claim. At six foot two, she was easy to spot. Even in a country where everyone was astonishingly huge and fair, she was striking. Her bobbed bright white hair was a beacon, guiding me through the sea of heads and right to her side.

"Elsa," Grandmother said, kissing both cheeks. "You're getting so tall. Almost as tall as me." Graham and I took almost completely after her side of the family, resembling not only our father but also his mother, Hilda Overholt—I realized it more and more every time I saw her.

"Well, about four inches shy," I replied, amazed that my grandmother still looked so young. Despite her white hair and old-lady spectacles, only a handful of wrinkles creased her face, and they were only visible when I searched for them. Grandmother Hilda was gorgeous.

"You'll get there, sweetling," she said, linking her elbow through mine. "Taller, that is. Then we'll see you in those fashion magazines."

"Right," I muttered. The last thing I needed was to be even more freakishly tall.

"Or tearing apart Tokyo?" she suggested, towing me through the crowd toward the exit. "Don't worry, Ellie, Godzilla still has an inch or two on me." She clucked her tongue. I'd forgotten how she did that when she was teasing. And that she'd always been able to read me too well. I had to laugh, pushing aside my jet-lagged crankiness.

Suddenly, I saw the two months stretching in front of me in a whole new light. Not that it wasn't always fun to visit her, but last time I'd been here was the summer before I started high school. I'd been just a kid. This time, things could be different. Grandmother Hilda had always been cool. She let me wander through town at all hours, no questions asked. That was never permitted in LA, under my mother's ever-watchful, all-seeing eyes. Even Graham would have more freedom in Skavøpoll, with the nonexistent drinking age.

That line of thought opened up a whole world of unwelcome anxieties, like whether Graham would loosen up. And how on earth I'd share a roof with Tucker Halloway for two weeks straight. But I knew I'd manage somehow. I always had.

MY GRANDMOTHER LIVED on the top of a hill a mile outside of town, in an old gray farmhouse nestled at the edge of a pine forest and surrounded by gardens that would put most professional landscapers to shame. A stone fence taller than Graham traced the property line, surrounding all two acres, making it feel almost magical, like we were set apart from the rest of the world. The calm and quiet of her house were so consuming that the day before Graham arrived was really the first time I ventured out for anything other than a morning run through the surrounding fields.

The morning was bright and warm, and after my run, I decided to explore the town. Not much had changed during the two years since I'd last visited Grandma Hilda. Downtown Skavøpoll was still a long row of family-owned shops lining a narrow main street. One side of the road backed into the water, while the other was built along the base of a slope that stretched up behind the town, dotted with homes and farms until it disappeared into the mountain. The stores along the water's edge were scattered, fading into docks and rickety fishing sheds.

I wandered toward the wharf and waterfront, where the

fishing crews were unloading their morning catch. With every step I thought about my grandfather, who had taken me down to those same piers each morning when I was young. We'd buy warm croissants from the bakery and watch as salmon the size of German shepherds were wrestled out of the cargo holds and tossed ashore.

The fishing crews had been up since the early hours of morning, hauling in nets full of fish, and it was amazing to see how much work they'd already done. While the rest of the country was still rubbing the sleep from their eyes, the fishermen had already unpacked their wares and were preparing the fish to be frozen and shipped all over the world.

The men patrolling the decks and hauling on ropes and pulleys were every bit as barnacled and battered looking as their weather-beaten boats.

Or so it seemed.

As I leaned forward over the metal railing along the dock, watching the work progress, I felt someone watching me. So I turned. A boy, an older boy, was on the deck of a boat farther down the pier.

Words utterly failed me. Except "wow."

Disheveled blond locks peeked out from beneath his baseball cap. He grinned when he caught my eye—a flash of pearly white in an otherwise tan face.

I looked down, wondering if I'd been staring or if he had. Even though he'd seen me first, I'd definitely given him more than a casual glance in response.

I started to walk away, down the pier, but I heard a deep

voice behind me, slightly out of breath from jogging and saying something incomprehensible. My stomach dropped, but I managed to look composed as I turned to face the blond boy. He smiled expectantly, waiting for me to reply to whatever he'd just said.

"I—I only speak English," I said, ashamed that most of the Norwegian I'd picked up over the years was food related. I was hardly going to ask that boy to pass the bread.

I finally looked up to meet eyes that were the breezy blue of a sun-drenched tropical sea, which was ironic in such an arctic climate.

"You're Hilda Overholt's granddaughter?" It was more of a statement than a question, delivered in flawless English. He could have been a boy from any town back home, with that Wonder Bread smile. Maybe from a small town in the Midwest where they hold their vowels just a second longer.

"Yes," I said. "I'm here for the summer."

"I thought so—I saw you running the other day, up in our neighborhood. I've been meaning to stop by. I live just down the road."

I nodded.

"We met once before. But you were about eight years old. You probably don't remember."

I shook my head. It was surprising that I could forget a face like his, even if I'd been just a kid.

"You know," he said, covering for my awkward silence, "you look just like your grandmother did when she was young. At least, in her pictures."

I felt warm. Once upon a time my grandmother was supermodel caliber. The pictures on her wall made that more than clear. I didn't really know what to say. But I rarely did when I was talking to boys other than Graham and Tuck—and they hardly counted.

Fortunately he didn't seem to notice. He extended one hand. "I'm Kjell," he said, then repeated it, "Ch-ell," carefully enunciating the first part, since the Norwegian *ch* sound is harsher than its English counterpart. "I'm here for the summer too."

"Really." I was determined not to blow a chance to make a friend. Better yet, a boy who didn't see me and think of Graham. So I took a deep breath and forced myself to be bold. "And where do you spend the rest of the seasons?"

He laughed. It was a noteworthy event—his teeth were so straight, it wouldn't have surprised me if he said he'd had braces twice. But his smile was crooked. It was the best possible combination.

"Oslo," he replied. "At the university. I'm studying medicine, so eventually I'll work summer shifts at a hospital. But for now, I'm navigator on my father's boat. There." He pointed to a newish-looking fishing boat a hundred feet down the pier.

"That's not at all impressive," I said. "I mean, I've been a doctor since I was twelve. And nautical navigation? Kid stuff."

His smile took a playful turn. "I've heard you Americans mature quickly."

I wasn't sure what to make of that. Given our obvious age difference, it triggered an uncomfortable association with the romantic disasters my mother's art students got into during her summer program in Europe. It seemed that older Italian men also thought that Americans matured quickly. That comment wound away into awkward territory, so rather than replying, I pretended to be interested in the crates being lifted off the boat in front of us.

"Are you free tonight?" Kjell asked rather abruptly. Then, a touch embarrassed, he added, "Some friends are going to a pub. Nothing fancy, but it's better than sitting around Hilda's doing nothing."

"I don't know," I said on reflex. Hanging out with a boy, even in a group, meant wanting it bad enough to fight for it. On the one almost-date I'd had that year, Graham and twenty of his closest friends had miraculously ended up at the same movie. As if my bio lab partner had been plotting for weeks to murder me in the dark.

It took a second for it to sink in that there was no one there to stop me. Graham was five thousand miles away. And what he didn't know wouldn't hurt him. I felt a smile building inside as I realized I was free to do whatever I wanted. "I don't usually go out with strangers," I said, even though I had every intention of doing just that.

"But I'm not a stranger to the rest of your family," he replied. "Your grandmother used to babysit me."

Even though it was beginning to sound less like a date and more like my grandmother had nudged him into taking pity on me, I held my smile and said, "Okay."

He rewarded me with another flash of straight white teeth.

"I'll pick you up at seven."

Before I rounded the corner and he disappeared from sight, I glanced back at Kjell. He was already at his father's boat, easily stepping over the four-foot span of water that separated the deck from the pier.

He was tall, cute, and smart enough to be in medical school. What more could any girl ask for? I paused to imagine what Graham would have done if he'd been there to witness the whole exchange. If he scowled when I was asked out by boys he'd known since kindergarten, I couldn't imagine what he'd think if a college boy asked me out—a heart-wrenchingly adorable college boy. Graham's certain disapproval was a point in Kjell's favor.

But Graham wasn't there. And until he showed up, I didn't have to play obedient little sister. Or listen to his comments about boys and their one-track minds. As if he wasn't one too. For now, I was Ellie Overholt, an American girl in Norway, and I'd finally get to do things *my* way. Even if I wasn't sure exactly what that was quite yet.

I just knew that I, for one, couldn't wait to find out.

I HAD PLANNED to jog back to Grandmother's house, but after my encounter with Kjell, I decided to prolong my window-shopping, savoring my newfound feeling of freedom. The bakery still had a few fresh croissants displayed in the window when I passed, and even if Grandmother had probably eaten breakfast five hours ago, I knew she wouldn't be able to resist our favorite treat.

When I pushed the door open, everybody turned and stared.

And by everybody, I mean the three old women occupying one of the two café tables, sipping espresso from doll-sized cups, and the two burly fishermen still sporting orange rubber pants misted with seawater. I pretended not to notice how they watched my every move. In a small town, newcomers are endlessly fascinating.

So I wasn't surprised when one of the old ladies rose and wobbled toward me, her carved birch cane tapping along the checkerboard floor.

The baker leaned forward with a polite, expectant smile. He must have known who I was, because he didn't bother trying to talk to me in Norwegian. Instead he nodded mutely as I pointed at the croissants and held up two fingers.

The old lady reached me, so I turned and smiled, struggling to remember how to say sixteen in Norwegian, since holding up fingers for my age hadn't cut it for a while.

"You shouldn't be here," she said. Her English was thickly accented, and it took a moment for the words to register, even though the malice behind them was unmistakable. "Stay out of our town."

I took a step back, my eyes flashing to the fishermen for help. Maybe this woman was senile. Or maybe she thought I was someone else. But whoever she thought I was, the fishermen were similarly mistaken. Because they narrowed their eyes in suspicion like they expected me to rob the place.

"I don't understand," I said. I truly didn't. Last time I'd been in Skavøpoll, people had stopped me on the street to ask questions about life in LA, listing celebrities I might have spotted or wondering if I knew their distant cousin who lived in Tennessee. Sure, Grandmother kept to herself, but that didn't stop the town from being curious about me.

The baker turned, handing me the package of croissants. His voice was sharp as he said something to the woman in Norwegian. I heard my grandmother's name, but that was all I caught. The old woman scowled back at him. Whatever the baker had said made her even angrier. She muttered something about my grandmother that didn't sound like a compliment as she lifted her cane and slammed it down on my foot. Hard.

Pain shot up my shin.

The fishermen burst into laughter.

"Stay away. Or *you'll* be the next to disappear."

There was a lump in my throat the size of a croissant as I realized everyone but the baker was rejoicing in my humiliation. They were all in on whatever strange inside joke was unfolding around me.

The old woman turned and waddled back to her friends. The baker's eyes were apologetic as they returned to me. "Tell Hilda she still has friends. Not all of us believe the rumors." He shook his head, refusing the money I slid across the counter toward him. "Run home, and don't pay her any notice." He inclined his head toward the table of old ladies, who looked like they were contemplating a second assault.

The baker certainly didn't need to tell me twice. I had no intention of staying to be abused by a crazy old lady. Or mocked by a bunch of rude fishermen. It seemed that even if the town looked the same, some things about Skavøpoll *had* changed.

AT SEVEN O'CLOCK that night, there was a soft knock at the door. I'd told my grandmother about what had happened at the bakery, and she'd laughed like it was the best joke she'd ever heard. Apparently the old lady was angry about something that happened at last year's garden show. She'd spread rumors that Grandmother had cheated. Attacking me seemed like an over-the-top reaction, but as Grandmother showed me daily, flowers are important to old ladies.

When I mentioned my plans with Kjell, Grandmother didn't seem at all surprised. Even though it confirmed my suspicion that Kjell was acting under her coercion, nothing prepared me for her behavior once Kjell finally arrived. She could be a bit abrupt with most people outside our family. Which, come to think of it, might have had something to do with how the rest of the people at the bakery had acted that morning.

Grandmother rushed through the entry hall to greet Kjell before I was even halfway out of my chair. She opened the door and pulled him into a bear hug—which was no small undertaking.

I tried to understand what they were saying but only got the general gist that he'd been back for just a few days and she hadn't seen him since the holidays. Kjell was clearly a favorite.

I stood there, feeling stupid and silent, until finally my grandmother mercifully switched to English. "I'm so glad you two met," she said. "And I know you'll take good care of my Ellie."

"Of course I will," Kjell said. "But she seems like the kind of girl who can take care of herself, too."

His response earned him more than a few points. As did the fact that Kjell looked even better when cleaned up—and far too sophisticated, in his dark slacks and sweater, to be seen with someone like me.

"Ready?" Kjell asked.

"Let me just grab a jacket."

I ran upstairs and dug through my suitcase for a sweater that would make me look slightly less like a high school girl who had no business hanging out with a cute college boy. Which was impossible. I finally found a black sweater that Tuck always said made me look like a little old lady. Far from ideal, but at least that meant it made me look older.

When I was halfway down the stairs, I heard Kjell and my grandmother talking in low voices. Something about their tone made me reflexively pause to listen, even though I wouldn't understand. I strained my ears, but the only words I could pick out were Odin and Valhalla. And only because I recognized them from my grandfather's bedtime stories.

Whatever Kjell said made my grandmother break into a peal of laughter. Oddly enough, it sounded forced. I wasn't sure what could be so funny anyway, given that Odin was basically the grim reaper in Norse mythology and Valhalla was his home. From what I remembered, anything involving Odin was pretty creepy and gory.

The step beneath my feet creaked as I shifted, trying to creep closer. Their conversation ended abruptly.

One look at Grandmother's arched eyebrow as I walked

down the stairs told me that my attempt at stealthy eavesdropping had failed, to say the least.

I wouldn't have given their whole exchange a second thought . . . well, maybe not a third . . . if my grandmother hadn't stood there a moment longer, blocking the door.

"Just be careful, Kjell," she said, switching to English and snaring my curiosity once and for all.

Kjell nodded, giving Grandmother a loaded smile. "I promise I won't disappear. I'm too big for the fairies to carry away."

"Even ridiculous rumors spring from a seed of truth," Grandmother said.

"What rumors?" I asked. If she didn't want me to know, she shouldn't have dangled a big juicy carrot in front of me.

She shook her head and smiled as she tucked my hair behind my ear.

"Nothing you need to worry about," she said.

I turned to go. In the reflection in the window beside the door, I saw Grandmother slip a small velvet envelope into Kjell's hand, the kind that jewelers use. He upended it, and something silver slipped out onto his palm. Both of them clearly thought I hadn't seen. But I was tuned into every single thing she did, given the way their conversation had made me reconsider Grandmother's explanation of what had happened in the bakery. Rumors and disappearances seemed to be the new theme in Skavøpoll, and something told me they had nothing to do with last year's garden show.

"We'll head to the pub in a bit," Kjell said as we climbed into his compact European hatchback. "First we have to pick up my friends."

We drove through town and stopped in front of a narrow alley that snaked uphill, disappearing into an older part of town. I heard the rattling metal under their feet before I saw the two shapes scampering down a fire escape and jumping the last four feet onto the uneven pavement below.

"Look, Elsa, if they—if they say anything strange, just ignore it," Kjell said. I could see his lips pressed into a thin line. He was nervous. "I've known them forever. And they're great once you get to know them, but ever since I came home, they've taken up some, um, strange ideas."

"No worries," I said. "I'm sure they're great." Out of everyone in the whole world, I was the last person to judge his friends.

It can be hard to find people you can trust, and when you do, you hold on to them, imperfections and all. Most of my supposed friends were wannabe Graham groupies who didn't make the cut. Even my best friend always flirted like crazy with Graham's friends. Especially Tuck. I hated how much that bothered me— forcing me to admit things to myself that it was far safer to suppress.

By then, the two shadows had reached us and were cramming themselves into the narrow backseat. One was a girl with a round face framed by chin-length red hair. There was something wholesome and open about her wide brown eyes that made me like her at once. Kjell introduced her as Margit. The boy, Sven, was standard-issue Norsk—blond, blue-eyed, and with teeth so white they practically glowed in the dark. Margit whispered something, making Sven smile and lean in close to hear the rest.

Was this some sort of double date? Butterflies in my stomach were stretching their wings, preparing for flight.

Margit slipped a nylon backpack from her shoulders and set it in the middle of the backseat. The bag was straining at the seams, its taut fabric struggling to swallow something roughly the size and shape of a microwave.

"You're joking," Kjell said, sticking to English. "You aren't bringing that with us."

"You bet I am," Margit replied. First in Norwegian, then repeating it in English, presumably for my benefit, even though, surprisingly, I'd understood her the first time. She pulled roughly on the zipper until it opened just enough to reveal a bulky electronic box. Then she reached further inside and slipped a smaller object out of the bag that looked like a tiny remote control, only it was made of clear plastic decorated with fluorescent yellow trim. She pressed a flat green button on the front of it, and a white light inside snapped on like a flashbulb. Sven leaned in close and whispered something in Norwegian. I could tell they were testing it, making sure that whatever it was, it was working.

"What is that thing she's holding?" I whispered to Kjell

Kjell sighed as he glanced over his shoulder. "That's a personal locator beacon," he explained. "We use them when we fish. If you get thrown overboard, lost, you activate it. That way the rescue helicopters can find you." He paused. "And in the backpack is an old radio she pulled off her father's boat. Seriously, Margit, don't tell me you're bringing those. This is taking it too far."

"You never know when you'll need to call for help," Margit snapped. "I have some extras—you might consider carrying one, too. It's not like I'm the one who should be worried."

I couldn't help it; a laugh slipped right out before I could stop it. "I think I'll pass on the rescue choppers, thank you. Pepper spray will suffice," I said, patting my pocket. The most dangerous thing that could happen to me in Skavøpoll was a mountain goat attack. Still, Grandmother had insisted. But then Margit's comment settled into place next to my grandmother's cautioning Kjell to be careful, and suddenly Margit's behavior wasn't quite so funny. Perhaps Kjell was actually in some sort of danger.

Margit peered at me from around the side of the headrest. Her eyes narrowed and her nostrils flared, like I'd repulsed her somehow.

"Elsa Overholt." Margit said my name like it belonged to a celebrity whose claim to fame was eating live puppies. "You look like your grandmother." It felt like an accusation, so I glanced at her in the rearview mirror. Her hair was a vibrant scarlet.

"So I've heard," I said, deciding to proceed carefully since she was predisposed to hate me. One sideways look at Kjell reminded me that he was definitely someone worth being jealous about. But it wasn't like I hadn't marched a million miles down that road—with all the time I spent with Tucker, feeling irrationally jealous of other girls when I knew I had no right to be. Fortunately for Margit, I was pretty sure she was misreading Kjell's level of interest. "Personally, I think my brother looks more like that side of the family than I do," I said, settling on the most innocuous thing that crossed my mind.

"Maybe that's a good thing," Margit snapped back. "My grandfather always said your grandmother is a witch. That a pretty face doesn't say a thing about what's inside a stone-cold heart. You'd do well to remember that, Kjell."

I sat bolt upright. Even if Kjell was the love of her life, I wouldn't expect this kind of hostility. I'd spent less than fifteen minutes with him.

"Margit!" Kjell hissed, followed by something gruff in Norwegian.

Back home, I wasn't the type of girl who fired back, unless it was against Tuck. Maybe it was because being Graham's sister meant I'd never really needed to, or maybe it was because I'd never done something daring enough to really garner this sort of reaction. Either way, a whole new Ellie simmered beneath the surface, rising to meet Margit's challenge.

"It's funny you bring that up," I said. "In some countries, red hair was considered a sign of witchcraft. They actually burned people at the stake for it. Can you imagine? Just goes to show that a little ignorance can go a long way—if you let it go unchallenged, that is."

The entire car went silent, and for a moment I wondered if I'd gone too far, and if every one of them could hear me struggling to swallow the nervous lump in my throat. Then Kjell threw his considerable weight behind me.

"You're way too sweet if you feel guilty." He shot me a reassuring big-brother smile that made me think of Graham. "She deserved it."

While I was grateful for the moral support, I would have preferred he keep his eyes on the road as the car started the steep ascent into the narrow mountain lane outside of town.

For the first time that night, but far from the last, I wished I'd just stayed home. Particularly when I peeked in the rearview mirror and saw the sulky, bitter scowl on Margit's face. The hate in her eyes when they met mine told me she had no intention of letting me off so easily.

We drove around a dark and narrow road that traced the fjord, past shallow rowboats bobbing at the ends of rickety docks and stilted boathouses clinging to the shore. An occasional fishing trawler, anchored close to shore, cast a dark shadow across the shimmering water. Not a single car passed us during the drive from Skavøpoll to the tiny town of Selje, its nearest neighbor.

What Kjell had called a pub was actually the bar of the only hotel in town. And it was surprisingly crowded for a Tuesday night. Kjell found a barstool for me, after Margit somehow managed to straddle two stools, making sure I couldn't sit near her. And I was uncomfortable when Kjell then ended up standing himself. Especially when Margit scowled at me, like I'd forced Kjell to do that.

Margit immediately launched into a hushed conversation

with Sven, who cast a few apologetic looks at me and more than a dozen at Kjell. It made me feel even worse, since she was making a fool of herself over a boy and alienating him at the same time.

After one last questioning glance at his friends, Kjell seemed determined to make up for Margit's behavior. He kept me entertained—so entertained, I was surprised to glance at my watch and see it was already eleven. I'd promised Grandmother I wouldn't be out too late, since we had to leave for the airport first thing in the morning to pick up Graham.

When I looked up again, something in Kjell's face gave me pause. He was staring over my shoulder, his mouth slightly ajar. His expression was slack and distant, as if his brain had gotten up and walked away, leaving a vacant body behind. It was unsettling. Which is why it took me so long to notice that Kjell wasn't the only one staring at the door. Sven and Margit were similarly fascinated by something or someone directly behind me.

Naturally, I turned.

Two girls roughly Kjell's age were framed in the open doorway, scanning the interior of the bar with cold, appraising eyes.

The first thing I noticed was their appearance. They were impossibly beautiful. And tall. While Norwegians are known for both qualities, these girls decimated anyone I'd seen during all my time in Norway. Or anyone I'd seen in any magazine or movie screen—ever. They were breathtaking and heart-stopping all at once.

They walked slowly into the bar, letting the door close

soundlessly behind them. Every movement was lithe and graceful, yet with an edge of casual confidence that seemed almost predatory. Like lions circling their prey.

Both girls were dressed strangely. That was the second thing I noticed. They were wearing all leather—from the plunging necklines of their skintight jackets to their knee-high, fur-trimmed boots. Not the slick black leather of a biker or even the shiny metallic leather of Eurotrash nightclub girls. This leather was beige and natural, a coarse, untanned suede. While I'm personally an Ugg boot addict, there was something off-putting about an entire Ugg catsuit.

There had to be a logical explanation for their clothes. Parts of Norway are still rustic in the most charming way. Herds of goats wander the mountain roads and constitute traffic jams. Entire families live in houses so remote, they can only be reached on snowshoes. Perhaps these girls didn't look as odd to the rest of the room as they looked to me. Maybe that was normal attire for hardy Norwegian mountain folk who happened to look like supermodels.

One quick glance around the bar told me I was hardly the only curious one. There was something extraordinary about those girls. Extraordinary and terrifying. I watched, transfixed, as, one by one, heads turned throughout the bar. Conversations faded into silence, punctuated by the occasional speculative whispers, until the bar was dominated by the obnoxious American country music pumping through the speakers and the loud guffaw of the man in the corner who was too drunk to notice anything except the pint of beer in his hand.

The girls stepped forward, scanning every face as if they'd need to re-create each one from memory when they got home. If they noticed the effect they were having, they didn't care.

As she stepped to the side to get a better view of the booth in the corner, the first girl's jacket slid open just enough to reveal a gun secured against her hip in a low-slung holster. There was a long serrated knife strapped to her calf by a thin leather cord that snaked all the way up her leg. Just when I thought things couldn't get any weirder, a strange voice sounded in my head, one that was me and wasn't me. Like it came from a new part of my consciousness I hadn't had the chance to meet yet. It told me she was an expert with both weapons. Lethal. Her companion was similarly dangerous, but not nearly as skilled as the blond one. It was the way the other girl stood, bearing too much weight on her left leg. And her holster was half an inch too low. The fraction of a second she'd waste drawing her gun could mean the difference between life and death.

And I had no idea where that knowledge came from. I'd never even held a gun. But the truth of it was undeniable. Seeing those girls was like pulling a muscle I didn't even know I had. It stirred something that terrified and electrified me. I felt as if I was fully awake for the first time in my life.

Then the rational Ellie weighed in, reminding me of where I was and how unbelievably strange this moment was. Especially when I glanced back at the lobotomized expression on Kjell's face.

"Is this some sort of local militia?" I whispered, watching the girls move toward the bar, their eyes scanning the room, ever vigilant. Kjell didn't reply. He didn't even acknowledge that I'd spoken.

Before I had a chance to nudge Kjell back into the present, the drunk, guffawing man took three wobbly steps right into one of the girls, the blond one, and stumbled backward, dropping to one knee to catch his balance. He must have been stupid as well as drunk, because somehow he missed the weapons strapped to that model-perfect body. As he rose to his feet, he gave her a very thorough once-over. When his eyes finally reached her face, a lewd smile spread across his lips as he reached out and let his fingertips trail along her thigh.

The blond girl's retaliation was fast as lighting and every bit as deadly. She grabbed him by the hair. Her knee came up as she slammed his head down. There was a sickening crunch as his face met bone. The move was as graceful and smooth as a ballerina's pirouette, but no one could mistake the brutal, incalculable force contained in those long limbs. Or the cold blood pumping through Blondie's veins.

The man crumpled at her feet when she released him, blood pouring from his shattered nose and pooling into a puddle on the floor.

"Kjell," I whispered. "Your medical training . . . shouldn't you help him or something?"

Kjell's eyes never left those girls, even when I shook his arm hard, trying to snap him out of it. He was staring at them with an odd sort of determination. The set of his jaw told me that now he only had eyes for those two.

"Kjell?" I repeated, annoyed and a bit scared when he

swatted me away with one arm. "If you're staying here to watch the ultimate fighting floor show, can you at least tell me how to get home? Can I call a cab or something?"

When Kjell finally looked down at me, his eyes were as cloudy as opals. The boy at Graham's party had looked the same way, right before he almost pushed me into the pool.

As Kjell stared at me, his eyes cleared, and he recovered enough to remember his manners. "I'm sorry," he said, shaking his head the way you do when water is trapped in your ear. "I seem to have dozed for a sec."

Right. Years of hanging out with Tucker and Graham had taught me more than enough about boys and their attention spans. Particularly when supermodels were wandering around. Kjell was hardly in danger of falling asleep anytime soon with those two sirens in the room. But for the moment, his eyes were back on me. And I needed to seize the opportunity to secure my ride home. I wanted out of there immediately.

I'd barely opened my mouth to speak when manicured, fire-red fingernails curled over his shoulder. One of the leather-clad bobsled girls was standing at his side, her lips framing a devastating smile.

"How old are you?" she asked in Norwegian. It was one of the few complete sentences I knew. Hopefully, next she'd ask for the time or directions to the airport. But I had a feeling this conversation was about to soar past my repertoire of memorized phrases.

"Nineteen," he replied in a flat, monotone voice.

Really? I thought. Graham would die. A nineteen-year-old

boy had taken me out. To a bar. Even if the story was about to end with that boy ditching me for someone more in his age category, I almost regretted I'd never get to see the look on his face.

The beautiful girl shifted closer as she trailed her fingers from Kjell's shoulder down his chest, probing, as if she'd find buried treasure beneath his shirt.

I had to admire the speed with which she closed in on what she wanted. But the way her fingers continued to expertly weave across his torso reminded me more of a butcher inspecting a side of beef than an attempt at seduction.

I started to laugh. I couldn't help it. In light of the man still washing the hardwood floors with his blood, a groping session seemed ill timed. At home, the LAPD would be all over the place by then. As I glanced around the bar again, no one seemed particularly bothered by any of it.

The catatonic expression had settled back over Kjell's features, like he wasn't fully cognizant of what was happening.

The second girl joined her companion. She curled one hand over Kjell's cheek and started saying something in Norwegian. It was about time, I thought. In my book, a few words of small talk ought to precede a full body massage.

I caught the word doctor. Somehow they knew about medical school. Perhaps these were Kjell's friends from Oslo? Kjell tipped his head to the side, watching the blond girl in absolute rapture. Beautiful as she was, it was wrong. So wrong. She pulled him two steps forward, leading him toward the door like a puppy on a leash. I knew I had to do something about it. I had to stop them.

"Kjell, are you okay?" I asked, putting my hand on his wrist protectively.

Instead of replying, Kjell glared down at me. Like he had no idea who I was or what I was doing there. But I held his gaze, steady and trying not to be frightened by the furious intensity in his eyes. He blinked, three times, fast, as if waking out of a dream.

Frantically he dug for something in the pocket of his jacket—something small and silver. It looked like the tiny object my grandmother had dropped into his hand earlier that night. It was a small metal disk, with a series of raised lines and curves that resembled letters, only from no alphabet we'd ever learned in school. Kjell held it out in front of himself. Like a priest exorcising the devil. Except his eyes were firmly closed, clenched tight.

His other hand reached out and found mine, his fingers snaking in between all the digits, squeezing so tight I thought my knuckles would pop like balloons.

The blond girl took a step back, staring scornfully at the object resting on Kjell's palm. Her hand flew out as if she was planning to snatch it away from him. But the instant her fingers touched metal, she whipped them back like she'd been burned. Then her eyes shifted to me. She looked me up and down as the strangest feeling flooded me, a surge of power and knowledge nipping at the periphery of my consciousness, fighting to get in.

A slow, cruel smile spread across Blondie's face. I felt as if I was an amusing, albeit annoying, pet. One that she was about to back over with her car. On purpose.

She extended her index finger and pressed it hard against my forehead. My skin burned under her touch, but I was paralyzed by whatever current seemed to flow between us. And for a horrifying instant, it made me question whose side I should take in this encounter. After all, I barely even knew Kjell, and these girls were something truly remarkable. Longing filled my heart, a burning desire to go with them. To follow the blond girl anywhere she chose to take me.

I fought against the intrusive urge, because it came from someplace that I didn't trust. I grabbed her wrist but couldn't knock her finger away.

"Valkyrie," she said in clear, ringing accents. The word unleashed a double roller-coaster ride of exhilaration in my veins. It was so foreign, yet so familiar, both the word and the feeling it triggered. The effect must have been plain on my face, because the blond girl smiled. While her expression was far from warm, it was the first thing she'd done that didn't chill me to the bone.

My hand flew to my forehead when the blond girl released me. The skin where her finger had been was still hot to the touch.

Everyone in the bar was watching us by then—maybe because of the gorgeous supermodel who'd practically burrowed her finger into my brain, or maybe because they'd noticed that an underage American was in their midst. Either way, the eyes that met mine were a strange milky white. I swallowed hard, fighting back panic, as I realized that Kjell and I were alone with those lunatics in a room full of vacant, slack faces.

The blond girl said something else, a torrent of angry

Norwegian that left me confused, breathless. "I don't understand," I said, shaking my head. "But I think you should leave." After a moment, I added, *"Blad."* I'd either told her to leave or called her a car.

"How fascinating that you exist," she said, switching languages effortlessly. Her accent was different from that of everyone else I'd met in Norway. Antique. Like she'd studied English three hundred years ago. "Information so valuable that I'll forgive you this once."

"Astrid," her friend said, a protest brewing in her voice. Something flashed between them as their eyes met. I felt the silent argument roll back and forth the way you can sense motion in the water even when it's far away.

Astrid glanced from me to Kjell as if weighing her options. So I took a step in front of him, like I'd actually be able to protect him from those two if they were determined to hurt us.

"No." Astrid surveyed my defensive posture and gave me a patronizing half smile. "Let her live. There's no justice in punishing the ignorant. And they understand just enough to carry an important message home." She locked eyes with me. "Consider this a one-time courtesy." The last word stuck to her tongue as if it were the vilest combination of letters in the dictionary. "Next time you won't be so lucky. When I hunt, I kill anything that gets in my way—predator or prey."

Astrid turned on her heel and strode toward the door without hesitating and without looking back. Her friend fell into step behind her but cast one last angry glare in my direction. Their boots pounded against the hardwood floor in unison.

With military precision. It was the only sound in the bar other than my shallow jackrabbit breathing.

The moment the door closed behind them, Kjell leaned forward onto the counter and exhaled as if he'd been holding it in for an aeon.

"I can't believe that just happened," he whispered. He stepped forward, putting his hands on my shoulders. "I don't know how you did that. But thank you." Then he kissed me, quickly, so lightly, on the lips.

"You sure?" I challenged, keeping my tone casual and hoping to distract everyone from the fact that all the blood in my body had just relocated to my face. "Tuck, er, my friend, would scream at me right about now—say that I got in his way when he could have gotten laid."

"Laid?" Kjell made the word sound even dirtier than it was. "Is that what you think was happening?"

If there was one thing I couldn't stand, it was being talked down to. "I don't know what to think," I said frostily. "And I really don't care. I just want to go home."

"I see." Kjell was looking at me like I was four years old, which was the other thing I couldn't stand. "Didn't your grandmother tell you about the rumors? Your brother arrives tomorrow, right? After what happened here tonight, he'll need to be very careful."

"What rumors?" I asked. "And what do Graham and my grandmother have to do with you picking up girls?" I said it even though I was beginning to realize that there was more at stake here, there were deeper implications that I couldn't even begin to grasp. Like denying it would make it go away.

Kjell's eyes widened in surprise. Or maybe it was disappointment. "It has nothing to do with picking up girls, and I think you know that. They would have kidnapped me if you hadn't stopped them. I owe you my life."

"Dramatic much?" I pulled my hand away when he reached for it, alarmed by his sudden intensity. "Look, you don't owe me anything," I said. He clearly did owe me an explanation, but I was willing to wait until we were in the car, especially if he was going to act so peculiar in public. "Except maybe a ride home."

"Anything you say."

Fifteen minutes ago, he had observed a careful enough distance that I figured the age difference was too much for him. But those baby blues now told me they were seeing me in quite a different light. It was such a complete one-eighty that I couldn't help wondering how much of it was beer goggles or some sort of misplaced gratitude for supposedly saving him. Either way, I didn't like it one bit.

Kjell's blue eyes were still bright with excitement as he turned to Margit and Sven. "We should go." In all the chaos of the last few minutes, I'd forgotten they were even there. "I believe you now," Kjell said. "But we'll be okay. Elsa just drove them off. She saved me. It was incredible. You saw, right?"

Margit was glaring at me with so much loathing, I was surprised I hadn't felt it, even with my back turned. Sven, who'd seemed nice enough before, was now staring at me like I'd just sprouted bat wings and a third head. I almost touched my shoulders to make sure I hadn't.

Kjell didn't seem to notice their less-than-enthusiastic reactions. He was already pulling me forward. "Let's get out of here." As the people around us were shaking off the strange fog that had settled over their pupils, they started conferring in whispers. More than a few unfriendly faces had already turned my way. "C'mon, Margit, Sven."

"We're not going anywhere with *her*." Margit stood, shaking her head. "She's one of them."

Kjell and I had reached the middle of the room, and Kjell fired back an angry torrent of Norwegian. The words were fast and furious, and I was surprised to find I could catch a few. Kjell was calling Margit stupid, demanding to know why I would have stood up for him if I was one of them.

Whoever *they* were.

The important part, the touching part, was that Kjell was begging Margit to give me a chance. I looked back at Margit, more curious about her reaction than anything else. Given the undercurrent of jealousy that had swept through the evening, I was pretty sure Kjell was making it worse by defending me.

"Don't you even look at us," Margit snarled, covering Sven's eyes with one hand. "You already have my brother. Isn't that enough? Besides, Sven's too young, remember? That's what they said last time. You have to be eighteen." She took four quick steps until she was right in front of me, dragging Sven behind her.

"Too young for what?" I backed away, right into Kjell. "And I've never even met your brother. I just met you tonight." I couldn't believe I'd been stupid enough to get myself into this position. I was alone in a bar in Norway with a weird boy talking in riddles and a paranoid stranger who was preparing to wring my neck.

Margit's finger was in my face, practically poking my eye out. "She can't be trusted." She hurled the words at Kjell. "I told you. What she did proves it. She's just like her grandmother."

"You say that like it's a bad thing," I shot back, surprising myself yet again that night.

Margit was dying to hit me. But that wasn't what scared me. I was horrified by the image that flashed through my mind, courtesy of the new voice that had stirred to life inside me. My retaliation would be swift and brutal if she even tried.

Sven shook his face free of Margit's hand and grabbed Kjell roughly by the shoulder.

"We can't let you leave with her," Sven said. "You'll thank us for this tomorrow."

"Back off." Kjell knocked Sven's arm away and shoved his chest, just hard enough to send him back a few paces.

Margit pulled the personal locator beacon out of her pocket.

"Don't you dare," Kjell hissed.

But without even hesitating, Margit pressed a flat red button on the front. This time, a red light on the top blinked to life, flashing in time with my thundering pulse.

"Turn that off," Kjell said, taking a step toward Margit and making a grab for it. Sven blocked him. "You're gonna have the Royal Navy out looking for you," Kjell said. "That's not a toy."

"No," Margit said. "We changed the frequency to one the navy won't pick up. You can't pretend this isn't happening now," she added, suddenly all smug self-satisfaction. "You've seen it too. No more thinking you're so much better than us, Dr. Perfect back from Oslo, acting like you know everything." The tangible resentment in her words surprised me and made me wonder if I'd been misreading Margit's behavior all along. Because bitter wasn't the best way to sweet-talk your crush.

"I know what I saw," Kjell said, rubbing his forehead with his palm. "But that doesn't mean Ellie's part of it. She has no idea what's been going on."

"Fine." Margit glared at me, and I started inching my way toward the door, pepper spray in hand. "If she's innocent, she can prove it to the others when they get here."

"What others?" I asked.

But Margit's focus had shifted back to Kjell, who made one more grab for the emergency transmitter in her hand.

"Turn that stupid thing off," he said. Sven pushed him away. Hard. "If she was part of it, why would she have saved me? Think. You're letting prejudice cloud your judgment." Sven and Kjell glared at each other, hands balled into fists, teetering on the brink of an actual punch-throwing fight.

"Interesting that you're defending her." Margit's mouth pressed into a thin line. "Snap out of it. She'll seduce and kidnap you too."

"Seduce?" I asked as a flush crept up my neck. That accusation was certainly a first. "Kidnap?" I whispered.

"Kjell." Margit's voice broke over the plea. "Please."

And then I knew, all at once, that her hostility toward me had nothing to do with an unrequited crush. She was scared for

Kjell. She truly thought she was protecting him. The scraps of odd behavior I'd collected over the day, from the angry old lady in the bakery to Margit's flaming hostility, were shuffling inside my mind as I tried to piece together what everyone was so afraid of.

"Let's go," Kjell said, pulling me behind him. "Before their *new* friends get here."

"What do you mean?" I asked. "Who's coming?" I didn't like the way Margit was standing, hands on her hips, a smug smile on her face, like we were stupid if we thought we were going anywhere.

Kjell's long strides dragged me to the door at a half run, and he didn't slow down when I stumbled, which was when I realized maybe there was a reason we needed to get out of there fast. Whoever Margit had summoned with that transponder was someone Kjell wasn't all that eager to meet.

It was impossible to ignore the stares that followed us across the bar, but I kept my eyes glued to the door, counting down the distance between me and safety with each step.

"Hope we see you tomorrow, Kjell," Margit called after us. "But if not, at least we know where to find *her*."

3

The air outside was crisp. I inhaled deeply, surprised yet grateful for the clarity it brought. Even at the height of summer, the night in Norway holds a hint of what's to come in the long, hard winter months. My senses were unusually sharp that night. I could hear everything—from the stream two miles into the woods to the dog barking in the next town over. The metallic taste of danger lingered in the air, dissipating in the night breeze off the fjord. I tried to pause, wanting to savor the sensation, but Kjell towed me toward his car as if we didn't have a moment to spare.

The low hum of engines filled my ears. Headlights flickered through the trees like lightning bugs. Four sets of high beams traced the road along the fjord, still a few miles out but approaching fast. Given the astronomically steep penalty for speeding in Norway, it had to be an emergency for them to risk going that fast. Almost hidden by the normal car sounds, I caught the faint rattling of metal, the grating sound of guns bouncing in a truck bed, concealed by something—a heavy blanket, judging by the way the sound was muffled. Don't ask me how I knew, I just did. My supersonic hearing bothered me considerably less than the way that violent voice was urging me to arm myself. To prepare an ambush.

I shook it off, pretty sure I'd be ending the summer in a padded cell.

"Come on," Kjell said, tugging on my arm. "Get in the car."

He didn't need to tell me twice.

This time, there was no gentlemanly opening of my door, no polite pause while he waited for me to fasten my seat belt. We were backing out of the lot before my door was even closed.

I didn't have to ask why. The proximity of danger had my pulse thrumming, but this time part of me embraced it. I told myself it had to be shock, the way I wanted to stand my ground, the lack of the fear my rational self knew I should have, given that four trucks armed with rifles were hurtling toward us at a breakneck pace.

Deep grooves of concentration creased Kjell's forehead as he backed the car out of the parking lot, keeping the headlights off. He hesitated, looking a long time in both directions, seeming torn about whether to head back toward Skavøpoll, crossing paths with the approaching trucks, or to drive off into the blackness on the other side of Selje.

Then he settled on a compromise. He drove up one of the residential roads and paused behind a dented white cargo van. His car had just come to a stop when three battered fishing trucks flew past and pulled into the parking lot of the hotel. They were still weighted down with mesh crab traps, and for a moment I thought that explained the rattling metal I'd somehow heard from miles away. But then two men exploded out of the cab of the first truck before it had even come to a complete stop. One reached into the truck bed and pulled out a rifle. He tossed it to his companion before pulling out a second and switching off the safety.

They sprinted around the side of the building while the second and third trucks circled the hotel in opposite directions, toward the water, out of sight. And the fourth truck just slowed as it continued past, off into the darkness on the far side of town.

My new, strange instinct told me they were coordinated, that they had carefully planned and rehearsed this attack, even though they were vastly underprepared to take on anything but an oversized salmon. They were afraid. The cloud of fear was thick, clinging to their pores, no matter how headlong and recklessly they rushed forward to confront the object of it. But as they moved, something else drifted through the night, overpowering it.

Courage.

I hadn't known things like fear or bravery had a smell, much less a taste, until that moment. Something strange was in the air that night. Something that was affecting me, subtly shifting my senses. And it had me terrified. More than anything, I wanted to be back in my bed at my grandmother's house, where I could bury my face under a pillow and block out the whole world forever.

Kjell sighed next to me. Or maybe he just exhaled. Then, without saying anything, he eased the car back onto the narrow road that skirted the fjord and led back toward Skavøpoll. He kept the headlights off until at least five miles separated us from those men.

We drove in silence, our eyes drifting to the rearview mirrors every few seconds. It wasn't until we were halfway home that Kjell's shoulders finally lowered back to their usual height.

"I suppose you're wondering what happened back there," Kjell said. His voice was distant, like he was still tangled up in his thoughts. "And to tell you the truth, so am I. There's a theory. I'm just worried you'll think I'm crazy."

"Try me," I said, looking out the window at the pale moonlight rippling across the fjord. It would take a lot to surprise me after what I'd just seen. But somehow he succeeded.

"If you want to believe the legends and the gossips, well, then, those girls were Valkyries." He said it fast, the words sprinting out of his mouth.

"What's that?" I interrupted. That word had hit me, again, with an almost tangible force. It was the question that had been burning my brain since Astrid had put her fingertip to my forehead. "What's a Valkyrie?"

Kjell's silence lasted so long that I looked over to make sure he hadn't fallen asleep behind the wheel.

"You'll think I'm crazy," he said. "I know before tonight, I thought everyone else was."

I glanced at his profile, surprised by how frightened and uncertain he sounded. It was a far cry from the sunny, carefree laughter of just an hour ago.

"Back in the time of the Vikings, soldiers were encouraged to embrace death without fear," he said. "And according to their religion, according to what is now considered myth, Valkyries were beautiful women who hovered around battlefields, and when brave fighters were killed, they took their souls to Valhalla—a fortress ruled by Odin, god of death and war and knowledge. From a military standpoint, it was a brilliant belief system. The idea of being rewarded by Odin and his Valkyries took away the fear of death, so that people would fight without regard for personal safety. Because if they were brave and reached Valhalla, they were rewarded, but they were also on call in case Odin needed them. They became part of Odin's army."

The mention of Odin tied my stomach into a double knot. Kjell and my grandmother had been talking about Odin in hushed voices in the entry hall that very night. It was far too timely to be a coincidence. It wasn't like my no-nonsense grandmother was a mythology buff.

"You're joking, right?" I asked. "I mean, about there really being Valkyries?"

The eyes that searched my face in the darkness were tense, as were the hands gripping the steering wheel. He was about as serious as it gets.

"Sure, those girls were . . . unusual, but that doesn't mean they're mythical beings," I said, even though I knew it couldn't be yet another coincidence that Astrid had used the word

Valkyrie when she'd stormed the bar. I didn't like how neatly the pieces were fitting into an impossible explanation.

When Kjell didn't answer right away, I realized that maybe I'd offended him. "So is it a cultural thing—like people here still believe in all this mythology stuff? Because then I guess it's not such a leap of logic." As the words slipped out, I realized I'd probably just offended him even more.

Kjell laughed. "This may be a small town, Ellie, but we don't worship ancient pagan gods, if that's what you mean." He paused. "Look, I don't want to frighten you, but some guys from the area have disappeared. At first, everyone thought it was no big deal. Kids run away, get into drugs, whatever. But lately it's gotten worse. Boys being taken away. In public, right under everyone's nose. Like what almost happened to me tonight." His voice cracked and he cleared his throat. "When things start happening that can't be explained, even rational people, who should know better, fall back on old superstitions. They're scared. And there's no logical explanation for what's happening."

While part of me was grappling with what he was saying, the rest of me was half expecting the hidden cameraman to pop out any minute.

I must have been quiet way too long, because Kjell sounded defensive when he added, "You know there was something weird about those girls."

"Even if I accept that those girls were, um, special, they weren't the only strange thing tonight. Why does Margit hate my grandmother?" I paused, because for some reason the next part made me unfathomably sad. "And me?"

Kjell was quiet again, as if he wasn't sure where to start. "She doesn't," he said. "She's just looking for someone to blame. Ever since her brother disappeared, she's been different."

Hardly a complete answer, as much as I sympathized with what she must be going through. But given the grim frown on Kjell's face, it was the best I was going to get.

"Okay, then who were those guys in the trucks?" I pressed on. "Lemme guess. Leprechauns?"

"Don't worry about them," Kjell said, reaching over and covering my hand with his in a way that should have made my heart flutter but instead just made my stomach churn. "I'll handle them."

"What's to handle?" I asked, sliding my hand out from underneath his and crossing my arms. The universal signal to back off. "Who were they?"

"The holy inquisition," he muttered, "on a modern-day witch hunt, apparently."

The word witch carried me back to the bizarre things Margit had said about my grandmother. And about me. And the whispered conversation between Grandmother and Kjell in the entryway. Either it was all tying together or Margit's paranoia was as contagious as the plague. A symptom of the epidemic sweeping the town. "Is all of this why you were talking about Odin with my grandmother?" I demanded. "Why she told you to be careful?"

"Your grandmother knows everything," he said. "I just wondered what she thought about the rumors. And what has been happening."

"And what did she say?"

"She didn't seem to want to talk about it," he said softly. "So she just laughed. I was surprised. I've never known her to be anything but blunt. I believe you overheard the rest." He glanced at me from the corner of his eye.

"Then I'll ask her myself," I said, my resolve hardening like amber. "I'll tell her what happened tonight. I can promise she'll have an opinion when it comes to my safety."

"No," he said, suddenly way too loud for his cramped car. "I mean, you'll get in trouble. We both will. We weren't supposed to leave Skavøpoll tonight. She laughed about the Odin stuff, but at the same time she said to stay in town. She'll kill us both if she finds out."

"Great," I muttered. "Maybe you should have told me that before you dragged me into that den of lunatics." I was furious that Kjell had led me into breaking pretty much the only rule Grandmother had ever set for me. But more than anything, I was absolutely steaming that my grandmother had set that rule with someone other than me. Just like how my mother always counted on Graham to enforce my curfew when she worked late. Like I was some sort of simpleton who couldn't tell time.

"I'm really sorry," he said. "I thought—I thought it would be okay. The rumors just seemed so ridiculous. And Margit and Sven insisted. Probably because they have this weird plan to fight back." He got quiet. "I didn't mean for this to happen," he finally said. "And I really, really hope you don't tell your grandmother. Or at least wait a couple of days until I figure out what's going on."

"It's really my problem, not yours," I said. "The most she can do is get mad at you. Me, she can ground."

That comment nearly backfired when I saw the desperate look in his eyes.

"Then you can't tell her," he urged. "Because if you're grounded, I can't see you tomorrow."

Suddenly grounding didn't seem like such a bad option. It would extract me from the awkward situation that was clearly brewing between us. Then I realized it also meant I'd probably miss out on things I might actually want to do once Graham arrived.

"Fine," I said. "But you should have told me and let me make my own decision." Mentally, I added that Grandmother should have told me too. I'd never known her to be indirect about anything.

Fortunately, my tone sealed the tomb of our conversation for the rest of the drive. Which was just fine with me. It wasn't like I'd been getting any useful information out of Kjell anyway. Nothing but myths that should be saved for bedtime stories.

What I wanted was answers.

WHEN I GOT home, I wasn't as quiet as I could have been, half hoping Grandmother would hear and come out to say good night. Just to make sure I hadn't been out partying or getting into trouble, the way my mother would have. Graham and Tucker's antics had made Mom strict, especially after my father died, even though the worst she'd caught me doing in the middle of the night was smuggling ice cream into my room.

But the house was silent, other than the squeak of my shoes on the polished pine floors. I passed my room and walked all the way to the end of the hallway, until I came to a stop outside grandmother's closed door. It would be so easy to knock. To tell her everything that had happened. I curled my hand into a fist, ready to do just that. But then I tried to picture what would come next. And couldn't. I had no idea how to even start. Or what exactly I was expecting her to tell me.

Plus, being awakened in the middle of the night to the news that Kjell and I had disobeyed her and walked right into some sort of freak show in a bar in the next town over hardly seemed like the best way to get her to trust me and open up.

So I backed away from her door and headed toward my room, this time hoping my footsteps wouldn't disturb her slumber.

Exhausted as I felt, once I crawled into bed, I couldn't sleep. The events of the night played through my mind in a constant, seamless loop of beautiful bobsled girls and vacant zombie eyes staring at me from Kjell's brainwashed face.

I'd have the chance to talk to Grandmother in the morning, when we drove to the airport. By then I would think of a way to ask her about what had happened without incriminating myself. And if I couldn't find any answers, perhaps Graham could. Grown-ups actually listened when he spoke. He could help me find an explanation for what had happened that night that wasn't based on crazy myths and lore.

But the thought of Graham investigating sent a jolt of adrenaline down my spine. I sat up in bed at the spark of it. Whoever or whatever Astrid was, she was dangerous, and in a way that even Graham wouldn't be able to handle. I couldn't tell him what had happened—for his own safety.

I knew it was true, could feel it in the way the violent voice was awake and growling at the possibility of Astrid getting those manicured claws on Graham.

It was the first time in my life I'd ever thought of Graham as anything less than invincible. No matter what was at the root of what had happened that night, I would do whatever it took to keep Graham away from it.

4

At five thirty the next morning, Grandmother was in my room, pulling back the curtains and humming a tune so painfully cheerful, I almost crawled out of bed just to get her to stop. Of course, that was her plan all along

"Breakfast is ready downstairs, Elsa," she said brightly before disappearing through the doorway. "It won't stay hot all morning."

"All morning," I repeated. "It's basically still night." Even the sunshine streaming in through the window was pale and weak with slumber. So I pulled the blanket up over my head, deciding I'd fake sick and stay home. It wasn't like Graham would get up at dawn to come and greet little old me.

But the moment Graham's name formed in my mind, the

memory of what had happened in the pub in Selje slammed into me like a linebacker. Just like the realization the night before that I had to keep Graham safe. I shuddered again at the image of Astrid's fingers cupping Graham's cheek, as they had last night with Kjell.

Suddenly I couldn't have been any more awake.

How had I put it aside, even for a moment—even in sleep? You'd think those girls could dominate everything, including my dreams. But maybe they had. Because faint, hazy images followed in a line, on the heels of the things I knew were true. The things I remembered. Or thought I remembered. There was no way I'd made up the way the whole bar had gone catatonic at the sight of those girls.

Yet as my thoughts roamed backward, separating the fact from fantasy and the truth from PTSD, I suddenly wasn't so sure where to find the line. Maybe Kjell's eyes hadn't gone milky white. Maybe they'd just glazed over. And it didn't quite seem possible that no one had cared when the blond girl, Astrid, had broken that man's nose and left him bleeding on the ground. Things like that just didn't happen today in civilized society.

"Ten minutes," Grandmother called up the stairs. "I packed your breakfast. And I'll pack you up too if you're not out soon. Something tells me you won't want to show your face in public wrapped in an old lady's tracksuit."

I couldn't imagine how so much time had passed while I'd been just lying there, thinking. I rolled out of bed, whipped my hair into a ponytail, and threw on the clothes I'd worn the night before, ignoring the cigarette smoke still clinging to my sweater.

Once we were in the car, my thoughts seemed even more tangled, memories melding into dreams, mixing things I wished had happened—like me throwing Astrid right through the window—with visions that horrified me, like me abandoning Kjell and walking across the bar to stand behind Astrid. Dying to learn everything she was willing to teach me. Wanting to be just like her.

I never get carsick, but my stomach felt abandoned by gravity as Grandmother guided her sedan along the roller coaster of mountain roads.

"Something on your mind?" Grandmother asked, clearing her throat first, as if breaking a tense silence that somehow I hadn't noticed.

I traced the slats of the air vent with my index finger, realizing I'd been adjusting them for the last fifteen minutes. Switching the air current back and forth and up and down was oddly soothing.

There was a long pause.

"What is it you'd like to ask me?" Grandmother asked.

I shouldn't have been so surprised. She'd always been way too able to read me. And she knew it. Because I didn't realize until that moment, until she asked me dead-on, that I'd made up my mind to tell her. And I'd been waiting for the chance, deciding how far I'd take my story. In my heart I'd always known I had to tell her what had happened, even if it meant getting Kjell and myself in trouble. After all, why would I keep secrets on behalf of a boy I'd known less than twenty-four hours? Especially when he knowingly broke her rules?

I shifted until I could covertly watch her reaction as I backed up and dumped a whole truckload of crazy at her feet.

"I was just wondering"—I paused to decide exactly how to proceed—"about Valkyries. Kjell told me there are rumors about them, um, being around. Last night I think we saw two of them." Blunt seemed the best way to break the ice.

"Where?" Grandmother asked.

"Just a pub in Selje," I replied. "Inside this old hotel."

The expression on Grandmother's face could not have been more neutral, which made me squirm in my seat.

"Right next to the water? Old Johann's place. Strange that Kjell took you there when I specifically told him not to leave the boundaries of Skavøpoll."

So many things about that statement were odd. Not only was she focusing on the least important part of what I'd just said, she acted like it wasn't strange at all to impose a rule on me through a boy I barely knew. "In the future, I expect you and your brother to obey that rule unswervingly. Am I clear?"

I nodded. It was unsettling indeed that she was suddenly so interested in our whereabouts, given everything Kjell had told me.

Grandmother lapsed back into silence, and it took every inch of my spine to demand, "What about the rest of what I said—about the Valkyries? Kjell also said people have been disappearing."

"Kjell was just trying to scare you," Grandmother replied dismissively. "There's no such thing as the boogeyman, either. Boys will tell all kinds of stories to impress a pretty girl. Make that heart of yours flutter. Kids run away from small-town life. Or go on a trip without telling everyone. It doesn't mean they disappeared. Or were carried off by fairies, trolls, or Valkyries. Time to increase the sensitivity on your bullshit detector."

That was exactly the kind of response I'd expected from her. The irony was, my bullshit detector went wild at the way she delivered it. "You're hiding something," I said, before I'd fully thought through what I was accusing her of. "I heard you telling Kjell to be careful. Now suddenly we can't leave town without you? You can't pretend nothing is going on."

But it seemed like she had every intention of doing just that. Instead of replying, she clicked the wiper switch forward, dousing the windshield in fluid. Even though the windshield couldn't be more clean.

"Some kids from town went with us," I said. "They called you a witch. And said I'm one too. They accused me of trying to kidnap Kjell. What aren't you telling me? I need to know."

Grandmother glanced at me, true surprise in her eyes. "I'm not telling you how disappointed I am in Kjell for breaking my rules, and for befriending idiots who repeat ridiculous stories," she said, her voice getting softer at the end. "Yes, some boys have left town, and the gossips are doing what gossips do best—speculating and spreading rumors. And even after fifty years of knowing me, half the people in this town still whisper that I'm dangerous, all because I came to town alone, with no family. And early on, there were some misunderstandings." She paused, a strange ferocity glinting in her eyes at some distant memory I hoped she'd share. "There was an avalanche, and a year later a devastating boat accident. And in my years of travel I had learned a few things about survival. I thought I was helping when I rescued those people. But instead I set gossiping tongues in motion. And they never really stopped. If I can rescue a drowning boat crew, what's to stop me from kidnapping a few boys?" Her lips curled in a wry smile as she reached over and patted my hand.

At least I now knew the real reason the old lady had attacked me in the bakery.

"But no matter," Grandmother said. "Let's let small-minded people live within the confines of their small-minded assumptions while the rest of us carry on with our lives." It was clear she thought those words closed the topic. And any other day, the magnitude of what I'd just learned about her might have been enough to keep my brain busy for a while.

But not that day. "Still. The girls we saw—they just weren't normal. I'm sure of it," I pressed.

Grandmother sighed. "An example, please."

"Well, first, they were ridiculously pretty. Unbelievable. Then one of them hit this guy when he grabbed her leg. I think she broke his nose. Then she walked right over and started talking to Kjell. She knew all about him being a medical student even though he hadn't told her, and . . . and she tried to force him to leave with her." It sounded so inexcusably ordinary, even to my own ears.

Which is probably why Grandmother interrupted me. "Kjell is a nice-looking boy. You can pardon another girl for taking a chance," she said. "As for the hitting, I'd look the other way if you defended yourself in bar."

"There's more," I said, taking a deep breath and holding it so that the rest practically exploded out of me—because this was the part of the memory I still distrusted. "Everyone's eyes turned white. Solid white. And one of the girls, named Astrid, put one finger to my forehead and said Valkyrie."

"Astrid saw you?" she asked. Her voice was unnaturally calm.

"You know her?" But I didn't need her answer. I could hear the familiarity of the name on my grandmother's tongue.

But "No," she said. "It's surprising this Astrid girl would go after Kjell if you were standing there, that's all." If I hadn't been staring at her hands on the steering wheel, I might have accepted her explanation. But I'd seen the way her fingers tensed around the leather like talons strangling their prey. The skin across her knuckles was stretched so thin, it almost melted away, leaving just bone behind. The hands of a skeleton.

"That's all you have to say?" I demanded. "What about the Valkyrie part?"

"These supposed disappearances have the whole region on edge. Fabricating outlandish explanations. Name-calling. Sounds to me like Astrid was exploiting their fears. Really, Ellie, you're smarter than this." She paused, slowing down and changing lanes. Driving like a confused old lady—something my lead-footed grandmother never did.

"Speaking of fears, I'm terrified I'll miss the airport exit. Last time I went ten miles before I realized I'd gone too far. You're in charge of watching for it."

Her explanation was a cover-up, followed by a blatant attempt to change the subject. Still, I let her words slip right into my ear unhindered. Maybe if I let them sit there long enough, I could start to believe them myself, because the truth was getting weirder by the second. Grandmother was holding something back, something big. And it wasn't going to be easy dragging it out of the usually blunt and brazen Hilda Overholt.

WE PULLED UP to the curb at the main terminal, and after a few minutes of evading airport traffic cops, we saw Graham stroll through the sliding glass doors. I jumped out of the car and ran to greet him—so intently focused on Graham, I didn't see Tucker Halloway until I ran smack into him. Actually, he ran right into me. In typical Tucker fashion, he stepped in my way the second before I would have reached Graham.

"Tuck?" I came to a stunned stop as my shoulder slammed into his chest. I took a step back, wishing my skin wasn't so hyperaware of that brief moment of contact. "What are you doing here?"

"Missed you, Ells," Tuck said, leaning way too close. "It was torture. I changed my ticket just to see your smiling face."

"Then you're out of luck," I said, determined not to let his flirting confuse me. "With you around, it'll be a while before I smile again." I passed him by and folded myself under Graham's extended arm.

"I missed you too," Graham said, squeezing my shoulder. "Didn't Grandmother tell you Tuck was coming early? Guess she didn't know it was the start of World War Seven. Or are we already on Seventeen? Either way, there was a change of plans. Summer school starts in two weeks." Graham gave Tucker a pointed look. "*Some*one skipped too much English class to get credit."

"Actually, that's still open to debate," Tuck told me. "They have yet to produce a single shred of evidence that I wasn't there. Everyone knows old Ms. Turner is so nearsighted, she wouldn't know if it was me or a shrub planted in my seat."

"Please tell me you didn't actually test that theory," Graham muttered, even as he cracked a grin and headed toward Grandmother's car, keeping his arm draped over my shoulder.

"No hug for me, Ells?" Tuck fell into step beside us and tugged at my sleeve like a puppy.

"How about a hug around the neck with my hands?" It slipped out before I realized how harsh it sounded.

But Tuck laughed. "Easy there, tiger." He gave me his flashiest grin. "Save some ammo for later. We've got two weeks. And you're already throwing some pretty heavy shrapnel."

After what had happened the night before, slipping back into my routine with Tuck offered the best kind of release I'd ever imagined. It was amazing I'd never appreciated it before, how Tuck could frustrate me and make me laugh all at once.

Even thirteen hours of airplane travel couldn't take the shine off him. I had to bite my cheek hard not to smile right back at him as I prepared to fire the winning shot.

The words never made it past my lips. "Stop," Graham ordered. "Mandatory truce. Effective immediately." Then he lifted his arm from my shoulder and took the five remaining steps toward Grandmother alone, crushing her in his arms. As tall as Grandmother was, she looked dainty next to Graham's broad frame.

"Mrs. Overholt—or may I call you Hilda?" Tuck said, ramping into overdrive as he gave my grandmother a hug. He hadn't seen her for more than four years, but Tucker was never one to be shy. "Now we see where Graham and Ellie get their good looks." He winked at me.

I rolled my eyes.

Then I looked at Graham standing beside her, trying to restrain Tuck before he said something even more inappropriate.

Even though my instincts warned me against it, now that Graham was actually here, it seemed so easy, so logical to tell him what had happened with Kjell in the pub.

He'd know exactly what to say and do to make Grandmother tell us everything she knew. But that moment of temptation was immediately followed by a horrifying image. Graham staring at me from white-on-white eyes—if that was what had really happened. My memories were still confused, tripping over themselves. All I knew was those girls were dangerous, and knowing the truth about them hadn't helped Kjell or Sven one bit.

It was better to wait and watch, and if I ever saw those girls again, I'd keep Graham and Tuck as far away from them as possible. Without either of them ever being the wiser. Because Graham and Tucker weren't the kind of boys who'd just back down or run away from trouble.

So I bit my lip, hoping ignorance would be enough to keep

them out of the line of fire. Even as the new voice in my head assured me it wouldn't be.

WE ATE DINNER early that night, and Tuck and Graham went to bed immediately after. They'd practically fallen asleep at the table. After my own war with jet lag just one short week earlier, I could sympathize, but I still felt a pang of disappointment as Grandmother and I settled down to a quiet game of cribbage— alone. All day, we hadn't even acknowledged the conversation we'd had in the car, and I wondered if the tension between us was all in my head or if she felt it too.

At eleven I went up to my room and wrote down everything I'd noticed or overheard about the disappearances and those girls in the bar. But try as I might to find a rational, real-world explanation for everything I'd seen, nothing fit. And a rudimentary search for Valkyries on my phone had led me to video-game blogs and dating websites I'd rather not know existed.

Before long I was staring out the window. The world seemed clearer, more alive than ever that night, as if it would whisper all the answers to my questions right into my ear. Suddenly my skin itched to be out under the starlight. I'd always found it easier to think up on the roof—which drove my mother absolutely nuts. Fortunately, she wasn't there to voice her opinion.

I pushed the window open as wide as it would go, smelling the jasmine in my grandmother's garden mingled with the trees in the pine forest beyond. I stepped onto the window ledge and tested the rain gutter and steel shutters to make sure they still held my weight. Sure enough, they were as solid and still as a ladder put there just for me. In three quick steps, I was up on the roof, overlooking the fjord.

I leaned back against the steep slant of the peaked roof, picking at the blades of long, weedy grass. The sod roof was my favorite thing about my grandmother's house. In Norway, living roofs were pretty standard, and I'd even seen the neighbors put a goat on their house, to give it a trim. The night was that much more magical when I was suspended in the air, two stories above the ground, yet at the same time securely rooted to earth and green.

I'd been sitting there for about ten minutes when I heard a tapping noise to my right. I crawled along the edge of the roof and peered over until I saw its source.

Tucker.

He was looking up at me or, more specifically, at my ankle hovering above the lawn.

"Ells, move back. You're making me nervous," he said, leaning out his window.

"Shouldn't you be in bed?" I asked, even though I welcomed the company.

"I wish," he said softly. "I was thirsty. Now I can't get back to sleep. Then I heard this scampering noise, like a mouse. And there was your shoe dangling out in space." He paused. "That's dangerous, you know."

"Lots of things are far more dangerous," I replied, leaning back on my elbows and dangling both my legs off the edge of the roof.

"Don't," Tuck gasped. Which made it all too tempting to tease him like that. I sat up and scooted forward until I was perched precariously on the edge, looking down at him.

Tuck made a funny noise in his throat. "God, Ells. Seriously, please, just lean back again."

"Of everyone in the whole world, you're the last person I'd expect to be so uptight," I said, leaning forward farther still.

"If I come up there, will you lean back?"

"If you come up, I'll jump."

"Oh." He sounded hurt. His head disappeared back through his window.

"Tuck?" I called softly—actually feeling sorry. Tuck so rarely displayed any emotion other than impenetrable arrogance that I wasn't quite sure how to deal with his reaction.

"I was just kidding," I said. "I won't jump. I promise. Join me. It's incredible—you can see the whole fjord. You just need to mind your manners. This is about silent appreciation." I slid backward, making room for him.

"I'm all for silence," Tuck said as his hands appeared on the edge of the roof seconds later. He hauled himself over the side. "And appreciation." His teeth flashed white, and I could picture how he'd look if I could turn on the lights—perfect smile, rumpled T-shirt, and the myriad assorted details that made him our Tuck.

"Really?" I said.

"Of course," Tuck replied, like he couldn't fathom the meaning behind my sarcasm.

"Pardon me for being skeptical," I said softly. "It's just that parties and senior cheerleaders are usually more within your purview than quiet moonlit contemplation."

Tuck just settled on the grass next to me, like he hadn't heard. "Wow," he whispered, looking out over the twinkling lights of the slumbering town. Beyond that, the water of the fjord reflected the path of the moonlight and the dark mountains straining toward the stars. "You weren't kidding," he whispered.

I leaned back again, pressing my elbows into the soft sod of the roof. "You should listen to me more often."

"Amazing," he said. "I was thinking the same thing." I braced myself for the jab that would follow. He'd most likely rattle off a few examples of times I'd suggested something stupid or childish. Life with Tuck was a never-ending chess match— you had to plan ahead at least ten moves or you'd be toast.

But Tuck was silent as he stared out into the night. His profile was so serene and un-Tuck-like that I did a double take.

I couldn't help but wonder what Tucker Halloway was thinking about while sitting alone in the dark with me.

As if in answer to my unspoken question, he said, "It's funny. Norway almost reminds me of Oregon. My father and I went on a few fishing trips, back before he got remarried. I loved it there. I think I love it here, too." I could hear the smile in his voice as he added, "Thanks for sharing your roost with me."

"It's not like you gave me much choice," I said, even as my mind was scrambling to figure out what he was up to—why he was acting so bizarre. Sure, Tuck sometimes decided to be sweet, but it was usually a side effect of whatever ridiculous thing he'd set out to do in the first place. "If I'd left you downstairs alone, you'd probably be halfway through the bottle of schnapps Grandmother keeps under the sink." As I said it, I reached over and pinched his arm just above the elbow, like he always did to me.

"Nah. Would have gone back to bed." Tuck glanced at me out of the corner of his eye. "Would have been a shame to miss this." He slipped his hand over mine as I set it back down on the grass. I did my best not to let it be strange when he just left it there.

But it was.

More than a few anxious minutes passed as I waited for the first—or any—shoe to drop, but gradually, inch by inch, I started to relax. It was as if we were just two friends sitting on the roof in the middle of the night.

Tuck was so still that if not for the warmth of his fingers pressed against mine, I could have forgotten he was there. I was alone with my thoughts of Valkyries and white-on-white eyes. Something about Tuck's steady, constant presence at my side made everything that had happened, everything other than that moment, feel a million miles away. Like it had taken place in a dream.

The silence wrapped its arms around us until a drop of water brushed my cheek. I looked up at the sky. While it had been clear minutes ago, a storm had rolled in from the ocean, and my upturned face was instantly coated with a thin film of droplets. Each was smaller than a grain of sand, more a mist than rain.

"We'd better go in," I said. "Slippery is not a good thing

when you're climbing down from a roof."

"I guess," Tuck said as I scooted forward. "You need a hand?"

"Nope." I gripped the edge of the roof and expertly shimmied down the side of the house. "Do you?" I looked up as I reached the windowsill and sat with one leg dangling outside and the other resting securely on the hardwood floor of my room. All I could see was the flash of his teeth in the darkness as he peered down at me.

"Is that really all you've got?" he asked, grabbing the edge of the rain gutter and lowering himself back into the window of his room without using his feet. It was an impressive display of upper-body strength.

"Show-off," I said.

"I'm glad you were impressed." His head popped out the window just enough to look at me. "And for the record, I hate heights."

"Is that meant to dazzle me even more?" I replied.

"Dazzle? Overshot my mark."

I rolled my eyes, even though he couldn't see. It was a reflex born of years of enduring Tucker Halloway's ego. "Good night," I said, ducking my head back under the window frame and lowering the window enough to keep the rain out while letting the breeze in.

"Night, Ells."

I could hear Tuck moving around in the adjacent room, searching for something in his suitcase. Then I heard the scrape of the chair he dragged to the window, probably to look out over the fjord awhile longer. I curled up under my comforter and closed my eyes. Even though Tuck spent all his time in our house back home, he never stayed overnight. What was the point when he lived two doors down?

That night, his proximity was a splinter in my brain as I drifted off to sleep. I kept straining my ears for any sounds from his room. Finally I was rewarded with soft footfalls as he padded across the hardwood floors, followed by the creak of the bed under his weight. Only then was I able to sleep.

THE NEXT MORNING, the sun woke me at six, shining right into my face. Early as it was, by the time I made it to the kitchen, Tuck and Graham were scarfing down their breakfasts like they were in a speed-eating contest. There was a soccer ball on the table, wedged between the saltshaker and a vase of flowers.

As I sat down, Graham rose.

Something metal flashed around his neck. "What's that?" I asked, pointing at the thin chain sticking out above his shirt.

Graham gave me a sheepish smile. "Grandfather's old good-luck charm." He pulled the small metal disk out of his T-shirt. It was identical to the necklace Kjell had carried the other night to ward off Astrid. The charm Grandmother had given to him.

"I promised Grandmother I'd wear it always," he said, sounding none too pleased about it. "Guess I'll humor her for a few days."

"You should at least wear it the whole time you're here, then," I told him, gathering one more scrap of evidence that Grandmother was guarding some hefty secrets. "You don't want to hurt her feelings."

"I s'pose." Graham shrugged. "We're going to find a field to practice," he said. "You want to come?"

"Nah," I replied. "I thought I'd finish my book. Maybe go for a run."

After braving Margit's hostility and being attacked by an old lady in the bakery, I wasn't all that eager to venture into town. But I wasn't about to tell Graham. That was exactly the type of problem he'd be determined to help me solve.

"You're in Europe. Right outside is the kind of stuff people write books about. You can't sit around reading all day." Tuck nudged the spot between my shoulder blades with his knuckle. "Come with us."

I narrowed my eyes, wondering why he cared—what he was up to. We fell into an awkward silence. I waited for him to tease me, to steal my book or yank the rubber band out of my ponytail. But he didn't. He just smiled like it was perfectly normal for us to get along. And then I realized he was waiting politely for me to reply. Which was just too weird. It was as if the unspoken truce we'd forged the night before had carried into the daylight.

Suddenly I wasn't sure how to act. What to say. It was horribly unfair that he was changing the rules on me. I had enough things on my mind already, without being hyperaware of Tuck's hand brushing mine when he passed me the box of cereal.

"I'll come later," I said, rising to escape Tuck's scrutiny by pouring myself a glass of orange juice.

The screen door snapped shut behind Graham. He was

already outside, talking to Grandmother while she watered her flower beds. When I turned back toward the table, Tuck was standing in the middle of the room. Waiting for me.

"Promise?" he said.

"Promise what?" I asked, honestly confused.

"That you'll come later."

His disconcerting gray eyes were watching me, unreadable as ever. I'd never noticed the way his eyelashes cast them in shadow, making them even harder to pin down. Then again, I'd never stood this close to him before unless we were exchanging fire—when all my concentration was channeled into what I'd say next.

For an instant, my natural reaction was held in check by the memory of the roof the night before. The sweetness of our shared silence. But then the words came tumbling out anyways. "Only if you promise to tell me why you're suddenly pretending to care," I said. "You're up to something."

"I won't deny that." He flashed a private smile that sent my stomach floating away, like someone had just reached out and switched off gravity. It made me feel wary and confused and a little bit hopeful, all at once. "But it doesn't follow that it's something bad." It was the flirty voice he usually used on everyone but me.

"I've known you too long. Yes, it does." Fortunately, my voice held steady even if my hands wouldn't.

He frowned. His forehead creased with an emotion that I couldn't quite place—I just knew it wasn't a happy one. But Tucker Halloway was never one to dwell too long on anything unpleasant. He shrugged, and that troublemaker's grin settled back into its rightful place. Then he was gone.

By the time I glanced out the window, Tuck was jogging to catch up with Graham, who was already halfway down the long, rocky driveway. I watched as Graham tossed Tuck the soccer ball and Tuck bounced it off one knee, sending it flying down the hill. They both tore after it—until Graham took Tuck out with a brutal shove that sent him crashing into a shrub.

Boys.

I opened the fridge again, debating what to eat. There was a slip of paper secured to the side by a ceramic magnet I'd made in first grade.

ELLIE—KJELL HAS THE DAY OFF WORK AND WANTS
YOU TO CALL HIM IF YOU ARE FREE.

Beneath was Kjell's cell phone number.

I took one more look at Graham and Tuck as they disappeared around the corner toward town. My eyes lingered on Tuck, on the square, determined set of his shoulders and the way his hair looked brown but had streaks of gold in the sunlight. It was strange I'd never noticed that before. Then again, I'd been looking at Tuck a lot more carefully lately.

I removed the magnet, crumpled my grandmother's note, and dropped it in the trash.

I SPENT MOST of the afternoon reading in the kitchen or, more accurately, using my book as cover to mull over my crackpot theories without having to chat with Grandmother.

Fortunately, she seemed to be avoiding me, too. She spent the entire day in her garden, only coming in for lunch, so the whole morning we set eyes on each other only once.

As the afternoon wore on, I couldn't shake the feeling that something wasn't right. I had the oddest sensation that someone was watching me. And the second time I went to the front window, just to check, I saw Grandmother standing in the middle of the driveway, hand shading her eyes as she stared off in the same direction I kept glancing myself.

I opened the screen door, and Grandmother's eyes snapped to mine. "Thought I saw a raven," she said. "Strange to see them this far north." Not only was her delivery off, so were her facts. It was like she'd reached into a bag of excuses and read the very first one aloud without thinking about it.

She stood there a moment longer, hands on her hips, before she turned and attacked the weeds in her vegetable beds like they might attack back.

I wasn't the only who had that itchy feeling under my skin.

Her behavior was just further proof that my grandmother knew something, and the more I thought about it, the angrier I got that she'd sidestepped my questions the day before—especially if Tuck and Graham were in danger. Still, every time I rolled our conversation around in my head, I couldn't think of a way to make it end differently. No matter what I said, Grandmother would just clam up and change the subject all over again unless I found the right leverage—something that would force her to talk. Fortunately, given her lame explanation about the raven, I had a feeling it wouldn't take long for her to slip up and tell me everything.

GRAHAM AND TUCK didn't come home until late that afternoon, as the warmth from the kitchen had nearly lulled me to sleep. When they finally arrived, they took the house by storm. They barged into the kitchen and I jumped, sending my book tumbling to the floor.

"Plans tomorrow?" Graham asked, reaching into the fridge for something—anything—to eat. "Met some guys at the pickup game. We're going out on a fishing boat tomorrow morning. You in?"

"I don't know," I said slowly, wondering if it would just be a repeat of the first and only time I had hung out with boys from this weird Norwegian town. That was an experience I wasn't all that keen to repeat.

"Why not?" Graham asked. "You love fishing boats."

I hesitated, wondering if it was safe. Wondering if we'd run into Margit and her friends, or worse, the strangers who'd invaded the bar. Strangers who were much scarier to me than a girl with a grudge and a locator beacon.

"Of course she's coming." Tuck grabbed my book and opened it to a page at random. "She just wants us to beg. Make her feel special."

I tried to grab the book back, but Tuck held it up and away, out of my reach. I told myself it was a relief to have him acting like normal again, but part of me also wondered how long we'd be keeping up this Jekyll and Hyde act. It wasn't fair how he kept resetting the terms without warning.

"I'm shocked, Ells. Shocked and appalled that you'd be reading this smut. What is this?" he asked after a moment, flipping back to the cover.

"*Lolita*. Nabokov."

"For AP English?" Graham asked, glancing over at me.

I nodded.

"So it's about a younger girl," Tuck said, skimming the blurb on the back. "And the older guy chasing her? Sounds right up my alley." He shot me a private smile that almost jolted me out of my chair. If he was any other boy, that would have sent Graham into DEFCON-2. But he was Tuck, and he always flew underneath the radar.

"Not just a younger girl—a child." Graham shook his head. "You read that last year. I'm glad Ellie's getting a head start on the reading. It's a tough class. Stop pestering her." With that, he disappeared down the hallway.

"Am I pestering you?" Tuck asked, smiling sweetly as he handed me back the book, and keeping his hand on it a few beats too long. Like he didn't want to let it go.

"No," I said, hating myself for how much I savored his attention. "But you're confusing me."

"You're not the only one," he murmured, turning to leave. "Not sure I've been stood up before."

"Stood up?" I repeated, so bewildered I didn't even know where to begin.

"You never came today. You promised."

I just stood there, my jaw hanging half open like a door with a broken hinge.

"C'mon, Tuck." Graham called.

Tuck's quick, light footsteps echoed as he followed Graham up the stairs. I exhaled, realizing I'd been holding that breath for ages.

5

My alarm went off the next morning when I could barely convince my eyes to open. If the thought of spending the morning on the open ocean in a fishing boat hadn't brought back a thousand memories of my grandfather, I would have said screw it and fallen right back asleep.

Grandmother had a hot breakfast waiting when I stumbled into the kitchen. She'd always kept unconventional hours, since she'd spent decades helping Grandfather manage his fishing business. Awakening at what most people considered the middle of the night was old habit for her, so I tried hard not to growl my replies as she cheerfully chattered and I stifled yawn after yawn.

As we approached the docks, Kjell was standing on the deck of his father's boat, dressed head to toe in an orange rain suit with long reflective strips along the arms and legs. He heaved something over the railing, and a rubber sack landed on the ground at Graham's feet.

"Hey, Kjell." The way Graham greeted him made it all too clear that Kjell was our host for this adventure. I wasn't so wild about that, but it was too late to back out now. Graham lifted the heavy bag onto his shoulder. "What's in here, lead bricks?"

Kjell's eyes had barely left my face long enough to nod toward Graham and Tuck. "I was hoping you'd come," he said to me. "I thought you might if your brother did."

Graham stiffened. "You know each other?" Frost cracked the edges of his voice.

"Didn't Ellie tell you we went out the other night—before you arrived?" Kjell asked.

All three of them looked at me, all at once. I wanted to walk right off the edge of the dock and sink to the bottom of the ocean.

"No, she didn't." The chill in Graham's voice could have grown icicles. "Is that why you pushed so hard to take us out today?"

"So it would seem," Tuck said, looking at me even though I couldn't bring myself to meet his gaze.

"Can you blame me?" Kjell asked, smiling.

From the frown on Graham's face, he did.

Kjell just carried on, oblivious to the fact that every word he said carried him closer and closer to one of Graham's talks. Only this time, Graham faced an adversary not only his size but also a whole year older. I'd love to be a fly on the wall for that macho showdown. Even if I was ambivalent about the outcome.

"All the gear you need is in the bag," Kjell said. "And a bench over there if you need it. The boots can be tricky." He pointed toward a dirty-looking café with a flickering neon coffee mug in the window. Other fishermen were loitering around outside, drinking out of chipped plastic thermoses or leaning on packing crates full of a dizzying array of ropes, nets, and mesh traps.

The rubber rain suit was at least three sizes too big for me. Even with my jeans underneath, I had to roll the waist four times to keep the pants up, and they still dropped down around my ankles when I tried to take a step. Tuck nearly fell into the water laughing at me.

"Here," Kjell said, vaulting down from the deck of the boat with some black cords trailing from one hand. "This'll keep your pants up." The black straps turned out to be suspenders that he quickly fastened in place with two snaps in front. I thought that was the end of it, but then he started reaching around my waist to fasten them in back, too.

"I can get that," I said. But he moved closer, his hands groping around under my jacket for the snaps on the back.

"Let me help," he said. "You want to make sure it's right so they don't fall down and trip you on board." I turned to make it easier for him to reach those buttons, but his hands were still all over me for what felt like an eternity. Neither of us needed to have Graham walk in on a scene like that. Finally he straightened. "Perfect." He squeezed my shoulder before returning to the boat.

"That was the lamest excuse to paw a girl," Tuck said, coming up behind me. "I'm surprised you went along with it."

"What was?" I challenged. "Preventing me from tripping and falling overboard?"

"A pair of suspenders can do all that?" he said. "Would they also keep you from falling into the pool, or do you still need me for something?"

"You got me there," I said. "But at least they could double as a noose if you get on my nerves."

"Never took you for the tying-up type." Tuck smirked back. That playful smile curled his lips, the one that crossed the line Graham so vigilantly maintained on my behalf. "I like this new side of you."

I should have been mad, or at least pretended to be outraged, but all I could do was stare at him, utterly baffled that he would push this game so far into dangerous territory. I couldn't imagine what he was thinking.

"Don't get so deer in the headlights. I know you can keep up." His eyes were elusive as ever. "And if you're planning to go through life looking like that, you'd better."

I didn't need a mirror to know I was blushing. Which just made Tucker laugh as he slipped his hand into mine and pulled me toward the boat, where Graham and Kjell were waiting. For once, I was all too happy to indulge his blatant attempt to secure the last word.

KJELL'S FATHER MET us at the side of the boat, ready to welcome us on board and to offer us a hand. My shoulder nearly popped out of its socket as he swung me up past the railings and onto the painted metal deck. His accent and slow, deliberate speech reminded me of my grandfather. As did his bright blue eyes, set in the deeply creased face of a man who'd divided his years between scorching sun and biting arctic winds.

He gave us a quick lecture on safety and a tour of the bridge, which was just a glorified shack on the deck, crammed to the ceiling with navigational equipment, radios, and other beeping and pinging devices.

The boat pushed off at five o'clock sharp, and as we motored out into the fjord, I leaned against the railing, watching the green hills drift past, polka-dotted with white cotton wisps of sheep. The fjord we traveled through was just one of many winding inlets riddling the coast. Norway is a country of stark contrasts, from the impossible height of its steely mountain peaks to the dizzying depths of the icy blue water churning underneath the boat's engine. Most unexpected were the massive waterfalls that appeared every few miles, spanning hundreds of feet, crashing down from the steep rocky bluffs and feeding the fjords below.

I counted seven other fishing boats making the same pilgrimage through the harbor toward the open water beyond. White-capped mountain peaks in the distance dwarfed the nearby hills—it still amazed me that there was so much snow in the summer. But Norway is home to glaciers and everlasting winter.

"This is my favorite part," Kjell said, coming up and leaning his back against the railing. "Another day has started and nothing awful happened to me during the night."

"That's morbid," I said.

"Is it?"

"I mean, what would happen to you?" I instantly regretted my question.

"Apparently nothing, when you're around." He shifted closer, and I involuntarily took a step away. The intensity in his eyes gave me goose bumps, and not in a good way. "And that's part of the reason I asked your brother to come today—and hoped you'd come too." He glanced around to make sure we wouldn't be overheard. "I drove by your house three times yesterday. I wanted to see you again—no, I needed to see you again." His hand brushed mine along the railing, and my goose bumps grew goose bumps of their own. That might explain why all afternoon I'd felt like I was being watched. And suddenly I wanted off that boat so badly, I found myself glancing longingly at the lifeboats.

Kjell was dangerously close to sounding like a stalker, particularly when he grabbed my elbow to emphasize his next words. "I'm worried about you—about your safety. You heard what happened yesterday?"

"I'm assuming you mean other than Grandmother's flower beds being pillaged by a family of deer?"

"Your grandmother didn't tell you how much worse it's gotten?" he asked, his eyebrows furrowed and his lips pursed like he'd just tasted something bitter. "Did she at least warn your brother to be careful in town?"

The genuine concern in Kjell's voice made me feel guilty about how I was treating him. It also made me wonder, for the millionth time, what exactly my grandmother was keeping from me. I shook my head again.

"What can she be thinking?" he muttered to himself. For an instant, he looked so young—his wide blue eyes were too boyish to carry the weight of so much worry. "Like I said the other night, people have been disappearing for weeks," he said softly. "But the last few days it's gotten worse. Before it was never here, never in Skavøpoll. It was always something you heard about happening in the distance. Somewhere else. But now it's like the town is under attack."

"That's terrible," I said softly. "I had no idea."

"And it's getting more public," he said. "Yesterday three crew members from my dad's boat disappeared all at once from the dock. One minute they were there, and the next they were gone."

"I'm so sorry, Kjell—but you should focus on yourself, then. Don't worry about me," I said. "I won't disappear too."

"No, I don't think you will," he said drily. "They only take boys. Boys around my age. And they take the best. The strongest and smartest."

Fear stirred to life deep in my heart. No one fitted that description better than Graham. "Well then, no reason to worry about me, huh?" I replied, trying to sound lighthearted. Like what he was saying hadn't sent me into a cold sweat.

"That's not why I'm worried about you," he said. "No one's been able to stop them—until you did. According to legend, only a Valkyrie can defeat another Valkyrie." He paused and looked me straight in the eye. "That's why my friends think you're one too. Because of what you did."

I stood there in stunned, stone-cold shock.

"Plus, every single boy who's disappeared was last seen in the company of two or three girls—tall, beautiful girls who make people stop and stare."

"So naturally they thought of me."

The eyes he turned to my face were completely devoid of humor. "No, I mean . . . yes, you're young, but you fit the description," he said. "These things weren't happening *here* until you came."

I started to incoherently defend myself, but he interrupted. "Look, I know you'd never do anything to hurt anyone." He paused, and his fingers brushed my cheek. "But I'm biased. I don't think I'd care if you did."

The conversation was cruising right past creepy and taking a hard left into horrifying. "It doesn't matter," I said. "It's not true. Your friends are nuts." I started to move away, seriously needing to be by myself. Because as the shock of the accusation subsided, I found myself wondering how I *had* stopped those girls from taking Kjell.

"There's more," Kjell said, grabbing my arm again before I could take another step back. "And you need to know this." His tone warned me I would not like what would come next. "Margit and Sven have, well, joined this group—they're keeping watch on the bars and sports clubs. Places where people have disappeared. They're planning to put a stop to this."

"Like vigilantes?"

"Exactly."

"Interesting." A shiver rocked my spine as I realized where this was headed. "That's who those guys were. The guys who came to the bar the other night after we left?" The guys who were armed with rifles and fully prepared to use them.

Kjell nodded. "They've been watching you."

"Excuse me?"

"They've been watching you."

"I heard you," I said, annoyed. "I just wish I hadn't." At least now I knew my instincts the day before had been dead-on. Spying on the Overholt household was the new national pastime.

"They think you're dangerous."

"That's ridiculous."

"I know," he said. "But they're scared." He paused, and said the rest in a voice so low, I had to strain my ears to catch it all. "There've always been rumors about your grandmother. That she has some sort of powers. Fifty years ago, when she first moved to town, she rescued the crew off a sinking trawler. Most of the town was grateful, but others were suspicious. They said what she did was impossible. And some of them, well, they never let go of their fear, even after she married your grandfather. You heard what Margit said. They think she's a witch."

"She's not," I said, shaking my head like that would drive away his words.

"I know. I've known your grandmother my whole life. But the old people in this town have been saying this. For years. And now, well, other people are suddenly listening. After that incident at the pub in Selje, I've heard your name whispered a few times, too."

A pool of panic was filling in my chest. I wondered what the change fee would be for my ticket home if I just hopped into a taxi and hightailed it to the airport.

The fishing boat's engines revved as the boat accelerated into the open ocean beyond the mouth of the fjord. "I need to go," he said, squeezing my arm. "Be careful, Ellie, but don't worry. I'll be watching you too."

Somehow that didn't make me feel any better.

I was nauseous, and not from the waves, as I walked around to the front of the boat, staggering to keep my balance on the rocking deck. There had to be a place on that stupid trawler where I could be alone. Where I could put my head between my knees and try to stifle the mayhem in my mind.

A burly sailor rounded the corner in front of me. There was resentment in the eyes that met mine. He sped up, gaining momentum before ramming his shoulder into mine. Throwing me into the fire extinguisher lashed to the railing. It would definitely leave a bruise.

"Go back to America." The words were thick and awkward, like he didn't speak English but had memorized that phrase just for me. How touching.

As he straightened, moving away, an image flashed across my mind—of how easy it would be to grab the sailor by the arm and flip him over my back. One quick step to the left would be enough to clear the railing, hurling him into the churning water of the sea, where he'd disappear forever.

A wave of anger and aggression washed over me, frightening in its intensity. I did the only thing I could: I turned and walked away, wrapping my arms around myself, like that would stop them from bringing my daydream to life.

My legs were shaking like a colt's as I made my way toward the bow, hoping I could avoid everyone for the rest of the morning and seriously contemplating heading back to shore in one of the lifeboats.

The boat turned sharply as we passed through the mouth of the fjord and headed south, hugging the coast. Jagged gray cliffs stretched above us, softening into green pastures that lined the bases of the mountains beyond. I grabbed the thick railing along the side of the bridge and used it to pull myself around the corner. And came face-to-face with Tuck.

I could have told him right then. Everything that had happened was on the tip of my tongue and fighting to get out. In my fear and shock, I almost let the words come tumbling out— last night it had seemed like something between us had changed. Maybe he would take me and my crazy-sounding problems seriously.

Until he reminded me exactly how overly protective he and Graham could be.

"You're getting pretty cozy with Captain Ahab," Tuck said, proving once and for all he could irritate me on command. Although Kjell had passed him the baton with a hefty head start. "Who needs prom when you can clean fish?"

"For your information, Kjell is in medical school."

Tucker frowned. He didn't like that answer one bit.

"For your information, Graham will rip his head off if he tries to play doctor with you." His face softened just before I would have smacked him for that last comment. "What were you two whispering about, anyway?" he asked. "You looked upset."

If he was this pushy about someone talking to me, I couldn't imagine what he'd do if he knew people were blaming me for bizarre crimes I didn't commit. And that realization was all it took to get my emotions back under control.

I threw a decoy in his path. "Apparently he can't stop thinking about me." I kept my tone neutral, not letting Tuck know how disturbed I was by that and everything else Kjell had told me.

"Really?" One eyebrow arched, but the rest of his face was bland, flawlessly indifferent. "After one date? That's a pretty heavy line, even for a fisherman. But maybe he thinks you're stupid enough to bite."

"Not everyone runs around throwing out insincere compliments like you do," I snapped back. "Maybe he means it."

"It's possible," Tuck said, his voice and expression so controlled he could have been thinking anything. "I think it's more likely he assumes you're naive and wants to take advantage of that."

"Only because that's how you operate." I started to turn away. The danger of standing near the side of the boat in choppy water couldn't compete with my desire to be as far away from everyone as the boat would allow.

"Ells, wait," Tuck said. His fingers trailed along my wrist, as if that would be enough to stop me. "Don't be mad. I'm not saying he wouldn't adore you if he had the chance to get to know you. Is that really what you want? For Kjell to like you? Because just now you seemed freaked—"

But the rest of what he said was drowned out by a loud, metallic grinding. It sounded like the time my mom stripped the transmission in her old station wagon—only ten million times louder. And it was coming from the engine room.

Tuck pulled me out of the way as three crewmen pushed past, running toward the source of the noise.

The boat jerked to one side at a precarious angle. Then it tipped the other way just as quickly, rocking back and forth like a Tilt-A-Whirl. The sudden shifts threw me to the deck. Before I could even wrap my mind around the possibility of what was happening, I was sliding down the deck feetfirst, scrambling to grab on to something, anything. The rain boots and rubber suit were useless on the slick surface of the deck—absolutely zero traction.

At that speed, I'd hit the water with a spectacular splash.

I closed my eyes and took a deep breath, bracing myself for my grand entrance into the freezing-cold water. But the toe of my boot hit the railing and I pushed off hard, buying myself a few more seconds to think.

I'd barely managed to catch my breath before strong hands slid underneath my arms and pulled me up onto my knees.

"Tuck!" Graham shouted, his voice sounding impossibly far away given how small the boat was. "Get her away from the edge!"

As Tuck helped me to my feet, the boat heaved again, violently rolling onto its other side. But Tuck stood firm and steady, as if the ground beneath our feet weren't bucking like a rodeo bull. With one arm locked around my shoulders, he took three huge steps forward and grabbed the railing of the bridge, pulling me with him. He pinned me against the wall of the bridge with his body, wrapping his hands around the railing and wedging one foot behind a crate. We were pressed together so tight I could barely breathe.

"What's going on?" I asked as the metallic grinding gave way to a high-pitched mechanical wail. Three more fisherman ran past at full speed—or as fast as was possible, given the waves.

"Engine broke down right as we hit a rough patch of water. It's all part of Captain Ahab's plan to get in those sexy rubber pants," Tuck replied, a smile in his voice. "Danger is hot. A daring rescue is even hotter."

Only Tuck would turn this into a joke.

"But you're the one who rescued me." The words were out before I realized the implication.

"Backfired," Tuck replied. "Poor Ahab." The screeching engine was so loud, I could barely hear him as he added, "Don't worry—this is the safest spot on the boat. The most stable." The words were warm against my cheek, as was the scent of reckless summer radiating from his skin. Up close, Tuck had his own gravitational pull. It tempted me forward until my nose and forehead rested against his throat. I heard his sharp intake of breath, his surprise, but I couldn't help myself. Even if it meant I wouldn't be able to look him in the eye when this was all over.

It seemed Tuck's theory about danger had some merit.

The boat rocked back and forth like a teeter-totter, picking up speed each time. A wave broke over the railing, sending a spray of ice-cold water over our heads, but Tuck held on to the railing with both hands, locking me in place. I looked around for Graham but couldn't find his face among the running crewmen.

That's when I smelled the smoke. At the same instant, a deep voice bellowed one of the handful of Norwegian words I knew.

"Fire," I repeated. "Tuck, there's a fire. We've got to get out of here." I started to push him away, just as another wave hit us and the boat rocked so hard, I thought it would flip right over.

"Don't move," he urged. "We'll be fine. Promise. I saw lifeboats if it comes to that, but these guys know how to handle emergencies—they're pros."

Over Tuck's shoulder, I finally caught a glimpse of Graham. He was hauling himself one-handed along the railing, struggling against the force of the rocking waves. He had the tarp from one of the lifeboats wrapped in his other arm.

Someone was shouting orders in the distance. After what felt like an eternity of being tossed back and forth and slapped with ice-cold water, the engines roared to life. The boat started to turn, slowly at first, but before long it was facing directly into the waves. While we still bobbed up and down, it wasn't like it had been before, when the boat was utterly at the mercy of the ocean. The deck just swayed back and forth like a hammock in the breeze, so gently I could have stretched out and taken a nap—if my heart weren't still thundering to a techno beat.

Tuck sighed and relaxed his arms. I finally uncurled my fingers from the railing. They ached with the strain of holding on so tight.

"Do you think they put out the fire?" I asked.

"I'm guessing we'd know by now if they hadn't," he murmured. "But why don't we stay here a sec? They got the engine working, which is a good sign, but it could be rock-and-roll time again if it stalls."

"Okay." I glanced up at him, and he smiled. Suddenly my situation hit me with an almost tangible force. Tucker Halloway was standing mere inches away from me, his legs tangled with mine. His forearms pressed against my waist. And even though it was all in the name of safety, for some perverse reason, I wanted to stay that way a little bit longer.

As if he sensed my thoughts, his smile widened. "This is strictly business, Ells," he said with a wink as one hand released the railing and found its way up my back. "Try not to enjoy it so much."

Leave it to Tuck to say something shocking and arrogant at a moment like that.

"Then again . . . I am."

My eyes flew to his face, but he was already turned away, looking out toward the water. He was concentrating hard, like he was listening to something in the distance. But his eyes shifted back just in time to catch me watching his profile and wondering if there was a single angle or plane that wasn't textbook perfect.

I said the first thing that popped into my head. "Do you think Graham is okay?"

"Of course he is." Tuck's faint smile was inches from mine. His head tipped to the side, just enough that if he kissed me, our noses wouldn't get in the way. It was a ridiculous thought, but really, I couldn't help it when he was looking at me like that.

"Graham is always okay—you know that," he said softly. "He's half Superman, half Double-Oh-Seven. Just think what a great story this'll be." He pulled his face back a few inches, restoring my ability to breathe. The teasing smile I knew all too well was back. "Only, do you care if I spice it up? Maybe add in a squall?"

"I could still fall overboard. And you could jump in after me. Really give them something to talk about."

"I would, you know."

Even though I knew he meant it, I laughed it off. "Whatever, Tuck. Embellish away."

I lowered my face, away from his. It was best to remove all temptation to look up into his eyes again. I'd already flirted with enough danger that day.

The boat lurched into high gear and turned in a wide arc until we were traveling fast with the waves, back toward the port of Skavøpoll. I never thought I'd be so happy to see those squat, rundown buildings again.

When we pulled in to the dock, it was clear word had gotten out that we'd had an incident on the high seas. It looked like the entire town was lining the pier. Even my grandmother was there, one hand shading her eyes as she searched the deck for Graham and me.

Grandmother pushed her way through the crowd toward us, collecting suspicious stares as she passed but holding her head high, daring them to do stop her. She pulled me into a smothering hug. "The harbormaster called and told me what happened. I worried a wisp like Ellie could just tumble overboard in all the commotion."

Only my six-foot-two grandmother would call me a wisp.

"Hilda Overholt," a deep voice said behind us.

"Knut!" Grandmother caught Kjell's father's hands in both of hers and squeezed them before letting them drop. Stoic as he seemed, Knut winced at the pressure. "I thought my grandchildren would be safe with you—what happened?" Grandmother's smile softened the accusation, but she was a lioness protecting her cub when she wrapped an arm around my shoulders.

"An oil fire in the engine room," Kjell's father replied. "Would have been fine, but the boy who inspects fire safety never showed up for work yesterday."

My grandmother's hand tensed around my shoulder.

"It's a good thing Graham knew how to handle it," Kjell's father added. "While everyone else was rushing around, he mixed some cleaning acid with an old box of baking soda, ran into the engine room covered with a wet tarp, and threw it on the fire. It went right out."

"Really?" I asked, looking up at Graham in awe.

He waved one hand dismissively. "It was just like this lab we did in chemistry. Liquid and carbon dioxide smother the flames. No big deal. Anyone would have thought of it."

"Right. Of course," I murmured. Tuck nudged my shoulder with his, and I bit my lip not to laugh.

"Well, in my book, it was impressive." Kjell's father smiled. "Quick thinking. The current was fast today, carried us toward the cliffs. A spot of rough water I avoid during the high summer winds."

Next to me, my grandmother made a sound that almost sounded like a growl.

"It's a good thing for you my grandchildren made it out of there safely," she said, an edge of warning in her voice that made the air around us feel heavier. I had to fight harder to breathe.

"Yes, it is," Kjell's father replied, eyeing her warily. "We only hit a few of the biggest waves. Your grandson was quite the hero." And with that, he gave Graham a solid thump on the shoulder and turned to walk away.

"No vacation is complete without Graham playing hero and rescuing us all," I said drily, trying to lighten the tension that had descended after my grandmother's weird behavior. Tuck nudged me again, and this time I giggled.

A shadow crossed Grandmother's face, and she glanced around the parking lot like the pavement had ears. "Don't say things like that out loud, sweetling," she said, so low only I could hear. "You never know who could be listening."

I couldn't imagine what that meant, but when I looked up, something caught the corner of my eye. Across the parking lot, a tall, graceful silhouette stood motionless in the shadows. Watching us. A solitary streak of sunlight turned her blond hair into a river of molten gold. A raven perched on her arm, its talons digging into her bare forearm.

Astrid.

My heart rate doubled at the sight of that hauntingly beautiful face.

She lifted one arm, releasing the raven. It spread its wings and flew upward into the sky, circling overhead like a buoy marking our position from above.

I no more than blinked, and she was gone. I rubbed my eyes. It had to have been a trick of the light.

Grandmother's hand on my elbow snapped me back to the present. "Let's go home." I followed her as if in a dream, my eyes still locked on the spot where Astrid had stood moments ago.

Grandmother loaded us all up into her car, rain suits, Wellington boots, and all. "We'll take your gear back to Kjell later," she said, looking at me in the rearview mirror. "Right now I just want to get you home—and warm. I see you shivering back there, Ellie Overholt. Your hair is sopping wet."

I put my hand to my head. She was right. Also, my fingers were turning blue.

We were just pulling out of the parking lot when Kjell came jogging over, blocking our exit. For one inexcusably cruel moment, I wished Grandmother would just hit the gas and blow right past him. But no, he approached and knocked on my window. I rolled it down slowly, resenting the cold air that followed.

"Sorry to hold you up, Hilda," he said. "I won't keep you long." He turned to look at me. "Ellie, will you come out tonight?" His head poked through the open window.

"Sure," Graham said, even though Kjell was looking right at me.

"You too?" Kjell asked, reaching through the window and touching my shoulder.

"Maybe," I said. Tuck cleared his throat, shifting in the seat next to me, and suddenly I just wanted Kjell to go away.

"We'll be at the restaurant next to the hardware store at seven. Promise you'll come," he said, still staring at me too intently. "Or if you're too tired from this morning, I can come over instead."

That was the last thing I needed.

"Okay," I said. "I'll go." It would be better to face him in a crowded restaurant than on my grandmother's narrow love seat.

Kjell straightened, and I rolled up my window—more quickly than was polite.

"I think someone has a crush," Graham murmured.

"More like an obsession," Tuck whispered loudly.

"Whatever," I said. "It's none of your business. Either of you."

I felt someone staring at me and looked up, only to meet Grandmother's eyes in the rearview mirror. She was watching me. The feeling that followed was unlike anything I'd experienced before—it was as if she were reaching inside my head and probing my emotions. An unsettling, guilty feeling pinched my heart, as if I'd somehow been unfair or even cruel to Kjell. Even though all I really wanted from him was enough space to figure out what was going on in that backward town. While keeping Graham and Tuck from figuring out what I was up to.

ONCE WE WERE home, a hot shower fixed all my problems. At least the physical ones. I hadn't realized how sore and bruised my muscles were until steaming water poured over them, washing away the grime and sea salt.

By the time I made it down to the kitchen, Graham and Tucker were gone. Apparently our morning brush with death hadn't been enough activity for one day. They were off at some field, doing soccer drills.

I made tea and sat at the kitchen table, prepared to crack open another book. But every time I tried to focus on the page, my thoughts would drift back to what Kjell had told me on the boat. The possibility that his creepy friends were spying on me. That thought had particularly plagued me in the shower. I'd double-checked the curtains three times.

"Ellie?" Grandmother called up the stairs as she walked into the kitchen. "Are you hungry?" When she saw me already sitting at the table, her hand flew to her chest. She looked startled, but also like she was prepared to do something about it. I wondered who else she thought might have wandered into her kitchen. "You scared me, sweetling," she said, forcing out a laugh. "I didn't hear you come downstairs."

"I was just reading." I set my book facedown on the table.

"Can we talk for a moment?" Grandmother settled onto the window seat and folded her legs up underneath herself. She was amazingly flexible for a woman her age—actually, for a woman of any age. "While the boys are out of the house," she added.

That last comment grabbed all of my attention. "Why?" I asked.

"Some conversations are better had when you can't be interrupted," she said softly.

My heart started to thunder in my ears. It seemed my patience was finally paying off. I knew she was hiding things—

information about the disappearances and maybe even about Astrid.

And I was burning to have her come clean. But even if she didn't tell me everything, hopefully what she did say would help me pull the rest of my information together.

I held my breath as she started talking. "You've grown up so much in the past two years," she said. "So much that I was shocked when I saw you walk through the airport. And you look so much like your father—your Norwegian blood is coming through, loud and clear."

"I know," I said. "People almost don't believe Mom and I are related sometimes." An awkward pause followed, but I waited, certain she'd get to the important stuff soon.

Grandmother looked down at her hands. "What I'm trying to say . . ." She paused. ". . . is that I'm not the only one who'll start to notice now that you're grown up. Kjell seems very aware of the fact—and he won't be the last."

I swallowed hard but still couldn't force my disappointment back down my throat. Not only was it not what I was hoping to hear, it was a nightmare. Under no circumstances did I want to have this particular conversation with my grandmother.

"Certain people will find you irresistible. Particularly if you want them to. Do you understand what I mean by that?" Her eyes were sharp as she searched my face, but I just looked down and shrugged, hoping she'd take the hint.

She reached over and touched my hand. Trying to get me to meet her gaze. "From now until your eighteenth birthday, well, things will change a lot for you—in some unexpected ways.

I want you to start paying very close attention to the types of things you say to boys. Always be aware of your tone of voice and the way you look at them."

A modesty lecture was honestly the last thing I ever expected from my grandmother. She'd always seemed so much cooler than that. I just kept staring at my knees, praying it would end.

But Grandmother would not let the subject drop. After a pause, she pressed on. "You've never done anything wrong, darling—that's not what I'm saying. There are certain things you need to understand about how a special tone of voice can be, well, hypnotic. Other people abuse that power—use it for their own gain. I don't want you to make that mistake. I want you to respect it. The way I did. Sweetheart, trust me. You haven't even begun to realize what you're capable of."

The silence stretched more painfully than the rack.

Until the screen door exploded open and a soccer ball ricocheted against the table leg, spinning to a stop in the middle of the floor.

Graham was a half second behind it.

"Sorry!" he panted, grabbing the ball and tucking it up under his arm. "Just came back to grab something to drink."

He had nothing to apologize for—I could have kissed him. I seized my chance to escape.

"Can I come too?" I asked.

"Course," he said, eyes widening in surprise. "Grab your shoes."

"We'll talk later—right, Grandmother?" I said, rising.

She nodded, but I could sense her hesitation, like she didn't want me to go. I felt bad fleeing, but really, she couldn't expect me to sit through that willingly. It's one thing to be close to your grandmother, but quite another to discuss your love life with her. Or lack thereof.

Yet as Graham and I walked away across the yard, I glanced back at the house. Grandmother stood just inside the screen door, her shoulders tense and her face creased with worry. Seeing her that way, I almost wondered if I'd underestimated the importance of whatever she'd been trying to say.

6

When we got to the restaurant that night, Kjell was the first person I saw—mostly because he flagged me down like a taxi. He was sitting on the far side of a long, crowded table.

"Ellie, here," he called out, motioning to one of his friends to shift down. "There's room for you right here."

"Such a stalker," Tuck muttered under his breath.

I nudged him with my elbow, and he nudged me right back. Graham frowned the way he did when he was about to play dad, so I slipped away from Graham before he could say something that would put me in an even worse mood.

The space between the table and the wall was narrow, and I used hand gestures to let Kjell know it was too hard for me to make my way over there. Instead I pulled up a seat at the end of the table, right next to Tuck. I knew if I needed him to, he'd help me keep Kjell at bay, but unlike Graham, he'd do it without treating me like a toddler.

A boy at the end of the table raised a beer as Graham found a seat farther down, away from us.

"*Skål*—that's cheers, for the Americans—to Graham, who saved some of us from a long swim home." The words sent a shiver down my spine as it brought back all the memories of the fishing boat mishap. But that wasn't the only thought that made the trembling spread until my fingers shook. My grandmother's warning echoed through my mind: it wasn't wise to say such things out loud. Deeds like Graham's had a power, an allure all their own—I could feel it—and it was better not to draw so much attention to it. You never knew who or what it would attract.

The glimpse of Astrid at the docks flashed through my mind, and I shuddered.

"Only a true hero could save a boat and a goal on the same day," someone said, his voice drifting above the chatter at the table.

My chest tightened as the shadows in the room expanded, boxing us in, threatening to swallow us whole. The air was close and stuffy, like the inside of a parked car in the height of an LA summer.

The table erupted in laughter as another round of pint glasses slid into waiting hands, beer sloshing over the edges and onto the chipped Formica table. The ominous feeling deepened as the jokes continued, all focused on the multitalented Graham. I looked at my brother and fought the urge to drag him from the room and hide him away, someplace secret, someplace safe.

Unlike the other times I'd felt sick hearing Graham lavishly praised, this time my agitation wasn't tainted by resentment. I wanted to protect him, and my anxiety only got worse because I was still struggling to understand exactly what from.

And as the panic mounted, I turned frantic eyes toward the door, contemplating bolting. I would grab Graham and Tuck and flee back to Grandmother's house. But a man stood just inside the door, leaning against the window. He caught my eye and his hand slid inside his jacket. Exactly where you'd expect to find a gun. Maybe he was one of them, a member of the crazy group who'd been watching me. Or maybe I was being paranoid.

Given how weird my life had become, sanity was a distant memory.

I glanced back at the man, only to find him still staring at me.

Tuck's head tipped closer to mine. Inches away. "Maybe next they'll elect him mayor. Do we even need a vote?" He flashed a grin that in any other circumstances would have captured my undivided attention but in this case just served to return my focus to the table, where they'd started toasting Graham all over again. My brain moved sluggishly, grappling with Tucker's joke. Trying to act like everything was fine, even though it was the exact opposite.

"You okay?" Tuck's forehead creased. He turned and looked out the window, where I'd been staring. "You look like you just had a stroke. Want me to walk you home?"

"I'm fine." I shook my head.

Tuck frowned and opened his mouth to say something but then snapped it shut. His jaw twitched as he glared over my shoulder.

"Do you want anything?" Kjell appeared from behind me, pulling up a chair. "A drink? Or are you hungry?" Before I could even formulate my answer, he'd flagged down a waitress.

"Maybe just some water," I said, shifting in my seat as his arm draped around the back of my chair. I tried to keep my eyes on Graham, but Kjell leaned forward until his head was directly in my line of sight.

I glanced back toward the door, to see if that man was still staring at me. He was, and he was no longer alone. Five men now sat at the table by the window, making no effort to conceal their objective. They were watching me. It couldn't be a good thing that they were no longer trying to keep their surveillance covert.

Kjell followed my gaze. "Don't worry about them," he told me. "I won't let anything happen to you." The way he was looking at me made me slide my chair a full six inches away. I should have been blown away to have a boy look at me like that—especially a boy like Kjell. But there was no way I deserved the unswerving, puppy-dog devotion in those baby blues.

My grandmother's advice from that morning floated back to me, and I decided that as ridiculously old-fashioned as she'd sounded, maybe she was right about the power of a certain type of look or glance. Maybe I needed to watch my step around Kjell. Even though I spent the rest of the evening doing just that, Kjell stuck to me like a tick that hadn't fed in years. I wasn't sure who it irritated most—Graham, Tuck, or me.

By the time we left the restaurant, it was well past midnight. Everyone emptied onto the sidewalk and stood under the streetlamps, saying good night and gradually dispersing.

There was a tug at my sleeve as I was joking around with Tuck, and I turned.

"Ride home?" Kjell asked. He glanced over his shoulder toward two men who had followed us outside and were trying to look casual, smoking cigarettes. But they were staring straight at me.

Walking home might not be the safest idea.

Graham answered for all three of us. "That'd be great," he said. At first I was surprised. I thought I'd have to force the issue with Graham, after Kjell had been all over me at the restaurant. But the way Graham was frowning as he sized up Kjell made it all too apparent that he was prowling for the opportunity for a tête-à-tête. While that irritated me more than Kjell's stifling attention, it wasn't enough to overpower my sense of self-preservation. We needed a ride home.

When we came to a stop in Grandmother's driveway, Kjell turned to face me. "When can I see you tomorrow?"

I was mortified this was happening at all, but it was even worse to have it happen in front of Graham and Tuck. As if I didn't have enough to worry about. I was already anxious without having to let Kjell down gently in front of an audience.

"There's this new restaurant, serves really fresh fish. We send our best catch to them," he said. "Tomorrow night? I—I need to see you again."

That caught Graham's full attention. He'd opened the car door, but now he froze. Waiting. Listening.

"Just us. I won't bring my friends this time," Kjell added.

While I had no intention of hanging out again with Sven or Margit, this was also sounding too much like a very serious date.

In the rearview mirror, Tuck's eyes found mine, and I knew it wouldn't be fair to say yes when I was engaged elsewhere. Or at least wanted to be. Graham was watching me, too. His disapproval filled the car like floodwater, pressing the air from my lungs, suffocating me.

Which is why I said, "Okay."

Even though it wasn't an optimal way to assert my independence, it was the only route open to me—without causing a scene.

"She hates fish, just FYI, Ahab." Tuck slid out and slammed the door so hard the whole car shook. To make my misery complete, Graham didn't get out until he'd caught my eye and given his head a shake. I hadn't heard the last of this.

If Kjell noticed, he didn't care. He smiled like the conquering hero, which made me realize exactly how big a misstep I'd just taken. Who knew that acting out of spite could be every bit as limiting as having an overprotective brother boss you around?

"Great," Kjell said. "I'll pick you up at seven?"

"I've gotta go," I said, already wracking my brain for the out that I would deliver in the morning. "Good night." My eyes were glued to Tuck's retreating back. His posture was ruler straight, his shoulders tense, and when he didn't even turn around at the sound of my footsteps, I knew he was mad. But not as mad as I was at myself.

Everything that had happened during the last week was tearing at me from the inside. Just two short weeks ago, my relationship with Graham was the biggest worry on my mind— how to go from little sister to actual grown-up person who could manage her own life. Now it was the tiniest item on my pile of problems, from the lingering mystery of Astrid and her bobsled girl sidekick to Kjell's creepy behavior. Together, all these things fueled my inexplicable premonition that something dangerous was circling, moving closer to both Graham and me. And overriding it all was my certainty that I didn't have much time to piece it all together—to figure out what was happening and to fix it before something terrible happened.

As soon as Graham's bedroom door clicked shut down the hallway, I opened my window and climbed up onto the roof. I made enough noise that Tuck would be sure to hear me. Then I sat back, hoping he'd accept my olive branch. I knew he was mad at me for agreeing to go out with Kjell, even if his reasons were muddy. He could hardly expect me turn up my nose at every other boy just because he kept flirting with me. I'd seen Tuck in action enough times to know it was a fair bet he wasn't serious. And he probably expected me to be able to tell the difference. Still, it was hard to keep my feelings out of it, especially when Tuck and I were walking so very close to the edge.

After five minutes, I started to get angry that Tuck wasn't coming. It stung that he would just blow me off—like he didn't even need to acknowledge that things were weird between us lately. He was taking Graham's overprotective act to a whole new award-worthy level.

My temper was just getting warmed up when I heard a noise coming from the direction of Tuck's window. Then the warmth applied itself to a different feeling altogether.

Tuck's hands appeared on the edge of the roof, followed by his head and shoulders as he pulled himself over the edge.

He walked softly across the roof and sat down at my side, close enough that his arm pressed against mine. I knew I'd been forgiven. I leaned back on my elbows, his proximity soaking into every pore like a soothing balm.

We were quiet for a long time, for what seemed like ages.

"I don't like him," Tuck said. "Graham doesn't either."

It took a second for me to figure out what he was talking about, but when I did, I couldn't hold back an impatient sigh. "Do you really think that's going to win your argument?"

"Is it an argument?" he asked after a tense pause. "Because from where I'm sitting, it looks like you're trying to keep him at arm's length. Or is little Ellie playing hard to get?"

"Unlike some people, I don't play games with people's feelings."

"That's right," Tuck murmured. "You just go out to dinner with them even when you're not interested."

"Of all the people in the world, you're the last person who has the right to criticize anyone on this subject. How many girls are you dangling along right now?"

He looked at me in the darkness, and suddenly I wasn't sure if I had the courage to do it—to put words and a name on what had been happening between us. The flirting and the strange, private smiles. The way even now his hand was resting too close to mine.

"None." The word slammed into me, knocking every last breath from my lungs. Apparently it wasn't even worth mentioning—the weird games we'd been playing. "But we're not talking about me. Do you like him?"

I glanced at his profile in the darkness, but the expression on his face as he stared out over the fjord could have meant anything. Tuck could teach the Mona Lisa and the Sphinx a thing or two about mystery.

"Not like that," I said. "And honestly, I've got bigger things on my mind than boys."

He turned all the way toward me, shoulders too, until his face was so close that even in the darkness I could see the way his pupils expanded, devouring the gray from the inside out. Now they were watching me, unreadable as ever. One eyebrow arched. Waiting for me to elaborate.

"I only agreed to go out with Kjell to make Graham angry," I said, surprising myself. I hadn't had time to decide exactly how far I was willing to open up to Tuck. To tell him the full and complete truth about everything that was on my mind. "He doesn't get to run my life. He treats me like I'm too stupid to tie my own shoes. Or decide who I'll date or what classes I'll take."

"Graham doesn't think you're stupid," Tuck said softly. "Believe me. And if you're upset, just talk to him—he's a pretty smart guy, you know. The direct approach is bound to work better than revenge dating your stalker." He settled back against the roof, his shoulder pressed against mine, and on reflex I found myself leaning against it. "Graham's stubborn when it comes to you, but that can change. Just remember, to him, you're still the little girl who sniffled on his shoulder when Tommy Wallen pushed you off your bicycle."

"Well, I'm not that eight-year-old anymore." My voice cracked. I hated him for being right. And myself for being such a coward when it came to standing up to Graham.

"No." He shook his head without once taking his eyes off mine. "You're not."

His face was closer now, even though I didn't notice until his head tipped slightly to the side. It was a signal more universal than SOS and just as panic inducing. The devil on my shoulder told me to close my eyes, to let it just happen, so I did. Even with everything that was going on, I couldn't let this moment pass me by.

Tuck edged closer, so close I could taste the heat from his skin, so close the air I inhaled had also crossed those lips. So close I felt the passage of the few remaining molecules of oxygen he displaced as he leaned forward.

I held my breath.

I waited.

And I sat like that for a full count of ten. When I opened my eyes, Tuck had turned away. He'd pulled his knees up against his chest and wrapped his arms around them. His head disappeared into the hood of his sweatshirt.

The remnants of tension still lingered in the air, like ozone after a thunderclap.

"Graham's my best friend," Tuck's voice was muffled, far away. "Without him, I'd have flunked out of school. I can't ask for anything else."

"Maybe you don't have to ask," I said. The slow spreading sting of rejection was leaving a trail of red up my neck and across my cheeks. "Maybe some things aren't Graham's to decide."

"You think I don't know that?" He finally lifted his head and looked at me again. His face was so guarded, he could have been hiding anything. "But Graham's opinion *does* matter. Even when he's wrong."

I thought about that for a minute, but it seemed to me Tuck always got what he wanted—from anyone. He could outmaneuver Graham if he just tried hard enough. The real problem was that I'd misread the situation and forced Tuck into making awkward excuses.

And then I realized that even if there *had* been a moment between us, a spark, and Tuck had felt it too, maybe he wasn't ready to risk both Graham and me by acting on it. Either way, it added up to the same answer—complete humiliation.

I wished with all my might that the whole conversation would just shrivel up and die and its brittle carcass would blow away on the wind. From the way Tuck let it drop like a stone, I knew he felt the exact same way.

With that, we lapsed back into silence. And this time, not a comfortable one.

It was just one more devastating item to add to the pile of my problems. Even if I couldn't tell him what was happening, at least I'd had Tuck and this thing between us to make me feel less alone. Helping me bear the burden of all the secrets I was carrying around. All the crazy mayhem in my mind.

In one fell swoop, the feeling of closeness with Tuck was gone. There was no way to pick up the thread of the conversation, to act like an avalanche of awkwardness hadn't just buried our friendship alive. It would have been better to kiss him and let that make things weird if our friendship was in danger anyway.

So I sat on the roof next to Tucker Halloway, feeling miserable and alone even in the company of the one person I wanted to be with. Wallowing in an unfulfilled longing that so clearly wasn't reciprocated. I waited long enough that Tuck wouldn't know how hurt and embarrassed I was.

Then I rose. "Thank you for saving me today." I forced my tone to stay light.

"Anytime." He relaxed back onto his elbows. I caught a flash of white when he smiled. "But you'd have been fine without me."

"We don't know that, do we?"

"You're always better off without me."

I almost rose to that bait, offered up on a silver platter. Making it all too easy for me to take a cheap shot and let things slip back to the way they used to be. Our usual routine. But instead I decided to just let my honest answer come out. "No, I'm not," I said. "Everything is better when you're around."

Before he had a chance to reply and ruin everything, I scooted my way along the sod roof until I could lower my foot over the edge. I wedged my shoe into the drainpipe as I slid down the siding onto the window ledge. Tuck stayed where he was, propped up on his elbows, staring after me. He sighed and leaned back, looking up at the stars. I wondered how long he'd stay like that. After all, I wouldn't be able to sleep until I heard his window slide shut and his soft footfalls before he climbed into bed.

The next morning, my brain hurt from a night of restless, anxious sleep. I worried that things would be awkward with Tuck. I worried that I'd come home one day to find Graham staring back at me with white-on-white eyes. Or worse, that he'd disappear altogether. I worried that I was crazy for being so preoccupied with something that could be just a figment of my imagination, cultivated and nurtured by small-town gossips and mass hysteria. But as I scarfed down my breakfast, I mostly worried that if I loitered around the house, Grandmother would try to resume her modesty lecture. Or Kjell would call. I wasn't prepared to face either eventuality.

I grabbed a book and went to the nearby soccer field, where I knew I'd find Graham and Tuck. Fortunately, Kjell wasn't there—even though I recognized a few of his friends on the opposing team. I settled on the sidelines, watching the pickup game gel together.

During a pause in the play, when everyone else was catching their breath and grabbing some water, a tall boy jogged across the field and over to me.

"Hi," he said, glancing over his shoulder and shifting his weight from foot to foot like the grass was on fire. "Have you seen Kjell?"

I looked over his shoulder too. A group of boys was watching us. "Not since he dropped me off last night," I said, putting my bookmark in place.

"He dropped you off last night?"

I nodded.

"Then no one but you has seen him since he left the bar," the boy said. "Not even his mother."

"What do you mean?" I pressed my palms together. They slid, suddenly slippery with a thin film of sweat.

"Just that. No one knows where he is."

"Maybe he's fishing with his dad—or went on a trip or something?" It sounded pathetic, even to my own ears.

"Or maybe he disappeared." The boy was looking at me like he expected me to reveal my horns and spit fire any minute. "Just like the people in the other towns. The Valkyries have finally come here too . . . and so have you."

"I'm sure Kjell is fine," I said. "There must be a simple explanation."

The suspicion on his face was no longer thinly veiled. It was open and out there for the whole world to see. "Yes. I wonder what that explanation might be."

"You can't seriously think I have something to do with this?"

"There are some pretty interesting rumors about your family," the boy said. "And you're the last person who saw him."

"No, I wasn't," I said, rising to my feet, outraged. "Graham and Tucker were there too."

"You'd better watch your back. And if he doesn't turn up soon, you'll need to watch more than that."

Then he was gone, retreating to the safety of his herd. The other boys gathered in a circle around him, casting hate-filled stares back at me as he poured his lies and half-formed theories into their ears.

Two other boys joined him when he broke away from the group and walked to the middle of the field. "This game is over," he said.

"What do you mean?" Graham called back from the sidelines. "You can't quit while you're ahead like this. At least give us a chance to catch up."

"Sorry, Graham, but the rest of us don't feel safe here anymore." He fired a hostile look in my direction. "Ask your sister if you want to know why. She's caused enough trouble in this town."

Every eye on the field turned toward me. I was torn between wanting to curl up and die and wanting to march right out there and make that boy eat his words. The new, violent presence in my mind told me exactly how to do it.

"If you have a problem with my sister, you can take it up with me," Graham growled. His tone and posture introduced a side of Graham the world didn't get see very often. Apparently it was one thing to ask me out but quite another to insult me. If I ever needed confirmation that it was a good thing I'd kept my mouth shut about everything, this was it.

"It doesn't work like that," the boy replied, shrinking back as Graham straightened to his full height. "At least, *this* doesn't. But no hard feelings—at least not with you." He held out his hand for Graham to shake. It was trembling slightly.

Graham surveyed him through narrowed eyes before knocking the hand away roughly. It didn't look like he was going to let it stop there. He took a step forward, his hand curled into a wrecking ball. But Tuck grabbed his shoulder. After a second of standing and glaring, Graham let Tuck pull him away.

Graham walked across the field and wrapped me up under one arm like a mother bird protecting her chick.

"What was that about?" he asked as we started walking toward home. When I didn't answer, he added, "Does this have something to do with Kjell? If he's been saying things about you—you know you can tell me."

"No," I said, not really sure which part I was contradicting. "It's nothing. Just a misunderstanding. It's not Kjell's fault. Or anyone's, really."

"All the same, I'll talk to him." Graham looked back across the field, watching the other boys picking up their sweatshirts and water bottles. "Aren't you supposed to go out with him tonight?"

"Um, no," I stammered. "Kjell had to cancel. Rain check." I'd never, ever lied to Graham's face before. I wasn't sure I could do it, even if it was for his own good. But both boys swallowed my explanation without question—making me feel even worse. And even more alone.

"On the bright side," Tuck said, casting me a significant look and a wink, "he might never get the chance to cash it."

"You shouldn't wish bad things on other people like that." The angry words were out before I could stop them. Tuck had no idea how morbidly prophetic he might have been.

"You're so mean sometimes."

"Easy there, tiger." He said it lightly, like he didn't notice my over-the-top reaction, but his eyes locked on me and held on tight. "I didn't mean something had to happen to him. It just seems like a lucky break. You won't be spending the evening trying to let a two-hundred-pound Norwegian down gently."

"Right." I had to start controlling my emotions. The last thing I needed was Tuck trying to sniff out the truth. Kjell disappearing had rattled me to the core, and I couldn't afford to do or say anything that could put Graham or Tuck in danger of being next.

"Sorry. I guess I'm just on edge about the whole thing," I added.

Tuck didn't buy that, not for a second. He looked at me like I was a book written in a language he couldn't quite comprehend.

"He's too old for you—I mean, he's even older than me. And you're not ready for something this serious." Graham paused, then added, "Thought I'd have a chance to tell him that at the game today, but he was a no-show."

The reminder Kjell was missing would have made me feel even worse if the rest of what Graham had said hadn't set my remaining patience on fire. "Thanks, but I can handle it on my own," I said. "I don't always need you butting into my life, you know."

"I'm not butting into your life, but this is a lot for you to handle on your own." Graham tried to put his arm around me again, but I shifted away, just out of reach.

I wanted to scream. Graham had no idea what I was capable of handling, how many things I was already juggling all by myself—things far bigger and more important than boys. I was doing it all for him. For Graham. To keep him safe. My temper quieted, soothed by the logic that even if I wanted to strangle Graham sometimes, I didn't really want something bad to happen to him. If he found out everything that had been happening in Skavøpoll, and that Kjell was missing, there was no way I could keep him from trying to help out. Which could throw him directly in Astrid's path. I shivered as I remembered how Astrid had watched Graham after the fishing boat accident.

I couldn't afford to get into a fight with Graham.

"About the date today. I handled it," I said, smiling. "I told him I wasn't interested."

"I'm glad to hear it," Graham said, giving me a smile. "I'm proud of you for handling Kjell. And that jerk back there on the soccer field. It looked like you were standing up to him, too."

Silence settled over the three of us, and I looked back at them, relieved they'd finally let the subject drop. That's when I realized only Graham was satisfied by my explanation.

Tuck met my gaze, his steel-gray eyes cutting through my lies like a knife.

AFTER DINNER THAT night, we ended up sitting at the table, just talking. In my frustration with her, I'd forgotten how cool Grandmother could be—unlike my grandparents on my mother's side, who lived in Palm Springs in a house that always smelled like overcooked peas. Grandmother had traveled everywhere in her twenties and told stories that had us enthralled for hours, especially Tuck, who'd never heard most of them before.

By the time we cleared the table, it was almost nine, and I assumed we'd watch a movie or just hang out for the rest of the night. I'd been sharpening my cribbage skills for just such an occasion.

But Graham and Tuck were already conferring in low voices as they cleared the table, making plans to go out.

"You coming out tonight?" Tuck asked, bumping right into me with his shoulder as he loaded the last of the plates into the dishwasher. It caught me off guard, and water splashed out of the pan I was scrubbing, dripping down my arms.

"No," I said. "I'm tired." After the way Kjell's friends had treated me at the field earlier, I had no intention of going more than twenty feet away from the house.

"Ahab won't be there," Tuck said. "Or the asshole from the game today. It'll just be a select few."

A wave of dread washed over me. The town was so public, open to the eyes of everyone. It was so much better here, hidden in the woods, where we could see anyone approaching from miles away.

"Don't you think you could take a night off?" I asked. "Stay in?"

Tuck eyed me like I'd just suggested we rob a bank.

"Not when there's a girl involved," he said.

I tried to hide the way my heart lurched at those words. Judging by Tuck's grin, I did a terrible job.

"Not me," he said. "But big brother isn't *that* holy. And you know how determined he gets when he's got his mind set on something. A tall, blond something."

"Shut it, Tuck," Graham said, approaching, empty wooden salad bowl in hand. I was surprised to note that he was blushing. Must be one fantastic girl if she could throw Graham off balance. "Why would we stay in on a night like this?" he added.

"Because I'm afraid you don't have a choice," Grandmother said, making all three of us jump. "You'll have to cancel your plans, Graham. Whoever she is, believe me, she'll understand. All three of you will stay here tonight." Her voice sounded different. It was infused with command and the expectation of absolute obedience. Not that she hadn't always been self-assured, but this was a whole new dimension of confidence.

She stood in the doorway to the kitchen, dressed in jeans and a long, tailored coat I'd never seen before. Was it my imagination, or had the silver streaks disappeared from her hair? She wasn't the type of person to hide her gray, so I squinted, trying to decide if it was a trick of the light. As I did, I caught movement right outside the window. It was a raven, its black wing brushing the glass as it slid past in the darkness.

"Why can't we go out?" Graham asked, tipping his head to the side, like he too was startled by Grandmother's transformation. "You've never cared what we do."

"On the contrary," she said. "I've always cared far more than you realized. This is not open for debate." Her voice was firm, the way a general delivers orders to her troops. "You're welcome to do anything you want within my property lines. Scale the walls and camp out on the roof." She gave me a pointed look. "But do not go past the fence."

"But we have plans," Graham said, still staring at

Grandmother like he wasn't quite sure it was really her. "What's this about?"

"A good soldier doesn't question orders, Graham," Grandmother informed him crisply. Then she turned and strode back toward the living room. "They follow them without hesitation," she added over her shoulder.

"A good soldier?" Graham mouthed, raising both eyebrows. "That was just weird. This afternoon, I caught her hiding a rifle and a box of buckshot inside her winter coat in the hall closet. She claimed she's taking up skeet shooting." He dropped his voice to a whisper. "Do you think Grandmother is getting senile?"

"No, I don't," I said slowly. Grandmother was finally starting to tip her hand, revealing exactly how much she knew. Which meant under no circumstances could we disobey her.

"Well, she can't just decide something like that," Graham said.

The irony of that statement wasn't lost on me—coming from the same person who just last month had turned down my possible date for the junior prom without even consulting me.

"Grandmother wouldn't have done that if there weren't a good reason," I said. "And with everything happening around here, I kind of agree. I think it's safer if we all stay here."

"What 'everything' are you talking about?" Graham asked. "The delivery van that got a speeding ticket downtown?"

"The disappearances." It was the first time I'd openly acknowledged it to my brother. To Tuck. I looked at them both, half expecting their mouths to hang open, aghast at this revelation. "People have been kidnapped."

I'd kept my secrets locked away so long, it didn't even occur to me how feeble they'd look to the outside world.

"Kidnapped?" Graham repeated, trying not to laugh at me. "We're not twelve, Ellie."

"Not kids," I said. "Older boys. Your age. You must have heard about it. People just disappearing."

"Some of the guys said something about it," Graham said. "Trying to warn me about Valkyries or something. It was pretty weird. Look, kids get bored. Leave town. It just happens to be noticeable because Skavøpoll is small and everyone knows each other."

He took in the frown on my face and softened his voice. "Tuck and I can handle ourselves. If Grandmother asks, we went to bed. Jet lagged. Cover for us?"

The words sent a chill all the way to my toes. I couldn't believe he was spitting my own skeptical words back at me and sounding even more dismissive, more certain than I'd ever been that all of this was just some sort of small-town scandal blown way out of proportion. Fortunately, it didn't matter if Graham believed in what was happening as long as I kept him there, in the house. Safe.

"No, I won't," I said. "And Grandmother wouldn't have asked you to stay in without a good reason. You should listen to her."

"I forgot how easily you get scared," Graham said, laughing all over again. "Your eyes couldn't get any bigger right now. Remember when you slept in the hallway three nights in a row after I let you watch that zombie movie? Mom was so mad. Don't worry, Ellie. Tuck and I will protect you."

I'd been seven when that had happened. Even though he'd been just nine at the time, in his mind he'd grown up while I'd remained suspended in time.

I shouldn't have cared that he was making fun of me. It was just one more reminder that I was practically an infant in his eyes. I should have focused on the big picture—keeping him safe— and saved this fight for another day. But when he started in on another story, about the time I'd climbed a tree and been too scared to climb back down, my frustration broke free, exploding out of my mouth.

"I was really young then," I pointed out. "And it's not fair you're dismissing me today because of what I did when I was seven."

"I'm not dismissing you because of what you did then," Graham said, laughing and trying to wrap his arm around me. "I'm dismissing what you're saying because it's ridiculous. Although, now that you mention it, falling for some silly stories is something you would have done when you were seven. Still such a baby."

Tuck caught my eye and tried to hold it. He knew how that would sting. But having him acknowledge it wasn't enough. I needed Graham to acknowledge it, too. To understand. To see me and everything I was doing, everything that I could do, all the secrets I was keeping.

"I am not," I said, sounding far too petulant. "If you really think that, you don't know me at all. I'm so sick of how you do this—blow off my opinion. Like I don't know anything. Even when it's my life we're talking about."

Graham's smile faltered, like he wasn't sure if I was kidding but desperately wanted me to be.

"What are we talking about here?" Graham said, slipping seamlessly into his patient, saintly voice. "Is this about Kjell? Because even when you're thirty, I'll know way more about the inner workings of the male brain than you do. But you're not thirty. You're sixteen. And older guys have totally different expectations than you do. Trust me on this one. It's my job to protect you from situations like that."

The conversation had veered wildly off course and into the last place I wanted to go with Graham. I had a million more important worries on my mind. But then I saw the look on Tuck's face—complete and utter resignation. As if all the words Graham had said were directed right at him. And they could have been.

I thought back to last night on the roof, to how he'd pulled away from me because of Graham. I couldn't just roll over this time.

"So you're saying a girl my age wouldn't be safe being alone with you? That you'd just crawl all over her and take advantage of her? Because you were spending an awful lot of time with that sophomore cheerleader last fall. Anything you want to confess?"

Tuck made a strained coughing sound.

"Ellie," Graham said. Now his laugh sounded forced. "That's different. You know what I mean." He reached out and squeezed my shoulder.

"No," I shot back, taking a step away. "I guess I don't.

Unless you mean double standards are okay when you're on the winning side of them."

"I'm not saying everyone is going to attack you." He said it slowly, enunciating each word. Like I was stupid. Or, worse, too young to understand. "But there are plenty of boys your own age you can date. Plus, we don't know anything about Kjell. And driving around with him alone, in a dark car and in a foreign country, isn't the best place to find out."

"Maybe sitting alone in the dark is the best place to discover exactly how trustworthy someone can be."

Tuck's eyes snapped to mine. They were wide, wild, and begging me to stop. It was too close to the truth. Graham turned, catching the tail end of the exchange. He frowned, and I felt a twinge of panic too as I wondered exactly how much he'd understood.

Graham switched to his best placating voice, the one that never failed. "Look, there's no reason to get so upset. I thought we agreed on this—you're the one who turned Kjell down. We decided he was too old for you."

"We?" It was too much. The straw that broke the camel's back and severed its spinal cord. "This is my life, not something decided by committee."

"I really don't understand," Graham said. "I thought you didn't like Kjell." He glanced at Tuck for support, but Tuck was looking everywhere but at either of us.

"This has nothing to do with Kjell," I said, forcing myself not to shout. "You're the one who brought up Kjell. I'm saying you blow off my opinion. About going out tonight. About everything. Even when it's about my own life. You think you can control everything. You're even trying to control this conversation when you don't even really know what it's about."

"Okay. Then tell me," he continued in a forced-calm voice. "Please tell me what this is about."

"I just told you!" My voice was louder than I meant it to be. But I was angry, and my temper spiraled completely out of control. "But you weren't listening. Because you were too busy trying to tell me who I can't date. And as soon as we get home, it'll be nagging about my grades. Or the SATs. You're barely two years older than me—not twenty. It doesn't mean you get to boss me around. It doesn't make you Dad. It just makes you a jerk and a bully." The moment they hit the air, I tried to suck the words back in. But it was too late. They flew across the kitchen like poison-tipped darts.

Graham winced. The carefully controlled irritation that had twisted his lips a second before was gone, replaced with wide, shocked eyes and a half-opened mouth, like my words had frozen his response in place before it could leave his lips.

"Graham," I whispered, taking a step toward him.

He took a step back. "I think it's best if we stop this conversation right here." His voice was tight. Then he turned and left the kitchen. His footsteps sounded softly on the stairs as he climbed to his room.

I started to follow, desperate to explain myself. But Tuck caught my arm.

"Give him a sec," Tuck said. "You know, there's a middle ground somewhere in between lashing out and utter submission.

Might be worth exploring."

As if my guilt wasn't already enough.

"I know." My voice was smaller than a mouse. I'd made such a mess of everything—Graham did so much for me, with one parent dead and the other working all the time. I knew that. And now I'd thrown it back in his face. The weird flirtation with Tuck on the roof had ended in humiliation. And I was no closer to figuring out why people were disappearing or what my grandmother was hiding.

"Hey, hey, no reason for that." Tuck used his thumb to smudge away the water at the corner of my eye. "It doesn't have to be a bad thing. You got his attention. And even if it was harsh, it was something he needed to hear. Now you'll for sure have to talk it out. Explain yourself. And you guys will come out stronger on the other side. Promise."

I nodded and tried unsuccessfully to hold back a sniffle.

"Tell you what," he added gently. "Sleep on it. You both should. I'll go talk to Graham. Smooth things out."

He put his hands under my elbows, and for a moment I thought he might hold me, comfort me. His arms looked so inviting from where I stood. But his eyes were miles away from me and retreating further by the second. His hands did the same.

"I'll meet you on the roof at midnight," he said, tipping his head like he was listening to something in the distance. "I really should go after Graham. But don't worry, Ells. It'll work out."

I nodded, allowing myself to believe him. Tuck turned and slipped out the kitchen door and up the stairs, in pursuit of Graham.

7

After Tuck left, I stood in the kitchen, staring out the window into the night. I spent the next half hour building up my confidence for one more attempt at talking to Graham, practicing the things I could say to smooth over my harsh words while making it clear that things did still have to change—the middle ground Tuck had mentioned.

Just as I turned, prepared to mount the stairs in search of Graham, the roar of an approaching engine sliced through the quiet of the kitchen. My eyes flew to the window and the lengthening shadows outside. Headlights licked through the trees like flames. A car was winding up the road toward the turnoff to the house. It shouldn't have been strange to see a car passing by in the night, sparsely populated though the area might be. But it was. My pulse thundered in my ears as two more sets of lights appeared, sliding into place behind the first.

"Grandmother?" I called out. "Someone is coming. Cars."

She was in the doorway before I'd finished speaking.

The cars stopped at the base of the driveway. Doors clicked open and closed softly. A feeble attempt at stealth. The headlights twinkled again as the shadows of people crossed the paths of the beams. I counted twelve silhouettes gathering, conferring in the darkness.

"Get your brother and Tucker," Grandmother said. "There's a trapdoor underneath the red area rug in the basement. Get inside until I come for you."

"What?" I demanded. Alarming as her reaction should have been, I was outraged that she thought I'd just hide and let her face whoever was down there. Waiting. The jittering in my limbs came roaring back, like my body was spoiling for a fight.

"There's no time to explain. Just obey," my grandmother said, looking me squarely in the eyes. I'd usually question, or at least pause, but something in me switched on, triggered by the changes in my grandmother. She was right. At the moment, she had all the advantages—skill, experience, familiarity with the land, and most important, knowledge of what the threat might be.

Grandmother flicked a steel-plated light switch next to the door, one I'd somehow never noticed before. Floodlights poured into the yard, lighting the world like the midday sun. Then Grandmother stepped forward, into the night. Her footfalls were even, keeping tempo with an internal rhythm I felt too, vibrating through my bones until my heartbeat settled into place beside it.

A thought began to form in my mind. A horrible dawning realization that the answer had always been in front of me. What my grandmother knew about the disappearances and why. Because the more I watched her move, with lithe grace and cold confidence, the more she reminded me of Astrid. My thoughts drifted back to the way my grandmother had pronounced Astrid's name, like she'd said it a thousand times before. Whether those girls were Valkyries or just a renegade group of homicidal supermodels, my grandmother was one of them.

There was no time to dwell on what that meant, since I was pretty sure that whatever my grandmother was, she wasn't part of the whole kidnapping scheme. I ran through the house and up the stairs, leaping them three at a time.

Graham's door was closed, a ribbon of light peeking out from underneath it. I turned the handle. Rattled the knob. It was locked. My fists pounded the door. "It doesn't matter if you're mad at me," I said in a rush. "Open this door right now."

Silence.

I took two steps back and threw my shoulder into three inches of solid oak. It surrendered without hesitation, splintering the frame.

"Graham?"

The room was empty.

It made no sense. The door was locked from the inside.

Then I noticed the window was wide open. A cool night breeze led the long white drapes in a moonlight dance across the pine floorboards.

The necklace Grandmother had given him—with the rune-covered charm identical to the one Kjell had used to ward off Astrid—was discarded on his desk. It was warm to the touch, as if it had spent the last few hours resting on the radiator. Still, I slipped it into my pocket, silently cursing Graham for breaking his promise.

I don't remember leaving Graham's room. The next thing I knew, I was standing in Tuck's empty bedroom, staring at a bed made up with military precision and neatly folded clothes stacked inside an open suitcase.

My head felt like it would explode from the pressure—I had to find Graham and Tuck. I stepped into the hallway, wondering where to search next. A slip of white peeked out from beneath my bedroom door—a folded sheet with my name etched across the front in Tucker's square boy handwriting.

GRAHAM TOOK OFF. COVER FOR US.

It was the last thing I needed. The night was full of danger. I could taste it in the air, feel the adrenaline whisking through my veins in response. Astrid was out there. Waiting for her chance to strike. Against us. As were the strangers at the bottom of the driveway, blocking my route to town. And to Graham.

We had enemies pressing closer on both sides like a vise, and Graham and Tuck were out there in the middle of it, alone, unprotected, and without the faintest idea of the danger they were about to face.

I ran down the stairs and out the door, moving as silently as

I could. Grandmother was at the foot of the driveway, talking to someone, her posture straight, hands dangling loosely at her sides. Her casual stance was deceptive. She was ready for anything, poised for attack.

She stiffened as I approached, and turned her head to the side just enough to see that it was me. Then she relaxed. I wondered who else she thought it might have been, given that the yard was fenced in on all sides. She was guarding the only opening.

Two men stood at the boundary of Grandmother's property, staring up at her. I could sense the others off in the darkness, watching warily. Like sheep eyeing the wolf prowling through the trees in the distance.

"I'm not going anywhere with you tonight," Grandmother said in Norwegian. I was surprised by the ease with which I understood her. I comprehended her words like a switch had been flipped in my brain, pouring translations right into my ear.

"We just want to ask you some questions, Hilda," the man in front said as his gaze shifted to me. "The whole town is nervous, and I can't promise they won't do something rash that we'll all regret. You see, I can't guarantee your safety, out here by yourself tonight."

"It never occurred to me that you would be either willing or able to do such a thing," my grandmother replied. "Fortunately I'm not alone. Ellie and I are more than equipped to hold down the fort." She tilted her head to the side, laughter in her voice. It wasn't until I looked back at Grandmother's house that I got the joke. It was fortified indeed, complete with floodlights and painted steel shutters that latched on the inside. Four inches of thick oak secured the front and back doors, and a ten-foot fence surrounded the entire property.

And there were also the things that couldn't be seen, including the mysterious trapdoor in the basement that I'd just learned about. I had a feeling that the buckshot and rifle hidden in the closet were just the tip of the iceberg.

We were hunkering down for a siege, and Graham and Tuck were on the wrong side of the moat.

"You've got two options," the man said, letting his eyes drift from Grandmother to me. "Come quietly. Or if you don't, we're prepared to force you."

"Well, when you put it that way, the choice is clear." Grandmother flashed a smile that made the men in the shadows take a step back, their rubber soles scraping against loose rocks. "The second option sounds like much more fun."

The leader put his hand on his gun. I wondered if he had any idea how obvious he was, how thickly the fear and self-doubt clung to him.

"I didn't pick this fight, gentlemen. The first move is yours," Grandmother growled. "And the final one, I assure you, will be mine."

The leader looked back at his men, as if he'd find reassurances there, when even in the darkness I could feel their muscles tense with apprehension.

I took a step forward. Grandmother held up one hand and turned her head just enough to catch my eye. "Stay behind me."

While Grandmother was distracted, for an instant, the leader made his move. He rushed forward and grabbed her arm, jerking her forward roughly.

I didn't see what happened next, even though I was staring right at them. It was so fast, like someone had frozen time and rearranged the world while we stood by, unconscious and unmoving.

The leader lay flat on his back, ten feet away. Groaning like he'd just been dropped from the sky onto the pavement.

I was so focused on watching Grandmother, in my awe and pride, that I didn't notice the figure slinking through the shadows until he grabbed me. The gun in his hand swung around in slow motion until it pointed straight at me. My whole body went rigid with terror as my heartbeat shifted into a sprint, caught somewhere between fight and flight. I couldn't slow my brain down enough to think through a single course of action, so I ended up standing there, feet frozen to the ground.

"Now, Hilda," the man said. "I think we can come to a reasonable compromise here." The barrel of his gun nuzzled into my spine, stirring the new force inside me fully to life and crushing my fear into oblivion. "We just want to have a chat," he said. "I'm going to leave with your granddaughter, and I think you'll want to get in your car and follow."

He nudged me forward. Unpleasant as the gun was, digging into my kidney as we took an awkward step forward, I was far more concerned about letting so many minutes slip past while we dealt with this minor irritation.

"Graham and Tuck snuck out," I told my grandmother, shifting into English and hoping that would confuse at least a few of the men. "And Kjell disappeared last night. Someone needs to go after them right now. Make sure they're safe."

"I agree," Grandmother said mildly.

"Stop talking," the man hissed, shoving me forward.

"Which poses the question, Ellie, why are you wasting time?" Grandmother's eyes met mine. "Handle him. Now." I didn't know what she meant. Strong as I felt, I was pretty sure I wasn't bulletproof, and there was a gun pressed against my vertebrae. Safety off. One twitch of his finger, and I'd be dead. But when I thought about it, a trigger took an awfully long time to pull. It wasn't just the fraction of an instant it would take his muscles to complete the motion, but the solid seconds of hesitation I knew he'd suffer through. Without even realizing what I was doing, I twisted, bringing up my knee as I turned to face him. A shot exploded through the trees above us, sending birds streaking into the night as the gun flew through the air, disappearing into the shrubs lining the drive.

Grandmother was at my side in an instant, lifting the attacker off the ground by his collar. "How very bold to cross over into enemy territory," she said to the man. "Particularly when an old artifact like me doesn't believe in taking prisoners." The smile she gave him was wolfish and sure, and reminded me so much of Astrid I took a step back, not entirely sure if I should trust the woman standing in front of me.

She dropped him, and the man stumbled to keep his balance. When neither of us did a thing to stop him, he turned and ran. While we'd been busy with him, his friends had retrieved their injured leader and were helping him into the backseat of a car.

The few who remained clustered around, watching, hesitating, unsure what to do without someone giving orders. Especially after seeing what we were capable of.

Finally one of them moved into the headlights, his grim features cast in angular shadows. "We'll be back," he said. I had to admire how well he controlled the abject terror in his heart.

"I'll be waiting," Grandmother replied. She didn't pause to watch them climb into their cars and drive away. She was in motion, striding up the driveway toward the house. "We don't have much time," she said. "Go into town. Find Graham and Tuck and bring them back here. This house has many secrets that will protect you." She turned to face me. "If Astrid directly engages you, run. Even if it means leaving them behind. You're fast." She flashed me a proud, ferocious smile. "But not fast enough to defend yourself against her. Do you understand?"

I nodded. At that moment I would have agreed to anything she said.

"The three of you will stay here until I come for you." She flicked her wrist, and a long, serrated knife slid out of her sleeve and landed in her palm. She flipped it once, catching the blade and extending the handle toward me.

"Who are you?" I asked, wondering how many more times she was planning to shock me that night.

"I'm your grandmother," she said. "There are just a few things about my past I haven't told you yet. Things you're finally getting old enough to understand. Like who and what you really are. Take it." She was still holding the knife out toward me.

"I don't know what to do with this," I said, accepting it. "Except chop carrots."

"You're deadly with a knife. It's in your blood." Grandmother lifted one hand and pressed her index finger to my forehead. "Valkyrie," she said. It was exactly what Astrid had done to me in the bar. But this time, instead of burning, I was flooded with strength. The word meant something entirely different on my grandmother's lips. When she said it, it felt like a promise, a tribute to the old ways—to courage and sacrifice. "I left my home fifty years ago. To see the world. To learn," she said. "And I did. I learned that the world had moved on, had passed us by. And I was at peace with that. But I was the only one who saw it that way. And knowing my friends as I did, I've waited here."

"Why?" I asked. "For what?"

"For Odin to awaken," Grandmother said. "Astrid wouldn't do this on her own. And Odin won't give up the old ways without a fight. He'll try to drag us back into the dark ages. It's all he understands. I've feared this day for longer than you could possibly imagine."

At first I wasn't sure what she meant. But then I thought about what we'd learned in history class. About what the world was like a thousand years ago. When the strong took whatever they could. When justice was subject to interpretation. And minor thefts were punishable with death.

My eyes widened.

"I'll deal with Odin," she said as we reached the kitchen and she pulled a sword and three small daggers out from underneath the sink. "But I need to leave now, and I need to know you and Graham will be safe."

I knew what I had to do next, just as clearly as if she'd said it out loud.

"I'll protect Graham and Tuck," I said. "I won't fail you."

"It's Graham they're coming for." She held my gaze so firmly that it was impossible to look away. "It's revenge. Tucker is too young to interest Astrid. I should have told you the other day, but you're still so young yourself—you won't reach your true strength until you turn eighteen. I'd hoped this summer could be about teaching you these things slowly, but fate pushed my hand. I can't protect you from this any longer."

"I understand," I said. "We're stronger together." I knew it on instinct, remembering the way I'd felt in Astrid's presence, an ache that we were opposed, even though she terrified me. "Where are you going?" I asked.

"Hunting."

Her grin should have made my blood run cold.

Instead: *"Seire,"* I said, the phrase bubbling up from someplace deep inside my heart. *Be victorious.* Another word, a phrase I'd never learned, that had magically planted itself in my brain.

"I always am," she replied without turning back. "Go. You have a job to do."

I'd already wasted far too much time. I had to get to town.

While my logical self told me to take the car, something primal within me howled that I'd be faster and safer on foot. Invisible. Once the night air filled my lungs, my instincts were honed to a razor-sharp clarity. I could see each leaf on every tree. The wind whispered secrets, carrying to my ears the footfalls of the squirrels and deer in the forest. I could smell the salt in the air and feel the slightest shift in the wind's direction. Something was happening to me. It was as electrifying as plunging headfirst into ice-cold water—every molecule of my body was alert, awake, and screaming for action.

I lowered my head and ran, sprinting toward town at a speed I would never have dreamed possible. I was as fast and sleek as an antelope; power rippled through me.

Within minutes, I reached the outskirts of Main Street and passed silently by the shuttered doors of the hardware store and flower shop. There was a palpable tension in the town. I felt danger against my skin.

Graham wasn't at the restaurant we'd been frequenting all week—he was in the bar. I could feel his presence, feel the signature heat of each and every human in that building. Fire raged in my veins. No one would get in my way that night.

Not even the bouncer, who was the size of Graham. His eyes widened when he saw me jogging down the sidewalk toward the bar. Without hesitating, he pulled something out of his pocket. A cell phone. I couldn't afford to have him call in the cavalry.

"You don't want to do that," I said. The voice came from my mouth, but it wasn't my own. It was laced with power and poison. I was speaking Norwegian—a language I'd never bothered to learn came to the tip of my tongue with ease.

As soon as the words reached his ears, the bouncer's eyes turned milky as opals and his arm fell slack, letting me pass. I felt a twinge of confused guilt, but Graham's safety was on the line. I'd save my regret for another day, when I could afford that luxury.

Inside, the bar smelled like stale cigarettes and even staler beer. It hadn't been remodeled since the early eighties and hadn't been mopped in substantially longer.

I did a careful survey of the room, searching for Graham but also keeping alert for any signs of Astrid and her sidekick. My heart lurched when my eyes finally landed on a pale golden head, instantly recognizable even in that sea of blonds.

Graham.

He was in a booth at the very back of the bar, laughing with some other boys. Tuck was nowhere to be seen, but that was to be expected—there were lots of girls in the bar that night. No doubt he was off carousing with one of those gorgeous Norwegian girls who rolled out of bed camera ready.

Weird European pop music burned my ears. It felt like the entire room was moving to its odd, disjointed rhythm. As I took a hurried step forward, toward Graham, a hand grabbed my arm and yanked me back so hard my teeth rattled. Someone—a big someone—moved in front of me, blocking my view of Graham completely.

For one dread-filled moment, I thought it was Astrid and that I was too late. But it was a boy's voice that spoke. "You're either very brave or very stupid to come here."

I looked up into the face of the boy who'd accused me of having something to do with Kjell's disappearance earlier that day. My courage faltered—but only for an instant.

"There's a third option," I retorted. "Maybe I'm smart enough not to be afraid of little boys running around playing commando."

The boy lowered his face a few inches to my level; his voice oozed contempt. "Actually, smart ass, *that* would make you stupid. You should be afraid of me. I know what you are." Fear clung to him, sticking to his skin, twisting through his hair.

"And I know what you are," I said. "A coward. Now get out of my way."

His fingers dug into my arm. "I don't think so," he said. "I think we should step outside."

My stomach seized up. I wasn't prepared for this particular turn of events. "It's a bit chilly out there for my tastes," I said. I tried to summon that strange voice that had worked so well on the bouncer, but it came out more like a squeak.

The boy pushed my shoulder, knocking me toward the door. I took a step back to steady myself as Margit and another boy stepped into place behind him. My route to Graham was narrowing by the second. And even though that vicious voice in my head told me exactly which bones to break to get them out of my way, I knew hurting them would just make me every bit the monster they expected me to be.

Then Tuck stepped right into the middle of that mess, shielding me completely. "What the hell do you think you're doing?" He shoved the ringleader in the chest. While Tuck definitely had a temper, it always came out sideways, through jokes. It took me a second to recognize the look on his face as absolute fury. "I don't know what happens in this hick town, but where I come from, we don't push girls around." He knocked the boy back one more time, driving his point home.

"She's not a girl," Margit said, glaring at me with so much hatred that it almost hurt. "Filthy *Valkyrie*." Her tone turned the word into the worst kind of slander. "Don't look all innocent. I saw what you did to that bouncer."

The words ached. She was right and I knew it. But it didn't necessarily follow that I was evil.

"Tuck," I said, "I can handle this myself. It's okay." Even though I wasn't entirely sure I could, anything was better than having Tuck get into a fight.

"Right," he said. "I'll just step aside and let you face three psycho Vikings alone."

"They won't hurt me," I said, and this time the edge of power crept back into my voice. "We're taking Graham and leaving, and they won't do anything to stop us."

The ringleader looked at me, and the anger drained from his face. His pupils had that filmy, distant quality I was beginning to know far too well. He took a step back, and his friends and Margit followed suit.

By that time, with all the jostling and shoving, Graham had seen us. His forehead creased. Then his eyes narrowed. He was sharp enough to read the situation—Tuck's arms were extended, blocking anyone from coming near me. He was guarding me like a pit bull.

Graham's hands were resting on the table, but now they curled into fists the size of bricks as he pushed his way out of the booth. The guy sitting at the end couldn't get up fast enough, and Graham sent him tumbling to the floor. Once he was on his feet, Graham's entire posture shifted, stiffening until it was like every molecule in his body was aligned to one singular purpose—unleashing hell on those Norwegian boys. I needed to contain the situation—and fast. There wasn't time to get into a fight—I had to get Graham and Tuck back to Grandmother's house. I had to make sure both of them were safe.

And it was only a matter of time until Astrid found us. I could almost taste her presence drawing near. The same electric current that seemed to flow between us was licking at the edges of my consciousness. I didn't have a moment to spare.

Graham set aside his usually flawless manners as he shoved his way through the crowd. His eyes locked on me. I knew I'd been forgiven, no matter how much my words had hurt him, because there was a connection between the two of us, an affection born of a common childhood, the roots of our lives inextricably tangled. No matter how much either of us grew or changed, he'd always be my painfully perfect big brother.

When Graham was halfway across the room, he slowed. Confusion rippled across his features. His eyebrows drew together, and his lips pressed into a thin, firm line. Slowly, deliberately, he turned. His face was reverent, as if the entire universe centered on whatever he'd just seen.

My blood ran cold when I followed his gaze. The crowd parted just enough to give me an unobstructed view of exactly who was perched on the stools lining the bar. Waiting for him.

Astrid looked even more beautiful than before, which shouldn't have been possible. She and three other stunning girls were sitting in a row, shielded by a group of catatonic admirers. It was like a candy shop window—a display of glossy, blissful temptation.

There was no mistaking the malicious gleam in Astrid's eyes as she flashed me an ultra-white, ultra-wide grin.

This was personal.

"No!" I shouted, lunging forward as Graham took two long strides toward Astrid.

Tuck grabbed me around the waist and spun me to face him. "What's going on, Ells?" he demanded. "What just happened? What was with those guys?"

"Never mind," I hissed, wiggling my way free. In the mirror behind the bar, I saw Astrid lean forward, curling her manicured fingers around the back of Graham's neck. She tousled his hair playfully, as if he were her favorite new pet. Graham's eyes changed instantly, turning from baby blue to pearly white. It was as if she'd drained his very soul, sucked it out through her fingertips.

Graham's jaw fell slack, his easygoing smile fading into a grim scowl.

"Damn it, Tuck!" I screamed, still fighting against his restraining hands. "We've got to save Graham."

That got his attention. Tucker's arm went limp, and I surged toward the bar. I don't know where the strength came from, but I hit the nearest Valkyrie with the full force of a high-speed train. She was thrown off balance, but only for an instant. In the end, I was the one who tumbled to the ground. It was like hurtling into a brick wall.

Astrid reached down and pulled me up by the shoulder. Then she wrenched my arm hard, pinning it behind my back.

"I told you next time I wouldn't play nice." Her voice was an animal snarl. She shoved me hard, and my forehead smacked against the edge of the bar as I crumpled onto the floor. Hot blood dribbled down my cheek, but I managed to pull myself back to my feet. I wiped my face with my sleeve and squared my shoulders, turning to face her. It was exactly what Grandmother had warned me not to do, but did she really expect me to turn and run, leaving Graham and Tuck behind?

Astrid had Tuck's chin firmly in one hand. His eyes were distant, vacant. Long red fingernails pressed against his jaw, leaving crescent marks of blood in their wake.

"Too young," she said flatly. "A shame. This one's clever. And there's something unusual about him." She narrowed her eyes, scanning him more carefully. "Something unsettling." But it couldn't have been that interesting, because she turned away, leaving Tuck frozen in place like a statue. "Take the blond one," she ordered. "We were lucky to find him before Hilda could interfere."

"No," I said. The entire bar was watching, but as I glanced around, I saw milky pupils and pale zombie faces. I was the only one who understood what was happening. I was completely and utterly alone.

I felt for the short dagger tucked into the back of my jeans. "You can't hurt my brother," I said. "You'll have to kill me first."

"Hurt?" Astrid arched one sculpted eyebrow. "I'd never hurt him. I have high hopes for this young hero." She examined

Graham with the cold, efficient eyes of a Formula One mechanic. "It's been centuries since I've found quarry with this much promise."

One of the nameless Valkyries nodded at me as if this news should make everything all right. "He'll make you proud," she told me.

"You're not taking him anywhere," I told them, impressed that I could growl just like Astrid had.

"You forget your rank, Elsa. You have no right to question me."

Astrid was right. The truth behind her words was etched deep in my soul, right next to the knowledge that I should obey Grandmother. I had to actively fight the urge to slip into my proper place at Astrid's side.

Astrid pointed at Tuck. "We'll take this one too, just to keep Hilda and the girl in line."

"That's against the rules," her companion said, genuine shock flashing across her wide brown eyes.

"We abandoned the rules weeks ago," Astrid snapped.

"Why?" I shouted. "Why are you doing this?"

"Take him," Astrid repeated, glaring down the objection brewing in her friend's eyes.

A Valkyrie with raven-black hair grabbed Tuck roughly and pushed him toward the back door of the bar.

"No!" I shouted, struggling to push past her to reach Tuck. "Tuck! Don't listen to them!"

He turned toward me, his eyes darkening as they shed their milky white armor. Familiar gray stared back at me.

His eyebrows furrowed. He was trying to get a hold on what was happening. But I didn't have time to explain. The Valkyrie's hand was still curled around his biceps, dragging him away.

"Get away from her!" I screamed as I threw the dagger at the Valkyrie. I hadn't known I had that kind of violence in me until my fingers relaxed, letting the blade fly.

One manicured hand snatched the blade from the air without flinching. As flawless as the move had been, it forced her to release Tuck's arm for just an instant. But that was all we needed.

"Tuck—run!" I shouted.

Tuck was disoriented, but he obeyed. He shoved the Valkyrie hard, taking her by surprise. Then he pressed through the crowd, reaching his long arms out to shield me, just as Astrid raised one arm and struck me. It wasn't the type of slap you'd expect from a bone-thin, model-perfect girl. It was a brutal blow that sent me flying into the bar again. A stool collapsed under my weight. When I hit the ground, I actually spat blood, like an action movie star.

Astrid grabbed Graham and pulled him to the door. I watched, sprawled across the floor like a squashed spider, as Graham followed her, glassy-eyed and all too willing.

"Graham!" I croaked. My entire body was broken. My head was bleeding and my eyes couldn't quite focus on anything. I felt drunk, delirious, and utterly helpless.

Graham turned, but his face was stone and the eyes that met mine were milky white. He looked away without giving me a second thought.

I closed my eyes, defeated and in too much pain to move.

"Oh my God," Tuck said, suddenly at my side, "Are you okay? Can you hear me?"

"I'm fine," I whispered. "I've got to stop them. They've got Graham." I pulled myself up onto my elbows, gasping at the pain that stabbed through my ribs.

"No, don't move." He pushed me back down. "I'll go after them. Just sit tight. I'll get you a doctor as soon as I can."

"NO!" I roared, grabbing his arm and pulling him so hard, he almost fell on me. "You can't go after them. They'll take you too."

"I'll be fine," he said, flashing a smile that was dulled by fear and not at all reassuring. "But Graham won't be if he leaves with some girl who just hit you. Someone roofied him or something, I swear."

"Look around you." I winced as I somehow managed to pull myself to my knees despite Tuck's best efforts to keep me down. "Can't you see what's happening? They've all been hypnotized or something. You were too. I'm the only one who isn't affected."

Sure enough, as Tuck glanced around, his jaw muscle started twitching. Everyone in the bar was in varying stages of waking from a trance. Some were staring absently through partially clouded eyes, while others were shaking their heads and murmuring softly to themselves.

I rose and limped toward the back door. With each step, I pushed the pain further and further out of my mind, spurred on by the need, the absolute drive to save Graham. I flung the door open in time to see a black Range Rover peel past the bar. The enormous SUV was equipped for some serious off-roading, with roll bars on every exposed surface, spotlights, and massive tires that looked like they could climb right up the side of a cliff.

The red taillights disappeared around a curve in the road out of town, vanishing into the trees.

Graham was gone.

8

Tuck and I stood alone in the deserted alley behind the bar, utterly stunned. I stared at the distant trees that had swallowed Graham and the Range Rover whole, knowing I should move, should force myself back into gear. But there was no point. By the time I found a car to follow them, they'd be on the highway—halfway to anywhere.

I slid to my knees on the sidewalk. Failure paralyzed every muscle.

"Ellie?" Tuck sank down to my level. He put his hands on my cheeks. His fingers tangled in my hair as he tried to make me meet his eyes. "Snap out of it. Look at me. Where are they taking him?" He was practically shouting, like he already knew it was my fault. My cruel words had all but thrown Graham into their arms.

"I'm so sorry. So sorry," I said, fighting a losing battle against the terrible, hateful lump in my throat. The fear and anger on his face were too foreign. They almost made him a stranger.

But then his eyes softened, and he was Tuck again. "Hey, hey, stop," he said, his voice back under control. "Crying won't help. It just makes you impossible to understand." The smile he flashed just then was a few kilowatts shy of the usual, but even at its best, it wouldn't have been enough to erase how resoundingly I'd failed Graham. And Grandmother.

The tears came pouring out—along with everything that had happened to me since I'd arrived in Skavøpoll. I told him about my first encounter with Astrid at the bar, Kjell disappearing, Grandmother's strange behavior, and my certain knowledge that they were all connected. That Astrid had hunted Graham down.

Tuck took it far better than I'd expected. He didn't question my sanity—not once—which surprised me given how wild it all sounded. Even after what he'd just witnessed firsthand, I half expected him to break out a straitjacket.

Instead he got quiet, so quiet that his silence unhinged me. I'd expected questions, interruptions, exclamations of shock. Yet there was only one question he had for me, after I'd dumped about a dozen crazy theories out onto the sidewalk between us, followed by Graham's necklace, which I pulled from my pocket.

"You should keep this," I said, surprisingly eager to release it into Tucker's care. Not only did it burn my skin, something about the symbols on the front made the hair on my neck stand on end. "I think it'll keep you safe. Although maybe not. It didn't exactly work for Kjell."

He gave me a funny half grin before slipping it into his pocket. I was instantly more at ease with it out of sight.

"Is that everything?" he asked. "Is there anything you're not telling me? We can't have any more secrets if we're going to fix this."

My heart started racing in my chest. There was. Even if he'd taken the rest in stride, I wasn't ready to share the whole truth. The things I was learning about myself and my grandmother. What disturbed me most of all was how my grandmother and I could be so much like Astrid. I had to believe in my heart that we were different—despite the violent voice in my head and the weird way I felt in Astrid's presence. How could I tell Tucker Halloway all of that?

"No," I lied.

He studied my face carefully, in a way that almost made me wonder if he somehow knew. Maybe he could see the change in me and guessed what I was trying to hide. Lately, Tuck had been inconveniently observant. But then he touched the dried blood on my temple.

"I should have dragged him back to your grandmother's house," he said. "By the time I caught him, he was halfway into town. So I just followed."

"Well, he wouldn't have gone into town in the first place if I hadn't provoked him," I said. There was no way I'd let Tuck take even an ounce of the blame. It was all mine.

"It wasn't your fault either," he said. "You really think

your grandmother's rules would have stopped him? Sometimes you seem to forget Graham isn't actually perfect. After all, he's friends with me. You've gotta assume we've got something in common." Tuck's fingers curled around mine. "But right now, we need to go to Hilda's house," he said. "And we need to call a doctor."

"No . . . I actually think I'm okay." While we'd been sitting there, my strength had returned. Either I was going into shock or Astrid hadn't hurt me as badly as I'd thought.

Tuck looked at me for what felt like forever. I waited for him to object. To call an ambulance. Instead he asked, "Can you walk?"

I was on my feet by the time he finished saying it.

He just stared at me again, like I was one of the seven wonders of the world. Like I was a stranger, exactly like how I'd felt a few minutes ago, when I'd seen him shed his practiced poise.

I couldn't bring myself to meet his eyes, hoping he wouldn't guess that the source of my new strength was the same as Astrid's.

A car door slammed on the street. Three more slams followed in rapid succession. I could sense the tension on the air, the fear in the men as they approached. Margit had called her friends.

"We should get out of here," I said. "We don't have time to fight these guys off too."

"What guys?" Tuck demanded, but then he frowned as shouts echoed through the deserted streets. Without asking another question, he grabbed my hand and we started running down the alley in the opposite direction, toward the older part of town, where the roads snaked their way up into the foothills. It was the long route home, weaving through the residential area, but we had no other choice.

While my mind screamed that I should be hobbling along, barely able to walk, my body said quite the opposite. Strands of moonlight filtered through the trees, soaking through my skin and deep into my veins. They recharged me, fueling every cell until my body nearly shook with the power of it. If I needed to, I could run for hours without tiring. I could do anything.

Given what we could be facing to get Graham back, I hoped that feeling wasn't just the head injury talking.

As we approached my grandmother's house, there was a sudden shift in the night air; it had faded before, but once again I could taste the bitter edge of danger on the wind. Every nerve in my body hummed to attention as I shifted from a run into a flat sprint. Suddenly I couldn't get to the house fast enough. Grandmother had said we'd be protected there, but the warning snapping at the corners of my mind told me that might no longer be the case.

I barely broke a sweat as I sprinted harder and faster up the road. The air vibrated with violence, both recent and close. Violence involving two of us. Valkyries. Whatever power connected us was like a bat's sonar. Silent communication and coordination that echoed through the night. While I couldn't interpret it, I could sense it was there.

By the time I reached the driveway, I knew I was already too late. It was no longer the smell of battle that singed my throat, but its acrid aftertaste.

I ran up the driveway and slowed to a stop, standing just outside the circle of light cast by the porch lamp.

"What's wrong?" Tuck was breathing hard when he finally caught me. He actually looked annoyed that I'd smoked him running home.

"Something bad happened here," I told him.

"Well, things can't get any worse, can they?" Tuck shrugged and started walking up the stairs toward the door.

"Careful," I whispered, grabbing his arm and pulling him back down the stairs. My throat was dry. My legs and hands were trembling from the adrenaline.

"Easy, Ells," he said, rubbing his forearm as I released it. "When'd you get so strong—and paranoid?"

"When I started to realize how much danger you and Graham were in," I replied. Then, on instinct, I sniffed the air. All was quiet. Whatever had happened here was over. The house was empty. I could sense no one within.

"It's safe," I said.

"Nice work, Lassie." It had felt so natural, I didn't realize how strange it must have looked until I saw the wariness in Tuck's eyes, the way he hesitated before he put his hand back on my arm.

"Promise one day you'll tell me what's going on with you," he said. "Because that's the only way I'm letting it slide right now."

I nodded, grateful he understood I didn't want to talk about it.

"Hilda?" Tuck's voice echoed through the deserted rooms. There would be no answer.

The emptiness of the house was lead in my limbs. Grandmother was gone—she'd said she was leaving in pursuit of Odin. But whatever fight had just ended on these grounds might have changed things. Maybe her mission had been thwarted, or perhaps this meant it was well under way. Who had fought and who had won?

I didn't know how to use these new instincts to find the answers I so desperately needed.

Tuck hurtled up the stairs, two at a time, and I followed more slowly, searching for anything that would give me an idea of what had happened in Grandmother's house. "She's not here." Tuck's voice broke off abruptly, making me double my pace.

Tuck tried to intercept me when I reached the top of the stairs. "I don't think you want to go any farther," he said, stretching his arms across the hallway, like that would stop me. I pushed past. "There's a lot of blood."

Of course there was.

That's what I could sense—the physical aftermath of a brutal victory.

"I need to see it."

"Her room is trashed—broken furniture, the works. It's like there was a biker brawl in there." His words were rapid-fire as he followed me down the hallway. When I froze, coming to a stop at my grandmother's door, he hovered, expecting me to snap and have a meltdown any minute. From the looks of it, he was on the verge of one himself.

My grandmother's room was exactly as Tuck had described it: a disaster. The dresser was facedown in the middle of the rug, and the curtains looked like they'd been shredded with a chainsaw. Even more disturbing than the puddle of blood inside the door was the broad gash in the thick oak door frame. It looked like it had been struck with a super-sized ax.

"We should call the police," Tuck said.

"And tell them what, exactly?" I asked. "That we think Valkyries kidnapped my brother? And attacked my grandmother? Maybe we should interrogate all the other fictional creatures, starting with the Easter Bunny?" I knew I wasn't being helpful, but my frustration was screaming for an out.

"Leave the Easter Bunny out of it," Tuck murmured. "I know that dude has an alibi."

I wanted to hit him for making a joke just then, but I knew he hated feeling helpless even more than I did. No matter what problem I'd ever run into, he and Graham had had a solution at the ready. And I knew when it came down to it, Tuck relied on Graham as much as I did. These were uncharted waters for us both.

I knelt down by the blood. It smelled different from the nauseating metallic tang of raw meat in the grocery store. The blood on my grandmother's floor was familiar and distinct, the way a slept-in sweatshirt can smell like the boy it belongs to. Before I really knew what I was doing, I reached forward until my fingertips hovered above the blood. Suddenly I knew it wasn't smell I was responding to, it was something else—a signal of pure energy that my brain was still struggling to unscramble.

"What are you doing?" Tuck wrinkled his nose in disgust.

"I don't know," I said. "But this isn't my grandmother's blood."

"How do you know that?" he asked. "Whose blood is it, then?"

"I don't know," I repeated. "But I know it's from one of us." I felt strange, almost dizzy.

"One of who?" His scrutiny of my face couldn't have been more thorough if he'd used a microscope.

I'd said too much. "It just slipped out," I hedged. "Something's wrong with me, Tuck. I feel strange." And I did. I rocked back against the door frame as the room spun slowly around me like I'd boarded a lazy merry-go-round.

"It's probably that head injury," Tuck said, concern creasing his forehead as he leaned in for a closer look. Fortunately, it seemed to distract him completely from the other things I'd said. His fingers trailed along my hairline, igniting a totally inappropriate spark of warmth across my skin. "Come here a sec—lemme see." He pulled me into the bright light of the bathroom, where I took my first look in a mirror. And wished I hadn't. Who knew I could bleed so much without needing a transfusion?

Tuck put his hands on my shoulders. "It's probably not as bad as it looks."

He moved my hair aside, searching for the wound.

"I don't get it," he muttered, right as I was getting worried that his silence meant it was really bad and I'd be ending the night in a hospital bed instead of searching for Graham. "You're fine. There's nothing here. No cut, no bruise, nothing. I can't find anything wrong with you."

"And you won't," a deep voice said, coming from my left.

Tuck and I jumped. A tiny scream slipped out—I couldn't help it.

I whipped around to see a strange boy standing in the hallway, watching us through the open bathroom door. He took a step back, leaning against the wall and crossing one leg over the other—the classic James Dean pose. And that was hardly where the resemblance ended.

But as I looked at the boy, stunned by his beauty, his features seemed to shift until he was no longer recognizable as the same person. I rubbed my eyes, trying to force them into focus, but his face was a spinning kaleidoscope, unwilling to settle for too long on any one set of features.

My head injury must have been worse than I'd thought.

The boy looked past me, at Tuck. "Her kind heals quickly," he said. "And she's still young. She'll get stronger."

Tuck and I were both too shocked to speak. But Tuck recovered first. He stepped in front of me and said, "What are you doing here? Who are you?"

The boy smiled. The way his lips curled up into dimples in each corner was oddly familiar. "One question at a time."

"I know you," I said slowly. "I don't know how, but I do."

"Of course you do," he said softly. And his face changed completely. I gasped.

"Grandfather?" I asked in a tiny voice. "But—but you're dead."

"Yes, yes, he is," the boy's voice said, coming from my grandfather's weather-beaten face. "That wasn't very nice of me, dredging up those memories. Can you give me someone else? Let me check for something better." He tipped his head to the side and stared at me without blinking, like he was reading something etched on my forehead.

Suddenly, Mrs. Sherman, my second-grade teacher, was standing in front of me, exactly where my grandfather had been an instant before.

"Tuck," I said, burying my face in his shoulder. "I need an MRI. That guy changed into Mrs. Sherman. I'm going crazy."

"Possibly," Tuck said. "But that isn't one of your symptoms. I see her too. Hated Mrs. Sherman. Always smelled like mothballs."

I looked at Tuck. Even though he was doing his best to sound brave, there was fear in the way he held his shoulders back, in the new line between his eyebrows.

Mrs. Sherman's mouth twisted into a dry smile. "Hard to rattle, aren't you?" The strange boy's smooth voice slid from between Mrs. Sherman's lips. "I wonder why that is."

Then Mrs. Sherman was gone. In her place was the boy again. Now that his features were still enough for me to get a good look at him, I realized he was about our age. But that was the only detail I could truly remember. It was a face that could be lost in crowd even if I was holding a picture of it. Yet when he smiled, it was the same curl I'd seen before. Framed by the same symmetrical dimples that looked like they'd been sculpted by a plastic surgeon.

And the boy smiled now, larger than life. "Let's start again." He took my hand and held it in both of his. "Ms. Elsa Overholt," he said. "I'm Loki, your grandmother's dear, dear friend—even though she hasn't talked to me in fifty years. But what's fifty years to creatures like us?" His laughed softly at the joke I didn't quite get. "I'm delighted to finally meet you. That is, delighted to have you finally know I'm me. I've checked on you from time to time—pardon the curiosity. I couldn't imagine my Hilda playing grandma." His gaze lolled around as he spoke, never quite landing on anything at all. "Where is she?"

"I—I don't know," I stammered, meeting his eyes as they snapped to me. They were the dark, woodsy green of a pine forest. And I could have lost myself in them forever. I finally had to force myself to look away. "She's gone."

"Gone?" he repeated. His smile took on a hungry edge. "Fascinating. She left you here all alone?"

"Not *all* alone." Tuck cleared his throat. "Maybe Loki can help us?" He nudged my shoulder.

"Probably not," Loki said, walking down the hallway toward Grandmother's bedroom. "Not particularly interested in other people's problems." He looked at Tuck like he was less than roadkill. "Particularly human problems."

"Human problems? What, as opposed to squirrel problems?" Tuck shot back. The flash of anger showed how fragile his veneer of calm actually was.

I put my hand on his elbow, just in case. Something told me Loki wasn't someone he should bait. Once Tuck got started, he was impossible to stop. But he ignored me and aimed those inscrutable gray eyes right at Loki. "So what exactly are you?"

"Not really sure," Loki said, indifferently flipping through the family photo album he pulled down from the bookshelf in the hallway. "I've always been me. Like you've always been you. You'd maybe call me a god. Humans have done that in the past. If you ask me, I'm ordinary—and you, well, humans are subordinary. No offense." Loki's gaze transferred to me and stayed there for an uncomfortably long time.

"None taken." Tuck sent me a look that said he wanted to believe Loki was loco. But there was a trace of doubt, like he was begging me to double-check his sanity.

Loki no longer paid us any heed. He wandered through the hallway, blandly perusing the framed family photos decorating the walls and examining the paperweights and knickknacks displayed on a narrow table. Finally he came to a stop in front of the puddle of blood.

I felt a surge of panic. My grandmother was gone, and there was a pool of blood in her vandalized bedroom. Maybe Loki had something to do with it, or maybe he'd suspect that Tuck and I were delinquents who'd taken Grandmother hostage. I didn't know who or what Loki was, but my instincts told me not to trust him.

But Loki's grin brightened the room like a camera flash. "Hilda's been fighting again, hasn't she? It's long overdue. Valkyrie power is a fickle thing—use it or lose it. And she was skating dangerously close to the latter." He strolled around the room, assessing the rest of the damage. "I wonder what brought her back. It would take something big to summon Hilda out of retirement. Or shall we be frank and call it what it was—hiding?"

"Hiding?" I repeated. "But she's been living here for the last fifty years. That's hardly hiding."

Loki didn't answer. He was too busy examining the thick gash in the door frame. "Hilda still can swing a sword, you've gotta give her that. But who knows how far that will get her these days? Most of the modern girls prefer semiautomatics." He paused. "More discreet," he mouthed, as if it should have been obvious.

Tuck's eyes were tracking every millimeter of Loki's progress around the room, until he stepped forward, visibly impatient with Loki's circular chatter. "What girls? And who was Hilda hiding from?" he demanded. "What are you talking about?"

Loki walked slowly through my grandmother's room, muttering about our appalling lack of education while searching for something. "Ah, here it is." He lifted an antique-looking book from underneath some papers on Grandmother's desk and flipped to a page, seemingly at random, then handed it to me.

It was open to a black-and-white sketch of a woman pointing a sword at the back of an armored soldier, marching him up a hill. Another woman waited farther up, with a wolf at her side and a raven perched on one arm. There was a sword in her other hand.

Loki cocked an eyebrow and looked down at the book in my hands. "Things have changed during Odin's absence. Modernized. But those are Valkyries, in their more traditional role. Until recently, when she went AWOL, your grandmother was their leader. The best and most brilliant of them all. Something Astrid can't forget even though, by default, she's their leader now. Hilda managed to keep herself hidden from the others for half a century."

"Excuse me?" Tuck said.

Loki shifted impatiently, as if he was explaining the obvious and resented every second he was wasting doing so. "Valkyries are far and away the most ferocious fighters you'll ever meet," he said, aiming his words at me as if Tuck wasn't even there. "For centuries, your grandmother hovered over battlefields, rewarding the soldiers who fought ferociously and faced death without flinching. She escorted them to Valhalla. To the afterlife."

"Afterlife?" I repeated. "As in dead?"

"Most certainly," Loki said. "How else would Odin build an army powerful enough to one day destroy the world? That's his burning desire, you know. Been at it for ages, and frankly, it gets a bit old. Unfortunately, undead soldiers don't. That's how he keeps his ranks up. Otherwise he'd barely get them trained, and poof, they'd be gone. He gouged out his eye in exchange for the wisdom of the ages, and that strategy is the only evidence I've seen that he actually got anything out of the bargain."

"That's not my grandmother," I said, casting a nervous glance at Tuck, who was still staring at the open book in Loki's hand. "Even if she was a Valkyrie, she wouldn't help Odin build an undead army. Especially if he wanted to use it against the rest of the world. She hates war. Besides, that book's a hundred years old."

Loki cracked a mocking half grin. Calling me an idiot without uttering a word.

The room felt hot and close, a nursery designed to hatch my wildest fears. Fears that surrendered all too willingly to exhilaration. And something else—pride. I shook my head again and again as I backed away from him, not sure if I was more terrified by what he was telling me or by my own desire to revel in the truth of it.

"You know what your grandmother is." Loki's mouth twisted into a dry smile. "Just as surely as you now know what you are. I see your guarded posture, the way you're watching my hands for any hint of pending attack. You're enjoying your heightened senses every bit as much as you should. There's nothing wrong with being fast and strong. With being invincible. Savor it. You're the first new Valkyrie I've seen in a thousand years. It's nearly impossible to make new ones, you see. Not many gods wandering around these days, tampering with mortals. Creating half bloods. And even when they do, only a select few have what it takes. But you do."

He was right. And it was written all over my face. My lips curved into a smile at his word choice. *Invincible*. It felt too good to deny, the surge of power and knowledge. And as the rest of what he'd said hit me, I realized that accepting what I was didn't necessarily mean I was evil, like Margit said. Because I was still me. Ellie. The violent voice yielded to me when I stood up to it. My Valkyrie instincts were an adviser, not a dictator. If my grandmother could control them, so could I.

Loki was grinning ear to ear, as if my thoughts were being

posted on my forehead like a stock market ticker.

"Of course you can choose your own path, Elsa," he told me. "You haven't made any promises. You owe Odin nothing. And I'd advise you to keep it that way. Unless you envy Astrid's state of servitude."

Tuck had an odd, pinched expression, like if he scrunched it up tight enough, the truth wouldn't be able to sneak its way into his ear. For once, his face was all too readable. He frowned as all the weird things I'd done replayed in his mind, settled into place, and fitted Loki's explanation just perfectly.

I held my breath, waiting for him to react. Given what he'd seen that night, I couldn't blame him if he was angry I'd lied. Or was afraid of me. But Tuck met my gaze as he said, "Let's focus on the real issue here—it's got nothing to do with what Ellie and Hilda are or aren't."

Loki scowled, disappointed by Tuck's reaction. Or lack thereof. "By all means, enlighten me," Loki snapped. "What *is* the real issue? Other than the amazing creature standing next to you." Something dangerous flashed in Loki's eyes when he looked at me. Greed. Like I was a precious museum piece.

Tuck and I exchanged a nervous glance. "We need your help," I said. "Valkyries took my brother."

"That wouldn't surprise me," Loki said, losing his last remaining shred of interest in the conversation. "Any grandson of Hilda's would be a great hero. I'm sure he's in Valhalla as we speak. How did he die? Was it noble? Brave?"

"Die?" The word was thick as peanut butter on my tongue. "Graham didn't die. He was out at a bar with his friends, and these girls, Valkyries, they just came and took him. One of them was Astrid. And I want to get him back."

"Astrid." Loki grinned lasciviously at some memory I sincerely hoped he wouldn't share. "It's been centuries. Lovely girl. I haven't seen her since the time Odin had me chained and tossed into the ocean—right into the Mariana Trench. It took a decade to get out of that one. She tied me so deliciously tight." He tugged at his chin with his index finger and thumb. Then he stared at me with a disturbing intensity, as he finally processed the rest of what I'd said. "Your brother was *alive* when Astrid took him?" Loki's tone made me flinch, even though I was pretty sure his anger wasn't directed at me.

"Yes, of course," I said. "Otherwise I wouldn't exactly be able to get him back, would I?"

Loki's features were a mood ring. His face twisted into a mask of abject fury. "They're allowed to take only the dead to build their army—that truce is three thousand years old. Astrid knows better." He paced around the room.

"Well, apparently she doesn't," I said, standing up straighter. His outrage introduced the hope that maybe he'd help us. "She took my brother and our friend Kjell. And I want them back. Along with all the other living boys they've taken. Because there are a lot. Who do I report this, um, truce violation to?"

"Me," Loki said in a flat, even voice. "Astrid would never do something like this on her own. That means Odin is awake. And, once again, he thinks he can take whatever he wants."

"That's what my grandmother said, too," I whispered. "Right before she disappeared."

Loki's eyes finally focused back on me, like he'd just remembered I was in the room.

"And Hilda would know," he muttered. "No wonder she let them take her prisoner. She's so predictable. Even if what she's probably plotting works, it won't be enough to stop Odin. He's a complete maniac. Obsessed with an archaic prophesy about the end of the world that clearly didn't come true." He regarded me with thoughtful eyes, as if he was weighing the various courses of action laid out in front of him. "Given the state of modern warfare, at least he won't get too far outside this county. I'll make sure of that." His clothing shifted into a military uniform. The kind that high-ranking officials wear, weighed down with stripes and gaudy medals. "I'll keep it old-fashioned. Ground forces and light artillery. Out of respect for the elderly." His eyes were glittering with a caliber of excitement that made my stomach drop through the floorboards. "Besides, smart bombs are so anticlimactic," he added as an afterthought.

"What about my brother?" I challenged. "You just said if the Valkyries took Graham, he's with Odin. You can't attack him. Graham could get hurt."

"It's not a possibility," Loki murmured. "It's a certainty. He's as good as dead already, if he's in Astrid's hands. She was always Odin's favorite general. Because she'll fight to the very last soldier." Loki paused and squeezed my arm. "At least he'll have a glorious death. Astrid has a flair for the dramatic."

Amazingly enough, Loki seemed to think that would appease me.

"I'm afraid that answer won't work for us," Tuck challenged

him. "We need Graham back alive."

Loki laughed. "Maybe I should ship you off to Valhalla too, little boy. Takes some nerve to stand up to me, but then again, you don't really know what I'm capable of, do you?"

My new, sharper instincts confirmed that Loki was more venomous than a snake and every bit as slippery. I took a step forward, just enough that I'd be able to intervene if he tried to hurt Tuck.

"If you want Graham back," Loki said, "you'll have to get to him soon. I don't have time to trifle with one measly soldier's safety. How very selfish of you to forget all the other boys and innocent bystanders who'll die if Odin makes his move. Is Graham more important than they are?"

"No," I said. "We want to save them all." I had to believe there was a different solution, something that would save all the kidnapped boys. "We have to stop Odin before it comes to a fight."

I glanced down at the image of my grandmother in her Valkyrie glory. I wished with all my might that she'd appear right then and save the day. But she didn't. For the first time in my life, there was no one there to fix things but me. And now it wasn't just Graham and Grandmother I had to worry about. I had to save the innocent people who were getting tangled up in Astrid and Odin's net.

As I stared at the book in my hands, sifting through every scrap of information I'd collected over the course of the past week, a word on the opposite page caught my eye: Loki. It was all Norwegian, a tangle of words with too many vowels, and armed with umlauts. But as I stared, the words connected themselves with meaning in my mind. Not a translation, not the way it was when I read Spanish in class. I recognized the words just as surely as I knew my own name.

Two paragraphs were dedicated to the moody madman standing in front of us. Loki was a jokester, a prankster. He was the Norse god of mischief and could change shape at will. But like all other Norse gods, he had a healthy streak of war-loving Viking violence. For centuries he and Odin were locked in a battle of wills, of cruel pranks and brutal retaliation. Vying for control. And bragging rights.

It was pretty clear that Loki was looking forward to this opportunity to crush his nemesis.

As sister to the most popular boy in the world, I'd known plenty of guys like Loki over the years. Arrogant, conceited boys who always got their way. While Loki was more dangerous than your average lacrosse player, a boy is a boy, and I knew better than anyone how to manage their raging egos.

"Loki, wait," I said as he sidestepped around Tuck, who had shifted back into Loki's path, bracing for a confrontation I preferred to avoid. "I know the stories about you and Odin," I bluffed. "Your history of fighting. Back and forth for centuries. And it seems to me you need an outside perspective. You haven't exactly been able to keep the upper hand for very long on your own. You're gonna just take out his army when you know he can't do much damage anyway? Not all that humiliating, if you ask me. Not flashy enough. He'll just come back for more one day."

A shadow passed across Loki's face. Apparently *someone* didn't take criticism very well.

"This time you need to hit him where it hurts," I said.

Loki's eyes betrayed a glimmer of interest. "I'm listening," he said.

I inhaled, steadying myself. Then I caught Tuck's eye and held it. He winked—so calm and collected, no matter what was happening around us. Or at least pretending to be. It gave me the infusion of confidence I needed to deliver my next words.

"We'll free the soldiers who are still alive, who've been kidnapped, and we'll lead them against Odin. You can bet they'll be pretty mad, right? I mean, this is beyond military conscription, and people get pretty worked up about that. Having all those people he kidnapped inside his army, inside Valhalla, would be like a Trojan horse he built himself." I paused, scrambling to throw this plan together on the fly. "Odin would be humiliated because a bunch of kids beat him, and you would prove once and for all that you're more than some silly prankster he can just dismiss. You're a military mastermind who can beat him at his own game."

Loki narrowed his eyes. "You overplayed your cards," he said. "I can spot manipulation a thousand miles away. I invented the concept. Yet your idea amuses me. Tell me, Elsa Overholt, how would you propose to free so many mortals, with Astrid and the others there to undermine your efforts? You do realize all those boys aren't just lounging around playing video games. Astrid keeps everyone on a very tight leash. Her influence gets stronger with each passing day. Graham and the others will be completely loyal to her." He leaned against the door frame, his features settling into arrogant perfection.

"Easy," I said, bluffing with the best of them, even as his words made my heart crack. "I've done it twice now—stolen a boy right back from under Astrid's nose. I'm stronger than she is, and she knows it."

Loki laughed. "Maybe in five hundred years you could challenge her, but not a moment sooner. What if she just decides to kill you? Or your brother? Don't tell me you think you'd be a match for her in a fight. I'll know you're lying."

I couldn't help it, my eyes widened at that. I remembered all too well the feel of Astrid's bone-crushing blows.

Loki laughed even louder. "It might be worth my while to let you try. Better even than the Battle of Bayeux, perhaps." He sized me up lazily. "What would humiliate Odin more than destruction at my hand?" He chuckled to himself. "You have until Thursday at dawn." His tone made it all too clear that he considered it the most lavish of favors. Even though his deadline was only twenty-seven hours away.

"What happens at dawn on Thursday?" I demanded, mentally adding ". . . if I fail."

"If you keep wasting your time interrogating me, there's a good chance you'll find out," he glanced at his wrist even though he wasn't wearing a watch. "Tick-tock."

As Loki turned to leave, for real this time, his face rearranged itself into that of a boy I recognized from Graham's pickup soccer games in town. He grew three inches all at once. With a quick bow and an even faster smile, he disappeared down the hallway.

"Loki?" I called after him. "Wait! One more thing."

"You already have everything you'll get from me today." He gave me a slow once-over that sent all the blood in my body straight to my face. "Although I could come back when you're alone and let you practice your powers of persuasion."

I swallowed my disgust and chased after him down the hallway, catching his arm. "Wait. Loki, please. How do we find Odin and Astrid? Where is Valhalla? How do we get there?"

He paused. "Your grandmother didn't tell you?"

I shook my head.

"Wonderful." Loki's grin was cruelty incarnate. "If you'd told me that from the start, I wouldn't have thought twice about approving your proposal. Fate is truly on my side this time." His eyes glassed over, lost in thought. "Yes, my second plan is even better. Genius, if I do say so myself. And I have remarkably high standards." He turned away, not bothering to explain whatever second plan he was talking about. "I'll await you at the finish line—or at your brother's funeral. If the two aren't inextricably intertwined."

Loki snapped his fingers and disappeared into thin air, leaving me standing there, utterly confused, confounded, and without the slimmest sliver of hope.

When I returned to my grandmother's room, Tuck's mouth was drawn into an uncharacteristically grim line. "How do we start, then?"

"Start?" I repeated numbly, feeling like a deer caught between headlights and a high-power rifle's scope.

"It's Valhalla or bust," Tuck said, a spark of his usual fire flaring beneath his somber surface. "Until we wake up from this acid trip, I guess we play along? Please tell me your new Spidey senses will tell us what we do next." He pointed at the alarm clock on Grandmother's bedside table. "It's midnight. Dawn on Thursday is barely more than a day away. Good news is, I'm fantastic under pressure."

I'd never in my life been so grateful for Tuck. For his confidence—even when it defied logic. He looked like he was unraveling at the seams, but he was making a valiant effort to hold those edges together. And that was enough to snap me into gear.

Even though Grandmother had told us to wait here, there was no way we could obey. She hadn't known Graham would be taken or that Loki would appear, claiming he knew her plan would fail.

"My grandmother would know—apparently she had quite a life before my father was born. Maybe we can find something that will point us in the right direction." I glanced around the room, grasping for something that would point me in *any* direction.

A floorboard had been pried up at one corner. A thin metal rod was wedged underneath, propping up the wooden slat just enough that I could see beneath it.

"Tuck, c'mere," I said as I tugged at the board, dislodging it the rest of the way. The nails made a stripping sound, like Velcro, as they were wrenched from the subfloor. Before Tuck had a chance to reach me, I'd already pushed the board aside to reveal a hidden compartment below.

Inside was a sword. It was ancient looking, with crude carvings along the blade and handle. They were difficult to make out underneath a layer of dust as thick as frosting, but at first glance, it almost looked like the engravings told a story—with scenes and characters arranged in panes like a stained-glass window.

I lifted it out of the concealed compartment, and a scrap of paper followed, fluttering to the ground at my feet, faceup. Grandmother's handwriting was scrawled messily across the page in a rush. Judging by the torn edge, she'd ripped it hastily off the corner of a larger page.

YOU MUST BEAT ONE OF US BEFORE YOU CAN JOIN US.
VICTORY LIGHTS THE ROAD TO VALHALLA.

"She left this note here for me," I said. "Left the board wedged up like this so I'd find it."

"A sword?" Tuck said. "And a cryptic note. Well, now I'm not worried at all. We'll have Graham back in no time." I shot him a nasty look, and he muttered, "Sorry, but maybe she could have been more direct."

"She was," I said. The scribbled words just confirmed that things had changed in the last hour. Even if she'd originally told me to wait here, she'd left another, more important message since. "She wants me to fight Astrid. Beat one of them. It says it right here," I said. Even though we still didn't know where she'd gone, I was sure she'd left this here for me to discover. Her coat and glasses were discarded messily on a chair. She'd left in too much of a rush to be any clearer.

"That's the stupidest thing I've ever heard," Tuck said. "Astrid just pulverized you. Your grandmother wouldn't put you in that kind of danger—with some antique to defend yourself with."

"She wouldn't have left that note here if she didn't think I could do it," I said. But I didn't tell him the rest of what occurred to me as I stared at the blade. Maybe she didn't have a choice. When faced with the danger Graham and the other boys were in, maybe Grandmother thought it was worth risking my life for a chance to stop it.

And I agreed.

A moment passed in silence. I knew Tuck was waiting for me to figure out what we should do next, and I was stalling, not wanting to tell him that I really had no idea. I thought about the way I felt in Astrid's presence, the unity. I was a part of something that was larger than myself, a network of shared energy and camaraderie that flowed between the Valkyries. I wondered how my grandmother had hidden from the others for so long, if that was truly what she'd been doing. Because even as I stood there, most likely miles upon miles away from Astrid and the others, I could feel the space they'd occupied in town a mere hour ago. Traces of Astrid's presence lingered, dissipating into the night but still present enough that I could reach out with my mind. And suddenly it seized me, like a super-sized wave at the beach, knocking me off my feet and sucking me under into the darkness.

"Ellie? Are you okay?"

I tried to tell Tuck to back away. I had no clue what was happening to me. But my tongue was frozen in place, every muscle in my body held rigid, waiting, as a thought that wasn't mine wormed its way into my brain. Unlike the voice that couldn't decide if I should crack Astrid's skull or join her, this was completely external. Alien.

Tuck grabbed my arm, and I wondered distantly if I was fainting. The world went black as an image settled in my mind's eye, painted by whatever force was raging through me. I saw a boat, a massive navy destroyer. It smelled like bravery, like victory, an aroma that was suddenly as irresistible to me as Tuck's lingering scent of grass and sunshine. The boat was anchored in a harbor, and I strained to see more, to understand. It was all too familiar—the town built up around the narrow port.

"Ellie?"

I must have looked pretty strange, because Tuck was in a flat panic, squeezing my arm so hard, it might have hurt a normal girl. Slowly I snapped back to myself enough to say, "I'm okay. I think I know where Astrid will go next."

Tuck raised one eyebrow.

"It's hard to explain," I whispered. "But when I'm near them, there's this energy that flows between us, connecting us. And I have to fight it, because otherwise it might convince me to join them." I laughed nervously but stopped when I saw how Tuck's frown deepened. I wasn't sure if he was afraid *for* me or *of* me.

"That sounded worse than it is," I fibbed. "The important thing is, I think I just picked up a signal or something that Astrid is sending to the others. Of where to go next."

Tuck's eyebrows drew together. My explanation hadn't reassured him at all.

"Where?"

"Bergen," I replied. I'd recognized the wharf and the hills beyond, with the strange glass tram that tows tourists to the top to take in the view. "There's a military destroyer anchored there. Full of exactly the type of soldiers we . . . I mean, Astrid . . . would want."

"Bergen," Tuck repeated. "That's where the airport is, right? That's far. We can't afford to make a mistake like that. How do you know that's where they'll go?"

"They won't be able to resist. I can feel it too. The water's chummed; now we just wait for the sharks."

"Can you pick a different analogy?" he asked, shivering. "I mean, technically, I'm chum."

"Not old enough," I said, surprised by how firmly I could feel the difference, even though Tuck was every bit as brave. These bursts of insight, this understanding of the rules of my new being, were embedded somewhere deep in my brain. Waiting for me to stumble across them, one by one. "Eighteen is the age of knowledge. The age a Valkyrie attains her true power. You're not old enough to be useful yet."

Tuck stared at me for a long moment before cracking a playful grin. "Glad we settled that," he said. "Because after being rescued and outsmarted by you all night, my self-esteem was getting tired. You know, hanging on for dear life."

"I didn't say you're not useful to me."

"Useful?" he repeated. His smile broadened when I started

to stammer an explanation. Because useful didn't even begin to describe how I felt about Tuck.

"Relax, Ells. I'm kidding. Have you forgotten I hang out with Graham? Suppose it doesn't matter which Overholt outshines me."

"Stop it," I said, rolling my eyes because I knew he wouldn't stop until he'd gotten a reaction. "We'll go to Bergen, then. We find Astrid. Unless you have a better plan."

"Plan? That's not a plan, that's just looking for trouble," he replied. When I just stared at him blankly, he added, "What exactly are we gonna do when and if we find her?"

"I need to fight her."

"You can't be serious." His hand slid up my arm. "You're not gonna fight that lunatic. We'll find another way." He touched the side of my forehead, where a few flakes of blood were clinging to my hair. The reminder was clear. Astrid had crushed me like a bug without even breaking a sweat. I'd have to be insane to take her on again. "I have news for you, Ms. Ellie," he added. "You'll have to get through me first."

I didn't have the heart to tell him exactly how easy that would be. I knew, thanks to the voice in my head that seemed to be constantly tabulating people's physical weaknesses and exactly how to exploit them. "Bullying me might work for Graham, but this isn't up to you," I told him. "We're going after her."

"No."

Ordinarily, the raw anger on his face might have made me think twice, but there was no backing down now. So I matched his glare, flame for flame. It would take more than one stubborn boy to hold me back.

We stood like that for what felt like a year, locked in a silent battle of wills that each of us was determined to win.

Until finally I did.

"Fine," Tuck muttered. "We'll go after her, but no fighting. And I mean it. At the first sign of trouble, I'll drag you out of there. No matter how tough you think you are now, you wouldn't hurt me."

Of course he was right, but I wasn't going to admit it.

"We find Astrid and follow her," he said. "And hope she leads us to Graham."

9

Once we hit the freeway, it was almost a hundred miles to Bergen. Tuck drove, making impressive time along the winding, unfamiliar mountain roads.

When we reached the outskirts of the city, it was past two in the morning. Downtown Bergen was built around a square harbor, flanked by old clapboard row houses that tipped slightly to the right, in unison, like a group of old, drunken men propping one another up for the long walk home. Although they were once family homes, they'd long since been converted into tourist shops and expensive restaurants. The sidewalks along the front, skirting the harbor, were lined with café tables and benches, giving it an open Parisian feel. The Bergen castle, a medieval fortress on the hill overlooking the town, was a dark shadow against the glow of the approaching sunrise on the horizon.

Even though it was later than late, the bars along the harbor were in full swing when we turned onto the waterfront drive. Each café had an enclosure of tables in front, with people sitting outside, drinking and smoking. It was so alive and vibrant after the solitude of Skavøpoll that, for a moment, I let myself forget why we were really there. I was caught up in the excitement of being in a city again.

Tuck drove slowly through the narrow cobblestone streets until he found a parking spot across from a church—just a few blocks from the center of the action. He'd always had ridiculous parking karma. That counted for a lot in LA.

As I closed my eyes, silently praying I hadn't led us dangerously astray, I suddenly knew Astrid was close. I could feel her signature vibration, along with the jittery anticipation I was beginning to recognize when danger drew near. Accompanied by the knowledge that I was ready and able to do something about it.

We hadn't made it more than a few blocks when Tuck grabbed my arm. "You remember our deal, right?" he asked. "We aren't fighting Astrid, we're following her. You've got your determined face on. And I know how you get."

"How do I get?" I demanded, sidestepping his question. Tuck was way too perceptive, given the direction my thoughts had been heading.

"Determined," he said. "Which is usually a little bit hot. But not tonight. Just—just cool those engines, okay? I don't want anything to happen to you." His fingers looped through mine.

The way my stomach flopped right then should have been from Tuck. In any ordinary world, it would have been. But instead it was the jolt of Astrid's presence slamming into my consciousness. An image flashed through my mind. A street sign. A name. It was a signal, coordinating whatever mission she was about to initiate. I squeezed Tuck's hand and tugged him into a run. We were catapulted into a dizzying race through the tangled streets of the town. Even though I barely knew my way around Bergen, something was pulling me forward, around one corner, up through an alley, then down another side street.

We ran until I knew Astrid was so close, I should be able to see her.

A shrill screech pierced the night, followed by the rumble of the loudest engine I'd ever heard outside of an airplane. Something big was moving toward us—fast. A massive Range Rover rounded the corner an instant later, followed by the shriek of rubber tires skidding across slick pavement.

It roared down the street, brushing a row of parked cars and setting off a symphony of car alarms. It didn't even slow to acknowledge the damage it had done.

I'd recognized the SUV in half a heartbeat. I knew I'd see it in my nightmares for years to come. Graham had disappeared into its backseat. Maybe it wasn't too late to stop Astrid from taking him to Valhalla that night.

Tuck grabbed my arm and pulled me down the street in pursuit. In my shock, I'd frozen and was standing stock-still on the sidewalk, staring after the disappearing taillights.

"C'mon," Tuck urged. "Some warrior you're shaping up to

be. Do I need to carry you?" He gave my arm one more tug—just enough to shift me into gear. I took off after him, running down the sidewalk and dodging the stragglers wandering home from the clubs. We rounded the corner as the Range Rover skidded to a stop in front of a crowded bar, leaving a trail of shredded rubber. It parked right under a sign that showed a car with a line through it. Woe to any tow truck that dared to enforce the law that night.

The passenger door opened and a booted foot emerged, followed by a long, slender leg. My heart pounded in my ears as I watched Astrid descend, her eyes never leaving the door of the bar. She had the bored, apathetic look of a supermodel forced to endure yet another catwalk. This time, she'd traded in her Ugg catsuit for jeans and a tissue-thin tank top with a long, red scarf looped once around her neck. The ends floated through the air behind her like plumes of poisonous smoke.

Only her boots hadn't been exchanged for more modern counterparts—she wore the same uncured leather knee-highs trimmed with white fur and crisscrossed up the front with thick laces. The kind of boots you wore in case you needed to stomp on someone's face, and from the way the night was going, that face would most likely be mine.

She was followed by a Valkyrie I'd never seen before.

Heads turned, one by one, until everyone at the outside tables was watching Astrid's approach. I noticed more than one glassy, vacant stare that had nothing to do with a night of drinking.

The thumping bass swelled as she opened the door and

disappeared inside, leaving behind confused and groggy bystanders who were trying to puzzle out what had just happened.

I looked back, expecting to see Tuck similarly stunned. Instead he watched me with a self-satisfied smirk on his face. As usual, all arrogance.

"You're okay," I said. "At least we know that necklace works."

"Maybe," he said. "But I was thinking about what happened in the bar when you called out my name. It's a mental game, really. Astrid kinda tugs at my mind. Some weird impulse makes me want to look at her—it's begging me to. But when I look at you, it goes away. You're more important to me than she is."

I thought about that for a second. While it made sense, something didn't quite fit. "I'm more important to Graham too, but I couldn't wake him up, no matter how hard I tried."

Tuck's eyes were wary, like he either didn't know the answer or didn't want to tell me. Then he shrugged, trying to make what he said next seem casual. "Because I think the power—the hypnotic power has its roots in desire," he said softly.

The words sank in with a weight my chest couldn't support. "Oh," I said, wondering how he could just stand there and turn my universe upside down so casually. Like it was no big deal.

But then I thought about desire, about what that word really meant. Especially since he'd been known to spread his desire around a little too liberally. Ultimately, what he'd just said was no more significant than the rest of Tuck's flirting. And it too wasn't enough. With Tuck and me, it had to be all or nothing.

Close on the heels of that realization was a stab of self-reproach. I couldn't afford to waste precious seconds plumbing the depths, or maybe the kiddie pool, of Tuck's feelings for me. Graham was in danger, and nothing else could matter.

"Go get the car, and I'll make sure they don't get away," I said. "They work fast, and we can't lose them—not tonight."

"You think I'm gonna just leave you standing here on this corner? Alone?"

"Yes."

"That was a rhetorical question," he told me. "You go get the car, and I'll stay here."

He was being ridiculous. The street was packed with people. As we stood there, frowning at each other, a group of older guys walked by, singing something in wobbly German. I didn't need to recognize the song to know they were off-key.

"Tuck," I said. "I can take care of myself. Really. Besides, what if they try to leave and you get all weird and hypnotized or something? This is the only way. Go."

"You don't move one millimeter," he said. "Stay right here." After one last scowl at me, intended to show disapproval but really just reminding me that pretty much nothing could mar those features, he sighed and started running down the street in the direction of the car. I watched his retreating back anxiously, particularly when three drunk-looking guys slowed, two of them eyeing me and whispering to each other.

It was the last thing I needed.

Luckily, instinct kicked in. "Don't even think about it," I said in Norwegian.

The boys stared at me openmouthed, their eyes switching

instantly to filmy white. "Go," I added, shooing them with my hand. They instantly obeyed, walking away slowly with strange, dazed expressions on their faces.

The edge of power had saturated my voice at my command. I'd barely had to think about it. For the first time, I felt in control of it. It didn't hurt that once again I'd slipped so seamlessly into another language.

I was intoxicated by the power I felt then. Maybe I really was invincible. What had happened earlier with Astrid had to be a fluke. I'd just needed to get my sea legs. Because the power coursing through my veins was undeniable, begging me to use more if it. To indulge. Promising that the more I tapped into my Valkyrie nature, the more I stretched myself, the stronger I'd grow. And it was so overwhelming, I was pretty sure it would explode out of me if I didn't do *something*—anything but sitting at the curb waiting for Tuck like a cocker spaniel.

I crossed the street, my new confidence howling through my veins. It was so all-consuming, so primal, that I never paused to question it. I just walked right up to the Range Rover and pressed my face against the window, not caring if the whole Valkyrie army was inside waiting for me. But the Range Rover was empty. Graham was nowhere to be seen. They must have put him somewhere else while they returned for a second helping of boys.

I tried to slip past the outdoor tables unnoticed, but conversations faded into whispers as I passed by. It was a strange feeling to be watched so intently—I couldn't bring myself to meet anyone's eyes, preferring not to know if they were milky white. It wasn't like I'd meant to do anything wrong.

Inside the bar, the music was so loud it threw me off balance, as did the darkness after the well-lit streets. A few faces turned toward me as I lingered in the open doorway of the bar, but other than that, no one inside took particular notice of me. The room was narrow and divided in half by the long, skinny bar along one wall. It was full to capacity, with everyone pressed shoulder to shoulder, except for a small clearing where three girls slithered to the music.

I pushed through to the counter and slid into a narrow space between the back of a tall brown-haired man and the wall. From there, I could surreptitiously scan the room for Astrid. There was no sign of her. I leaned on my elbow, trying to look casual while watching and waiting.

A champagne flute appeared at my elbow.

"It's on the house," a low voice quipped. I looked up, startled, into Loki's liquid green eyes. Even though the face was unfamiliar, I knew it was him behind the bar, dressed in a black, well-tailored shirt and slacks. "Did you miss me?" As I stared, his burly bartender's mug melted into a face that was reminiscent of Tuck's, even though the features never quite settled into place. I reminded myself that he was a shape-shifter and was using that ability to reel me in like a bigmouth bass. That made it easier to look at him without getting tangled up in his impersonation of my favorite smile.

"Go ahead," he said, nudging the flute closer across the bar. "It will help you relax. I've never met such an uptight Valkyrie."

"Relax?" I had to shout to be heard over the music. "You

can't threaten to kill my brother and act like we're friends meeting for a drink. We're not. If we were, you'd tell me how to find Odin and get to Valhalla."

The brown-haired man in front of me turned and stared, both eyebrows raised so high they disappeared underneath his bangs.

Loki chuckled and put one finger under my chin. "That wasn't your line, pet. I was hoping we'd end this one scene, at least, on a happy note." His soft voice carried perfectly, even in that noisy place. "I wish you'd try to be appreciative. After all, we're going to be such great friends. Now take a sip and thank me. Bonus points if you lean forward and look adoringly into my eyes."

"This isn't a game or a movie. It's my life, and it's real to me," I said. "I'm searching for Graham. I'm not here to entertain you."

"Yet you're managing both so competently," he said. "Quite a fortuitous side effect—winning so much of my attention. But I shouldn't keep you, dearest. You're about to have your hands full. I can't wait to see how you'll handle what's next."

Something over my shoulder caught his attention as he took two steps away, shifting back into the bartender's sour face. He took a drink order from a woman down the bar who didn't seem to notice that his nose was still adjusting itself as he poured her a beer.

I had nothing to lose, so I lifted the glass to my lips and drained it in one long swallow. As the liquid hit my throat, it left a trail of burning fire that ripped through my veins. I thought my heart would explode from the heat. It was filling me with strength. It took my new, heightened senses and catapulted them into the stratosphere. I could hear the quietest whisper, train my ears on each individual conversation in the room or listen to them all at once. I could see every particle of dust floating through the air and taste the cologne of the Eurotrash man across the bar.

But somehow, in the midst of all my amazing new observations, I failed to notice the stormy-faced boy plowing through the crowd toward me—until he grabbed me by the elbow and whipped me around to face him.

"Do you have any idea how freaked out I was when I came back and you were gone?" Tuck demanded. "And here you are, drinking champagne like everything's just fine!"

I was about to apologize. After all, he certainly had a point. But fate cut me off. There was an abrupt, tangible shift in the room. Something was about to happen. The something I'd been waiting for. Astrid was approaching. I could feel the energy that surrounded her snapping at the periphery of my mind. The air was electric with anticipation and the sweet, tantalizing smell of impending danger. On reflex, my muscles tensed, prepared and eager to face whatever was about to happen.

"Get behind me and look down at the bar," I said. "Whatever you do, don't look up until it's all over."

"Until what's all over?"

"The next abduction," I whispered. "They're coming."

Astrid stalked out of the back of the bar, followed by a tall brunette Valkyrie. The door they slammed behind themselves was painted black to blend in to the walls, so I'd missed it altogether. From the quick glimpse I caught of a dartboard and pool table, it must have led to a game room.

Two boys were a half step behind, with opaque eyes and faces wiped clean of all traces of personality. The crowd parted slowly at their approach, backing away without really understanding why. She paused in front of a broad-shouldered, baby-faced boy sitting on a bar stool. He rose immediately, and Astrid gave him a quick once-over. She must have liked what she saw, because seconds later she turned and led her captives toward the door. Without needing instructions, the new boy fell in line with the other two.

My heart tried to dig its way out of my chest as she reached the door. I couldn't afford to let her out of my sight again. I couldn't let this chance pass me by. The violent voice was back and screaming in my ear, drowning out all other thoughts. Including my promise to Tuck and the memory of the bone-crunching blows Astrid had dealt me mere hours ago.

Tuck's fingers scrambled to find a hold on my arm, but I pushed away, cutting through the crowd and weaving between the motionless bodies of the catatonic crowd. The room was as still as a cemetery. All eyes followed Astrid and the three boys. She opened the door, one booted foot settling on the pavement outside.

"Astrid." The harsh sound of my own voice surprised me. And caused every set of vacant, glassy eyes in the bar to shift to me. "I want my brother back."

Her eyes brushed over me without pausing, like I was no different from the rest of the faded decor. Then she took one more step forward and let the door swing silently shut behind her.

"You promised," Tuck hissed, trying to grab me.

I was too fast and way beyond being reasoned with. I would crush Astrid or die trying. Anger howled through me, fueled by the certainty that I could win this fight if I was clever and bold enough. By the time I reached the sidewalk, Astrid was halfway to her SUV, bringing the steady stream of people walking home to an abrupt standstill as she passed.

"Astrid." My voice was firm, cold. Just like hers. "Stop running away from me." Whatever was in that champagne Loki had given me was still working its magical way through my veins. It was the only explanation for my reckless behavior. The way I'd surrendered all control to the voice in my head that was roaring for this fight.

Because then I added, "Coward."

Astrid went rigid. As she turned, her posture changed and she crouched lower on the balls of her feet. She was coiled for action by the time she faced me. "You should have settled for trying to follow me. That, at least, wasn't worth my time to acknowledge." Her lips curled into a contemptuous sneer. Ironically, it made her even more beautiful.

Her words settled in the pit my stomach like a twenty-ton anchor. Tuck and I weren't nearly as sneaky as we'd imagined. But at least that made me feel marginally less guilty about breaking my promise to Tuck—it wasn't like we had stood a legitimate chance of secretly following her to Graham if she'd known we were there. It was up to me to do something before Astrid disappeared again. By the time Tuck exploded out the door, I was prowling closer, trying to get Astrid within arm's reach in case she started to slip away. The people on the sidewalk had stopped walking and had circled around, like we were a pair of street performers warming up for our big juggling act.

"Go," she snapped at her companion, motioning her and the three boys toward the car.

Astrid's voice was low and soothing when she turned back toward me, catching me off guard. "Why fight what you are, Elsa? You're a Valkyrie. You belong with me. Maybe if you made yourself useful, Odin would spare Hilda. He's not incapable of mercy."

It took an enormous amount of willpower not to react to her words. Knowing that my grandmother was definitely in Odin's hands really didn't change anything. Except at least now I knew my grandmother was still alive. "I'm okay with the Valkyrie part," I said. "But as far as joining *you*, thanks, but I'd rather die."

"Yes, that *is* the other option," Astrid replied. For the first time, her lovely features twisted into something less than runway ready. I had the fleeting impression I'd offended her. "But something tells me you'll change your mind when you understand exactly how painful that prospect can be."

"I want my brother back," I said, even though I knew this wouldn't be over until my grandmother was safe too and we'd stopped Odin's plans altogether. "I don't want to fight you, but I will if I have to."

"You have no idea who you're playing with."

Even though the look on her face should have chilled me to the bone, I stood my ground. "Then I guess you'll have to show me."

Astrid sighed as if she almost regretted what she was about to do. Maybe crushing skulls was getting old. But her hesitation lasted only an instant. The cold, efficient look in her eyes was back, warning me she was about to strike. I took a step away, but Astrid was far faster than I would have imagined possible. In a flash, she was behind me, her arm coiled around my neck like a noose.

"Swear loyalty to me and I'll spare you," she whispered in my ear as my throat closed under the pressure of her forearm.

While part of me wanted to use my last remaining breath to say anything that would make that arm go away, the voice in the back of my head told me that Valkyries can't break their word. Once promised, my loyalty couldn't just be taken back like a borrowed sweater. I'd never be able to rescue Graham and Grandmother if Astrid had that kind of power over me.

I twisted, desperate for just one sip of air, but Astrid was too strong. My field of vision narrowed. I was on the verge of passing out, but her grasp on me abruptly loosened as she pivoted to face something behind her. Tuck. He managed to shift out of the way an instant before Astrid's blow would have crushed his rib cage like a soda can. Instead, it glanced off his shoulder, sending him crashing to the ground.

With a flick of her wrist, a knife appeared in Astrid's hand. I struggled until my muscles ached from the effort but still couldn't gain even an inch of wiggle room. But the knife wasn't intended for me. As Tuck pushed to his feet, Astrid plunged the knife downward toward Tuck and, without so much as scratching his skin, sliced the chain of Graham's necklace. It slithered to the ground at her feet.

"Another one?" she snarled, grinding the metal disk under her heel. "Hilda certainly has been busy." When she took a step back, the necklace was a single, flat piece of crushed metal. The raised symbols that had adorned the surface had been replaced with tread marks from her boot. "You'll have to do better than that."

So much for the one thing we had to keep Tuck safe—other than me. And given how this showdown with Astrid was going, that didn't bode well for either of us.

The knife was still in Astrid's hand, and who knew what she intended to do with it next? I had to get enough room to maneuver and at least attempt to defend myself. I grabbed the low metal fence separating the bar's outside seating from the sidewalk and pulled myself toward it, my fingers slipping and scrambling for a hold. It was just enough leverage to pull me out of Astrid's grip. The crash as I slammed into the railing sent the people at the tables scattering. It clearly wasn't every day you saw an all-out brawl on the streets of Bergen.

I filled my screaming lungs with one long gulp of air just as Astrid's fingers dug back into my shoulder and wrenched me away. As I looked up, searching the crowd of spectators for a sympathetic face, Loki's green eyes were waiting for me. He was lounging in a chair, tipped up on the back two legs, an amused smile on his lips.

I grabbed the back of a flimsy aluminum chair and lifted it over the railing. As Astrid pulled me back into a vise grip, I swung the chair as hard as I could, hitting her dead-on. The chair crumpled on impact, as did my last remaining shred of courage.

"Poor little Elsa." Loki's voice seemed to come from all around us. "Hilda will be disappointed if you die like this, with so little fanfare."

"Thanks for your concern." I managed the sarcasm despite the searing pain as Astrid twisted my arm behind my back at a physically impossible angle.

Tuck was unsuccessfully trying to pry me free of Astrid's hold, but she just yanked my arm back harder then ever, until any move I made sent a wave of pure agony down my spine.

With no place left to turn, I caught Loki's eye, begging for help.

In the blandest possible voice, he said, "Astrid, darling, let her go. Pick on someone your own size."

The pain stopped instantly.

"I was hoping that wasn't really you," Astrid growled. "What are *you* doing here?"

"Babysitting," Loki drawled. "Hilda is back. It sparked my curiosity. And then Ellie ignited it completely. With a wild story about Valkyries abducting her brother. Alive. Now I'm quite caught up in the tragedy. I'm determined to help her find him, and Hilda, who seems to have disappeared again—right after coming out of hiding."

"I suppose you gave her mead—some liquid over-confidence?" Astrid said disdainfully. "You sent a sixteen-year-old girl after Odin because you're too scared to face him yourself." She looked right at me. "We give mead to soldiers sent on suicide missions."

I'd known Loki wasn't exactly on my side, but it was beginning to seem like he was my flat-out enemy.

Loki brushed Astrid's comment aside. "That hurts, Astrid. Everything I do is for Ellie's own good. I won't sleep a wink until I see her smile again." He set his hands on the railing and vaulted over. Then he approached Astrid until he was so close, I thought they might kiss. "We have a bit of a problem on our hands, don't we? You've been breaking the rules." As he spoke, he produced a roll of parchment from thin air.

"I don't know what you're talking about," Astrid snapped. But the vehemence of her reaction just made her fear that much more transparent. Never in my life had I thought I'd see one of the beautiful bobsled girls looking less than certain. She released my arm, and Tuck was there in an instant, hauling me out of her reach.

"Yes, you do." Loki's eyes never left Astrid's face. The tension in the air between them stretched so taut that I almost expected an audible snap when Loki finally broke it. "And I'll tell you what you're going to do about it—that is, if you want to save yourself. Not everyone is as forgiving as I can be. Not all the gods have been sleeping away the centuries like Odin. Apathetic as they may seem about the state of the modern world, imagine what would happen if I sounded the alarm in Midgaard. Odin's up to the same old tricks."

"What's your price, Loki?" Astrid forced the words out from between clenched teeth. "Even if Elsa didn't have such foresight, I'm not agreeing to anything unless you tell me all the terms."

"But you will, Astrid," Loki said, stretching. "Because your trust is a condition of my silence. When the time comes, rest assured that you'll have no choice but to give me what I want. Until then, your secret is safe with me."

Astrid actually looked startled as she eyed Loki. She growled low in her throat. "Cleverness won't mend a broken neck."

"Just like violence doesn't resolve conflict," Loki said. "It only begets more violence. It's unfortunate for you that the same isn't true of cleverness." Loki was the only one who laughed at his joke. "Odin may still delude himself," Loki drawled. "But I think you see the nuances of this modern world. You understand that true peace comes through negotiation. Compromise. And don't you worry, we'll reach one."

"Enough." Astrid made an impatient gesture with one hand before taking two long strides toward her car. "Summon all of Midgaard, for all I care. I'll give them a fight they'll never forget."

"Stop!" I said, trying to replicate her cold-blooded commands as she strode away. "I'm not letting you out of here until you give me my brother back."

"Let it go, Elsa." Loki groaned like it was a rerun he'd seen a thousand times. "Live to fight another day. It's all going according to our plan."

"No." I spat the word. Tuck reached out and wrapped one arm around my waist, in a silent reminder that this time he was prepared to stop me from fighting. "I don't know whose side you're on, Loki, or what crazy plan you're talking about. I can't let her get away while Graham is missing. I won't let Odin kidnap innocent boys and lead them to their deaths."

Astrid turned. Ice-blue eyes bored into mine. There was a well of infinite bitterness beneath her beautiful surface. "If I can't stop Odin, then you don't stand a chance."

Her reply was unexpected enough to stop me in my tracks—just long enough for her to reach the Range Rover, where the tall brunette Valkyrie and the three boys who had followed her out of the bar were still waiting.

"At least I'm trying," I said. "What you're doing is wrong. Now I know you realize it too. In my book, that's even more inexcusable."

The brunette studied me, open curiosity in her eyes.

Astrid scanned the crowd that had gathered to watch my pathetic showdown, letting her gaze wash over each and every face.

"Stop them," she said to no one in particular.

I surged after her, struggling out of Tuck's hold just as we were hit from the side by a burly boy in a university sweatshirt. He lifted me off the ground, crushing me against his ribs. Tuck reached for me but was grabbed from behind in a wrestler's grapple hold. The crowd of spectators had formed a hostile wall three bodies thick, trapping us while Astrid made her leisurely escape.

I broke free of the boy's arms only to be grabbed around the legs by two girls, while a third pinned my arms against my sides, and they lifted me, kicking and twisting. Astrid spared us one last backward glance. Her white teeth flashed, as if she found our situation particularly amusing. Then she climbed into the driver's seat and the Range Rover peeled away through the city streets, sending pedestrians scampering like mice as she accelerated through a crosswalk.

Given that I hated to use my full strength on these not-so-innocent bystanders, our predicament was doubly frustrating, but I shook my arms free while only bloodying the lip of one of the girls. Our struggle ended the moment the Range Rover was out of sight. One minute I was kicking, trying to free my legs, and the next I was falling through the air, hitting the concrete with a thud, and rolling, cradling my arms over my head. I'd had enough skull trauma that day to last a lifetime. The three girls who'd lifted me were looking down with wide eyes, as if they couldn't quite figure out what I was doing there, sprawled at their feet.

It appeared there was a whole new dimension to Valkyrie powers that I hadn't even begun to explore. It was one thing to turn people passive and catatonic, but quite another to force them to do your dirty work.

An unwelcome face hovered above me, grinning hugely. I didn't even try to stifle a groan at the sight of him.

"Well, at least I averted that catastrophe," Loki said, bending and yanking me to my feet. "Practice some self-preservation, at least for my sake. A dead Valkyrie is useless to me."

Tuck stood over another boy, offering him a hand up. Judging by the boy's swollen, bloodied lip, Tuck must have thrown a few punches to get himself free. Now the boy was confused, staring at Tuck like he wasn't sure whether to thank him or hit him.

"*Averted* a catastrophe?" I snapped. "Would have been great if you'd stepped in earlier." I massaged my throat. I was pretty sure Astrid's arm had partially collapsed my windpipe. "Plus you let Astrid get away."

"Believe me, Astrid could have left whenever she wanted to. And that doesn't matter for our purposes," Loki said. "I hate to be the bearer of bad tidings, but you weren't exactly winning that fight."

"No thanks to you," I hissed as the rest of what he'd said registered. "What purposes?"

The people who had assembled around us at Astrid's command were now fully awake and watching us suspiciously as they tried to piece their memories together. Like we'd tricked them into attacking us.

"Loki's right," Tuck said, dusting off the back of my sweatshirt. "You promised you wouldn't do that. You can't fight Astrid. She was crushing you."

Loki gave Tuck a smile that was somehow colder than his scowl. "You're not nearly as stupid as you look."

"So now I'm supposed to listen to Loki?" I shot back, ignoring Loki's comment completely. "Because he's got his own agenda. One that clearly doesn't include getting Graham back. You heard what he said to Astrid—he's using all of us."

"Can I help it if I'm the only one keeping my eyes on the big picture?" Loki flashed a condescending smile. "The best poker players are patient. They wait until it's a hand they know they can win."

"I'm a card in this scenario, right?" I said, seriously contemplating breaking Loki's nose.

"Would you prefer the term pawn?" he said. "I struggle to

stay abreast of what's politically correct."

"Anything other than chum is fine with me," Tuck murmured unhelpfully.

"Screw politically correct," I said, frustration threatening to overflow the confines of my self-control. "Let's focus on honest. How do I get to Valhalla? How do I get to Graham?"

"You need to be a full-blooded Valkyrie first," he said, surprising me by looking me straight in the eye and actually answering my question. "Then you can access their power. The energy that flows between them. Surely you can feel it."

"Aren't I a Valkyrie already?"

"Not until you've defeated one of your own kind. Either kill one of them or make her yield. That's the only way to enter Valhalla. Valkyries get stronger the more they fight, and this is day one, little Elsa, compared to Astrid's two thousand years. You need all the practice you can get before you face her again." His smile faded, and he took a step forward and curled one hand under my chin. "Fortunately, fate keeps throwing you test after test. Time to sharpen those talons, pet."

Loki's features shifted as he stepped backward, disappearing into the crowd. Try as I might, I couldn't latch my eyes onto him. It was the creepiest kind of camouflage. He could be anywhere. Anyone. My hand reached out, involuntarily, and found Tuck's. I knew he wouldn't appreciate this reminder of Grandmother's note. I had to defeat one of them to join them.

The people milling about had gathered into clusters of three or four and were looking less friendly by the millisecond. Angry mutters and narrow-eyed glares were an unmistakable sign that we'd outstayed our welcome. From across the street, a group of kids about Graham's age was studying us warily. Tuck took a few casual steps, as if we were just strolling slowly along the waterfront.

"They're following us," I said. It was too obvious, the way those boys had taken a step to the side all at once, mirroring us. They wanted to confront us. I could sense their building anger, mingling with fear and self-doubt.

I tried to seem disoriented too, like Tuck and I were just two more lost, confused souls, tangled up in Astrid's web. A blond boy standing in front of the group clutched a small electronic device against his chest. It looked exactly like Margit's weird transponder. A personal locator beacon. And it was blinking steadily, like the flashing lights on an airplane's wing, guiding it home.

It didn't take a genius to figure out who was on the other end of it.

"The car is ten feet up ahead," Tuck said. "When we get right behind it, I'll run to the driver's seat and you run to the other door, okay?" Out of the corner of my vision, I saw the group of boys keeping pace with us. Conferring in whispers, nudging one another into being the first to act.

"Stop!" one of them shouted, finally breaking ranks and running forward, faster than all the rest. But it was a domino effect. The others slipped into a sprint, following.

Without even thinking, I spun around. The leader was close, within five feet, so it wasn't hard to use his momentum against him. I waited until he closed the distance, then grabbed his arm and flipped him onto the hood of a parked car. My Valkyrie instincts howled for me to shove his head right through the windshield, but I pushed the urge out of my mind. He was panting hard, nostrils flared. He reminded me too much of myself moments ago, being pulverized by Astrid. The strained, determined look on his face mirrored my own desperation to find Graham.

Maybe this boy had lost someone he loved to Astrid, too.

I had him by the collar, so I looked straight into his wide brown eyes. "I'm going after them," I said, my voice firm and steady, deliberately steering clear of my tone of power. "I know who you are. Who your friends are. And what you're trying to do. And I'm your best bet if you want to accomplish it. I'm going to save my brother and all the rest of them. Now back off and let me finish what I came to do."

The boy lifted his hands in surrender, but his pupils were wild, darting around like minnows. His pulse raged beneath my fingertips. I doubted he'd processed a single word. He was useless, still cycling through the fight-or-flight instinct. I sighed and released his shirt.

"Graham is gone a few hours and suddenly you're brawling in the streets," Tuck said, pulling on my shoulder. Politely not pointing out the rest of what I'd just done. He had to notice how I struggled to control myself lately. "Now get in the car before I pick you up and carry you there."

I looked up. The boy's friends had frozen in place, watching, but at about the same time Tuck spoke, they shifted back into gear. Charging headlong at us.

"Get in the car." Tuck started to make good on his threat. But I wiggled free, diving for the passenger-side door as he jumped the curb and slid into the driver's seat. Who knew he could move that fast? The engine was running by the time I managed to haul myself into the car. Pounding footsteps echoed behind us. I glanced back as a glass bottle struck the rear windshield, sending spider veins across the window. No sooner had we locked the car doors than we were surrounded. A boy shouted in wobbly English, "You can't go until you tell us what happened—what your friend did to us."

"Sorry, dude," Tuck muttered. "But she's no friend of mine." Then he slammed his fist into the horn. The shrill blast pierced the night, and he used the distraction to whip the car up onto the curb in reverse, the only way to avoid hitting someone. Then he lurched forward, barely missing a sneakered foot. Three of the kids chased our car for six blocks, shouting things I couldn't quite catch, until Tuck's crazy driving finally shook them loose.

We drove in silence for a while, the car nosing through the deserted streets of Bergen like a shark in search of a nice fat seal. Only we were hunting predators—and they clearly weren't loitering around Bergen waiting for sunrise to give them a chance to strike again. Especially as most of the city had quieted down and gone to sleep.

"I think that's enough excitement for one night." Tuck was making a valiant effort not to sound discouraged. "We need to get some sleep. We'll figure out what to do in the morning."

"No, Tuck," I said. "We already know what we need to do. There's only one way. You heard what Loki said."

He was quiet, so quiet I knew he was preparing the winning argument. "Loki also said the more you fight, the stronger you'll get," he said. "Maybe we should make sure if it comes down to it, you can win. And I mean as a last resort. Because Loki also said you're not ready yet."

His reply was such a surprise that it took me a moment to realize we'd stopped driving. Tuck parked in front of a dimly lit hotel.

"What are we doing here?"

"Getting some sleep," he replied. "We can't just drive around all night hoping Astrid will give us a third shot at her. It's four in the morning." Without giving me a chance to protest, Tuck reached across me and pushed my car door open. "Even if we find her, it's not like we can do anything about it. Fighting her isn't exactly working. And you're in no shape for round three tonight."

I had to admit, he had a point.

Inside, an elderly clerk with beady eyes answered the bell at the front desk. "One room?" He asked, never taking his eyes off me. My cheeks were on fire—until I realized he was probably more curious about the blood on my face than the fact that I was checking into a hotel with Tucker Halloway in the middle of the night.

I nodded. "One room." The last thing I wanted was to be by myself in a strange hotel in a strange town. But at the same time, my stomach flipped as I realized how very truly alone Tuck and I would be.

The room was minuscule, but at least there were two twin

beds pressed against the walls, separated by a narrow nightstand and an old lamp. I collapsed onto the comforter, grateful for the plush feather duvet.

"How do you propose I get ready to face Astrid?" I asked, closing my eyes and savoring the feeling of my muscles uncoiling one by one.

"I have an idea, but we'll talk it through tomorrow." His voice was faraway and garbled, like he was talking underwater.

"Tell me now," I whispered, and even though I heard Tuck's voice, murmuring something important, the words were meaningless, floating past in random order. All I could think about was Graham and how fully I'd failed him.

"You're not even listening," Tuck said, his voice suddenly coming from somewhere above me. It was the only thing that penetrated the fog in my brain. Then he laughed and ran his fingers through my hair. "Just sleep, then."

The last thing I remember before lapsing into sleep was Tuck sliding the blanket out from underneath my legs and tucking it securely around me. It might have been just wishful thinking, but I thought I felt something brush my lips ever so lightly before sleep pulled me under for good.

10

When I opened my eyes the next morning, Tuck was sound asleep in the other bed. He was sprawled on top of the blankets with both feet hanging over the edge. I took a moment to smooth down my hair in the mirror. It was a wasted effort, but at least I looked marginally less mangled. I reached over and poked Tuck in the ribs. After three failed attempts to wake him like that, I shoved his shoulder—hard.

He sat up at once, rubbing his eyes with the back of his hand. If I needed any reminder that Tuck was quite possibly the best-looking guy on the planet, it was delivered on a silver platter when he smiled at me. It had my blood racing faster than any double espresso ever could. It wasn't a bad way to wake up.

"Ready to start training?" he asked.

"This isn't soccer camp, Tuck," I said. "Remember? Graham is missing. We've got less than twenty-four hours to find him."

"That's exactly what we'll be training for," he said. "Did I ever tell you that my dad didn't just take me fishing? I mean, I hated hunting. Never could bring myself to kill anything. But I'm a pretty awesome shot."

My jaw fell slack at that. Tucker Halloway in a hunting jacket, tiptoeing through the forest. It was either hilarious or a little bit hot. Even to a city girl like me.

"And you think you can teach me?" I said slowly. "So that I'll be able to shoot one of the Valkyries in cold blood?"

"Well, let's just see what happens—what I can teach you. You might not necessarily have to kill anyone. You just have to get Astrid to surrender, remember? From what I've seen of your new and improved reflexes, I think we can get pretty far in a few hours. Then it's happy hunting. I hear Valkyrie is in season."

IN LESS THAN an hour Tucker and I were standing in a worndown, deserted park just outside of Bergen. Weeds surrounded the soccer nets at either end of the field, threatening to devour them. An empty brown paper bag tumbled slowly across the overgrown grass, coaxed along by a light breeze. A stray, half-deflated soccer ball was the only sign the field had ever been put to use.

Tuck walked into the middle of the soccer field and pulled a handgun from the waistband of his jeans.

"Where did you get that?" I wished my voice hadn't squeaked.

"Hilda's house," he answered, not meeting my eyes. "I didn't want to freak you out. Thought I'd need to be able to protect us. Of course, that was before I figured out it would probably be the other way around." He gave me a sheepish smile. "Here," Tuck said, motioning me closer. "Hold it like this." He pulled me against his side, propping one arm against my rib cage as he guided my finger around the trigger. "Then just imagine it's an extension of your index finger as you guide it toward a target and pull."

A disturbing rush of exhilaration shimmied its way down my spine. Not just because Tucker Halloway was so close I could feel his heart beating in every single one of my vertebrae. It was also the gun, the force of the bullet fleeing the chamber. Feeding the stream of violence bubbling within me until it was threatening to overflow.

We spent the whole morning at the park, and I was amazed at how much stronger I felt after just a few hours of practice. It was getting clearer and clearer that whatever I was, I was built to crush any opponent. More than once, I caught Tuck watching me out of the corner of his eye, a weird smile that could have been either pride or admiration or a bit of both.

When the sun approached the middle of the sky, we drove back into downtown Bergen. We wound through the narrow cobblestone streets until we stumbled across a row of sidewalk cafés. Once I'd stopped moving long enough to catch my breath, I realized I was starving. We parked in front of a café, and while I grabbed an outdoor table, Tuck disappeared inside to order sandwiches.

When he walked back out to join me, Tucker was smiling like the Cheshire cat. He slid a newspaper across the table. The *Bergen Tidende*. It was folded in half to highlight the lead article.

"Look." He stood right behind me as he pointed at a photo of four uniformed soldiers standing in a row, one balancing a soccer ball in his hand. A shiny, important-looking medal was pinned to his chest.

"Seems the military has a soccer team. Playing a match at one against the local team." He pointed at the bolded text at the end of the article.

"What, so now you read Norwegian?" I demanded, even as I realized it wouldn't be that hard to guess what was going on, given the photograph of the Bergen stadium directly underneath.

"Course not." He smirked. "But I ran into a charming waitress who does."

He was trying to get under my skin, so I carefully schooled my face into a neutral expression.

"It would seem like a logical target for Astrid," I murmured. "Unless you're biased because you wanna watch a soccer game?" I looked up. Tuck grinned down at me, his face closer than I expected.

"Side perks never hurt."

"It's not the worst idea in the world," I said slowly.

"Tough crowd," he said. "I can't wait to hear *your* plan. Must be so much better. Here I thought you'd throw yourself into my arms in gratitude."

I hoped he couldn't tell how very appealing that option sounded just then, especially when they were draped so close along the back of my chair. Instead I picked a sugar packet and spun it on the table. "It's a great idea," I said, feeling a tingle of curiosity about these soccer stars that I hoped came from the Valkyrie part of me. My common link to Astrid. It was still hard for me to sort out which of my thoughts still belonged to me and which part was Valkyrie.

"See, it's not so bad admitting you're wrong." He reached across the table and put his hand over mine, bringing my fidgeting to an abrupt end. "And you don't even have to thank me—I'm happy do all that tricky thinking for both of us." Judging by his smirk, the words were intended to annoy me every bit as much as they did. But for some reason they also gave me the same thrill as when he touched my hand. It was as if the sweet side he'd been showing me in flashes and glimpses wasn't a game but rather Tucker unearthing one more layer to what we already had. A layer that in no way meant there wasn't room for me to smile and tease him right back

"Since most of your ideas end in potential felonies, I think I'll do my own thinking, thank you."

Tuck's answering smile was excruciatingly adorable. "There's my Ells. Feel better now that you've knocked me around?" He shoved my plate closer. "Now eat. If we run into Astrid again, we both need to be ready."

THE PARKING LOT outside the soccer stadium was packed. Families and groups of kids were arriving in cars and buses, on foot, and piled onto the handlebars or luggage racks of bicycles. I watched as a father lifted a young girl up onto his shoulders, just like my dad used to do with me. Two boys ran past our car, shrieking.

After circling the lot, Tuck found a spot just outside the main doors. It blocked a service entrance, making me question its legitimacy, but I decided to overlook this typically Tuckish approach to parking. I just crossed my fingers that we wouldn't get towed.

Inside, the arena was smaller than I'd expected, with only one tier of seats and a narrow ribbon of field along the outside for the benches. It was a far cry from Dodger Stadium back home. I went to the railing and looked down at the players scattered around the goal, warming up. Fans pushed past, making their way between the loiterers in the aisles toward their seats. Tuck and I scanned each and every face, hypervigilant for any sign of Valkyrie activity.

Thirty minutes into the first half, I started to worry we were wasting our precious time. It was almost two in the afternoon, and who knew what Loki was planning at dawn the next morning if we didn't find a way to rescue Graham and the others. Still, I hung in there, praying our risk would pay off. I couldn't be the only one who felt the allure of those players, how very right they would be for Astrid's purposes. Still, my watch was burning on my wrist as minutes fused into an hour—an hour we'd lost forever. An hour that took me that much farther away from Graham.

A strange heat crept up the back of my neck, the way it does when you know you're being watched. Only this time I recognized the feeling at once. It was the approach of one of us, the bond we shared tugging us closer. Astrid was drawing near.

Before I could warn him, Tuck inhaled sharply at my side and his hand curled around my wrist. "Don't forget your promise," he said. "No fighting. We follow her."

I caught a flash of brilliant blond, shining like a beacon. A tall, graceful someone was cutting a determined path toward the field. My eyes chased that bombshell head, trying to catch a glimpse of the face half concealed by artfully tousled locks. I didn't get my chance until Astrid had reached the edge of the field right by the army team's bench. She leaned over the railing, gazing down on the players below. Her hair dropped around her face like a curtain falling at the end of a play.

The moment she shifted closer, the atmosphere around the field changed. It felt sluggish, like we were moving through water, even though what was about to happen would be fast as a lightning strike. The players noticed first. I watched, fascinated, as the captain of the army team, a tall, muscular boy, stopped midfield and turned toward Astrid's spot along the railing. He was the star of the game, having scored three goals and made it look all too easy. Like the other team's goalie wasn't even there. His skill was infectious. Everywhere he went on the field, the rest of the team played better, rising to his high standards.

He was the heart of his team, but the boy abandoned the game without a backward glance. He walked toward Astrid, coming to a stop at the base of the wall. Astrid's long blond hair teased the tops of his shoulders as he reached up, wrapped his fingers over the edge of the wall, and pulled himself up to her level. He kicked one leg over the railing and in the blink of an eye was in the stands, at her side.

It was so daring, so bold compared to anything she'd done before, that I was frozen in place. Long gone were the days of making off with her victims in the night. Astrid had taken the stakes to a whole new level. I thought about the television crews I'd noted earlier, cameras trained on the field and stands. Sure, it was just a local broadcast, but it wouldn't stay that way for long. This was live-action footage. Irrefutable proof to validate the rumors and whispers flowing across the region.

Murmurs rippled through the stands—but just in the sections that were out of Astrid's range. Those closer had the vague, apathetic stare of a Valkyrie victim.

The grumbling in the stands turned to angry jeers as tense seconds ticked past. But it was too late. The captain of the team was already well beyond their reach. Astrid took the boy's hand. There was something tender about that small gesture that shocked me to the core.

The crowd parted, making way for them to pass. Heads turned, tracking their every move as they walked toward the stairs. Tuck and I slipped out of our seats. I breathed deeply, reining in the violent voice rattling the door of its cage, begging me to challenge her on the spot. Last time had taught me the dangers of getting a crowd involved—there was no way I could take on a stadium full of people. Someone would definitely get hurt.

"C'mon," I said, pulling Tuck behind me as we followed at a distance. I heaved a sigh of relief that Tuck had yet again avoided getting caught up in Astrid's spell, even without Graham's necklace. "Before people start to panic and get in our way."

No sooner had the words left my lips than a commotion erupted in the stands. Someone was jostling and pushing their way through the aisles in the back, up where the spectators were far enough away to be unaffected by Astrid and were still confused and shouting for the game to carry on.

A man leaped up on the brick wall framing the stairs and started jogging along the top, balancing precariously. Falling the wrong way meant a fifty-foot drop. But he reached the base of the stands nearest me in moments and jumped to the ground—just as two more men heaved themselves up onto the wall, following him and shouting for Astrid to stop.

Tuck's hand curled around my elbow, pulling me along as he slipped through the crowd, following Astrid from a distance. The second two men jumped down from the wall and pushed their way through the crowd, their eyes glued to Astrid's retreating back as she parted the crowd like the Red Sea. As the first man drew level with us, he pulled a transponder out of his pocket. While trying to activate it, he bumped into a girl about my age who stood frozen in the middle of the aisle. I assumed the girl was caught in Astrid's spell . . . until she spun and shoved him with a strength that made no sense coming from her spindly arms. Then she turned to face me. Forest-green eyes met mine, and pink glossed lips curled into Loki's smile.

But I didn't have time to pause and wonder what Loki was doing here—the first vigilante man was falling backward. The railing at his back wouldn't be enough to counteract his momentum. I could already picture how he'd flip over it and plummet down onto the concrete at the bottom of the stairwell. I caught his shoulder just in time, saving him from cracking his head open.

As I set him back onto his feet, his face contorted in terror. The moment he caught his balance, he lashed out at the side of my head with his fist in a frantic, poorly aimed blow that I blocked with one hand. He didn't even care that I'd just saved him. He was too busy scrambling away from me. I picked up the transponder.

And I turned it on.

It blinked away happily, but the man still refused to take it from my hand. He shook his head again and again, like he could shake the memory of what had just happened right out his ear.

"Leave him," Tuck said. "Ungrateful asshole."

He didn't need to tell me twice. I dropped the transponder on the ground at the man's feet and slipped after Tuck, moving slowly to make sure Astrid didn't see us following.

As soon as Astrid hit the pavement outside the stadium, the Range Rover appeared. It careened carelessly through the rows of haphazardly parked cars and slid to a stop just inches shy of Astrid and the soccer star. Astrid approached the driver's side, which—amazingly—was empty.

I pulled Tuck behind a narrow pillar inside the stadium door as Astrid turned. I'd known it was about to happen. I could sense the current radiating from her, the connection to her thoughts. It was snapping at the edges of my mind, trying to pull me in. She had to know where I was too. Presumably that meant I didn't pose enough of a threat for her to care.

The men who'd also been chasing her raced past us and exploded out the door, weapons drawn. Astrid shoved the soccer star behind her. I had the oddest impression that she was more concerned about the boy's safety than about keeping her quarry. If I could tell these men were unskilled with firearms, Astrid could too.

She crossed her arms and stood there for a long moment. It was a silent exchange, consisting only of Astrid tipping her head to the side. The men crouched to set their guns on the ground in front of them and kicked them away across the sidewalk. When they straightened, their eyes were vacant and glassy.

Astrid gave a sad smile, as if disappointed it had been so easy. Her eyes searched the walls and doors of the stadium, looking for anyone else lurking to attack her.

"Don't even think about moving," Tuck whispered, pulling me tight against him. "No fighting. You promised. Plus if she sees us, no way she'll let us follow her."

I nodded, refusing to be distracted by how Tuck's arms curled around me, fitting into place as if carved from scratch just for me, or by every inch of his chest pressed against mine.

"Let's go," he mouthed, just as I couldn't help but wonder what he'd do if I let my arms wrap around him too.

The screech of the Range Rover's tires filled me with shame. How could I think of anything but Graham at a time like this? Tucker Halloway was a walking, talking broken heart, and I was a selfish monster.

Fortunately, Tuck's arm fell away, removing the temptation.

"Get in." Tuck was already buckled into the driver's seat by the time I scrambled around to the passenger door. The Range Rover had disappeared around a corner, but Tuck's face was tense with steely determination.

My head knocked the ceiling as he slammed the gas and the car lurched over a curb.

"Seatbelt," he said without even glancing at me.

The Range Rover was already out of sight, but when I concentrated hard, I could hear its heavily treaded tires on the pavement and smell the exhaust snaking from its tailpipe.

My new Valkyrie talents made me half bloodhound.

Tuck was driving race-car fast, weaving in between cars without really looking at them. He narrowly missed a telephone pole as he cut a corner, and the car skidded three feet to the left. It was incredible that Tuck could pick up Astrid's trail when I was still freaked out that I could. At least I had an explanation.

"How do you know where you're going?" I finally asked, gripping the seat with my fingers. Like that would make any difference if we crashed at that speed.

He was silent for a long moment, and I thought his concentration was so complete that he hadn't heard me. But finally he said, "I don't know. I just do."

Normally I wouldn't let that answer slide, but my head smacked against the window again as he accelerated onto the freeway. It was best to let him focus on the road.

As we sped past a red delivery truck, I caught my first glimpse of the Range Rover in the distance. It popped into view for a second; the massive roll bars welded to the roof made it easy to spot. We kept it in our sights, driving with a grim determination.

Both of us knew we could be headed anywhere—including right into the open arms of a trap. I, for one, was ready for anything. And I recognized Tuck's game face in his narrowed eyes and the muscle that twitched in the corner of his jaw. It was a look of lethal concentration.

Time passed in silence, punctuated by whispers whenever Astrid changed lanes or sped up, as if she would hear our voices if they drifted above the roar of the engine.

It didn't take very long to figure out we were heading back toward Skavøpoll. After everything that had happened in that town over the last few days, I was hardly eager to get within ten miles of it. And I wasn't just worried about Astrid and the gang. Kjell's friends would probably kill me on sight.

But sure enough, the Range Rover took the exit for Skavøpoll. My skin tingled with anticipation, because it couldn't be a coincidence when there were so many other exits to choose from. Astrid knew we were following her.

The massive SUV slowed to a crawl as it entered the outskirts of town.

I rolled down my window and could taste the bitter, metallic edge of fear in the air, mingled with the scent of pine needles in the forest. The streets were deserted except for one solitary mountain goat that had seized this opportunity to raid the recycling bin in front of the hardware store.

Every shop and restaurant was closed, and corrugated metal gates shielded the doors, as if Skavøpoll was bracing for a siege. Regular closing hours weren't for two hours; the lockdown had everything to do with the recent rash of disappearances.

In the center of town, the Range Rover accelerated. The trawlers and fishing sheds were a frenzy of muted colors outside my window. It was a good thing the streets were deserted, because there'd be no stopping for pedestrians at that speed.

The mountain road on the far side of town was lined with manicured grass and a low wooden fence along one side that kept livestock out of the street. But as we passed the last storefront, something strange started to happen—the world as it should have been disappeared and was replaced with a glimpse of an older forest. Dirt and shrubs materialized underneath our tires, replacing the pavement. But only for an instant before we were back on the road as I knew it.

The car window was like a television switching back and forth between two channels, these two different vistas. Another world and another road slipped into view, parallel to the path we were traveling. And Astrid's tires were planted squarely on the hidden one. We glimpsed her Range Rover in flashes as it disappeared. There was a tangible distance between the two worlds; wherever Astrid was going, I knew we couldn't follow. I could feel her slipping away

"She's still in view," Tuck said, sliding his hand over mine. "We can still catch her."

I'd assumed I was alone in this hallucination, so Tuck's words surprised me. And gave me courage—like he always did.

The pavement narrowed into what could barely be considered one full lane. I wanted to close my eyes and crawl under the seat—one wrong move would send us hurtling down into a ravine. We were hemmed in by a solid wall of rock on one side and a hundred-foot drop down the mountain on the other. The road twisted uphill so tightly, we couldn't see more than five feet of road in front of us, but we could see the free fall down the cliff to the left that awaited us if Tuck made even the smallest mistake.

Up ahead, just beyond a sharp curve, I could sense something moving toward us at a breakneck pace. The warning was still forming on my lips when a wall of water tumbled down from the side of the mountain and slammed into the side of the car. We stopped moving, wrapped in the arms of a waterfall. The onslaught was relentless, battering the car and knocking it sideways, inch by inch. Closer and closer to the edge of the road.

"Go," I shouted. "Get us out of here."

But Tuck was already doing everything he could, pumping the gas pedal, trying to rouse the car back to life. The engine stalled, flooded with water. Metal groaned as the car shifted toward the edge. It was another inch we couldn't afford to lose.

"We're trapped," I said, pushing as hard as I could against my door. It was our only exit. Even if Tuck managed to open his door, there was nothing but empty space below. We were teetering over the drop-off.

The force of the water pushed against my door, pinning it shut, but I kicked and shoved and slowly made enough room to squeeze myself through the opening. Once I had half my body outside, I pressed off from the side of the car with all of my strength, bending the door backward until the hinges snapped and it was stuck that way. I stood for a moment, stunned by my own strength.

Jaws of life, eat your heart out.

Water poured through the open door, flooding the inside. The added weight made the car tip precariously on its side, rocking toward the ravine.

Tuck was struggling to pull himself out, so I anchored myself against the side of the car with one hand and grabbed his shoulder with the other, towing him against the current. Then we dragged ourselves along, using the side of the car like a rope. We'd barely cleared the spray when the car flipped onto its side and slid slowly over the edge. It fell so silently, cushioned and carried away on the envelope of water, that I almost didn't believe my eyes. I ran to the edge and watched as my grandmother's fuel-efficient European sedan fell through the air, so graceful it was almost floating. Until it toppled three pine trees at the bottom of the ravine and sent a shattering crash echoing against the surrounding cliffs.

Tuck was standing in the middle of the road, wringing out his sweatshirt. Like that would make any difference when the rest of his clothes were every bit as sopped. "You don't give a guy much of a shot at dignity," he said as he stretched the neck of his T-shirt to reveal a row of hand-shaped bruises.

"Sorry," I said. "I guess I didn't realize my own strength. You know—adrenaline."

"Adrenaline? Don't sell yourself short. Believe me, Ells, my ego is not at all threatened." He shot me one of his private smiles. "Remember what I said about danger, all those years ago—back on the fishing boat?"

Even though my clothes were soaked through and freezing,

I felt warm at that particular memory.

"What you did back there? Hot." He shook his hair like a wet dog. "And since you've got such superhuman strength, how about a piggyback to Skavøpoll? It's gotta be ten miles. And something tells me there won't be a car along here for a while."

He was right. We were stranded on a rickety old road that looked like even the mountain goats had forsaken it.

"Can you do that?" Tuck pointed at the waterfall, since once he got started he simply couldn't stop. "Because a waterfall could do wonders for our neighborhood. Maybe when we get home you can make landscaping history."

"That wasn't Astrid. That was older magic," I said, amazed that Tuck truly could make light of anything—including a near-death experience.

My thoughts were still stuck on the way the second road seemed to hover just out of reach. It was leading someplace else, and I would wager the rush of water was one of many surprises that lay in wait if we tried to follow Astrid again. "She led us into a trap. I think this is the way to Valhalla."

Tuck's whole posture changed at that, all traces of playfulness evaporating on contact. "Let's go, then." There was urgency in his voice as he turned back in the direction we'd been heading. "This is what we've been hoping for." He glanced back at me, eyebrows furrowing in frustration when I shook my head and didn't budge.

"It's not that simple," I said. "I know the pathway is here, I just don't know how to find it. We could spend forever searching for it. Astrid's not going to appear again on this roadside with an engraved invitation—we need to go back to town to have any chance of finding her. Plus I don't think it's safe to loiter around here. I doubt the waterfall was the end of it." My limbs were still jittery; while adrenaline would readily explain it, I couldn't dismiss the possibility that there were other dangers in store for trespassers.

"You want to just leave?" Tuck demanded. "When we're so close to finding Graham?"

"We're not," I said softly. "Finding the road is one more thing I can't do unless I'm a full Valkyrie. Which means . . ."

I have to fight one of them. I finished the thought silently.

I looked up, and Tuck was watching me. Waiting for the words that had frozen on my lips. "Nothing," I said, shaking my head. "It just means we're back to square one."

Tuck's eyes hardened. He knew the second half of what I'd been about to say. Because there was only one way to follow Astrid up this road to wherever they were keeping Graham. Everything was steering me toward the same ultimate conclusion. I had to fight a Valkyrie and win. *Victory lights the road to Valhalla*, my grandmother had written. *You must beat one of us before you can join us*.

And I had every intention of doing just that.

"We should start walking," I said, forcing my tone to stay light. "And by that I mean both of us. No piggybacks for all-state athletes."

"I don't like it," he said. "There's got to be another way."

"Sorry, Tuck," I said. "I'm afraid you'll just have to walk."

"That's not what I meant," he told me, shooting a not-so-friendly look from the corner of his eye.

We lapsed into silence as we trudged down the winding road, back toward town. Oddly enough, even though we didn't say a word out loud, it felt as if the argument raged on between us. Each of us had to decide on our own how much we were and were not willing to sacrifice to save Graham and the others. And as I realized that, all I could think about was how this time, when it was clear I was planning to fight Astrid, Tuck hadn't said he'd stand in my way.

11

It took two hours for us to walk all the way back to my grandmother's house. Hours we couldn't afford. The afternoon had turned into evening when we finally made it to the base of her long, sloped driveway. The kitchen door was slightly ajar—as if someone were home, waiting for us. But that was just wishful thinking. We must have left it that way when we'd raced out the door less than twenty-four hours ago. We'd had bigger things on our mind last night than burglary.

Inside, it was unnaturally quiet, particularly with the lights blazing overhead and the mug of now-cold tea my grandmother had abandoned on the coffee table. I walked over to her chair and sat down, wishing there was some way the walls that had housed her for so many years could impart her wisdom, because we were running out of ideas—and out of time. Now that I knew what I had to do, I craved her advice more than ever. I couldn't believe just two days ago I'd been avoiding her and had refused to listen when she'd tried to give me advice I'd now kill to hear.

And I had no idea what was happening to Graham or to Grandmother—where they were and whether they were safe. Or even alive. I couldn't think of any reason they would hurt Graham, but Grandmother was another story. It was pretty clear she and Astrid weren't exactly on good terms.

While Tuck was in the kitchen, foraging for food, I seized my chance to slip upstairs and into Grandmother's room. I already knew what Tuck thought of my plan, so I moved stealthily across the floor, wincing each time a floorboard creaked. My stomach churned as I sidestepped the pool of half-dried blood that had probably permanently stained the light pine floors. Grandmother would have to sand it out when . . . if . . . she came home.

The sword was still where we'd left it, resting in its hiding place. I slid it out and turned it over in my hands, wondering if I'd know how to use it to challenge Astrid. Or if I was about to do something completely stupid.

There was a not-so-polite cough from the door.

I turned, keeping the sword behind my back.

"What are you doing?" Tucker asked, his eyes drifting toward the pried-up floorboard.

"Nothing," I said. "Just looking around. Seeing if there's anything I missed. You know. Clues."

"You don't really think you're fooling me, do you?" Tuck

leaned sideways to peek behind my back, where the sword was not so hidden.

"No," I murmured. "I just wanted to test it out." I set it down on Grandmother's feather duvet.

"Did you know you always bite your lower lip when you're lying?"

Sometimes I really did hate Tucker Halloway.

"Listen." He sighed. "About this whole full Valkyrie thing. I've thought about it, and I can't let you do this."

I looked away, trying to keep my face neutral, so he couldn't read it.

"Why?" I demanded, for the first time actually letting my temper sneak around my guard. "You don't think I can win."

"Course I do," he said. "I'm just not willing to take the risk."

"Well, I am."

"If Graham were here, he'd agree with me. Two against one."

"I'm assuming you know I like being bullied by you even less than I like being bullied by Graham."

"And I'm assuming you know losing you scares me more than anything." The words seemed to surprise him as they tripped out of his mouth. "Just promise me you won't try to fight Astrid."

"Then why did you spend this morning trying to teach me how to fight?"

"I taught you long-range weapons," he said, his voice sharper than I'd ever heard it. "Which that is not." He waved a hand in the direction of the sword. "It's not worth it. Not even for Graham."

The words settled uncomfortably between us.

"I'll find another way. Promise you won't try to fight Astrid," Tuck said softly. "You can't distract me away from this."

He stared at me, so serious and unsmiling it made me squirm. It was like he'd suddenly turned into an entirely different boy. One who didn't smirk or tease. One who was honest and earnest and put all his emotions out there for the world to see.

I had no idea how to deal with this new Tuck. Or how to avoid making a promise I was pretty sure I wouldn't keep.

Fortunately, I never had the chance.

Tuck's eyes narrowed, focusing on something behind me. "What the hell?" Then he dived forward, throwing aside the curtains and sliding the window open. His head and shoulders craned over the sill, looking at something below. "Oh, no, you don't!" he shouted. He straightened and took off running down the hallway and thundering down the stairs. I followed.

Tucker flung the front door aside and jumped all five porch steps at once. Someone in a black hooded sweatshirt was scrambling down the side of the house, but when he saw Tuck closing in, he let go of the rain gutter and fell the remaining six feet, landing heavily on his side. In an instant, he was up and shifting into a run, but Tuck took him out with a sliding tackle.

"Nicely done," I said, approaching the pile of tangled limbs. I pulled the sweatshirt hood back from the trespasser's face, and a mess of red curls popped out.

"Margit?" I gasped. "Were you spying on us?"

She looked at me, absolute terror in her pale blue eyes, but just as fast, she constructed a stony wall of loathing, balling her fists and narrowing her eyes in revulsion.

"Why did you come back?" Margit demanded, pushing herself up off the ground.

"Believe me, I don't want to be within a hundred miles of this town," I said. "But we didn't have anywhere else to go."

"Because your friends ditched you earlier?" she snarled. "That was pretty crazy driving. You know, kids live on those streets. But I guess it shouldn't surprise me that you'd disregard human life."

"What did she say?" Tuck asked. It took half a beat for me to realize Margit hadn't been speaking in English. Comprehension had come so naturally. Just like fighting had. Every time I thought I had a handle on the changes I was undergoing, one more detail unveiled itself.

"Of course we didn't want to hurt anyone," I said, switching to English. "We didn't have a choice. We had to catch that Range Rover."

Margit's jaw clenched even tighter. I was wasting my time.

"Never mind," I said. "You wouldn't understand."

"I understand perfectly," Margit hissed in Norwegian. "You're a filthy Valkyrie—evil. Just like your grandmother."

"You'd better watch your mouth." Tuck crossed his arms and leaned back against the house. "I caught enough of that part to know. We've spent the last twenty-four hours chasing a bunch of psychopaths who kidnapped Graham—and Kjell, I might add. No more bullshit from you. One more bad thing about Ellie or her grandmother, I let her break your neck. We clear?"

Margit glared at me. Her eyebrows twitched like angry

caterpillars, daring me to even try. Even though she had done nothing but harass and annoy me, I had to respect Margit's courage, especially since she seemed to truly understand how dangerous I could be.

"Threats of extreme violence on my behalf," I said, annoyed that Tuck had enflamed the situation even more. "Not the way to warm a girl's heart."

"Maybe not." Tuck smirked back. "But I figure it's probably the only way to catch a Valkyrie's eye."

Just as I was about to point out that this wasn't the time for his inappropriate jokes, Margit pushed her way between us.

"Wait. Did you say Graham?" she interrupted, wide-eyed. "Your brother?" The burning skepticism in her eyes dimmed a few watts. "He was taken too?"

I nodded, backpedaling our conversation. Margit had no way of knowing everything Tucker and I had been through since last night.

"Didn't your grandmother protect him? She gave Kjell that necklace, the one with runes. Not that it worked. Still, you'd think she'd do better for her own grandson." The curiosity in her voice switched back to bitterness, as if she'd just remembered she was supposed to be angry. "But I guess witches' blood runs cold. Even when it comes to their own family."

"You do realize you're insulting a Valkyrie," Tuck said. "To her face. Not something I'd care to do. Personal preference. Like keeping my nose in this particular location."

"Stop," I hissed, nudging his shoulder.

He held up one hand. "Well, I think she should be warned

that I've seen you rip a car door off its hinges and flip a dude bigger than Graham over your shoulder."

"I was right, then!" Margit jumped to her feet. The minor headway of moments ago was gone. "Filthy Val. Your kidnapping days are over."

"Before they even started." Tuck shook his head slowly, with false regret. He was having way too much fun, given the circumstances. "Don't be so narrow-minded," he added. "Not every Valkyrie wants to abduct people. Some of them just want to hang out and read paperbacks all summer. Go to prom. That sort of thing."

"Look, Margit," I said, trying to glare Tuck into silence. "I know you and your friends have been spying on me. I also know some of you are tracking the Valkyries. Trying to stop them. I've seen people with your transponders three times now, at the sites of abductions. There's no reason we can't work together."

"Oh, really?" Margit said. "Because I can think of a few." But she didn't mean it. I'd caught her off guard. Her eyebrow arched. She was curious.

"We need to know where Astrid, er, the Valkyries are likely to strike next," I said. "Can you help us?" The hostile set of Margit's jaw relaxed, settling into a sulky, stubborn scowl, so I softened my tone. "I haven't hurt you now—and I saved Kjell in that bar. I've given you more reason to trust me than not to. What have you got to lose? We just need to know how to find the Valkyries."

Margit tried to maintain her anger, but she was visibly wrestling with my words in her mind. "They've been talking about you. Over the radio. That's how we communicate—the groups in different towns. I heard you fought a Val in Bergen last night. And at the soccer game, we heard you tried to help. I'm just not sure if it's a trick or if you're really not one of them." She spoke as if it were a physical effort to force the words out, each syllable inflicting a different breed of pain. "Why should I trust you?"

I motioned to Tuck to handle this part. Not only was Margit predisposed to hate me, Tuck could teach most politicians a thing or two about persuasion.

"You already told us why. All the reasons you just listed," he said softly. "Trust those sharp instincts. Help us." He cast his most irresistible smile. It was a lure no one could resist, including me. For once, I was relieved instead of resentful as I watched another girl bat her eyelashes a few extra times when she looked up at Tuck.

"Help you what?" she asked. Apparently the half-life on her hostility was a mere two seconds in Tuck time.

"Find them. The Valkyries. They'll lead us to Graham and the others. And then, well, we'll cram for that exam the night before, right, Ells?" He winked at me. I wished he'd give some sort of warning before he decided to make my heart skip a beat.

"Last night was the night before," I pointed out. "We only have until dawn."

"Why?" Margit asked, looking from me back to Tuck. "What happens at dawn?"

"We don't know," I replied. "We just know it won't be good."

"Promise you'll get my brother back," Margit said. Her

voice cracked at the end.

Tuck looked at her, really looked at her, and I knew he had this one in the bag. "What's your brother's name?" His voice was deep, soothing. The way he talked to nervous freshmen before their first big game.

"Eric."

"And they took him too?"

Margit relaxed. Millimeter by millimeter, her shoulders lowered. "Yes," she said. "He's been missing for almost a month."

"We'll get him back. We'll get all of them back." Tuck's face was so earnest, so open. No one could deny him anything when he was at his best. Even I had to believe what he was suggesting was possible. "I promise."

Margit smiled back at Tuck. Actually smiled. With teeth. "Can I use your phone?" she asked.

Within ten minutes, Margit had made a flurry of brief phone calls, and we sat in the kitchen while her phone tree of contacts grew and thrived, branch by branch. As we waited, Margit explained that there was a network of people from the surrounding towns working together to stop what Margit glibly referred to as the Val attacks, with satellite groups as far away as Denmark.

The groups had been monitoring bars and big public events, and they evacuated potential targets when Valkyries were sighted nearby. So far, it had worked only once—when they'd pulled the fire alarm to empty a restaurant in time. Every night for the past week they'd had at least one Valkyrie sighting, even if they arrived too late to rescue the victims. But advance evacuation was the only strategy that had worked. Once the Valkyries had their prey in their sights, no one had ever been saved—except Kjell, when I'd rescued him. Margit carefully avoided looking at me the entire time she was talking, but she glanced at me, just for a moment, when she delivered that last fact.

She still didn't like me, but at least she was beginning to realize that I might not be evil incarnate.

Tuck perked right up when Margit explained the emergency locator beacons. They used them instead of cell phones because they conveyed the location even when the person holding one was rendered unconscious. Margit's ultimate plan was that someone holding a live beacon would be taken. The range was hundreds of miles, and the signal could transmit through water, earth, and stone. I had to admit that it wasn't an altogether stupid plan, given that they had no way of knowing it would be impossible to follow Astrid down the invisible road without a Valkyrie to guide them.

I started to remind Tuck of that, but he cut me off and volunteered. "I'll do it," he said. "I know I can plant a beacon on one of the Valkyries. We just need your help finding them."

There was no way Tuck would think their plan could work, given what we'd just discovered on the road outside of town, when Astrid had given us the slip. As if sensing the objection on the tip of my tongue, Tuck looked me straight in the eye. "We're running out of time."

"We *are* running out of time," I whispered as soon as Margit picked up the phone again. "Which is why we can't afford to make a mistake. You know this won't work."

Tuck shrugged. "We'll figure it out," he whispered back as

soon as Margit's attention returned to the phone. "We don't have anything to lose at this point. And no matter what we do, we need their help finding Astrid. So we go along with their plan." There was something unsettling about how he refused to look me in the eye when he said it.

"You're up to something," I said warily, recognizing that intentionally expressionless look on his face too well. "What aren't you telling me?"

"That you look incredible in that shade of blue." The flirty smile was back. "It brings out your eyes."

The eyes he was still so carefully avoiding.

"Tell me what you're really thinking," I said. "You can't flirt your way out of answering."

"Bet I could if I really tried." He dropped his voice and leaned in closer. I had to admit, under any other circumstances, he would have knocked my eye right off the ball.

"Nope." I crossed my arms.

He sighed. "If I tell you, your fake reaction won't fool them," he said, all traces of playfulness gone.

"Fool them?" I hissed. "This isn't a game you're playing with one of your cheerleaders, Tuck. These are violent people."

"You need to give me more credit. I have a serious side too," he paused, visibly composing his response in his mind. "You know, sometimes it's like you think I'm hiding a harem," he added, actually sounding hurt. "At this point, if I haven't earned your trust, you need to adjust your standards." The way he said it, out loud when we'd just been whispering, sent a shiver down my spine.

I suddenly wasn't sure what we were talking about. The comment about a harem clearly had nothing to with Astrid unless Tuck was delusional to the point of insanity.

But Margit caught the important part.

"If you don't trust him, I'm not sure why you expect me to," Margit snapped, bringing an end to the argument. "We're putting people at risk to help you." When neither of us said anything, she seemed satisfied. "We'll find the Vals for you tonight," she said, looking me dead in the eye. "I'll keep my promise, and you keep yours."

"Fine." I forced myself to nod. Letting Tuck believe, at least for the time being, that I would let him do whatever he wanted. It didn't matter, since I already knew what I had to do—even if Tucker Halloway wouldn't approve.

"One condition," I said, turning to Tuck. "I'll be the one to plant the beacon."

"Whatever you say, Ells." His smug smile hit a chord I thought had faded between us. The secrecy. The games. And made me realize that maybe he had been able to flirt his way out of answering my question after all. All it took was the cryptic line about a harem and earning trust, and my traitorous imagination had absconded with the rest of my brain.

In a situation like we'd be facing, there was no room for error. I now not only had to defeat a Valkyrie and rescue Graham, I also had a sneaking feeling I'd be protecting Tuck from his own overconfidence. I'd do anything to keep him safe. Whether he liked it or not.

12

Margit drove, and within a half hour, we were climbing the fire escape to Sven's apartment, which was the de facto headquarters for the Skavøpoll branch of the Valkyrie hunters. My stomach was in a nervous knot that pulled tighter with each rattle of the metal stairs under my feet. We were walking into a nest of kids who insulted and threatened me every chance they got. And who were probably in cahoots with the mob that had tried to drag my grandmother into town for questioning.

"Doesn't Sven have a front door?" I asked, looking down at the ground, three stories beneath us.

"Yes," Margit replied. "But this is faster."

Even with my new confidence coursing through my limbs, I hesitated on the threshold, unable to see past the dimly lit kitchen. Anyone or anything could be hiding in the rooms beyond, waiting to attack. And unlike when I'd faced Astrid, I really didn't want to hurt anyone.

Tuck grabbed my hand and urged me gently forward. "C'mon." He squeezed my fingers and I yielded, letting him guide me. Inside, the apartment was dark and dank and smelled like unwashed socks and boys. Tuck sensed my hesitation and wrapped one arm around my shoulders.

"They're harmless," he whispered, making my disembodied feeling worse by letting his lips hover a millimeter from my ear. "A bunch of kids. We could take 'em if we had to. But who knows, maybe they can help us find Graham. That's worth taking a chance, right?"

"Just don't leave me alone with them," I whispered back. "They hate me."

"It's impossible to hate you," Tuck said, surprising me with his earnestness. "Just use those huge baby blues and you'll have them eating out of your hand in two seconds flat. It'll be all too easy. Promise."

Yet sure enough, when we walked into the living room, we were greeted by five pairs of hostile, suspicious eyes. Sven was sitting on the couch with another boy I recognized from the pickup soccer game and three girls who had taken the mean-girl stare to a whole new level.

"Just so you know," Sven said, rising and looking only at Tuck. "If she tries anything, we have no problem taking her out."

"Mind your manners." Tucker's tone was heavy with threats,

even though he kept his response simple. "Or I'll mind them for you."

One of the girls rose and stood beside Sven, watching me like I was a sleeping saber-toothed tiger. She put one hand on his arm possessively, and I wondered if she was more worried that I'd hurt him or that I'd steal him for myself.

Sven squared his shoulders, trying to look tough, but the hand that hovered near his pocket was shaking. I could smell the metal and gunpowder of the nine-millimeter handgun he thought he'd hidden so well.

"Is this it?" I asked, looking around. "I expected more of you. Who were the men who tried to arrest my grandmother?"

"They're getting ready to spend another night chasing after your relatives," Sven snapped back.

Tuck took a quick step forward, his right hand balling back up into a fist. I caught it and uncurled his fingers until they rested flat against my palm. He met my eyes and kept his hand there, weaving his fingers through mine.

"Leave it, Tuck," I whispered.

"Manners," Tuck reminded Sven. "Lessons are complimentary and exquisitely painful."

Sven's eyes flashed down to our clasped hands. "I guess not everyone has to be hypnotized into obedience."

Sven's friends laughed nervously.

"It's not obedience," I told Sven as I squeezed Tuck's fingers and he squeezed mine right back. "It's friendship. Tucker's known me forever—the real me. That's why he trusts me. Look, I am what you think I am—I'm a Valkyrie." It was the first time

I'd said it out loud, and I felt an unexpected surge of exultation as I claimed my birthright. "But I'm not like the others," I added. "I'm not evil or out to get you. In fact, I didn't know I was one too until the other night, when they took my brother. What I am didn't change anything. In fact that's why they took him in the first place. But it could change how this ends."

Margit had been standing behind us, and as I finished speaking, she cleared her throat authoritatively. "I believe her. They caught me and let me go."

Sven snorted. "She tricked you into leading them here."

"Why would she do that?" Tuck demanded. "If the other Valkyries didn't want you, why would she?"

Margit gave Tuck a dirty look that actually made him shut up.

"You heard what happened at the soccer game," she said to Sven and the others.

The entire room went silent, listening to her.

"We need to help them find the Vals tonight," Margit continued. "They say they can plant a beacon on them. I think we should trust them."

Stunning words coming from someone who utterly despised me.

"I don't like it," Sven said. "How do we know you're not hypnotized too? This could be a trap."

"Because you know it doesn't work as well on girls," Margit retorted. "It would never last this long."

Which was an interesting tidbit I filed away for future scrutiny.

"Do you really think I'd need to go to these lengths to trap you?" I asked, feeling the power tingling in my fingertips. "If I were your enemy, you'd all look like this, and the argument would be over."

I snapped my fingers in the face of the boy to Sven's left, and his eyes went milky white. One more snap, and he was back to normal, blinking in confusion. Until that moment, I hadn't known I could do that.

I thought I might have gone too far, terrifying and probably alienating them. Instead, Margit gave me a quirky grin. "That settles that," she said smugly. "We need a strong ally like this."

When I gave her a tentative smile, she added, "Besides, if anyone's going to be in the line of fire, it might as well be a filthy Val."

"That's more like it, Margit," I murmured. "I was beginning to worry we might be friends."

"Not likely," she growled. I tried not to look down at her fingers. Because she was snapping them softly, like a tiny part of her begrudgingly admired my power.

"See," Tuck murmured. "No one can resist you."

I nudged him to shut up. He was dangerously distracting when he dropped his voice and whispered so close to my ear. And at the moment, all our attention needed to be attuned to Sven and his friends, who were conferring quietly in the corner and glancing back at us suspiciously from time to time, like they thought we'd make off with their TV.

"We'll help you," Sven said at last. "We have enough coverage that we'll find them if they're within three hundred miles. What you do when you get to them is your business, as long as you plant our beacon."

"That's a polite way of saying you're on your own," Margit added. "We can't help you if things go wrong."

"We understand," I said. "Thank you for helping us."

"You're welcome." Sven nodded, which just made his girlfriend glower at me again.

"The others are coming," Margit said, glancing at her phone when it chimed with a new message. "I think we should talk to them before they see you. Alone. Go home. I'll pick you up when we're ready."

We followed Margit to the door leading out onto the rickety fire escape.

"Thanks, Margit," I said. "For helping us, I mean. I know it was hard to take a leap of faith—to trust us."

"I'm not doing it for you," she replied. "Bring my brother back. And Kjell. Or don't come back at all."

WHILE WE WALKED back to my grandmother's house, Tuck and I decided to check out the trapdoor in the basement. I kept hoping we'd find some secret Valkyrie neutralizing machine. Something that would let me defeat one of them, because I needed all the help I could get. My ribs ached at the memory of my last encounter with Astrid. Still, I had to find a way to become a full Valkyrie, stand my ground against Astrid, and follow her to Graham when I did.

And I had to do all that while keeping Tuck as far away from Astrid as possible. I'd seen Tuck be so reckless over the years, back when the biggest consequence he faced was suspension. I was terrified to see that edge in him now, when the stakes were so much higher. I wondered if he realized it or if he was past the point of caring. In the end, it didn't matter. It just meant I needed to be prepared for anything.

All we found in the basement was enough canned goods to last us a month, water, and an arsenal that belonged in a museum.

I was too frustrated and restless to keep rooting through the shelves of neatly labeled boxes, so I slipped upstairs to my grandmother's room and grabbed her sword. A few swipes with the hand towel in the bathroom removed most of the dust. I carried it outside to the backyard, where I could try it out without having to worry about taking out an armchair or two.

I curled my hand around the hilt and carved the blade through the air in a wide arc, not even noticing the weight of it. As heavy and bulky as it looked, it was light as a feather when extended in my palm. The instant, organic connection gave me the confidence to try more and more elaborate stunts. By the time Tuck appeared in the doorway, I'd worked up the nerve to toss the sword into the air like a drum majorette. It rotated once before the hilt found its way back to my palm, clicking into place like a magnet. When I was ten, Tuck had wasted a whole week trying to teach me to juggle. We'd given up when I broke the mirror in the dining room. It was amazing how fast my entire being was changing.

"Looky here," Tuck said, wandering out the back door with an old-fashioned crossbow resting over one shoulder. "It comes with arrows you light on fire. You know, in case we want to burn down a medieval village." He propped it against the garage and walked toward me, moving slowly, like we had all the time in the world. "Think I'll stick with weapons from this millennium."

"Probably best," I murmured, hoping Tuck hadn't seen how very comfortable I actually was with antique weapons. "You could hurt yourself with that."

"Well, you're one to talk, Zorro. Or are you auditioning for some sort of circus act?"

I blushed so completely, even my toes partook of my shame. "I was just experimenting."

"Looked like you know what you're doing, though." He caught my wrist and turned it over to examine the way my fingers curled around the leather-covered handle. "Interesting," he said. "It's almost like a lacrosse grip, but more stable. Where'd you learn this?"

I shrugged. "I was just goofing around. Trying to keep my mind off tonight."

"Just one more incredible thing that comes naturally to you." His voice was low, meant only for my ears, even though there was no one else within miles. "I know it's hard not to be scared after what Astrid did to you last time, but I don't think she'll hurt you unless you come at her directly. She seems to kinda ignore you otherwise."

"What makes you think that's what I'm trying not to think about?" I asked. "I'd be pretty hard to seriously injure anyway. Because I heal so fast." My next words would annoy him, but I couldn't get my worries out of my head, so I threw them at him in a rush. "But you don't. And I might not be able to protect you this time. What if they hurt you?" I had to take a deep breath to force the next words out. "Or kill you, even."

Tuck sighed. He lifted the sword out of my grasp and set it on the ground. Then he wrapped my hand in both of his. I tried to pull away, not wanting to be soothed like a kid, but he just shifted until he was standing right in front of me again. He caught my other wrist, locking me in place with his fingers resting right along my pulse line. There was no way to conceal my jackrabbiting heartbeat. "I'm comfortable with that risk," he said. "You're the only thing I care about right now. And Graham. I'll get him back for you even if it kills me."

I couldn't bring myself to look up at him, so instead I stared at his chest, following the groove of his collarbone to where it connected to his shoulder. The kind of strong shoulder you could rest your head on forever. Even through his shirt, I could see the lines and planes of him. It was difficult to concentrate on anything else when he was standing so close. I wanted to wrap my arms around his neck and press my face against his throat. And not just because I was scared—although I was terrified of losing him, too.

"That wouldn't solve anything," I said in a small voice. I buried my longings so deep, it would take an excavation team to drag them out of me, because this was about something deeper than his flirty words and playful smiles. This was about a lifetime of friendship and rivalry that had somehow turned into so much more. At least for me. "You're just as important to me as he is."

Tuck's fingers tightened around my wrists, and I wished instead they'd tighten around my whole body until I was so close I wouldn't be able to think about anything but Tuck and his flawless smile and the fact that his arms were wrapped around me and felt just like I'd imagined they would. Graham and everything else would just disappear.

Tuck's voice was hesitant, almost bashful, when he finally asked. "Do you mean that?"

I nodded. "I love you both. So much." My eyes hit a glass ceiling, still refusing to drift above his collar. The idea of looking up at him just then terrified me. Of seeing whatever smug smile was waiting to declare his easy victory. One more heart to add to the discard pile.

"Ells, look at me. Please," he said. Even though I'd never heard anything approaching doubt in Tuck's voice, I recognized it instantly.

His unreadable gray eyes were waiting when I lifted my gaze, this time, offering everything I most desperately hoped to find.

When Tuck kissed me, it was a question—a question I'd known the answer to for so long. And I had my response at the ready. My fingers traced along the muscles in his arms as they tightened around me, to where they joined his shoulders, and finally came to rest around his neck. So that he could never get away. It was impossible to imagine ever letting him go, and from the way his body wrapped around mine, I knew he was thinking the same thing.

I didn't let myself wonder what that kiss meant in the grand scheme of things, or about the fact that Tuck's hands were everywhere, pushing things pretty far past anything resembling friendship. Maybe this would ruin everything. Maybe Tuck just wanted me for that day—to slash and burn the undergrowth of longing that had rooted itself in our friendship. And maybe even if we wanted more, it would never work in the real world, back where Tucker Halloway was my brother's best friend and a boy who collected crushes like other boys collect comic books.

But I didn't care. All that mattered was then, that moment. All I knew was I wanted him too. I'd wanted him for so unbearably long that I ached with relief to finally stop fighting it.

We must have been like that for a half hour, pressed against the railing of my grandmother's porch, until I heard the crunch of gravel beneath tires. Margit had arrived—ready to drive us to our doom.

"Crazy about you, Ells," Tuck said, breaking away and kissing my forehead. "Been fighting it for as long as I can remember." He towed me toward the front of the house, but I dragged my feet, not ready for the night to begin and seriously needing a moment to fix my shirt.

"Why? Why didn't you just tell me?"

"Scared."

"Of what? Me?"

"You don't go after your best friend's little sister." His voice was strained. "Especially when he's Graham. No one was ever good enough for you."

Even though I dreaded the answer, given that he'd used past tense, I had to ask, "So what's different now?"

"Nothing."

We both knew he was lying. There was an army of bloodthirsty Valkyries standing between us and Graham's disapproval. Valkyries who might very well kill all three of us before the night was out. If I pushed my line of questioning any further, I knew I wouldn't like the answers I got.

Margit had climbed out of her car by the time we reached her. "Were you two just kissing?"

"I know, right?" Tuck grinned. "It was even better than I imagined."

Margit rolled her eyes. "I don't care."

I was mortified, but Tuck smiled at me like I was a sunset he'd painted all by himself.

He dragged me into the back of Margit's car, and I did a double take at the enormous radio consuming the entire passenger seat.

"It's from a fishing boat. The range is hundreds of miles," Margit said, following my gaze. "We've made contact all over Norway. If the Vals act tonight, we'll know. We just have to hope they hit close enough that we can get you there fast. Not everyone agrees we should delay evacuation for you. Since no one's actually in charge, there's not much we can do to force the issue. We'll stick to the central highway—best route to everywhere."

"I really appreciate everything you're doing," I said. "Thank you."

"Don't think you can be nice and win me over," Margit growled, but all the edge was gone. "And I still don't care what happens to you tonight. No puppy-love act will change that."

That made Tuck laugh as he reached out and wrapped one long arm around me. For once I was glad European cars were so cozy. I could have sat like that all night, with my head resting against his chest. It was enough to make me forget everything and to just relax into a moment of pure contentment, even if it lasted only for an instant

We drove up and down the highway for thirty minutes before we heard anything over the radio other than static. The first crackly voice that broke through the sizzling silence was just calling for a status check. Each of the surveillance teams radioed in to report that they'd seen nothing. I counted twelve different groups out stalking the Valkyries that night. I had to believe it would be enough, and that we'd find them.

"What if they don't show up tonight?" I whispered. We'd put everything on the line. It was just five short hours before dawn. This plan could not fail.

Tuck squeezed my shoulder, but that was hardly enough to reassure me as minutes fused into a half hour. Just when I was ready to explode from impatience, the radio crackled to life a second time and a voice spoke excitedly in some sort of code. A series of numbers that sounded like coordinates. "They've found them," I said. This was it—our last chance. The jittery feeling was back, shooting through my body like electricity.

Margit whipped across three lanes of traffic, almost sideswiping a station wagon, and flew up the nearest exit ramp. She sped across the overpass and accelerated onto the freeway in the opposite direction, weaving through traffic like a suspect in a high-speed chase.

"Where are we going?" I asked, as if it made any difference which town would host our final showdown.

"Bodahl," she said, hitting the gas—hard.

Fifteen minutes later, we pulled into a typical Norwegian fishing village. It skirted the sea, just like Skavøpoll, but instead of a narrow marina hugging the land, Bodahl had a broad pier extending deep into the fjord and disappearing into the darkness.

Not a single window on the main street through the town cast light out onto the vacant street. It would have felt deserted if not for the rectangles of illumination cast through the trees by the homes on the surrounding hills. But not for long. I could sense Astrid and other Valkyries, speeding closer through the night, energy flooding the shrinking distance between us.

Margit eased her car into a parking spot in front of the only bar in town. She clicked off the headlights and slid down low enough in her seat that she couldn't be seen from the road. "The Range Rover must have just driven into town," Margit whispered as the radio crackled to life again and a deep voice echoed through the car, telling us to hold position. "You're on your own," she said. "But we'll pull the bar's fire alarm if anyone is in danger."

"Right," I said.

"I almost forgot. Take this." She tossed me a small handheld radio. "The range is only one kilometer, but at least we'll hear what happens inside. Not like there's much we can do to help if things get ugly."

"Thanks." I slid the radio into my jacket pocket. I was surprised when she met my gaze and nodded in the rearview mirror.

"Good luck."

We had to move fast, before Astrid and crew snatched whoever they were coming for and left. I followed Tuck across the street and into a world of pounding bass. A nightclub like that was honestly the last thing I expected to find in such a seemingly silent small town—and it was packed. Everyone was older than college age and was dressed in the hip, sleek clothes you'd expect in a city, but that were oddly out of place in the middle of nowhere. It had to be the hot spot for every village within fifty miles.

The moment we entered, a bouncer pounced on us. Before he had a chance to block our path, I looked him right in the eye and shook my head. His pupils widened before taking on a vacant, disinterested glaze as he settled back onto his stool by the door.

"There's something I need to tell you," Tuck said, turning abruptly and grabbing me by both shoulders. He hesitated. The eyes that had been open and warm only moments ago retreated, back to the heavily guarded territory I thought we'd left behind. He was up to something—there was no other explanation for that half smile. "I love you. Whatever happens tonight doesn't change that. Just don't forget it. No matter what."

"What do you mean?" I asked. He had buried the most important part in a forest of vague statements that unleashed liquid suspicion right into my veins. "This isn't the time for one of your games, Tuck. This is serious."

"I should have just told you. Now I waited too long." He swore under his breath as he stared off through the crowd. "They're here. Take this." He pressed a folded slip of paper into my hand. "It's Norse. Old school. Back to the Vikings.

It represents separation—when a Valkyrie leaves the fold, so to speak. Hilda put it on those necklaces she gave to Kjell and Graham. But you can put it directly on your skin. Preferably in a place they can't remove without killing you. It's worked for me, at least. When Astrid crushed that necklace, I did this." He slid the sleeve of his T-shirt back just enough to reveal a series of crudely inked symbols on his shoulder blade. Like he'd drawn it while looking in a mirror.

"How do you know all that?" I demanded.

"It's complicated," he said, still avoiding my eyes. "You'll have to trust me. And if I don't get the chance to explain, my mother will."

"Your mother?" I repeated, utterly astounded, given that his mother had nothing to do with any of this. Knowing Tuck, it was a safe bet he'd only called to let her know when he'd arrived safely. Plus he was talking like we'd never see each other again. "Why wouldn't you be able to tell me?" I demanded. My heart was pounding so hard, it would have registered on a seismograph. "If you're planning something stupid, I'll kill you."

"Can't think of a better way to go." He cracked a lopsided grin. "You need to just trust me."

"You keep saying that."

"Because you're not doing it," he shot back. "Besides, it's too late. You have to do what I say or we blow this. It's our last chance."

The fire alarm exploded to life. It took everyone on the dance floor a solid thirty seconds to realize that the shrill screech wasn't just part of the music. When they did, we were crushed by a surge of bodies rushing toward the door. Tuck's hand disappeared, but he pushed his way back to me again and pulled us both into a corner sheltered from the mayhem. The crowd churned in panic, jostling and shoving. A pretty girl was shoved to the ground by a brutish boy who would have drooled all over her minutes earlier. Fortunately, another boy pulled her to her feet before she was trampled. There's nothing like an emergency to show your true colors.

The sounding of the alarm meant that Astrid was already here. If Margit had had anything to say about it, they wouldn't have pulled the alarm unless there was no other way to keep everyone safe.

"Game time." Tuck pushed the personal locator beacon into my hand. "It's too dangerous to plant the beacon on one of them. You can put it in their car."

He grinned, like he'd just had this stroke of genius. But his mouth curved up at one corner. He was still up to something.

"Where will you be?" I demanded.

"You get the dangerous part because you're faster. I'll stand guard out front in case they come out. I'll wait for you there." He said it like it should have been obvious. Which was step one of the Tucker Halloway bulldozing machine. Either I was being paranoid or Tuck was playing me. What thoughts were spinning behind his unnaturally serene smile?

Still, Tuck would be out front. Safe. Ultimately, that was all that mattered. While he waited for me, I'd have a golden opportunity to sneak back into the club and confront Astrid. Tuck wouldn't know a thing about it until it was too late.

Tuck grabbed my hand and plunged through the crowd, pulling us both through the flow of people. Once outside, I held my breath, eyes searching the road outside for any sign of the Range Rover. People cluttered the sidewalk; girls in clubbing dresses and high heels hugged themselves and shivered in the night air. No one noticed the two of us, huddled together by the door.

"There," Tuck said, pointing toward the alley a half block away. The glow of headlights reflected off the asphalt. "Hurry."

Astrid assumed no one was capable of an effective counterassault, which made my mission all too easy. I dropped to the ground on the pavement next to the back of the SUV and wedged the tiny transponder up underneath the metal bracket holding the bumper in place. Even a head-on collision wouldn't pry it loose.

I straightened, brushing the crusted dirt and oil residue off my fingers and onto my jeans. A rectangle of light on the alley wall marked the club's back door. I peered into the darkened club. Astrid was there. The connection between us clawed at the corners of my mind, urging me to join her. I would never get another chance like this.

Tuck would be furious when he realized I wasn't coming back and that I had my own plan. But I couldn't let that stop me. This was the only way.

I pushed the door open and strained my eyes, searching the club. In the corner, half hidden by a row of bar tables, four figures were clustered. My eye was drawn instantly to the tallest, the one with radiant blond hair. Even though her back was to me, I knew it was her. Astrid.

She had a stocky boy by the chin and lowered her face to look directly into his eyes. Her companions stood by, hands resting on the weapons I knew were concealed underneath their perfectly tailored jackets. They were standing with their backs to half the room. They had grown too accustomed to not being challenged, which I could use to my advantage.

Astrid's graceful movements were fractured by flashes from the strobe light. In those frozen moments, I watched the boy's eyes change from dark to milky white, just as Tucker Halloway stepped right up behind Astrid. Confidence incarnate. Like he was planning to tap her on the shoulder and ask her for the next dance.

I was so confused, it took me painfully long to unglue my feet from the floor. Tuck was supposed to be out front. Out of harm's way. But there he stood, larger than life. I lurched forward. But there was no way I could reach him before Astrid sank her manicured talons into him.

My stomach slammed into the floor as Astrid reached one arm behind her and grabbed Tucker by the throat without even turning to confirm he was there. Her eyes skimmed the room. Until they found me.

Suddenly I was running, not really sure what I'd do when I reached her but hoping I'd think of something. I'd forgotten how cold she was, a spider watching the path of a drunken fly bobbing and weaving right into her web.

Astrid's lips curled into a snarl. It made her look even more devastating.

"Still not dead?" She was so cool and calm. Like she was offering us another cup of tea. "Fortunately, I can remedy that oversight. Wait outside," she told Tucker, setting him down without a second glance. Assuming he was an obedient minion, under her spell.

But his gray eyes were clear and unclouded.

"No," he said, taking a step forward

Astrid turned and stared at Tuck, genuine surprise in her eyes. "You don't have permission to speak."

"I don't need it." He lifted his chin. "You don't hold much sway over me, Astrid, fascinating as I find you."

"I knew there was something strange about you," she said, tipping her head to the side, examining him like the answers to existence were scrawled all over his face. "Let me guess." Astrid turned ice-cold eyes on me. "He has family in Brittany."

I looked at Tuck, because I was pretty sure that was the region in France where his mother grew up. Then I turned back to Astrid. "So?"

"Stupid," Astrid hissed at me. "He's using you."

"No. Never," Tuck said to me. "I thought they were nuts. My mother's family. Until all this started happening. My mother was basically raised in a cult. They claim they're descended from a Celtic goddess, and they are obsessed with stopping the end of the world. As caused by you specifically." He looked right at Astrid. "I'll cooperate if you just let Ellie go."

"Cooperate?" Astrid made it sound like a dirty little secret. "Why would I have any interest in that? What's to stop me from killing you right now?"

"Nothing," Tuck replied. "But while I don't know everything about this feud between you and my family, I've figured out a couple of things. I know there's some bad blood between you guys, but I think you should talk to them. Use me as a mediator. Or a bargaining chip. Even if I avoid them, they've tried pretty hard over the years to get us back in the flock."

"What on earth are you talking about?" Shock made my words come out one at a time, as if they were disconnected rather than a cluster of sounds that formed a sentence.

"You really didn't know?" Astrid hissed. She took in my confused expression, and her lips curled into a disgusted snarl. "It's a disgrace. Hilda forced you to live in ignorance. It endangers us all."

I was surprised to realize that most of her anger at the moment was directed at Grandmother rather than at me.

"His family is our greatest enemy. He tricked you. I imagine he's been most gratified by your betrayal."

It was a lie—instead of crushing my bones, Astrid was going for my heart this time. At least, that's what I thought until I saw the way Tuck's eyes were still carefully avoiding mine.

"Have you lost your mind?" I demanded, wondering why he was playing along with Astrid. There was no way this could end well. "Tell her it's not true." But my words faltered as he looked down, away from me.

"But it is," Tuck said softly.

Astrid flashed a triumphant smile and prowled around me in a slow half circle. "You can't trust anyone, Elsa," she snarled. "How many times do you need to learn that lesson? Your grandmother. Tucker. Loki. I'm the only one who hasn't lied to you. And yet you distrust me most."

"I didn't lie." Tuck stepped toward me, but Astrid shifted between us. I wasn't stupid enough to think I could get past her if I tried, especially when her companions crept closer, watching my every move. "I just didn't tell you everything," he added.

"A meaningless distinction," Astrid snarled.

I hated that I agreed. Now all I could do was wonder what else Tucker was keeping from me.

Tuck held up both hands, yielding to Astrid even as his eyes finally met mine and he unleashed an explanation that just left me more confused than ever. "I hardly ever see Colette's weirdo family. Even if the handful of things I picked up from them were useful the last few days. Like how to use a gun. Plus I recognized the symbol on Graham's necklace once I got a closer look. I—I would have told you all this stuff earlier, Ells, but I still don't really know what it all means." He ran one hand through his hair, nervous, as his eyes finally met mine and he flashed his best smile. But for once it wasn't enough. My heart was a lump of lifeless granite in my chest. This couldn't be happening. The wonderful, albeit infuriating, boy next door was part of this whole nightmare too.

"I have a proposal, Astrid," Tuck said, shifting his gaze to her. "You don't have to take orders from Odin. There's another way."

"And end up like your ancestor?" Astrid's words dripped scorn.

"Just hear me out," Tuck said.

"No," Astrid replied. "I don't think I will." The side of her hand crashed down on the back of Tuck's head so fast, it was over before I even knew what had happened. He crumpled onto the floor. Unconscious.

I swallowed the scream that filled my lungs. Because it wouldn't help anything. Tucker had lied—he'd had a secret, just like I'd suspected. Only it was bigger than anything I'd imagined. All the ground I thought we'd covered on this trip disappeared in an instant, leaving a hole in my heart bigger than the hopes I'd harbored all these years. It had all been a lie.

I pushed the thought aside, because, ultimately, Tucker's betrayal was just one of my problems. Graham and countless others were still missing, and the clock was ticking down toward Loki's deadline. Dawn was four hours away.

"Take him," Astrid growled, waving her hand at the Valkyrie behind her. She'd been scary before, but nothing prepared me for Astrid in a bad mood. And apparently Tucker had plunged her into a foul one.

The sight of Tucker being taken away made me realize all at once that no matter how hurt I was, I couldn't let one more person suffer at Astrid's hands, especially Tuck.

I wracked my brain for a way to save him—I couldn't be left behind this time if I wanted to have any chance of rescuing everyone. I had to convince them to take me too. In a way, Tuck's painful secrets might actually make it easier to convince them I'd switched sides.

"I want to come with you," I said, looking Astrid squarely in the eye. "I want to learn how to be a Valkyrie. Learn to be like you. I can't—I can't take any more betrayal." My voice cracked on the last word, succumbing to the burning skepticism in Astrid's eyes.

"Interesting change of heart," Astrid said. "To what do we owe this stroke of luck?"

The words were saturated with sarcasm. She wasn't buying it.

"First my grandmother lied to me," I said, doing my best to sound bitter. "To keep me from the rest of you. I can feel it, the draw to be with you. It's like suddenly I found the family I was supposed to be with all along. Then Tucker lied to me." My voice shook with real emotion. "I can't trust anyone. Except you. Because, like you said, at least all along you've been honest."

Astrid's lips twitched into a flawless smile. It was impossible for teeth to be so straight and white.

Then she did something even more alarming than snarling or threatening me. She laughed. "You're a terrible liar," she said. "That would be lesson number one if I had any reason to train you."

"You have a reason to train me," I said. "I'm strong. And you know it."

Astrid stared at me without blinking. Like a lizard. The tension in the set of her shoulders was a potent reminder I was messing with someone who would snap my neck without a second thought. Or even a first one. Yet the words kept on coming. "I'm strong like my grandmother. You need me."

"I don't need anyone. There's a reason I'm in charge. I'm the best."

I could tell it wasn't working, so I took a deep breath and switched to a more aggressive approach. If nothing else, I could try fighting her again. On the infinitesimally slim chance I could win.

I relaxed the stranglehold I'd kept on my violent impulses, my Valkyrie side. As soon as I did, it sprang forward, seizing control.

"You *were* the best," I retorted. "Could it be you're afraid that if you train me, I'll be better than you?"

Astrid stepped forward, her voice low and dangerous in my ear. "Do you really want me to kill you?"

Soft enough that her companions couldn't hear, I growled, "What if you try and find you can't anymore?" My voice was terrifying, even to me. A wild animal was unleashed within me, savage and pure. "But that's not what either of us wants—you admire my strength. I know that's why you didn't kill me before. And I need your knowledge."

She moved closer still, until I shivered in the envelope of ice-cold air that preceded her. Her thumb absently traced a circle on the gun holstered to her hip. There was no room for error in this encounter.

"I'll prove I belong with you."

"You've had four shots at me, and each time you've only come out alive because I've let you," Astrid retorted.

I forced myself not to react to that revelation, because all along I'd been assuming she wanted me dead. "Not you," I said taking a step back just in case. "Her." I pointed one finger after covertly picking out the girl who looked the smallest. Because she only had two inches on me. And probably a thousand years of combat experience.

"It seems we finally have a learning curve," Astrid snapped. I felt the current that flowed between them, a silent communication, just out of my reach.

"She would be more than happy to kill you." Astrid stepped back, out of the way.

The girl flew at me before I had a chance to brace myself, and we collided against the mirrored wall of the club, shattering the glass into a million glittering pieces that trickled to the floor like rain. But surprise and a handgun were the only advantages she had. I could feel it, the superior strength and agility that were a gift from my grandmother's bloodline. I pushed her away by the shoulder, and it actually worked. She staggered back three steps before she caught her balance and lunged for me again.

There was a world of difference between fighting Astrid and fighting her lackey. The girl's hold yielded to mine as we grappled for control of the handgun.

This was a fight I could actually win.

And I did. All it took a flick of my wrist in the other direction, too quick for her to counter, and the gun was mine and pressed against the girl's windpipe. That stopped her dead in her tracks. It was so easy, I almost wondered if I'd broken some rule, and if that explained my victory. But no one raised her voice in protest as I pushed her hard against the wall, keeping the gun in place.

"Do you surrender?" I demanded.

Instead of answering, she just glared at me like she'd rather stay like this for the rest of our lives than give in.

"Surrender," I growled, but my voice broke this time. If she didn't, I had no idea what I'd do next. And still she just stared at me without blinking.

Her eyes were gray. Just like Tuck's. Was I prepared to shoot her, if that's what it would take?

"You'll have to kill her," Astrid whispered in my ear. I hadn't realized she'd crept so close until I felt cool fingers press against my forearm. "This is your chance, Ellie. Prove yourself to me."

I thought of Graham and my grandmother, locked up somewhere. I thought of Tuck, in mortal danger—even his deceptions couldn't erase years of memories and friendship. And I thought of everyone who'd been kidnapped from the surrounding towns. All the innocent people who would be hurt if I didn't find a way to make this right.

And I pulled the trigger.

I stared into the girl's wild eyes. She hadn't realized I had slid the gun to the side at the last second. She thought she'd seen the moment of her death, and that was enough to change her mind.

She whispered her surrender as Astrid spun me around to face her.

"Such a waste," she spat. And oddly enough, I didn't know who she meant—her friend for losing, or me for winning, then showing mercy. From the appraising look in her eye as she stared at both of us, it could have been either.

"You'll take me with you?" My heart was leaping in my chest as I wiped the sweat from my palms.

"Did you really think you could fool me?" she demanded.

"That I'd lead you right into your brother's arms? Unlike you, I wasn't born yesterday." As she spoke, her gun slid out of its holster. "You've put yourself in a very bad position."

"What do you mean?"

"I'd forgotten how young you are, in my excitement to find a brand-new baby Valkyrie I could train up in my image, like your grandmother did with me, until your boyfriend reminded me how dangerous your ignorance could be. I don't have time to housebreak you. Not with Odin barking at my heels."

The fire alarm stopped ringing. The only sound in the club was the thundering of my heart in my ears. I was staring straight down the barrel of a gun—all the way to Astrid's red-lacquered fingernail coiled around the trigger. It had to be happening to someone else, someone in a movie I'd seen somewhere, a long, long time ago. Not to me.

I closed my eyes, no more than a blink, as pain exploded through my head, fire raging from my neck to my forehead.

Then everything went black.

13

The pain was the first thing that told me I might still be alive. There was no way a dead body could suffer like that, even in the farthest reaches of hell. My head was pounding and spinning, and nausea slammed into my stomach. My limbs were full of lead, pinning me to the cold concrete floor like a frog awaiting dissection. It took another few seconds to feel the cool fingers on my wrist, pressing down against my pulse.

Somehow I'd survived.

"I've never known Astrid to develop such a soft spot for anyone." The voice was a ladder, and I climbed up it toward consciousness. Recognition flirted with the edges of my memory before hitting me all at once. Loki.

If Astrid had a soft spot for me, she certainly had an

interesting way of showing it. At the moment, the only soft spot I knew of was on the back of my head, right along the hairline. It felt like I'd been clubbed by a brick—or, more accurately, by a gun.

I opened my eyes just enough to confirm what I already knew, that Astrid was gone. I could sense only one other presence in the building, and that dreaded voice had already given me a preview of who to expect. So I sat up slowly, letting the flashing strobe pour itself into my retinas. Even if Astrid hadn't actually cracked my head open, it still felt like it.

I turned, scanning the dark corners for Loki. "I know you're here." My words echoed through the deserted club.

Sure enough, Loki stepped out of the shadows, chucking softly to himself. "You look disappointed, little Elsa. Did you really think she'd take you? That she'd fall for it? Astrid's too smart for that. Fortunately, I factored that into our plan before I let you face her one last time." He was walking in a slow circle around me, sizing me up in a way that made every nerve in my body stand at attention. And brace for an attack. "I didn't spend all this time preparing you just to have you end up chained in a dungeon somewhere."

"Preparing me for what?" I asked warily, trying not to shudder at the rest of what he'd said.

"Your shining moment," he replied. "Your real mission— saving Graham is the smallest piece of it. Now that you're a full Valkyrie, the real fun will begin. You can walk right up that second road winding through Skavøpoll. Lead an army up it, even."

I didn't like the sound of that one bit, or the way Loki was smirking at the thought of whatever he was plotting. I slipped my hand into my pocket, hoping Astrid hadn't stripped me clean of weapons while I was unconscious.

Then the rest of Loki's words trickled into my sluggish thoughts and were absorbed.

I had changed. I was a Valkyrie. Even if I'd failed at everything else, at least I had that one small victory to hold close to my heart. Along with the hope that my transformation might be enough to turn things around.

It was the strangest sort of irony, to suddenly know I was connected to the crackling energy binding the Valkyries together, and to know I'd have to use it against them. Because I sensed they didn't want to follow Odin's orders—they were bound by promises and traditions older than I could comprehend. The thought of standing against Astrid and the others made my heart ache almost as much Tuck's revelations had. I turned away, toward the door.

Loki narrowed his eyes. "Where do you think you're going?"

"I'm leaving," I told him. "I'm finishing this myself. My way. I don't want anything to do with your mission."

"*Our* mission," he corrected sharply. "You might be stronger now, you might even let your new power delude you into a false sense of confidence. But you're still less than a newborn when it comes to the ways of your world. *Our* world. You don't realize how fortunate you are to have me here. To guide you."

"I don't need you," I said, shaking my head and taking a step back. "I don't trust you. I never have."

"Trust." Loki's features shifted until he was wearing the one smile I'd have trouble wiping off his face: Tuck's. "Don't waste your time questioning *my* motives when a far bigger betrayal has been under way for years."

I took another step back, but Loki stood perfectly still. A statue in the middle of the deserted nightclub. "You don't know anything about Tucker," I said.

"Neither do you," he replied. "You can't trust anyone, Elsa. Least of all him."

I turned away again, ready to leave Loki and his tricks behind me forever. Even if what he was saying was true, I knew he'd find a way to twist it into something that wasn't. I needed time and space to process what had just happened, without Loki trying to interpret it for me.

"He's a descendent of the Morrigan," Loki said.

At that word, my blood turned to fire. I froze, hating myself even as I let Loki reel me back in. "What is that?" I asked.

"*Who* is that," Loki corrected, enjoying my impatience far too much. "The Morrigan was a Valkyrie—a long time ago. Her adopted name is spelled out in those runes that your boyfriend drew on his skin—and that are emblazoned on those necklaces Hilda has been passing out like candy. I'm surprised Hilda can stand to be near it—it's a physical manifestation of the heat of the Morrigan's hatred of our dear Hilda and her Valkyries— and of her separation from the energy that binds the rest of you together. Then again, perhaps Hilda made use of it herself—to ward off Astrid and the others."

"But I thought that symbol was protective—so Astrid's power couldn't work on whoever carried it."

"It is," Loki said. "If you're not a Valkyrie—a *full* Valkyrie. You see, it stops the Valkyrie magic from reaching inside you. But for a Valkyrie, it has entirely different implications— blocking the magic would also keep you from accessing all that wonderful shared strength and power you'll now be able to access. To Tucker and your brother, it represents protection." He flashed a predatory grin that made me take a step back. "To you and your kind, it means utter destruction."

"Why?" I demanded. "Why does she hate us so much? If the Morrigan was once a Valkyrie too, why would she create something that could hurt us?"

"She has more than ample reason to hold a grudge," Loki purred. "You see, she committed an unpardonable infraction in the Valkyrie world. She fell in love with a human who was fated by Odin to die in battle. Valkyries select and gather the brave, but only Odin decides who lives and who dies. The Morrigan spared her lover anyway, forcing Hilda to kill him instead. Hilda then tried to destroy the Morrigan too. Unfortunately, killing a Valkyrie is every bit as hard as it looks, even for Hilda. It's the energy that flows between you. Losing one is like losing a limb. My guess is the Morrigan's escape wasn't an accident, but she still swore revenge. A Valkyrie pledge is a powerful thing, as you well know. It becomes part of you. Runs in your blood. Mingles with the same energy and promises of sisterhood that make you strong. Invincible."

I shrugged, trying to pretend I didn't care, but Loki knew

he had a rapt audience and had every intention of drawing his explanation out. To torment me.

"That's what Astrid meant when she said she didn't want to end up like Tucker's ancestor. By disobeying Odin."

"It seems you're finally paying attention," Loki said, giving me a slow, condescending round of applause. "When she left the Valkyries, Tucker's ancestor went to Ireland and capitalized on local myths. It wasn't just her name she changed, it was also her nature. The Celts were remarkably easy to impress, and soon she became the all-powerful goddess of war. The Morrigan. But it wasn't until she fled to the Atlantic coast of France that she found her true power, tapping into magic that even I won't dally with—it was strong enough to fuse fire into the Norse runes that spelled her name. And for centuries, that was enough to keep Hilda and the others away. Eventually, she had a family—went native, so to speak. An irony of ironies that your grandmother later followed her example. Tucker has her blood in his veins, diluted over the generations until it almost shouldn't matter—you see how unremarkable it left him. Yet he was better prepared to meet his enemy than you were—he knew the old stories, handed down through his family, while you were raised in unconscionable ignorance. They remember the old ways and have guarded and cultivated their grudge through the generations, even if Hilda hasn't done the same. You're the granddaughter of his family's greatest enemy. Tuck would sooner kill you than kiss you, darling. Although who can blame him for exploring both options." Loki raised an eyebrow and gave me a smile that brought my knife to my hand.

"That can't be true," I said. "It doesn't make any sense. The boy next door doesn't turn out to be some weird villain from my grandmother's impossibly bizarre past." I spoke even as part of me was tabulating all the weird things I'd noticed about Tuck over the last few days. Like his unexpected familiarity with weapons and the fact that his senses at times seemed almost as sharp as mine.

Maybe his mother's Celtic cult wasn't so crazy after all.

"He may be American, but his mother is French." Loki drew out each word, making the statement take painfully long.

"Lots of people are," I said. "There's a whole country full of French people." Protest was futile, since Loki and I both knew I believed him. I finally let myself experience all the feelings I'd so carefully suppressed at Astrid's earlier revelation. A pain started in my chest and radiated down my limbs, searing all the places where Tuck's hands had been, where his lips had lingered. Every sweet thing he'd said. Here I'd been worried he wouldn't want to date me in the event we both make it home in one piece, when all along he was keeping secrets so big, they could swallow our friendship whole.

My thoughts were muddled by the pounding in my brain and the way Loki was circling around me, battering and bludgeoning me with his words.

"You're all alone. Even the other Valkyries don't want you. You need me. I can protect you from your own lack of experience. No one else will do that. I can give so much, and I ask so little in return. Just one small thing." While I had shrunk back, retreating in the face of his onslaught, Loki was growing larger and stronger, as if feeding on my pain.

But then I thought about Tuck, really thought about the way his smile filled me with light. And how he always smelled like sunshine and reckless summer afternoons. Even if sometimes he bulldozed through life and over people, there was something pure and sweet about him. Maybe he had some sort of ancient enemy bloodline—but I didn't care. I loved him. My heart had made that decision ages ago. It had just taken my head a while to catch up.

"What do you want, Loki?" I demanded. "Once and for all—just tell me."

"You." His purring voice curled up inside my ear no matter how much I tried to ignore it. "Your continued obedience. Really, when this is all over, we should stop and appreciate my generosity. All the things I've done to show you how strong you'll be with me to back you. Here you stand, Elsa, on the brink of disaster. Graham and Tucker are running out of time. And Hilda, well, her plan will only work if you set mine in motion. She's always been rash. And predictable. Once again, I've swooped in and saved the day."

"My grandmother had a plan?" I asked, a flip of excitement in my stomach. That there was a way out of this.

"Of course she did," Loki murmured. "No one could capture her unless she wanted it to happen. I'm surprised Astrid fell for it—even if Hilda did make one of her Valkyries bleed quite a bit before surrendering. If I know Hilda, she thinks that from the inside she can win her Valkyries back. They were fiercely loyal to her once. What she forgot is that change requires a catalyst.

Someone to bring things to a head. Force them to choose. A role you'll play magnificently."

"You've been driving me to this point all along," I said. "You know that now I'll do anything to get everyone back."

"Anything? Including a direct assault on Odin?" Loki asked, cocking one eyebrow. "Outstanding. Now let me carry you one step further, since you're a bit slow on the uptake. You need soldiers. One guess who would be all too willing to be led against Odin." He motioned his hand vaguely toward the half-open alley door. The sound of slamming car doors and running feet echoed through the streets. People were coming.

I stared at him, horrified. "You mean those people—the kids who've been hunting Astrid? Margit and her friends?"

"Of course. They're loyal, motivated, and entirely expendable. They, like you, will do anything to get their loved ones back. What they lack is a leader. And believe me, Elsa, no one can inspire courage like a Valkyrie. Now that you can cross over into Odin's world, you can lead them there. You were made for this role. Created for this day."

"Cut the crap, Loki," I hissed. "I was dragged to this day. And if you think they'll listen to me, you haven't been paying attention. They hate me. I'm all alone, as you keep pointing out."

"Things have changed," Loki said, leaning his shoulder against the wall and kicking one ankle over the other. "I arranged a few wonderful scenes in which you performed brilliantly. Showcasing your strength. The way you fearlessly defy Astrid. The miles you'd crawl to stop her. The man you rescued in the stadium. Oh, they saw it all. Even tonight, they listened until I destroyed that radio transmitter. Couldn't let them know about me. Once again, you were fantastic—brave and reckless in the face of heart-stopping danger. If you ever want to see Graham, Tuck, or your grandmother again, you'll capitalize on their trust and lead them right up the road into Odin's backyard." He tipped his head back against the wall.

"If I refuse?"

"You won't." All at once he was in front of me. He extended one hand and cupped my cheek. "Because there's no other way. It's what the townspeople want. You love your family and would do anything to keep them safe. It really is best for everyone. But if these stakes aren't high enough to motivate you, I'm happy to keep increasing them. Mother is in Italy, correct? No reason for her to miss out on all the fun." His angelic smile made his words so much more disturbing.

"Is that some sort of threat?" I tried to stand my ground, but my confidence faltered.

"No," he said, "it's a promise."

I knew I had no choice but to do as he said. Plus it wasn't like I had a better idea. There was an undeniable, brutal logic to what Loki proposed. It was the last resort for everyone. Still, the violent voice in my head was howling for Loki's blood, appalled that I was letting him push me around. Until another, more reasonable, tactical side of me weighed in. Cool and collected. Let Loki think he can use me. It would buy me time to come up with a way to get rid of him.

"Fine," I said, squeezing my eyelids shut.

I turned to leave, wanting nothing more than to get away

from Loki and his sneering smile.

"One more thing, Elsa," he said, catching my arm. His fingers felt like they'd been carved from ice, and I shook them off, recoiling from the cold as much as from his touch. "When the smoke clears, you will deliver Odin to me."

"And how am I supposed to do that?" I demanded. "Last time I checked, he was a god."

"And so am I," he said. "Don't fail me."

The threat was all too clear, as was the impossibility of what Loki had just demanded I do.

"It breaks my heart to see you so dejected," he continued. "You mean so much to me, Ellie. I've waited a thousand years for a shot like this at Odin, and almost as long for a chance to train up my own baby Valkyrie. Look at what a wonderful team we make already. Just think of how we'll shine together after a few centuries."

The words made me shudder. And doubled my determination to find a way to shake Loki off my jugular. There was no way I'd let him turn me into his favorite new pet. He'd have to kill me first.

14

As I left the bar and stepped out into weak light of the streetlamps, my head was reeling from everything I'd just learned. I could see the shape of Margit huddled over her steering wheel. Three other cars had parked behind her, and the passengers were peering out their windows, wide-eyed, like visitors at one of those drive-through zoos. Never in my life had I felt so alone. No Tuck, no Graham. No one to stand by my side if Margit and her friends suddenly changed their minds and turned on me.

Because like Loki said, I would need them on my side in order to save Graham and Tuck and everyone else. Even if I felt anxious and inadequate, I couldn't let Margit and the others know. I needed to be confident.

Margit stepped out of her car. "What happened in there?" she asked. "Did they really take Tucker?"

"Weren't you listening?" I asked. Then I remembered and pulled the small radio out of my pocket. It was damaged beyond repair. "Astrid knocked me out. Hit me over the head with a gun."

I expected a look of suspicion. After all, Astrid had left me behind, barely injured, while she'd skated away with two more boys. There was no way Margit could know that my head still felt like hell. But instead Margit frowned, and something that could almost be sympathy shone in her eyes. "We found this in the middle of the road. I'm sorry your plan didn't work." She handed me the transponder I'd hidden under Astrid's car. It had been wrenched from its hiding place and crushed like a soda can. "I bet we'll find them before dawn," Margit said, actually putting a hand on my back to soothe me. "If they're out there, we'll track them down." She inclined her head toward the massive radio crackling away in the passenger seat of her car.

"We don't have to find them anymore." My voice held an authority that I still didn't quite feel. "I know where they are," I added. "I need to talk to the people in charge of your . . . whatever it is, your network."

"No one's really in charge," Margit said slowly. "We just sort of call the contacts we have, then they call their contacts— anyone they know who wants to help. It's not like we had an emergency plan in place for psychotic Valkyrie attacks."

I ignored the jab as my fragile confidence deflated. I would need to mobilize a group of people who were even more disorganized than I'd imagined. Had I really once been afraid of these people? Was I really prepared to endanger their lives? Because even with only a couple of weeks to work with, you could bet Astrid and Odin had trained those kidnapped boys far better than the force I'd be leading. That didn't count the other soldiers they had—the ones with centuries of experience.

I couldn't let Margit hear my doubt. Confidence had a magic all its own, as Tuck had shown me hourly.

"I need you to call your contacts and spread a message," I said.

Margit narrowed her eyes. "What kind of message?"

I looked out across the fjord, toward the twinkling lights of Skavøpoll. The road through town filled my mind's eye, shifting in and out of focus, the way the world looked when I was young and tried on my father's half-inch-thick glasses. There were two roads in Skavøpoll, superimposed, one upon the other. I'd started to glimpse this when I'd followed Astrid, but now I could sense it so clearly. The second road was stripped bare of the shops and houses I'd come to know. Instead it was thickly wooded and untouched, the way the world must have looked in the aeons before human habitation.

There was something special about Skavøpoll—a reason my grandmother had stayed there all those years. It was a pathway, a portal to somewhere else. My grandmother's fortified house was a watchtower on the living side.

"What kind of message?" Margit repeated, snapping me out of my thoughts.

"To come," I said. "To gather in Skavøpoll an hour before

dawn. Everyone you've made contact with and everyone they've made contact with. Anyone with a vested interest in getting their loved ones back."

"Why?" Margit asked. "You said we need to find the boys before dawn. That would mean interrupting our surveillance. We can't afford the risk."

"Yes, we can," I said, surprised by the genuine command rippling through each word. "Because this ends now. On our terms. We're taking the Valkyries down."

At that, Margit's eyes grew bigger than the moon. I could hear the wheels spinning in her mind. I could taste her fear and hesitation.

So I reached deep inside myself, to the part that wanted so much to be as ferocious and invincible as Astrid, but as poised and righteous as my grandmother.

I blended it all together into something that was just me. Ellie.

"Something happened to me tonight, in the bar. I know where Astrid has taken them. I'm going after them. But I can't do it alone. We need as many people as we can get—we'll be facing an army. The people we're trying to rescue may very well be the soldiers who challenge us. They're under Astrid's control."

Margit was silent for a long moment, considering. "What if the Vals just hypnotize us all, too?"

I handed her the slip of paper Tuck had given me and watched as she unfolded it.

"It's from an opposing faction of Valkyries. Astrid's enemy. It represents protection. It'll keep everyone safe."

"This is what Tucker gave you?" she asked. There was open curiosity in Margit's eyes as she looked up from the slip of paper back at me. "I wondered about that part when I heard it on the radio. And about what Astrid said. I didn't understand—but then . . ." Her words trailed off when she took in my expression, and I seriously hoped she couldn't see how much I wanted to bury my face in my pillow like the girl I'd been three days ago. That wouldn't exactly instill faith in my ability to start a war. I wasn't ready to talk about Tuck.

"Thank you" was all she said. It was strange how much changed in that moment. Hate melting away entirely, giving way to trust.

"Make sure everyone carries it. So Astrid can't turn them against us, too. The best bet is to draw it straight on their skin. Not a limb. A place that can't be removed without killing them." My heart ached as I repeated Tucker's instructions. Making me wonder again about all the other secrets he hadn't had a chance to tell me.

Margit nodded, and I listened as she explained the plan to the others, the people who waited patiently in the cars idling behind hers. Cell phones and wireless radios were activated, sending our call for help out across the fjord, to all the people waiting and watching in the surrounding towns.

THE APPROACHING DAWN was painting the night sky in pinks and greens when I finally walked down the main street through town, heading toward the water. It was a permanent reminder of Loki's deadline, looming overhead.

It seemed too quiet, and I worried that Margit's call for help had failed, or worse, no one had any intention of following a sixteen-year-old girl on some crazy rescue mission.

Then I heard the voices. Like a crowd of people had just dropped from the sky into downtown Skavøpoll. Cars lined the street, double-parked, trapping one another in a mosaic of painted metal. Some had pulled right up onto the docks, perching precariously next to the deserted fishing trawlers. Even the fishermen had forgone their morning catch in order to gather in the streets of Skavøpoll with everyone else.

My relief at the sight of so many evaporated when they slowly turned, one by one, to look at me. Hundreds of expectant faces. Watching. Whispering to their neighbors. Words like Valkyrie and Odin and Hilda Overholt riddled my ears. They were gathered in the street in a loose crowd, spread across the street, under shop awnings and around the benches in front of the bank. It was odd to see such an assortment of people pulled together by one cause. A burly fisherman stood next to the elegant woman who ran the high-end clothing shop. I recognized the mayor and the waitress who'd served us at the restaurant.

They were all waiting for me to do something—to lead them. And that thought made me want to laugh and cry and crawl under the nearest bench to die.

I squared my shoulders anyway and continued walking, letting my gaze settle over them all, coming to a stop when Loki's wicked grin curled the lips of a paunchy middle-aged man. He gave me an enthusiastic thumbs-up before melting back into the rest of the crowd. That nudge of goading was all it took to bring my determination roaring back. I'd get Graham and the others back, and then I'd show Loki what happens when you try to manipulate me.

At the center of town, Margit met me.

"Incredible," I told her. "I had no idea you'd get so many people to come."

"They're all angry. Ready to do something about it." She gave me a wry smile, like she knew I was nervous and it made her like me a bit more. "Are you?"

I nodded as I surveyed the town. We were all focused together on this single task. An infusion of strength and bravery, pure and true, radiated out from them, and I magnified their energy and sent it back twice as strong.

We were ready. At least, as ready as we could be.

I walked to the far side of town, where I'd sensed the parting between the worlds. Eyes latched onto me and shoes shuffled along the asphalt as people followed, drawing together. Sven led a group of kids I recognized from town as they wove through the crowd to reach the front.

I took a deep breath and closed my eyes, willing the second road to appear. I pictured the empty road unfurling in front of me, wooded and winding its way through the world of the dead.

"Knock, knock, Astrid," I whispered. A tentative smile of victory curled my lips as I felt the breeze from another world whispering through my hair. I opened my eyes.

Instead of the deserted road I'd expected, Astrid was there. Five feet away. Flanked by ten Valkyries, five on each side.

I jumped back, falling over and scrambling away on my

hands, trying to get the space to maneuver.

"What is it? Are you okay?" Margit asked, dropping to her knees beside me. But she didn't have to wait for my explanation. Astrid stepped forward. To the rest of the world, she had appeared out of thin air. All alone. Only I could see that she'd brought backup. The other Valkyries remained just across the threshold of another world.

Astrid's eyes brushed impatiently across the faces in the assembled crowd before coming to a stop on mine.

"I'm afraid this will be a short-lived rebellion," she said. Her fur-trimmed boots were centered on the yellow traffic paint separating the road into two narrow lanes. "Disassemble your little pets and send them home. Or we'll do it for you."

She lifted one arm into the air. I winced, bracing myself for a blow. But it was just a signal, inviting the others to join her, crooking her finger above all our heads with enough flair that all of Skavøpoll got a front-row seat.

The other Valkyries stepped forward all at once, timing their appearance with a blinding flash of sunlight as it broke over the mountains—as if they needed anything to make their entrance more dramatic. Murmurs of shock and fear rippled through the crowd behind me, punctuated by a shrill voice screaming, "Run!" I couldn't blame them for being scared. Never in my life had I seen anything as awe-inspiring or terrifying as Astrid's squad in their full military splendor. Holstered guns strapped to slender limbs, vigilant snipers' eyes scanning the town through long Bambi lashes.

They were dressed alike, all in black, with the same fur-trimmed leather boots—the soles were heavy enough to serve as weapons in their own right. But that was where the resemblance ended. Each Valkyrie was unique, with varying shades of hair and skin and height.

"Oh, shit," Margit whispered, retreating to stand behind me. Like I'd be able to protect either of us. Yet nothing could have more aptly articulated the terror raging through the fishermen and shopkeepers who'd been stupid enough to put their faith in me. All courage and hope vaporized on contact, with the earth-shattering, annihilating finality of a nuclear explosion.

But just as the panic threatened to carry me off to its cave, another presence asserted itself in my mind. The violent voice was back. Only this time it was commanding me forward with cold, brutal logic. Because it was too late to back out now. We'd never get a second chance. The desperation in the people who followed me tore into my heart, but then I realized it was because they didn't know what to do next. They wanted to stay, they wanted to press forward and risk everything. But they were scared. They needed reassurance and an infusion of strength. They needed a leader.

Me.

"Stand your ground." I pushed my voice until it cracked, needing it to wash over the farthest reaches of the crowd. "Remember who is at stake. Picture his face. Know that we're bringing them all back." And then I did something even I didn't expect. My voice turned to ice as I added, "The Vals don't believe in what they're doing anyway. They won't stop us."

Astrid's eyes flashed with a rage so hot it would melt a

diamond, but I stared her right back down.

"You won't," I said, realizing the truth of it as the words skipped across my tongue. "Why else would you keep letting me live? I think part of you is relieved I'm here."

A few wisps of newly minted courage drifted back to me on the breeze. So I stood up straighter, taking a step toward Astrid and ignoring the thunderclaps of my beating heart.

"I'm afraid we're not open for visitors," Astrid said coolly, belying the fury I could feel radiating from her skin. Her lips twisted into a brittle smile as they drifted over the townspeople. "And there was a reason we left these people behind. They're useless. Our discards. What an utter cruelty to give them this false hope. You know I can't let you pass."

Her words triggered a ripple of jeers and protests. The crowd behind me pressed closer, drawn forward by the danger we now shared. Even the stragglers who'd watched from shop doorways or car windows now approached, joining the mob. The old lady from the bakery lifted her cane into the air and shook it at Astrid. She was fully ready to slam it into Astrid's toes just like she had mine. I never would have dreamed she'd be standing behind me one day, ready to fight.

"Can't?" I replicated Astrid's tone of pure scorn. "You can do whatever you want, Astrid. It's time to stop blaming Odin for your choices."

My imminent demise flashed across Astrid's face.

Her hand exploded into my peripheral vision, moving toward me, only I saw the blow coming this time. And I was ready. My forearm flew up, almost of its own volition, colliding with Astrid. For a moment, we stood there, locked in a contest of brute strength, until Astrid's lips curled into a slow smile and she took one long step back, away from me.

"What do you think would happen if I stepped aside? Do you really plan to lead this herd of fishermen against Odin? On his own turf?" Astrid's voice drifted over the crowd, echoing off the shops and through the deserted side streets of Skavøpoll.

"I was hoping you wouldn't just step aside," I said, surprising myself as the pieces of my plan finally slid completely together. "I was hoping you would join us."

The words dangled in the air between us like they were strung up on a gallows.

"No!" a man shouted. "Are you insane?" The shout echoed down the street, followed by a few catcalls.

"Elsa is right, Astrid," a familiar voice said. "She's doing what you should have done. Standing up to Odin."

The words came from a statuesque, blond-haired Valkyrie who stepped forward, appearing all at once, like the others had, in the middle of the street.

It took me shamefully long to recognize my grandmother. And when I did, I stared in openmouthed disbelief. A hush fell over the crowd as they placed her too. Even those from other towns had at least glimpsed her over the years, the beautiful, eccentric old lady from Skavøpoll. Only now she was half a century younger than when I'd last seen her. Her hair was a pale blond; all traces of silver were gone. The few wrinkles that had once framed her eyes and lined her forehead had disappeared without a trace.

"How did you get here?" Astrid snapped, growling low in her throat. I recognized the way her shoulders tensed, preparing to strike. Only there was a hesitation this time. Wariness.

Astrid was afraid of my grandmother.

"It seems I've kept a few friends, even after all these years," Grandmother said cryptically, even as the look she cast toward Astrid's band of Valkyries made me wonder if one of them had risked Astrid's wrath and released her. "We collect and lead the dead, Astrid. Not the living."

"Who brought her here?" Astrid demanded, her eyes piercing each member of her squad in turn. "I'd hate to think one of my loyal sisters disobeyed me."

"I brought her." The brunette Valkyrie I recognized from my skirmish in Bergen shifted anxiously on her feet, but she looked Astrid square in the eye as she said, "Hear Hilda and the girl out. I agree with them."

"See, Astrid, she too is doing what you should have done." My grandmother laid one hand gently on the brunette's arm. "She's questioning her leader when she knows her leader is wrong."

"How dare you?" Astrid growled, shifting to the balls of her feet as if she would lunge forward at any moment. "Don't you dare judge me for things I can't control. You left us too weak to stop Odin when you abandoned us—and your responsibilities."

"I've been right here this whole time, Astrid. Watching," Grandmother said softly. "I came back when you needed me. I never gave up my responsibilities. I just changed the way I upheld them. Because I have competing priorities now." Her eyes met mine, unleashing a ripple of pride that threatened to burst right out of me.

"Now it's your turn to reevaluate your priorities," Grandmother continued. "Because whatever spell Odin was under all those centuries, slumbering away, has driven him mad. And you can bet Loki planned it that way. So he could humiliate Odin, as he's tried to do so many times before. Do you really want Odin to start a war you know he can't win? And even if he could win, do you really think we should return the world to the old ways?"

Murmurs erupted in the crowd, until above the din, a man shouted, "No! Stop him and bring our boys back."

The other Valkyries looked from Grandmother to Astrid and back to Grandmother again, visibly unsure who to side with. But I could tell by the way their eyes lingered a few seconds longer on Grandmother that their loyalty was shifting.

Astrid had a frown on her face that reminded me of how I felt around Graham, when I was once again being shown how young and inferior I was. And I felt an unexpected twinge of sympathy.

"I can't stop him," Astrid spat. "He won't listen. But that doesn't mean I'll betray him. Not all of us cast aside our oaths as easily as you have, Hilda."

Grandmother looked away, a troubled crease appearing between her eyebrows. "I did what was right," she said, but her words were weighed down with regrets I couldn't even begin to fathom.

"But there are other, older promises you've made, Astrid," I said, picking up the thread of the argument. "Even I can tell that the connection between all of us is far stronger than any fleeting promises you made to Odin. And that's just after a few days of knowing what I am. You disagree with Odin. You belong with us, not with him. If I can feel it, I know you can."

Grandmother stepped up beside me, her resolve strengthened by my words.

Astrid watched me in that cold, dismissive way she had. But she looked almost longingly at Grandmother's hand as it curled gently around my shoulder. I couldn't give up just yet.

"In Bergen, you told me that I couldn't stop Odin because you'd failed," I pressed on. "You were right. Alone, I *don't* stand a chance. But now, together, all of us—with you—we can do it. Odin doesn't stand a chance against us if we're united."

As Grandmother approached Astrid, one hand extended, Astrid's expression hardened into a look I recognized as resolve. She'd made up her mind. I braced myself for whatever that decision might be.

But before Grandmother could reach her, the ground beneath us began to rumble, rattling windows and setting off a car alarm. A low, throaty chuckle rocked the earth until my bones rattled. "It seems Hilda's power can't be diluted. Even after two generations." It was a deep, disembodied voice that pulled at the newly discovered corners of my mind. But this was different from the way Astrid and the others made me feel, as if we were sharing a collective awareness of the world around us. This new force felt like it was sucking away my strength. And my will to stand up to it.

Odin.

I knew it was him. The recognition was hardwired into my bones.

The people gathered in the street began to scatter, running toward the trees or the boats bobbing in the water, crowding under awnings and in doorways, as if there was a way to take cover against a force with this kind of power.

"Odin is coming," my grandmother said as she looked up the road. "Stand together. He'll try to drain our strength. It's the only way he can keep control of his soldiers."

Astrid's fingers curled around my wrist and sent a jolt of warmth up my arm, building toward the numbing heat I'd felt all those days ago in the bar with Kjell, when she'd put her finger to my forehead. Startled, I tried to shake off her hand. "Stop resisting me," she snapped. "You want to stop Odin? Let me in."

I didn't know what she meant, but then the connection that was always snapping at the edges of my consciousness suddenly reached out and wrapped me in its arms.

There was a ripple of satisfaction as Astrid's decision spread among the other Valkyries. Their silent allegiance shifted, leaving Odin and locking in on Skavøpoll. They'd defend the town and the people gathered in the street at any cost.

Margit took a step forward, choosing her place in the front, right in the middle of the road. She may not have been a Valkyrie, but she was one brave girl. I smiled, fiercely proud to have her standing with us.

It was a grave tactical error that Astrid had been so focused on collecting boys, when the girls in this town were more than twice as worthy.

Other people followed Margit's lead, breaking away from their hiding places and making their way back to us cautiously, sticking to the shadows of the buildings. A group of kids climbed up onto the top of a delivery van to get a better view.

I could taste the fear in the air, see it in Margit's trembling hand and quivering upper lip, even as she stood straight and tall.

An uneasy silence settled over the town. Seconds ticked past until my muscles ached with eagerness to act.

Then my grandmother went rigid at my side. Not with shock, or fear, but with readiness. A man appeared, emerging from a mist that hadn't been there an instant earlier.

None of the other impossible things I'd seen over the last few days had prepared me for my first sight of Odin. He was massive and thickly muscled, with a broad chest and shoulders, like a rodeo bull. A gruesome network of crisscrossing scars covered his neck and arms. I couldn't believe anyone could survive so many wounds—if he had even been alive in the traditional sense. And when I looked into his lifeless eye, I definitely doubted it. I shuddered, imagining what was underneath the patch secured over the eye he'd traded for wisdom.

"Impressive," he said, letting his gaze drift over the town. "Winning my Valkyries back right under my nose. A simple, elegant plan." That merciless eye scanned the crowd until it landed on me, seeming to rake through my very soul.

"It's not often someone marches against me." He said it mildly, saving all his malice for his next words. "It's never."

Somehow that wasn't a surprise. Icicles were forming in my blood, crystallizing along my spine. "We don't want to fight you," I told him, somehow managing to control my terror.

"I don't negotiate," Odin growled.

Astrid's hand tightened around my wrist. "Stop talking."

It was too late. Odin had me in his crosshairs. "You will be an example. To them. This world. Of what happens when you challenge Odin."

"I'm not challenging you," I said, my voice cracking. "We just—we just want the living soldiers back."

"Are you certain?" Odin's lips curled into an inhumanly cold smile as he surveyed the crowd behind me. "That would be a fitting punishment indeed."

"Odin, don't do this," Astrid said. Her voice held an edge of desperation I never wanted to hear coming from someone so strong. "It's too cruel."

My heart stopped beating. Astrid's threshold for cruel was as high as the moon. Something monstrous was about to happen.

"You have no right to address me," Odin snapped at Astrid. "You surrendered your position when you sided with the deserter." His eyes shot pure, unadulterated malice right at Grandmother. "You've forgotten, too—you've all forgotten the old ways. *Our* way. Perhaps this will refresh your memory." Odin inclined his head, and a breeze drifted in off the fjord, carrying with it the scent of pine trees and the crisp, clean air from the glaciers.

Soldiers appeared in the middle of the road, armed and standing rigidly at attention. The other Valkyries shifted closer, preparing our defense. Somehow I knew my place in the coordinated motion. My role. It was the oddest sort of exhilaration, to be part of something so much larger and more powerful than myself.

My grandmother turned, meeting my wide-eyed look of wonder with a slow, ferocious smile.

The ragged force Odin had assembled was no match for us. We would crush their bones. They were young and unprepared; there was an obvious lack of combat experience in how they stood and how they gripped their weapons too tightly. But the very same moment I tasted our victory on the wind, their features emerged from the mist that seemed to emanate from Odin.

Forming faces I recognized.

This wasn't a bloodthirsty undead army. It looked more like a high school track team.

These were living boys. Our living boys.

There was a redhead in the third row who looked just like Margit. That had to be her brother, Eric. And the blond-haired boy who I'd seen working at the gas station was standing right next to a milky-eyed and scowling Kjell.

Anguished voices behind me called out to long-lost brothers and sons. Kjell's father had to be held back when he tried to rush forward. A tall blond woman with Kjell's pale blue eyes wrapped her arms around him, urging him to stay calm.

With mounting panic, I scanned face after face, desperate for a glimpse of Graham or Tuck.

"What's wrong, Elsa?" Odin asked. "Can't find what you're looking for?" He lifted one hand and curled an index finger, beckoning someone closer.

Just as motion in the crowd of frozen boys caught my eye.

Tuck stumbled forward, pushing his way through the frozen soldiers toward me. Relief was a physical force, practically knocking me off my feet. I couldn't believe our luck, that the soldiers were still as statues, letting Tuck slip around them like a stunt driver dodging orange traffic cones.

His eyes found me, latching on in surprise and relief. He too looked confused that they had let him pass.

But Tuck was no more than a few steps clear of the ranks of boys when a massive soldier stepped forward, materializing out of the mist. Unlike the untrained boys gathered in front of us, this was a real warrior. In his size and agility, I saw the powerful, dangerous adversary I'd feared all along. Odin was finally unleashing his finest on us.

With lightning-fast reflexes and deadly strength, the giant soldier reached out and caught Tuck's arm. Tuck jerked back, landing flat on the pavement. The giant stepped forward, the threat of pain echoing in each footfall. Tuck rolled over, pushing up onto his elbows with exaggerated care, as if he was still stunned from the impact.

Horror grabbed hold of my soul when the giant's face came into view. It was Graham, only now I was seeing him in a whole new light. As an enemy. Stripped of his easygoing smile, Graham was terrifying.

"My new favorite has something to teach Elsa and the rest of you." Odin locked eyes with me. "Loyalty. He'll follow my orders. At any price."

Then Odin's gaze shifted to Graham. His fingers moved lazily through the mist as it coalesced into a long serrated knife.

"Kill him." He tossed the knife, and Graham snatched the blade from the air with one hand.

"No!" I shrieked, sounding far more helpless than a Valkyrie ever should.

Graham looked up. His milky-white eyes carried only indifferent curiosity at who had just screamed.

Then Graham's entire focus snapped back to Tuck and the task he'd just been given. He would perform it with the swift and effortless perfection that had always made him Graham.

There was a flash of silver as Graham flipped the blade in his hand in a full rotation, like a juggler. If there was any doubt Graham wasn't in his right mind, that sealed the deal. Graham had never used a knife unless eating was involved.

Odin's voice rang out again, slicing my torn heart into two equal halves. "Kill them all." The mist returned, wrapping around Odin like a winter coat as his words settled over us.

In the world as it should have been, the colorful, churning mass of people in the street would have been a parade or a festival to be celebrated. Instead, a fight for survival had pulled together this mottled mess of grandparents and parents, brothers and sisters.

My path to Tuck and Graham disintegrated in a crush of charging boy soldiers colliding with the townspeople. Through gaps in the colliding crowds, I glimpsed Graham thrusting the knife toward Tuck's chest. Tuck managed to roll to the side, catching only the edge of Graham's boot as it lashed after him with rib-crushing force.

My stomach felt like I'd been the one who took that blow

as the first wave of boys crashed into us. A woman's tortured voice called out to her son, only to end in a howl of horror as he must have clashed with our group of Valkyries, in a blur of broken arms and dislocated shoulders. One-sided struggles erupted in the streets behind us as the first few kidnapped boys broke through our ranks. Tortured shouts and pleas to stop reverberated off the buildings. A middle-aged man to my right was trying to restrain a boy who had to be his son. The boy slammed his fist into his father's nose with a sickening crunch of cartilage. I pried him off just long enough for his father to secure his arms with a length of rope.

My heart was beating so hard and fast, it felt like a cage match in my chest. I was doing my best to hold my position, but my attention was torn between the fights raging around me and the flashes of Graham and Tuck I caught through the crowd. Tuck was putting bodies and space between him and Graham, using people as buffers to avoid fighting him directly.

There was resignation in Tuck's strategy, in the way he ducked and dodged, twisting out of Graham's reach without lifting a hand to defend himself. Fast as Tuck was, he had to know it was only a matter of time before Graham caught him. Tuck would never hurt Graham—or me. Loki was wrong. I'd seen it the moment Tuck's eyes had met mine, just minutes ago. But I knew it now in a whole new way. Tuck would give his life for us, Morrigan or not. And there was no way I would let that happen.

I had to stop them from fighting. Whatever it took. But if Graham was bent on killing Tuck, there was no easy way to restrain him; he was strong and fast, I could see that from here. If it came down to it, was I prepared to let one of them be hurt— or worse still, to sacrifice one to save the other? I was frozen in place at the thought, paralyzed by the mere idea of a choice I could never make.

"Go!" Astrid shouted, shoving me from behind. "Stop stalling. I know you don't want to choose, but you have to." I turned and caught her eye, surprised. She pointed toward Graham's golden head. A surge of ferocious power flowed from the other Valkyries straight into my heart. Reminding me that I wasn't alone in trying to save the town and everyone else. Astrid, my grandmother, and the others could hold their own while I stopped Graham and Tuck.

I catapulted through the crowd toward Tucker, knocking over a tall, lanky boy in a soccer uniform who tried to block my path.

"Get out of here, Ells." Tuck pushed me back, and not gently. "He could hurt you. Go away!"

"He could hurt you, too," I hissed back. "Graham, stop, it's me." I tried to knock the knife out of his hand, but Graham shoved me out of his way with the same minimal effort he'd use to brush the hair out of his eyes. It seemed Valkyrie blood did some pretty interesting things to boys, too. "You don't want to hurt us. I'm your sister." My voice broke over the words.

But Graham didn't hear me. At least not the part of him that I knew—the part that was my brother. His eyes were on the prize. Tucker.

Graham lunged with the knife, and it bit into Tuck's arm,

slicing a line of red from his elbow to his wrist. Tuck winced and dodged away, right as Graham pulled back, preparing to strike again. But Tuck recovered in time and caught Graham's wrist, dropping to the ground and using his downward momentum to slam Graham forward into a brick wall. Graham hit the corner of the building hard enough that it took him an instant to catch his balance.

Tuck fumbled in his pocket, looking for something. Then he pulled out a metal necklace like the ones Grandmother had given to Graham and Kjell.

"Hold him!" Tuck shouted. Without hesitating, I dived onto Graham's back in a massive bear hug. It took every ounce of strength I had to keep Graham in place, and even then he was thrashing like a fish on a line, shaking me off.

Fortunately, those few precious seconds were enough time for Tuck to slide Grandmother's necklace over Graham's head.

The instant the metal disk settled on his skin, Graham's brow furrowed, and he massaged his forehead like he had the mother of all migraines. Even though his eyes were still milky white, I could see his consciousness stirring to life behind them. He was fighting to clear the haze in his brain, and as he did, he gave up his struggle against my restraining arms. Graham sagged backward, against me, as if all his energy was focused on regaining control over his mind and not a single ounce could be spared—not even to keep himself upright.

"Where'd you get that?" I demanded, reaching toward the necklace but remembering at the last moment that I shouldn't touch it.

"Astrid kept one—she wanted to figure out what it was. Your grandmother managed to pass it to me on the inside. It seemed her mutiny was well under way by the time I arrived."

"What were you thinking, getting yourself taken?" I demanded as we lowered Graham to the ground, propping him up against the side of the building.

"Not sure I was thinking anything." He shrugged, trying to fake his usual casual confidence, but the eyes that met mine were full of apology. "I had nothing to lose except you. And it seemed like the best way to keep you safe."

I reached up and touched his face, still surprised I was allowed to do that now. "Use your sweatshirt to put pressure on that," I said, my eyes dropping to his injured arm.

Graham groaned, rubbing his forehead.

"Something tells me he's gonna wake up with a headache worse than my homecoming hangover." Tuck flashed a shy half smile. "You don't hate me?"

"Remains to be seen." But I let my smile give him the real answer as I straightened back up, knowing it was way past time to return to Astrid and the others. "You owe me a couple dozen explanations."

Tuck ducked his head in assent, his hands still resting on Graham's shoulders, just in case. The silver disk hanging from Graham's neck sparkled in the sunlight—a reminder of how very complicated our friendship, or whatever it was, had become.

"And a proper first date," I added, angling for one of his smiles. And it worked. I turned, feeling the pull of my Valkyrie sisters, needing me, needing two more hands to help hold back the onslaught that threatened to engulf us all.

"I have to go," I said to Tuck. "Keep an eye on Graham."

Tuck started to object, but his voice was drowned in the shouting coming from the street behind us. Twenty feet away, Astrid and my grandmother were standing back to back, surrounded by a wall of soldiers they were fending off with their bare hands. Astrid swept her leg behind the one in the middle. He fell and landed on his wrist with a crunch of broken bone. Astrid was visibly fed up with holding herself back when victory could be ours so easily. I was disturbed to discover that part of me could relate. But that wasn't our only point in common; judging by her actions, Astrid also shared my aversion to harming innocent people, a realization that made me like her a little bit more.

The pull to join Astrid and Grandmother was undeniable. My feet carried me forward, drawn by an impulse as basic as breathing.

But even as I raced forward, I realized that holding Odin back indefinitely was hardly a solution. We needed to break Odin's hold over those boys. And over us.

According to Loki, the symbol on Graham's necklace was the name of the Morrigan, the Valkyrie who had left us and withdrawn from our collective consciousness forever. The symbol blocked our Valkyrie magic from reaching her, just like it protected Graham from our influence.

If the runes on the necklace worked like that—if they could break the circuit of energy that bound us all together—then maybe we could use it to block Odin and his constant pull on our energy. And without our Valkyrie power to augment his own, he'd never be able to control so many soldiers. I could sense it, the way he drained the energy that flowed between the Valkyries in order to enforce his own will.

I turned and pressed back through the churning crowd toward Tucker, sidestepping a car door that one of the Valkyries must have ripped off and hurled into the middle of the road. I dropped to the ground at Tuck's side.

"Give me that necklace," I said.

Tuck's forehead creased. "Graham needs it."

"There are a lot of other people here who need it too. Trust me." When Tuck didn't move, I added, "Just do what you did to yourself—draw the symbols on Graham's skin. After all, that's what's important, not the necklace."

Tuck hesitated before sliding it back over Graham's head and handing it to me. Graham's eyes opened, focusing uncertainly on each of us before closing again. They were still confused, but at least they weren't milky white.

The chain reflected the sun's thin morning rays as it pooled on my palm, followed by the metal disk carved with three runes. But the instant the metal touched my skin, white-hot pain shot down my arm. On reflex, I jerked my hand away and sent the necklace tumbling to the ground. It felt like I'd just plunged my fingers into boiling water.

"What's wrong?" Tuck grabbed my wrist. The edge of the metal disk had burned my skin, leaving an angry red crescent mark that settled into a throbbing scar.

As the pain faded, I realized Loki wasn't exaggerating about the Morrigan's power. For the fraction of an instant the necklace had settled on my skin, the current that had connected me to the other Valkyries had flickered and dimmed, threatening to abandon me forever.

In the middle of the churning mass of soldiers, Astrid had stopped fighting. She stood stock-still, staring at me. A body slammed into her from the side, and she blocked the assault absently with one elbow, never breaking our locked gaze. She'd felt my absence. But then I saw the glimmer of realization, her blue eyes widening as she pieced together what had just happened.

"Ellie!" My grandmother's voice was frantic as she pushed through the crowd, running toward me. "Behind you."

I pulled my sleeve down over my hand and grabbed the necklace from its resting place on the muddy ground. As I straightened, the mist that had swirled around Odin was suddenly thick in my throat, depositing Odin right behind me. His eye burned into me like a red-hot coal, matching the heat from the necklace in my hand, which was scalding me through my shirt.

"Once again you have my undivided attention." Odin's voice was soft but deadly, like a snake's warning hiss. "Do you really think you can hide from me?"

As clever as Odin thought he was, he didn't fully grasp the implications of what I'd just done. Hiding was hardly my plan.

"Yes," I replied.

Odin's hand flew out, fast as a bolt of lightning. I tried to duck aside, already knowing it was futile. Fast as I was, Odin was far faster. He caught my throat in one hand and lifted me off the ground. The lack of oxygen slowed my thoughts until I almost forgot the details of my plan and surrendered to panic.

My eyes found Tuck. His eyes were wide, and his mouth opened to scream something. I clawed and thrashed against Odin's grip, trying to pry his hands loose enough that I could sneak in one last breath. I needed to steel myself against the grizzliness of what I was about to do. The sweet little Ellie who'd hidden during her brother's birthday party would never have done such a thing.

I lifted my sleeve-covered hand and pressed the burning-hot contents against Odin's forehead. And I held it there. The flat surface of the medallion pressed into Odin's skin. I would have sworn my hand was on fire if I couldn't see for myself that it wasn't. The metal scalded my skin through the fabric of my sleeve. His eye widened in shock, the iris a blue so pale it almost disappeared into the white around it. A howl of pain and anger roared from his open mouth. His grip on me slackened, and I sucked in as much air as my lungs would hold. There was no telling how long this respite would last.

Odin knocked the necklace out of my hand, sending it clattering down the street. But it was too late. There in the middle of his forehead were the raised runes from the necklace, seared into Odin's skin. The marks were surrounded by a red circle, the outline of the metal charm.

The scar on his skin deepened into an angry red welt.

"What have you done?" Odin growled. The shuffles and crashes of fighting slowed and finally crawled to a stop. Shouts echoed through the streets, but they weren't the cries of despair or panic. They were the celebratory whoops of victory.

"She separated you from your Valkyries," Astrid said, smug satisfaction in every word. "Let's see how long you stand without us to prop you up."

"This doesn't matter," he snapped back, still rubbing the scar on his forehead. "You belong to me even if I let you pretend otherwise. Get the troops back in formation. We're not finished with this town."

Astrid visibly vacillated. The tide could just as easily turn back on us if Astrid switched sides again. I found myself wondering what I'd do in her place. Would I be strong enough to defy a powerful god I'd obeyed for three thousand years when I could barely stand up to my own brother?

"No." The world hung in space between them. Odin's eye widened in surprise before narrowing dangerously. He had really believed Astrid would come back to him. "I'm through taking orders," Astrid snarled, finality in every syllable. "From you or from anyone. From now on, I decide what's right."

Grandmother stepped forward. "Let Ellie go, Odin." She flashed a wolfish smile that I found myself returning. Because if Odin refused, I was pretty sure the two of us could make him cooperate. "Unless, of course, you think you can face all of us."

Twelve Valkyries stood in an uneven line, squaring off against Odin. I curled my fingers around Odin's wrist and slowly, millimeter by millimeter, pried his hand off my throat.

"This isn't over." Odin's fingers traced the runes as his other hand struggled to keep its hold around my throat. "Revenge requires patience, Elsa. That is how Odin always prevails." The words had barely reached my ears before Odin hurled me to the ground. Four ribs and my left wrist shattered on impact. But nothing hurt like the bonfire raging in my right hand. I pulled back the sleeve of my sweatshirt and had to peel the cloth away from the raw skin beneath. My palm was red and blistered, and the circular edge of the amulet was seared into the skin between my thumb and index finger.

Even as my body set to work knitting the broken bones back together, I knew the burn marks on my hand would never heal.

Some scars are permanent.

By the time I managed to lift my half-healed self off the pavement to sit up, Odin was gone. A solitary ribbon of mist curled through the space he had just occupied.

Silence had settled back over Skavøpoll. The quiet was so complete, I could hear the waves lapping against the docks. Followed by hesitant whispers in the crowd. An instant earlier, the town had been locked in a battle to the death. But time seemed to have stood still the moment Odin had lost his power.

One by one, the people behind us rushed forward, embracing their kidnapped sons, who looked around in confusion, like they'd just emerged from a dream and weren't entirely sure why they were in the middle of the street. A lump grew in my throat as I watched Margit punch a groggy Kjell playfully in the shoulder, making him stagger a step to keep his balance. Then she took two more steps and crushed her brother in her arms. I knew exactly how she felt—the heart-swelling relief of finally having her brother back.

"We seem to be making a habit of this," Tuck said, helping

me to my feet, like he had so many times over the past few days. Except now he wasn't alone.

A hand closed gently around my injured wrist, and I winced.

"Ellie?" Graham's voice was scratchy, like he'd just woken up. "When did you get here? Did Grandmother send you?" His blue eyes widened in horror, and for a moment I thought he was remembering everything that had happened. But then he added, "She knows we snuck out?" He shook his head, looking down at his shoes. "It doesn't matter. I'm glad you came. I'll never sleep tonight if we're still fighting."

A laugh bubbled up inside me. Graham was stuck back in time, on the big fight we'd had the night Astrid had taken him.

"How did we get here?" he asked, looking around, wide-eyed as a newborn colt. "What time is it?" His gaze found Grandmother, and a spark of recognition fought its way across his synapses.

"Don't look so surprised, Graham," Grandmother said, taking in his stupefied expression when her voice came from the lips of that siren. She gave me a sly smile. "You must have noticed that there's something simply extraordinary about the women in your family."

"Grandmother is a Valkyrie," I clarified. "And so am I." Direct seemed the best approach, especially since Graham was still pretty out of it.

"Like out of the myths?" He laughed nervously, like he was already anticipating whatever punch line was waiting. But his forehead furrowed. The events that had just transpired were fighting their way forward in his mind, clamoring for recognition.

"Yes."

Graham opened and closed his mouth a few times, like a fish.

"The first new Valkyrie in a thousand years." The voice stopped me in my tracks. In my relief and happiness at driving off Odin, I'd forgotten all about Loki. Unfortunately, my memory lapse wasn't mutual.

"You're brave to show any of your faces here, Loki." Astrid moved to stand in front of us.

"Thank you." A smile curled Loki's lips. "But it's not particularly brave to show up for a fight you've already won." His eyes found mine, and he winked. "You've done beautifully, Elsa. Exceeded my expectations. Even *I* didn't think of branding Odin. Your only mistake was letting him escape."

"Mistake?" Astrid glared at Loki long and hard. "Ellie doesn't answer to you. Or anyone. Odin did what any wounded general would do when facing unfavorable odds. Retreat and regroup. Live to fight another day. We would never dishonor him by giving chase."

"I want Odin," Loki told me. He waved one hand behind himself, indicating the whole town. "This whole debacle more than establishes Astrid's incompetence. She's not strong enough to keep him under control."

"Neither can you," Astrid snapped, taking a step forward and looming over Loki by half a foot.

"On the contrary," Loki purred. "I've been saving a special surprise for him. Courtesy of the same wise women who relieved Odin of his eye in exchange for his supposed wisdom. For all the good it gave him. Odin should have traded that eye for cunning instead. Then perhaps he would have fared better today."

The crowd in the street was too caught up in reunions to notice what was happening—this new, unwelcome turn of events. Except for Margit, who started to approach warily, eyes widening in disbelief at the ever-shifting landscape of Loki's face. I held up one hand, warning her to stay back.

"You can't control Odin without me," Loki said, crossing his arms. "You have no choice. I made sure of that."

Again Astrid was wavering. She didn't know what to do about Odin, especially since her switch in allegiance was still new and raw. But no one in their right mind would trust Loki.

"Yes, you do," I said, my idea still crystallizing as I spoke. "Just leave Odin alone." My grandmother was the only one whose eyes didn't widen at my words. "He traded his eye for wisdom. Maybe we give him a chance to put it into practice. Let him travel. Learn. Come to grips with how the world has changed."

"Odin tried to make me kill Tuck?" Graham asked, rubbing his head like he could massage his brain back into full working order. "We can't let someone like that just wander around. Seems irresponsible. Was that really Odin, like *Odin* Odin? I can't believe I'm having this conversation."

I put a hand on Graham's shoulder. "It's okay," I said. "It'll take more than five minutes to catch up to the events of the past thirty-two hours. Even for you."

Astrid was nodding slowly to herself, her eyes scanning the road that led to Valhalla.

"Odin might be the god of war, but he's also the god of

knowledge," I added. "And I remember enough of Grandfather's bedtime stories to know he wasn't always cruel. Maybe time will help him figure out that the modern world is okay as it is."

Tuck's fingers squeezed mine. "Right. He can learn to surf. And if that's not enough to satisfy his megalomania, maybe take over a few South American countries?"

"I'm serious," I said, elbowing him. "We don't have any other option. He's immortal. He's got powers I can't even begin to understand. It's not like we can just lock him in our bathroom. And Loki . . . well, you can bet whatever he's up to will cause more problems than it solves."

Loki's face twisted in abject fury. I'm pretty sure he would have ripped out my throat on the spot if he hadn't been so outnumbered.

"Elsa is right," Grandmother said. "Odin isn't past repair. He just needs time. I'll keep an eye on him," she added. "Now that I don't have to worry about Astrid and the others, I'll have some time on my hands."

"Keep an eye on him?" Loki parroted back, his tone making it all too clear how stupid he thought we were being. "We need to *punish* him. Humiliate him. I've earned this victory. Give Odin to me."

"No," Astrid said. "I'm in charge here—not you. My word is final." Her eyes flashed, full of the possibilities that had just opened up in front of her at that moment. Doubt sucker punched me in the stomach as I remembered all the truly disturbing things I'd seen her do.

"We had an agreement," Loki growled. "Elsa, I'd hate to

think you're double-crossing me."

"Really? You should take it as a compliment. See how much I've learned from you in just two short days?" I replied levelly. "The only agreement we had is over. I've got Graham back. Dawn has passed. And it's time for you to find someone else to pester."

Astrid and the others shifted closer at once, into a half circle around me. Instantaneous coordination. With backup like this, Loki didn't stand a chance.

"I'll go to Midgaard," Loki said, a trace of whiny desperation curling through the words. "I'll tell them what you did. All the people you kidnapped."

"Good," Astrid replied calmly. "Tell them Valhalla is mine now. And if anyone has a problem with that, we'll be more than happy to convince them otherwise." She exchanged a slow smile with the brunette Valkyrie who'd released Grandmother, as if they eagerly awaited that opportunity.

"You and I aren't finished," Loki told me, even as his gaze switched nervously from face to flawless Valkyrie face. "This isn't over."

"Yes, it is," I said, more certain than I'd ever been before. "You can only push me around if I let you. I'm through with you, Loki."

Loki's features shifted, a spinning kaleidoscope of faces as he backed away, seeming to melt into the crowd milling about the streets of Skavøpoll. All the people were still embracing, reveling in their victory.

But Loki's voice drifted to my ears, carried there on the

wind, just for me. "We're not through until *I* say we're through. Just imagine. Right now I could be anyone and anywhere. I could even be the boy next door." The sound circled closer, suspended in the air, fading into soft laughter before disappearing entirely into the cool breeze drifting off the fjord.

15

"Ellie?" Astrid turned her glacial gaze on me. "You'll come with us?"

If my eyes were wide before, there was now a legitimate risk they'd fall out of my head altogether.

"Come where?" Graham asked, his usual sharpness returning all at once.

"Valhalla. She can come live with us now." Astrid talked down to Graham like he was too young and naïve to truly understand. A role reversal that wasn't lost on me. "She needs to learn to fight and lead."

"Don't be ridiculous," Graham said, even as he shrank back from Astrid's narrow-eyed glare. "She's coming home. With us."

"I wasn't asking *you*," Astrid informed him.

"She's my sister," Graham replied. "I'm not letting her run off to some commando camp."

He turned to Grandmother for confirmation, but her expression was blank. She was looking at me, and instead of guidance I saw genuine curiosity in her eyes. She wondered what I'd choose.

"Let her? You think you can stop her?" Astrid hissed. "You'll be lucky if she forgives you. Sulking. Sneaking out. Getting yourself conscripted. By me. Ellie spent the last two days being crushed by me in hand-to-hand combat, only to bring together an army of hostile vigilantes and march them right to Odin's front door. All to get you back. You're a liability she'd do best to dispose of."

"You did that?" Graham whispered in shock before remembering to use his fake Dad voice when talking down to me. "Something could have happened to you."

Astrid snorted.

"It did," I said. "A big something. I finally figured out who I really am. And being your sister is a part of that, but it can't be the only thing people see when they look at me. That includes you. You've got to stop trying to run my life. And paving over everything I say."

"You really think I do that? That I pave over you?" Graham asked. "Tuck? Do I do that?"

Tuck held up both hands and shook his head.

"You just asked Tuck to corroborate what I told you," I said, laughing at something that would have made me scream with frustration mere days before. Because suddenly I knew that Graham could boss me around only if I let him.

No one has power over me unless I surrender it.

"You're asking someone else," I pointed out. "Instead of listening to me."

"I guess, I mean, if you want to go with Astrid, you can." Graham looked at me hopefully, asking if that was the right answer, if these words would span this new distance between us.

Astrid made a disgusted noise deep in her throat before shifting impatiently from one booted foot to the other. "Come with us, Ellie. None of us think you require permission to do anything. The world will be what you make of it."

Then Graham shook his head, looking down at his shoes. "No. I get it. I get it. You're saying the permission isn't mine to give. It's yours. It's all yours to decide."

I met Graham's gaze, and I nodded.

And that's when it hit me. It was my decision.

Which meant I had to make it.

Everything went silent, except for the steady thud of my heartbeat in my ears.

In the weirdest way, Astrid's offer was exactly what I wanted. I could learn what I was. I could explore and master the strange whispers and violent impulses that had been urging me along this whole time. I knew how I'd be as a Valkyrie—daring and sleek like Astrid, yet wise and stoic like my grandmother. It was almost too good to be true.

Almost.

Because then I saw Graham and Tuck, staring at me like they'd just heard the sun would be leaving them for the foreseeable future.

It wasn't surprise I was feeling at Astrid's offer. In the background was the knowledge that I wasn't ready. Because before I could be strong with them, I had to be strong on my own. I'd be surrendering my new independence, my new self-awareness, before I'd even begun to truly understand what it meant.

I closed my eyes and let my vision of myself in all my Valkyrie glory float away on the breeze. "I'm still in high school. There's too much I'd be giving up right now." My eyes sought out Tuck, who was watching me, his eyes flawlessly unguarded and telling me everything I most needed to hear.

"I don't have time to train you anyway," Astrid snapped, but I caught a shadow of true regret before her features settled back to cold, hard stone. "What do we do with all the nosy mortals Ellie dragged into our private business?" she growled. "They know too much."

"Target practice," Grandmother replied, in a tone that made me seriously question whether she was joking.

Astrid laughed. "I'll clean up after you, just this once," she told me with a smile that could still chill me to the bone. "Although Hilda's suggestion isn't without its merits."

I took a step forward, ready to stop Astrid if she did something crazy. But Grandmother caught my arm and shook her head. She clucked her tongue like she always did when she was amused.

As Astrid walked away down the street, back toward the hidden road, there was something strange about the eyes of the people she passed. A wave of confusion swirled in her wake. Cloudy eyes, not quite milky but definitely not clear, stared off into space or out toward the water. A few people whispered to their neighbors, suddenly not really sure why they were standing in the middle of the street. Had it been an earthquake? Or a power failure that had driven them from their homes? Whatever it was, they were slowly casting suspicious glances at Grandmother. Soft whispers speculated about whether it was truly Hilda standing there, since suddenly she looked so young, followed by not-so-kind comments about her peculiar habits.

The old-lady spectacles appeared from Grandmother's pocket as she popped her high collar, making it impossible for anyone to get a close enough look to note the other differences in her.

As the whole town gathered and gossiped, Grandmother stood apart. Aloof. Feared. She was the one who'd saved the town, and yet again she was cast aside and distrusted.

Whatever Astrid had just done was a different breed of magic, not at all like how we seized control of people's minds. This felt older, primitive. I thought of the cascade of water that had nearly sent Tucker and me plummeting over the edge of a cliff. Gods had been around for centuries, weaving in and out of human lives without ever leaving concrete evidence of their existence. Perhaps there were other forces at work, guarding our deepest and most fundamental secrets. Forces even Astrid couldn't fully control.

The memories of everyone in town were being reshaped, sifted free of any recollection of what had just happened. While I was relieved I wouldn't have to discuss being a Valkyrie next time I went into the bakery or wandered along the pier after a morning run, there was one person who deserved to keep the truth.

"Not Margit," I said, out loud and to no one in particular. "She's earned the memory of her courage—of the day she stood with us and fought to get her brother back."

"Fine." Astrid's voice carried down the streets, and she gave me one last backward glance. "But rid yourself of this sentimental streak soon, Elsa. It's not our style."

Margit met my eye and gave me a tentative half smile. It seemed I'd found a real and true friend in the most unlikely place.

Astrid's footsteps faded as she disappeared into thin air, but twelve other pairs of boots picked up the rhythm. Marching to the steady thudding of my heart. Until they too vanished at the far edge of town.

A whole new breed of loneliness hatched inside my heart when Astrid and the others were truly gone. For a moment, I longed to follow. To join them.

But Tuck touched my elbow, appearing just when I needed him. As usual. The thrill that looped through me at his touch was all I needed to remind me of my life at home. The life I wasn't quite ready to give up.

At least . . . not yet.

16

My grandmother was in her garden by noon, watering her prize rosebush. Like it was any old day. I'd at least needed a nap after everything we'd been through. But not Grandmother.

I didn't know how to even begin to talk to her about what had happened. She suddenly felt like a stranger to me, and an intimidating stranger at that. I loitered in the kitchen, watching her and making tea. Working up the courage to say something.

But I should have known that she'd make it easy for everything to slip back to normal. After all, she'd had years of practice at pretending to fit in.

At my approach, she turned and smiled. "Feeling rested?" she asked. "I was hoping you could run to the hardware store for some new pruning sheers. I can't go into town looking like this." She motioned toward her dirt-flecked slacks.

Before I could reply to such a stunningly normal request, she reached into the pocket of her canvas gardening smock and pulled out a crisply folded piece of paper.

"I spent most of the morning trying to remember the words," she said as I unfolded the page and scanned her tidy script. It was a poem, written in Norwegian—something I was still surprised I could miraculously understand. "If memory serves, each word must be in just the right order to break the enchantment. It's been in place long enough that we need a strong remedy."

"Enchantment?" I asked, finally looking up from the page.

"You must have noticed the way Kjell was acting," she said. "I know it was an accident, Ellie. No doubt it happened the first time you saved him from Astrid—broke her hold and replaced it with one of your own. But we need to set it right, all the same. While I'm sure he thought you were pretty, I know Kjell well enough to know he wouldn't have such ridiculous intentions toward a sixteen-year-old girl."

"W-what do you mean?" I stammered.

"He came by while you were sleeping and asked if I'd mind if he proposed. Since your father couldn't be asked and I refused to give him your mother's phone number, he figured I was an adequate surrogate."

I choked on my tea.

Grandmother reached over and patted my back. Hard. She was making a valiant effort not to laugh at me. "Don't worry, he'll snap out of it quickly enough. Just nip this in the bud today, please. He said he'd be back at one to talk to you."

I glanced at my watch. That gave me exactly seven minutes to hide. But as I started walking up the path toward the house, a deep voice called my name. Kjell sounded so urgent, so excited to see me, that in light of my grandmother's news, I thought about running into the house and locking the door behind me. Or better yet, stashing myself underneath the trapdoor in the basement.

Instead I sighed and turned, smoothing my bed head down with one hand.

"Remember what I said, Elsa," Grandmother murmured as I walked past. "Take care of this. It's one of our more inconvenient talents. I promise the others will make up for it."

"Hi," Kjell said. He couldn't have smiled more brightly if he'd just swallowed the sun.

"Um, hi," I mumbled, doing my best to look bored. Unfortunately, we were well beyond the point that he'd pick up on hints. "Let's go for a walk?" I suggested, glancing back at my grandmother, who was standing in the yard, watching us with a bemused smile and both hands on her hips.

Kjell was all too eager to get away from my grandmother's watchful eye. As soon as we reached the base of the driveway and put a line of trees between us and Grandmother, he practically jumped on me. "I can't stop thinking about you," he said. "I can't sleep. I can't eat. Ever since you saved my life."

It was so melodramatic that it was hard to keep a straight face.

"Wait," I said. My stomach threatened to reject my breakfast as Kjell got down on one knee. "Before you do anything you'll regret, just hear me out."

"Of course. Anything you want," Kjell said, smiling like a drunken sailor. Which he pretty much was. Between whatever hold I had on him and whatever my grandmother and Astrid had done to erase the town's memories, Kjell was more than confused. "But after. First I have to tell you all about the plans I'm making for our future. We can live in Oslo, but I'll have to move out of student housing."

I took a step back. He scrambled to grab my hand, nearly knocking my grandmother's poem from my grasp. That would have been an all-out catastrophe given the stiff wind blowing down the mountain toward the fjord.

As Kjell held my hand in both of his and started saying something disturbing and completely inappropriate, I started talking too, raising my voice to be heard over his ridiculous proclamation of love.

By the time I reached the second stanza of the poem, Kjell had fallen silent. He was looking at me strangely. Like he had no idea where he was, how he had gotten there, and quite possibly who I was.

By the time I finished completely, he was shaking his head and pressing the heels of both hands to his forehead.

"I feel really weird," he said, almost tipping over as he tried to stand.

"You're okay," I replied, putting one hand on his shoulder and guiding him to his feet.

"What was I doing on the ground like that?" he asked. Then

he looked at me, as the memory of what he'd been planning hit him all at once.

"That was very funny, Kjell," I said, flashing my most innocent smile. "But I'm afraid that joke was lost somewhere in translation. Call it the culture gap or whatever, but in America our pranks aren't quite so elaborate."

"Right," he said slowly, still eyeing me warily. He knew I was lying, but he also had no incentive to correct me. "But you understand, right? That it was just a joke?"

"Of course I do." I was laughing now, hoping my smile would shoo away some of the awkwardness circling in the wings, waiting to pick our friendship clean. After all, I liked Kjell—just not like that.

"Well, one day I'm sure you'll have the chance to get back at me," he said, taking a step away down the driveway. I could tell he was still trying to untangle his thoughts, going back to that very first night in the bar. It was hard to imagine how bewildered he must have been. All the time he'd lost. "Because honestly, Elsa, you're just a little young for me. And we're both too young for all that down-on-one-knee business, right?"

"No explanation necessary, Kjell," I replied. "I can take a joke."

"Right," he said. But the eyes that scrutinized my face were skeptical and scrambling for a polite way to extract him from the entire situation.

So I gave him one.

"Look, I need to run an errand for my grandmother. But I think we're going out tomorrow night—Graham said he was gonna call you to get a game together."

"Thanks. That sounds great," Kjell replied. "But I'm going to visit some friends in Oslo. I won't be back before the school year starts." I could see in his eyes that he'd just made that decision on the spot, when he'd realized he was absolutely terrified of me. Even if he couldn't quite put his finger on why. I stood there for a minute, watching Kjell practically running away from me.

"Works like a charm," I said to my grandmother, waving the page in the air as I walked past.

"That's a good thing," she replied without looking up. "Because so does your smile. Keep it somewhere safe. You'll need it."

HER WORDS WERE dogging my steps as I walked up the porch stairs and ran straight into Tuck, nearly knocking the glass of orange juice out of his hand. I took a step back, not really sure what to do, since Graham was standing right behind him. In all the chaos of the past few hours, we hadn't exactly had time to talk about where things stood between the two of us.

"Hi," I said.

"Hi," he said back.

A long, awkward pause followed. Then Graham walked past, thumping Tucker hard on the back. "Don't hold back on my account," he said. "I'm not a complete moron. You're not as slick as you think—all those double entendres. Scampering around the roof in the middle of the night."

Tuck stared at Graham, and for the first time in his life, he didn't have a ready retort.

"Don't look so scared. Big brother is butting out this time. But if you break her heart, I'll break your arm. And maybe a leg." He laughed and shook his head. "Actually, she'll do it herself." He was still laughing to himself as he walked away, leaving Tuck and me alone on the porch steps.

It would take a while for Graham and me to figure out exactly what his new, laid-back-brother act would look like. I was just glad we were equally determined to find that middle ground together.

"Guess I'd better go talk to him," Tuck said, running one hand through his hair as he watched Graham stride away across the yard. "But we need to talk, too. Alone. Tonight? Same place?"

I nodded, not trusting my voice to be steady.

Even Tuck's playful grin couldn't ease the dread that had a stranglehold on my heart. Fortunately, Tuck's irritatingly astute skills of observation finally missed something. Like the way I forced my answering smile.

"C'mon, Tuck," Graham called. "We're late. Grab the soccer ball and let's go."

Then Tuck was gone, slipping down the porch stairs after Graham.

I should have been happy that everything had worked out the way it had. But my grandmother's words were echoing through my mind, and as Tuck glanced back at me, his smile was disturbingly sunny. A horrible realization was exploding into my consciousness, sending shock waves that threatened to shatter the rest of me.

Hard as it would be, I knew what I would have to do. I carefully folded the page with the poem into my pocket, keeping it close. Knowing I'd need it far sooner than my grandmother could ever have anticipated.

WHEN I CLIMBED up onto the roof that night, Tuck was already there. He was on his back with his hands behind his head, staring up at the stars. As I approached, he spread out his left arm, making a spot for me. I stretched out next to him, memorizing the way it felt to put my head on his shoulder and to have his arm wrap slowly around me, pulling me closer, until every inch of my side was pressed so closely against him that there was barely enough room for a molecule of oxygen to slide between us.

I touched my pocket, where the slip of paper was hidden. It was far too dark to read, and I couldn't afford to get this wrong, so I'd practiced this moment again and again, until I knew each line, each curve of my grandmother's handwriting, by heart. I closed my eyes, willing myself forward, telling myself for the thousandth time that this was the right thing to do.

Still, I couldn't help but wonder why the right thing felt so wrong.

"Penny for your thoughts," he said, rolling onto his side to face me. "Or would you prefer a different kind of barter?" Then his lips found mine, and I was sucked under. My grandmother's poem slipped away, dragged into the back of my mind by the other waves that were washing over me. We stayed like that for a long time, although all too soon, he was pulling back.

"Maybe that was a bad idea. Personally, my thoughts aren't

fit to be shared right now," he murmured. "Now talk. You didn't say a word at dinner. Does it have anything to do with Kjell? I heard he came over this morning and then left town. Guess I'm the jealous type, because I was relieved." Those unreadable and undeniable gray eyes were an open book, so full of longing and tenderness and a thousand other things I never expected to see there, at least not when they were looking at me.

Kjell had looked the same way that morning, but he'd snapped back to normal when he'd heard my poem. And I knew it would be the same with Tuck.

As much as I wished his feelings were real and could last forever, it would be unfair to trap Tuck, my Tuck, in such a state of servitude. I loved him too much for that.

I took a deep breath, and the first phrase slipped from my tongue. Tuck's eyes widened at the odd sounds and syllables pouring into the night between us. Even in the deep darkness of the roof, I could see how his face changed as the poem worked its magic. The dawning realization that something was happening, freeing his mind.

Before I knew it, it was over. I closed my eyes, bracing myself for what would come next. I didn't know what I'd do if he pulled away from me in fear, like Kjell had.

Tuck's arm disappeared. I felt him shift, rolling onto his side with his face angled away from me. The lump in my throat threatened to explode, and I hoped it would take the rest of me out with it. I couldn't bring myself to look at him, to see his reaction. Would he be horrified or confused—angry even?

Finally, breathing slowly to steady myself, I opened my eyes, prepared for anything. Anything, that is, except his reaction.

Tuck settled onto his back again, next to me, his chest shaking with laughter.

"Ells," he said, raising his voice above a whisper. "If you want to dump me, you'll have to do better than that." His arm wound its way around me again, rolling me over until I was on top of him. I could feel his heartbeat in my own chest, hear the way his breathing changed as his other hand slid through my hair.

"I—I don't understand," I said, drawing back even though every nerve in my body was begging me to do the exact opposite. "It didn't work. You should wake up now."

"Wake up? And have this be over? If that's a legitimate possibility, keep me knocked out forever." He kissed my neck, and it was impossible for me to concentrate on what I needed to do.

"I think I know why this happened—why you feel this way. It was that time in the bar, when Graham was kidnapped. I had to use my influence to break Astrid's spell. And I accidentally kept you under it all this time. That's why you feel this way. But it could have happened earlier, at home. You haven't had that mark on your shoulder for long."

"Interesting theory." He was laughing at me again.

I felt flushed and flustered. I couldn't figure out what was happening—how I'd failed. It had been hard enough the first time. The second would probably kill me. But I started reciting the poem again, this time looking him straight in the eye, willing the magic to find its mark.

But I was only a few words in when Tuck pressed his index

finger against my lips. "Stop, Ells, stop." His laughter faded. "Are you honestly worried that all this"—his arms around me tensed—"hasn't been real?"

Tuck flashed a sweet, disarming smile, and again I found myself wondering whether I really, truly had to give him up. "Actually, I'm disappointed. Aren't I worth keeping at any cost?"

The challenge in his eyes told me he didn't expect an answer. "I'm a hopeless case," he added, burying his face in my neck and murmuring the rest against my skin. "And it's got nothing to do with your wily Valkyrie ways. Because I've been this way for ages."

His smile was exquisite when he wanted it to be.

It took me a shamefully long time to process all of what he'd said. It seemed like too much all at once—that after spending all day worrying, I'd been so far off the mark. That everything that had happened and still was happening with Tuck was real. And that for the last two minutes, Tucker Halloway had been methodically unfastening the tiny pearl buttons on my cardigan.

"Finally," he muttered as he slid it off my shoulders.

I had only a thin T-shirt underneath, and the night air was cool against my skin. I shivered as he pulled me closer, pressing his lips against mine and ending the conversation once and for all.

But I wasn't cold for long—Tuck had more than a few very effective ways of keeping us both warm.

SAYING GOOD-BYE TO my grandmother was always hard. But the ocean that would separate us seemed bigger than ever now.

We'd grown so close that trip, in ways I was still just beginning to understand. For years I'd worried about her living alone. As other people's grandparents started to decline, I'd imagine Grandmother falling and breaking her hip, like so many grandmothers seemed prone to do. And there'd be no one there to bring her flowers in the hospital or take care of her. But at the end of this trip, as I looked at my grandmother, I knew that it would take more than a fall to bring her down. It would take more than an army.

Now that I knew the truth about her, the truth about us both, I couldn't believe how blind I'd been to the way people stared at my grandmother as she passed, awestruck by her height and the aura of power and confidence that surrounded her.

We said our farewells at the airport security entrance, and as Graham set his bag on the conveyer belt and watched it disappear into the X-ray machine, Grandmother caught my wrist.

"Don't forget, don't be complacent. Keep your skills sharp and do those drills I taught you." She smoothed my hair back, out of my eyes. "I'll come for Christmas, and more often now, so you'll be ready for whatever life, or Astrid, chooses to throw at you."

"You don't think Astrid will just forget about me—leave me alone?"

"Of course she won't, sweetling, not now that she's seen your mettle. She liked you far too much for that. Tuck won't be the only one vying for your affection—or your loyalty."

The thought sent a cold chill down my spine, but at the same time, I knew that I'd be able to handle anything Astrid, Loki, or the world could throw at me. After all, I was Hilda Overholt's granddaughter, and just like her, I was made of pure fire.

OUR MOTHER WAS there for us when we walked through customs, exhausted, jet lagged, and so thirsty that I swore my tongue was wearing a tiny felt jacket. While I couldn't wait to see him, I was relieved that Tuck hadn't come to the airport. I'd told him on the phone a few days ago that I'd meet him that night—after I'd had a chance to clean up. Somehow, Tucker Halloway was far scarier at home, on his turf.

It was surreal to be in our modern, oh-so-American home after the antique plumbing of our grandmother's old house in Skavøpoll. As I started carrying my bags upstairs, on the verge of collapse, my mother called after me, "Ellie, there is a package for you. I put it in your room."

That perked me right up. I never got packages—especially surprises. So I took the steps faster, itching with curiosity. The box was perched on the edge of my desk, wrapped in sturdy brown paper. Where the return address would have been, the name Astrid was emblazoned in an intricate script. There was no postmark, or any other sign that this box had ever been touched by a U.S. postal worker. In fact, the covering was perfectly preserved, free of creases, dirt, and any signs of wear and tear. I wondered how my mother could have missed such obvious oddities.

I backed away from the box slowly, like it would explode if not handled with care.

Graham's heavy tread pounded up the stairs, and his

bedroom door opened and closed behind him. For a moment, I thought about calling out to him, not wanting to be alone when I ripped into the smooth brown paper. Just in case. But Graham had been through enough, and he probably wouldn't understand the depth of what had transpired between Astrid and me and all the reasons I wasn't sure whether to be terrified or touched that she'd thought of me.

I used scissors to cut away the paper, buying time by folding it into a neat square and setting it on my desk to be recycled. It was a plain brown cardboard file box, the kind my mother used to store old tax receipts.

I lifted the lid slowly, scanning underneath for a trip wire.

Inside was a pair of all-too-familiar fur-trimmed knee-high boots. Thin straps crisscrossed over the front, lacing up the leg like ballet slippers. I smiled as I finally ran my fingers along the smooth tanned leather. The soles were a transparent rubberlike material I'd never seen before, and I touched their sticky surface, realizing that this level of traction would take me up the side of an ice-covered cliff without a hitch.

As I slid them out of the box, a slip of paper fluttered to the ground. Staring up at me, in the same curled calligraphy, was a note.

Train hard. Next time I won't go so easy on you. —A

"Ellie?" My mom knocked softly at the door. "Tucker's downstairs—he wants to see you."

"Coming," I said, slipping the note into my desk drawer. "I'll be right there."

After all, who needs sleep? Definitely not me. Especially when I'd missed Tuck every minute of the last five weeks.

As I unlaced the boots, I hoped his Morrigan blood would boil at the sight of the fur-tipped symbol of Valkyrie valor on my feet. After all, what fun would dating be if I couldn't still drive Tuck crazy?

I smiled at that thought, but then laughed out loud as I realized that the Valkyrie boots fit perfectly.

Just like I'd always known they would.

Acknowledgments

I want to thank my wonderful agent, Suzie Townsend, for finding such a perfect home for my book and for believing in me. A huge thanks as well to Brendan Deneen, who dug me out of the slush pile.

I will be forever grateful to my editor, Anne Hoppe, whose wisdom and insight helped me unlock aspects of my story and my characters that I didn't know existed. I've learned so much from Anne. I also want to thank Laurel Symonds, who provided invaluable editorial guidance.

Martha Flynn, Whitney Miller, and Heidi Kling, my amazing critique group, I couldn't have finished this book without you. I also want to thank Mary Kole and Alie Slavin, who read my earliest drafts.

I have been so fortunate to have an amazing group of friends and family who were conscripted to read countless drafts: David Paulson, Katharine Kivett, Katie Watson, Shin-e Lin, Lei Lynn Lau, Kerri Tarvin, Keith and Pamela Pugh, Kristin Bousquet, Tanya Marston, Georgie Hanlin, Kristen Harper, and my husband, Alex. I couldn't have done this without every one of you. Lastly, thank you to the Paulson women: Natalie, Kathy, and Grandma, who were with me on the fateful trip to Norway that started it all.